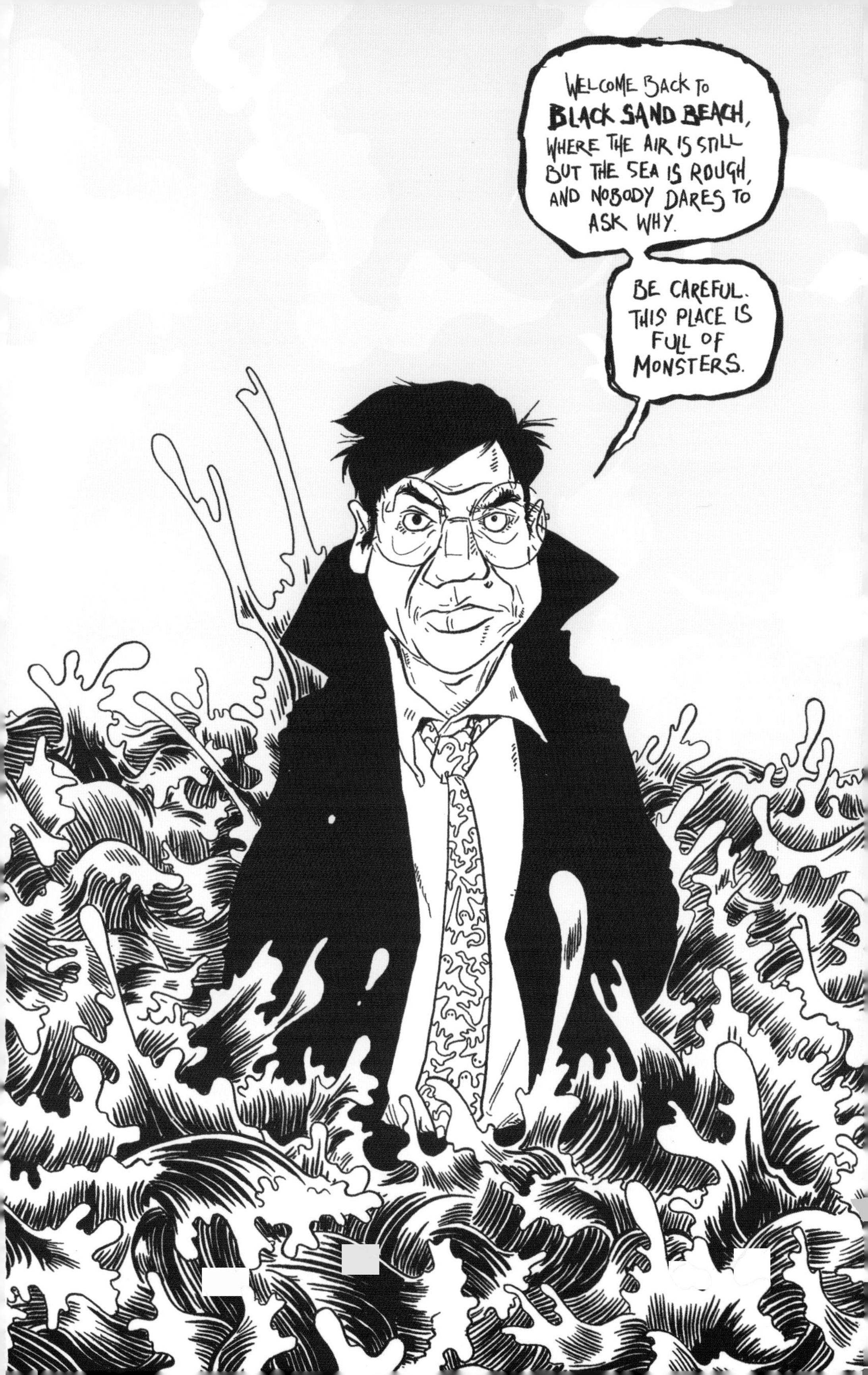
WELCOME BACK TO BLACK SAND BEACH, WHERE THE AIR IS STILL BUT THE SEA IS ROUGH, AND NOBODY DARES TO ASK WHY.
BE CAREFUL. THIS PLACE IS FULL OF MONSTERS.

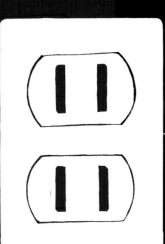

BLACK SAND BEACH

HAVE YOU SEEN THE DARKNESS?

BY RICHARD FAIRGRAY

For Dancer

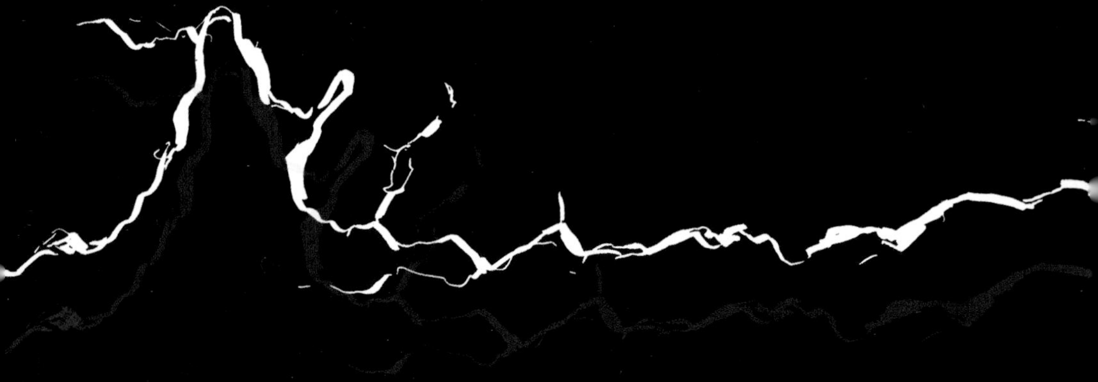

PIXEL INK

Text and Illustrations copyright © 2022 by Richard Fairgray
All rights reserved
Pixel+Ink is a division of TGM Development Corp
Printed and bound in January 2022 at Toppan Leefung, DongGuan, China.
Book design by Richard Fairgray
www.pixelandinkbooks.com

Library of Congress Cataloging-in-Publication Data

Names: Fairgray, Richard, 1985- author.
Title: Have you seen the darkness? / Richard Fairgray.
Description: First edition. | New York : Pixel+Ink, 2022. | Series: Black
Sand Beach ; 3 | Audience: Ages 8-12. | Audience: Grades 4-6. | Summary:
Told in alternating timelines, Dash and his friends try to use the
Darkness to capture the monster they accidentally freed, while in 1994
sisters Mabel and Kasey come face-to-face with the shapeshifting
creature their father is hunting.
Identifiers: LCCN 2021041404 (print) | LCCN 2021041405 (ebook) | ISBN
9781645950912 (hardcover) | ISBN 9781645950929 (paperback) | ISBN
9781645950936 (ebook)
Subjects: CYAC: Graphic novels. | Monsters--Fiction. |
Shapeshifting--Fiction. | LCGFT: Graphic novels.
Classification: LCC PZ7.7.F344 Hav 2022 (print) | LCC PZ7.7.F344 (ebook)
| DDC 741.5/993--dc23/eng/20211003
LC record available at https://lccn.loc.gov/2021041404
LC ebook record available at https://lccn.loc.gov/2021041405

First Edition
1 3 5 7 9 10 8 6 4 2

HAVE YOU SEEN THE DARKNESS?

PREVIOUSLY

After discovering his journal from the previous summer at Black Sand Beach, Dash thought he was finally going to be able to piece together the missing patches in his memory and (maybe) find out what it was that made him forget. But then Ramsays, the zombie sheep, grabbed the journal and disappeared into the woods.

The kids followed, picking up chewed fragments of the book along the way and reading parts of the story. It seems Dash had spent the previous summer bonding with his new stepmother and two local girls named Mabel and Kasey.

When they found Ramsays, he was caught in an ancient lock. As Dash read the rest of the journal, the kids debated whether or not to to help the trapped creature.

Mabel and Kasey turned out to be ghosts. They hadn't died, they'd just been near the Darkness for so long that they'd forgotten how to be alive. Dash had helped them, teaching them how to breathe again with the hope it might bring them fully back.

Of course, this is Black Sand Beach and things are never as they seem. Because Ramsays was not simply an unkillable zombie, he was something much, much worse.

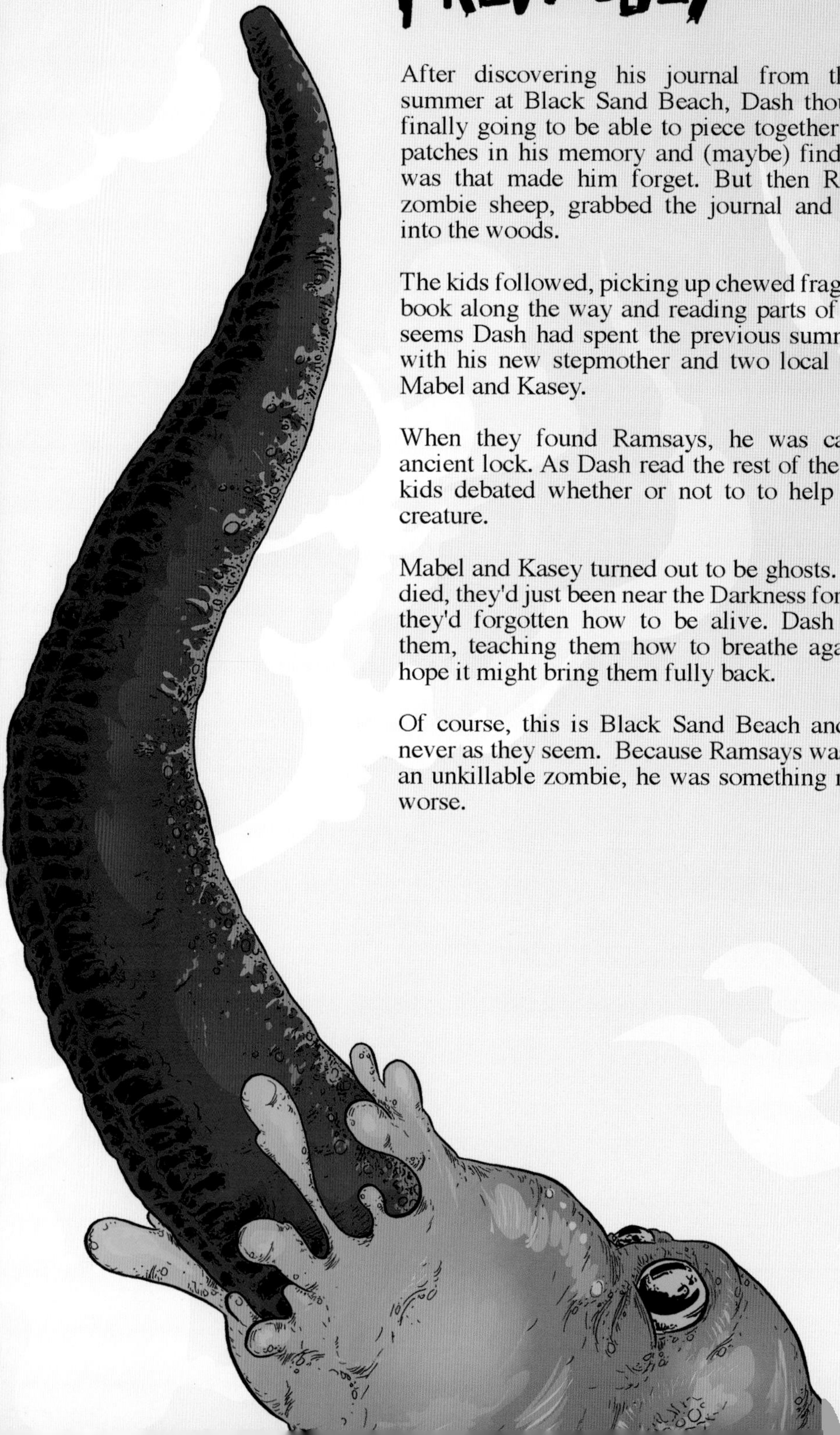

BEFORE THEY WERE

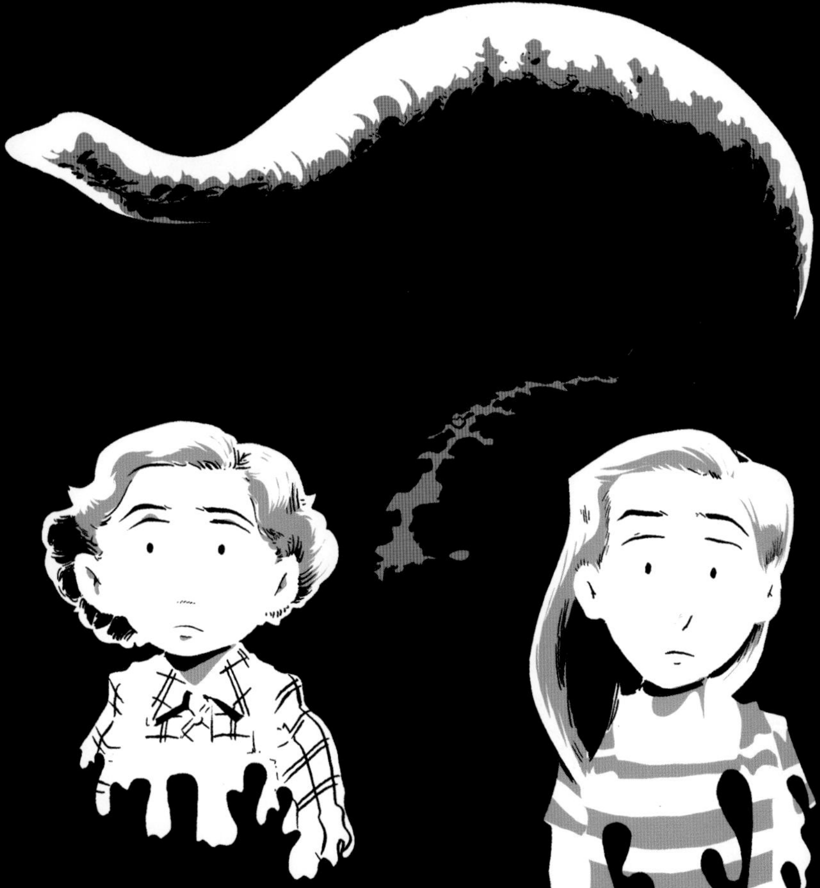

MONSTERS

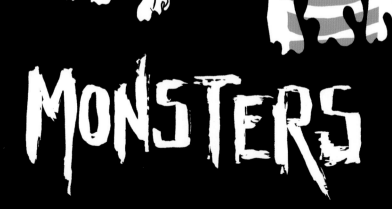

BEFORE THEY WERE

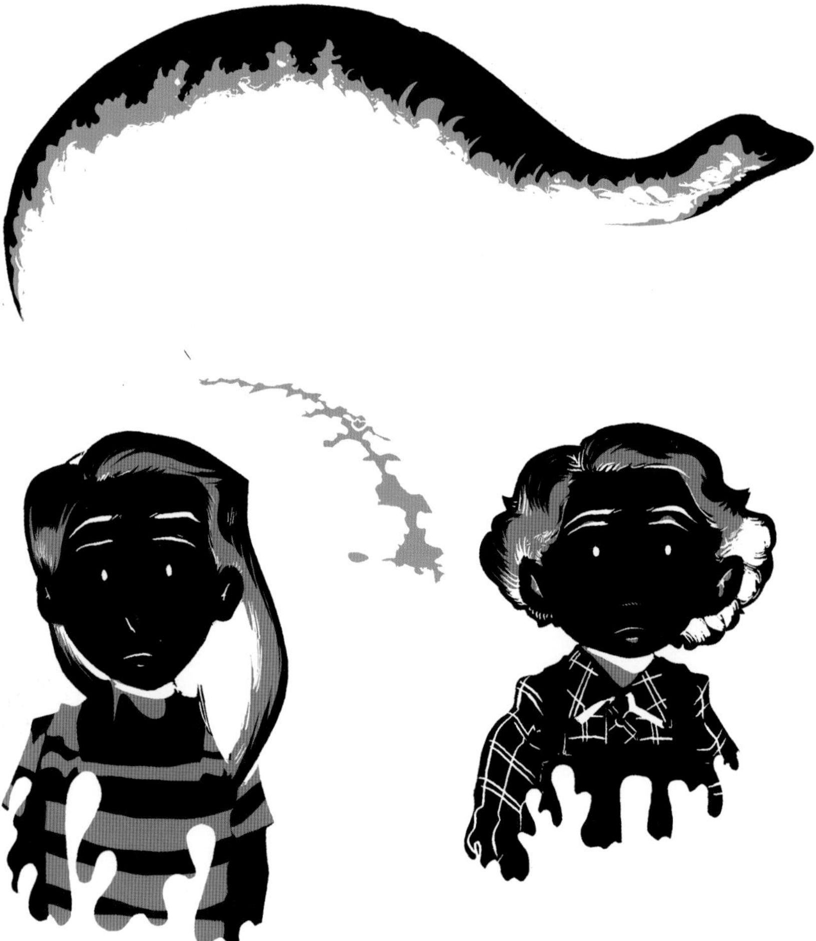

MONSTERS

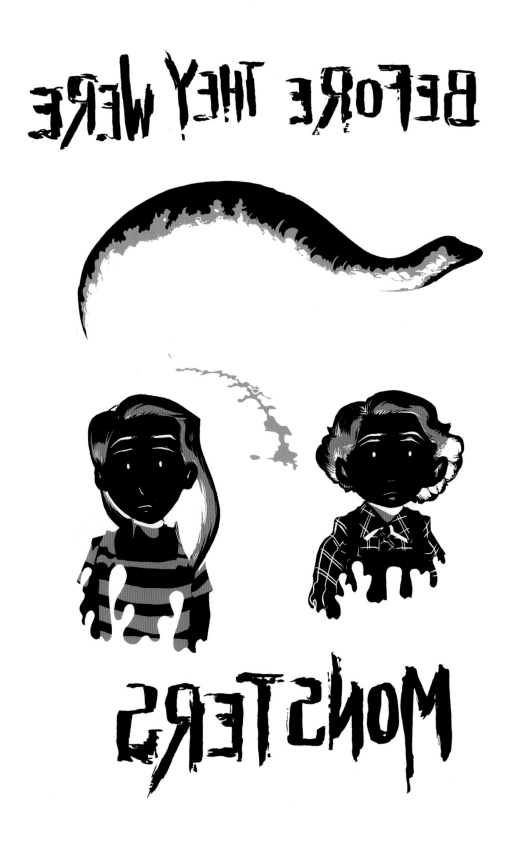

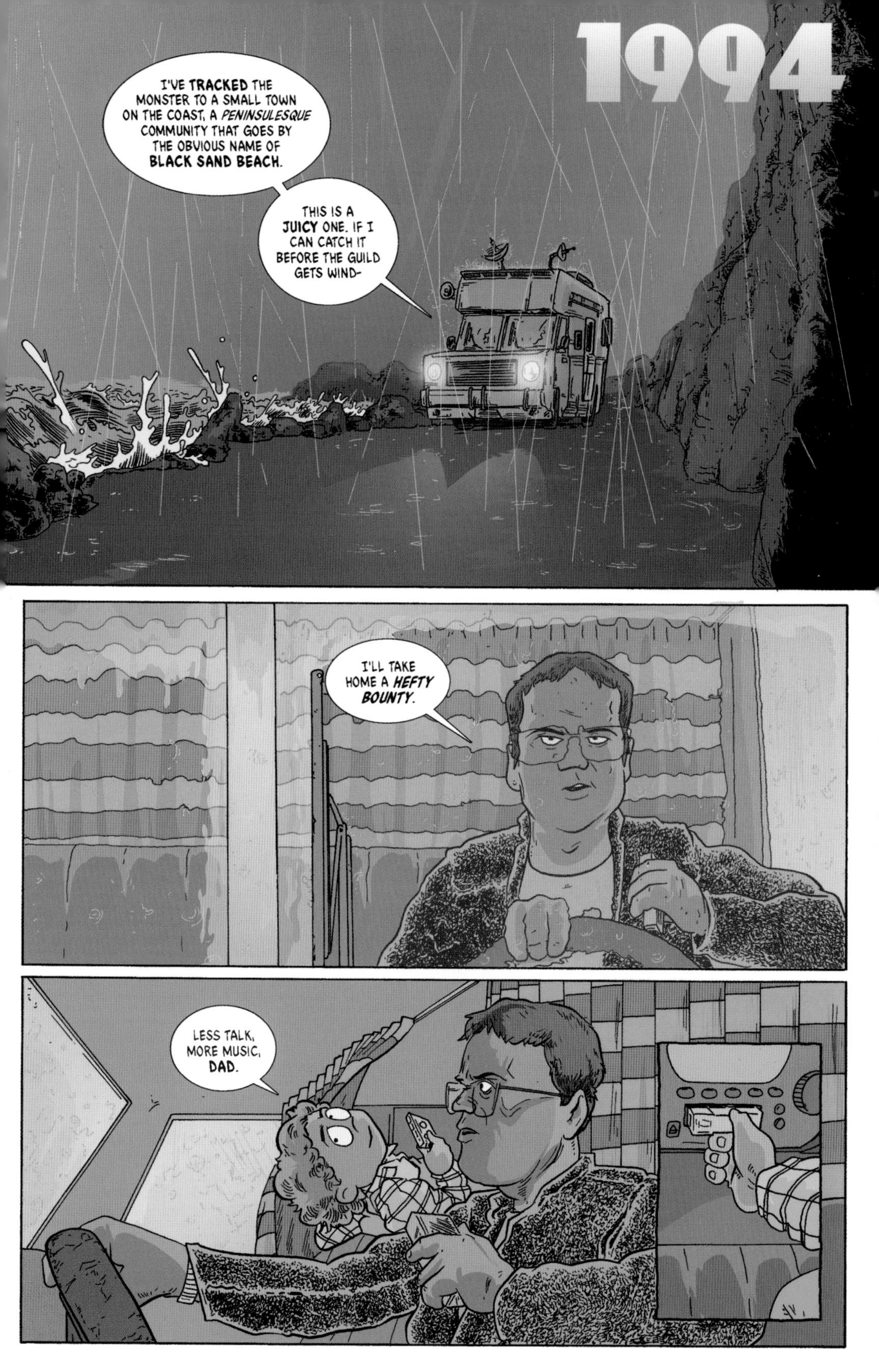
1994
I'VE **TRACKED** THE MONSTER TO A SMALL TOWN ON THE COAST, A *PENINSULESQUE* COMMUNITY THAT GOES BY THE OBVIOUS NAME OF **BLACK SAND BEACH**.
THIS IS A **JUICY** ONE. IF I CAN CATCH IT BEFORE THE GUILD GETS WIND-
I'LL TAKE HOME A ***HEFTY BOUNTY***.
LESS TALK, MORE MUSIC, **DAD**.

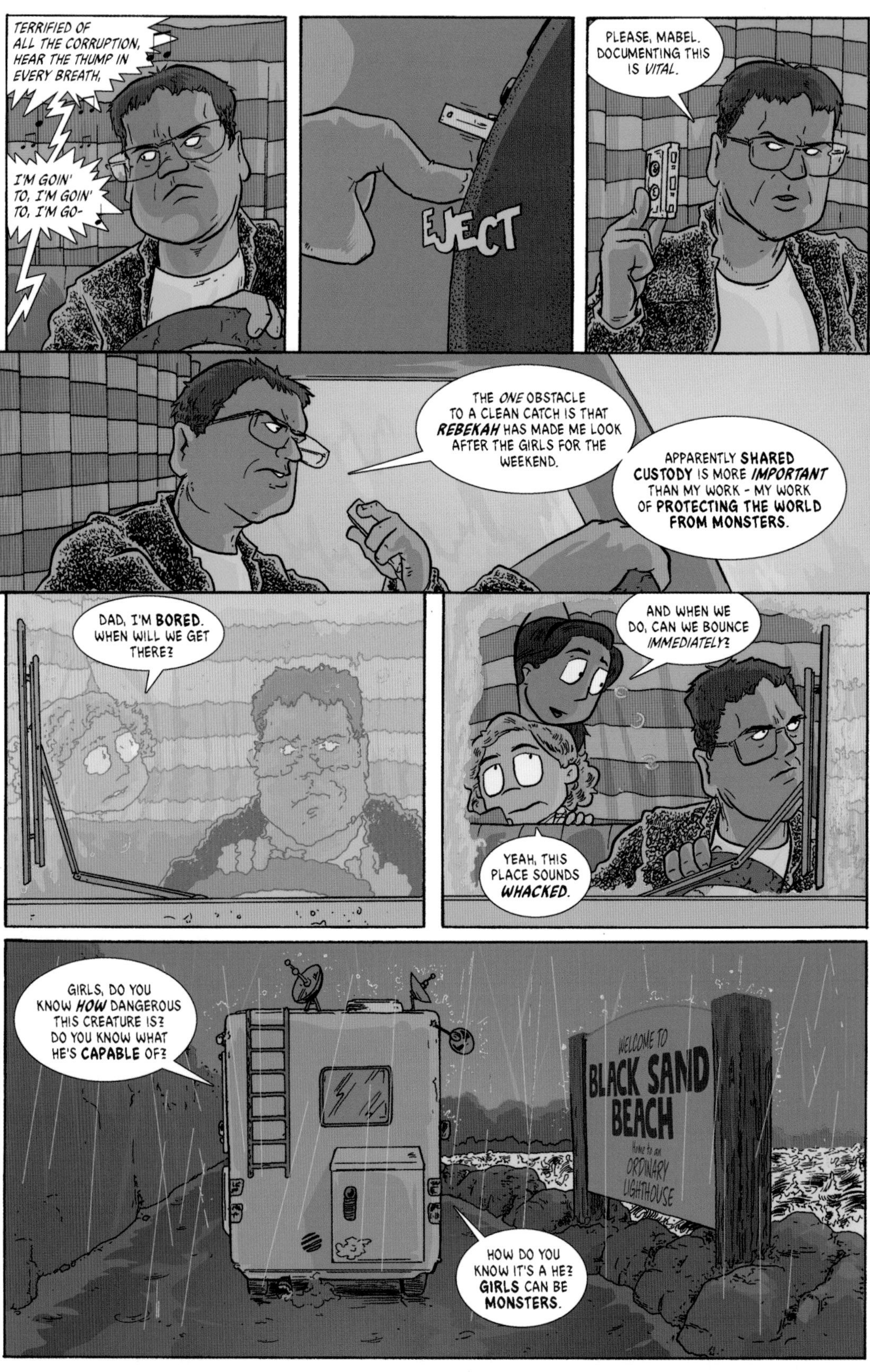
TERRIFIED OF ALL THE CORRUPTION, HEAR THE THUMP IN EVERY BREATH,
I'M GOIN' TO, I'M GOIN' TO, I'M GO-
EJECT
PLEASE, MABEL. DOCUMENTING THIS IS VITAL.
THE ONE OBSTACLE TO A CLEAN CATCH IS THAT REBEKAH HAS MADE ME LOOK AFTER THE GIRLS FOR THE WEEKEND.
APPARENTLY SHARED CUSTODY IS MORE IMPORTANT THAN MY WORK - MY WORK OF PROTECTING THE WORLD FROM MONSTERS.
DAD, I'M BORED. WHEN WILL WE GET THERE?
AND WHEN WE DO, CAN WE BOUNCE IMMEDIATELY?
YEAH, THIS PLACE SOUNDS WHACKED.
GIRLS, DO YOU KNOW HOW DANGEROUS THIS CREATURE IS? DO YOU KNOW WHAT HE'S CAPABLE OF?
WELCOME TO BLACK SAND BEACH Home to an ORDINARY LIGHTHOUSE
HOW DO YOU KNOW IT'S A HE? GIRLS CAN BE MONSTERS.

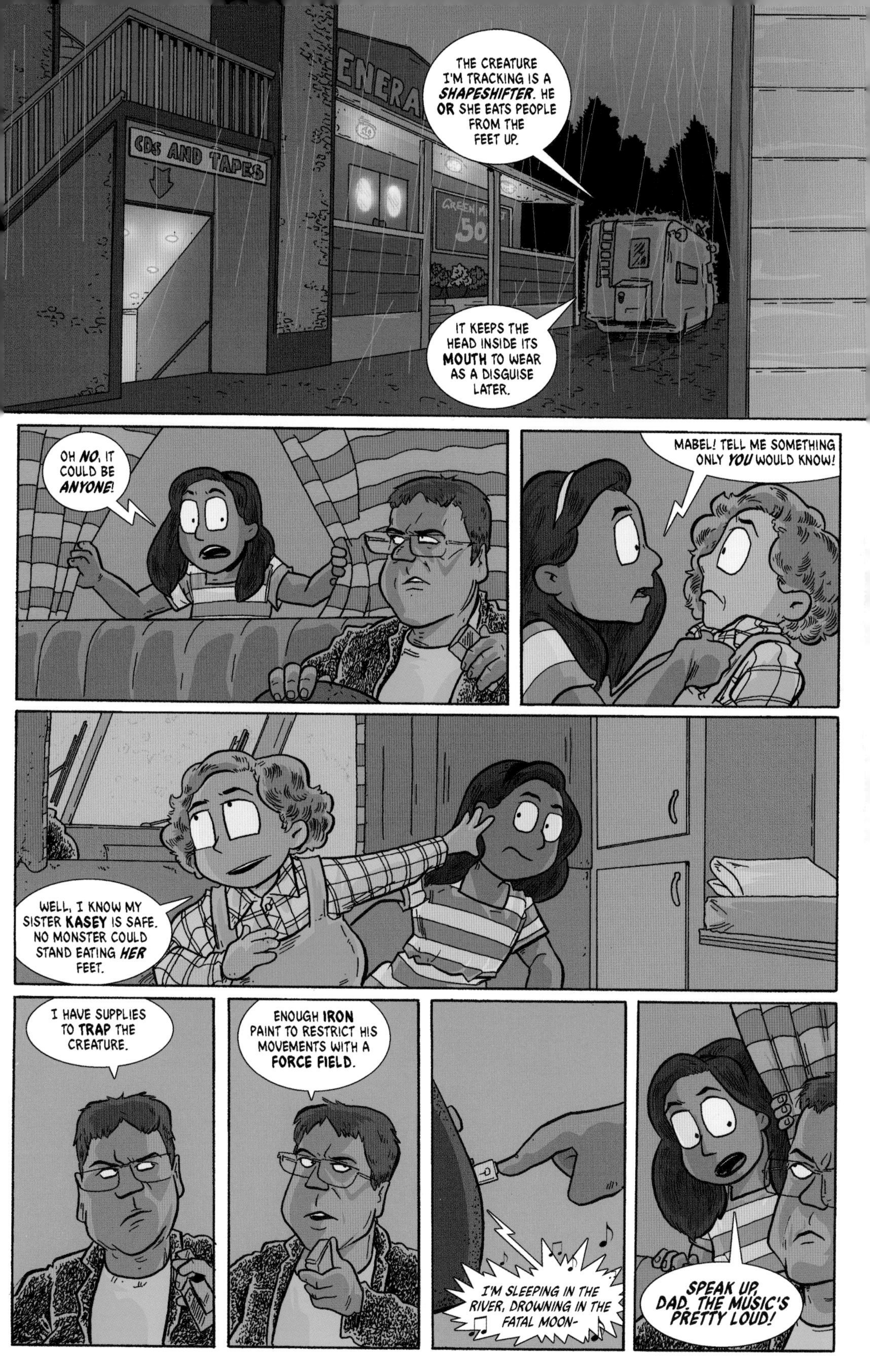

CDs AND TAPES
THE CREATURE I'M TRACKING IS A SHAPESHIFTER. HE OR SHE EATS PEOPLE FROM THE FEET UP.
IT KEEPS THE HEAD INSIDE ITS MOUTH TO WEAR AS A DISGUISE LATER.
OH NO, IT COULD BE ANYONE!
MABEL! TELL ME SOMETHING ONLY YOU WOULD KNOW!
WELL, I KNOW MY SISTER KASEY IS SAFE. NO MONSTER COULD STAND EATING HER FEET.
I HAVE SUPPLIES TO TRAP THE CREATURE.
ENOUGH IRON PAINT TO RESTRICT HIS MOVEMENTS WITH A FORCE FIELD.
I'M SLEEPING IN THE RIVER, DROWNING IN THE FATAL MOON-
SPEAK UP, DAD. THE MUSIC'S PRETTY LOUD!

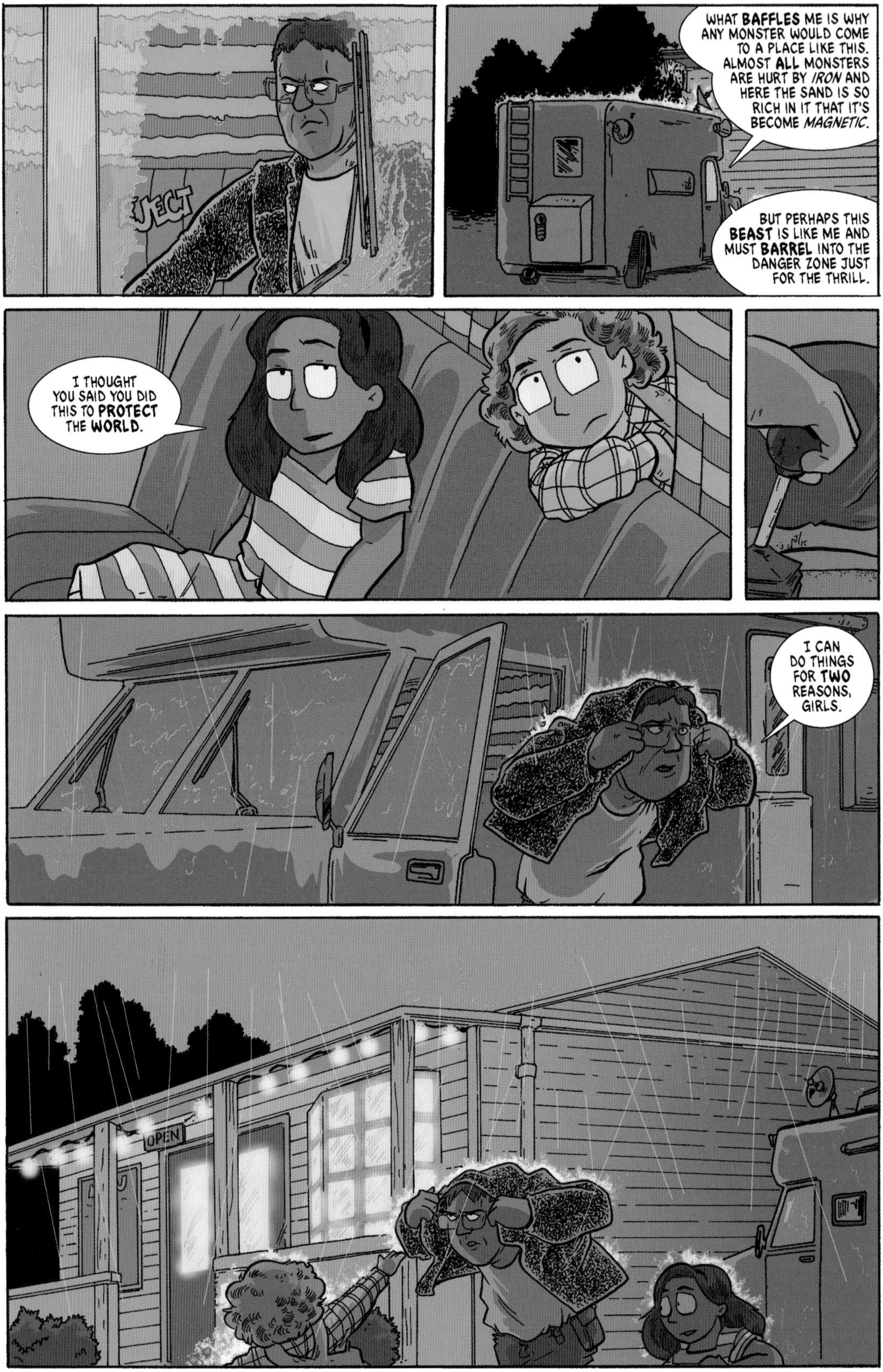

EJECT
WHAT BAFFLES ME IS WHY ANY MONSTER WOULD COME TO A PLACE LIKE THIS. ALMOST ALL MONSTERS ARE HURT BY IRON AND HERE THE SAND IS SO RICH IN IT THAT IT'S BECOME MAGNETIC.
BUT PERHAPS THIS BEAST IS LIKE ME AND MUST BARREL INTO THE DANGER ZONE JUST FOR THE THRILL.
I THOUGHT YOU SAID YOU DID THIS TO PROTECT THE WORLD.
I CAN DO THINGS FOR TWO REASONS, GIRLS.
OPEN

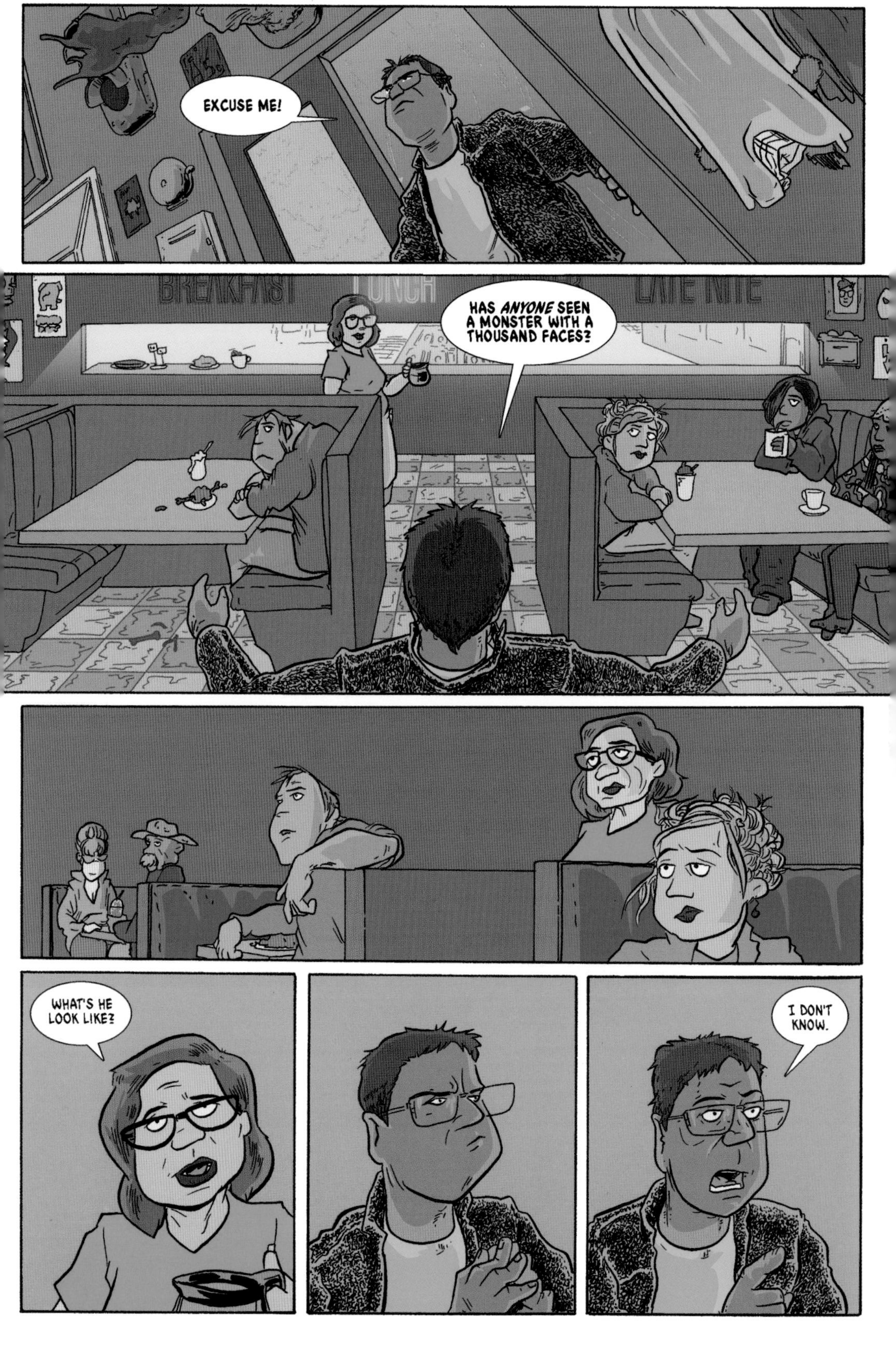

EXCUSE ME!
BREAKFAST LUNCH LATE NITE
HAS *ANYONE* SEEN A MONSTER WITH A THOUSAND FACES?
WHAT'S HE LOOK LIKE?
I DON'T KNOW.

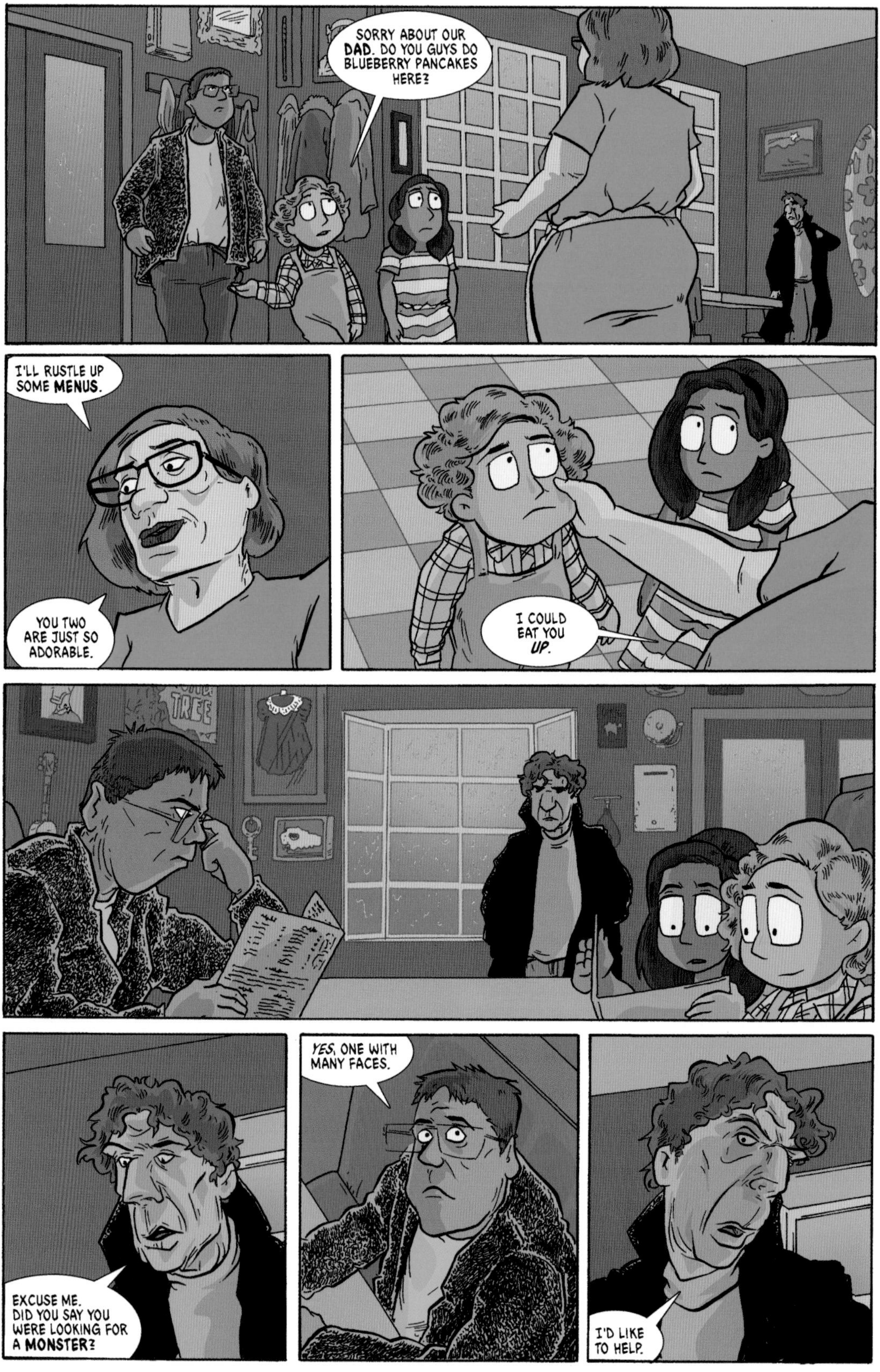
SORRY ABOUT OUR DAD. DO YOU GUYS DO BLUEBERRY PANCAKES HERE?
I'LL RUSTLE UP SOME MENUS.
YOU TWO ARE JUST SO ADORABLE.
I COULD EAT YOU UP.
EXCUSE ME. DID YOU SAY YOU WERE LOOKING FOR A MONSTER?
YES, ONE WITH MANY FACES.
I'D LIKE TO HELP.

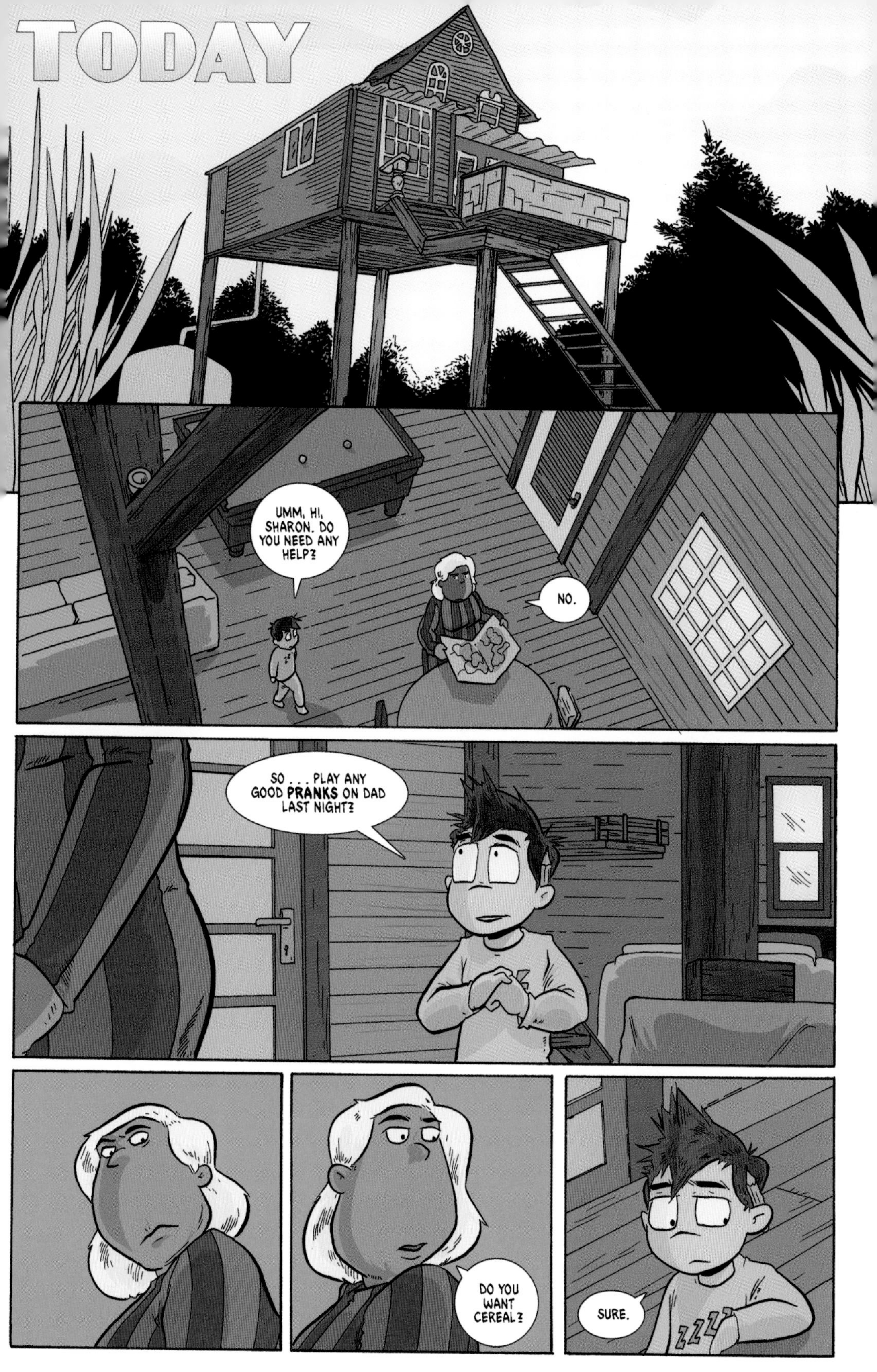
TODAY
UMM, HI, SHARON. DO YOU NEED ANY HELP?
NO.
SO . . . PLAY ANY GOOD PRANKS ON DAD LAST NIGHT?
DO YOU WANT CEREAL?
SURE.

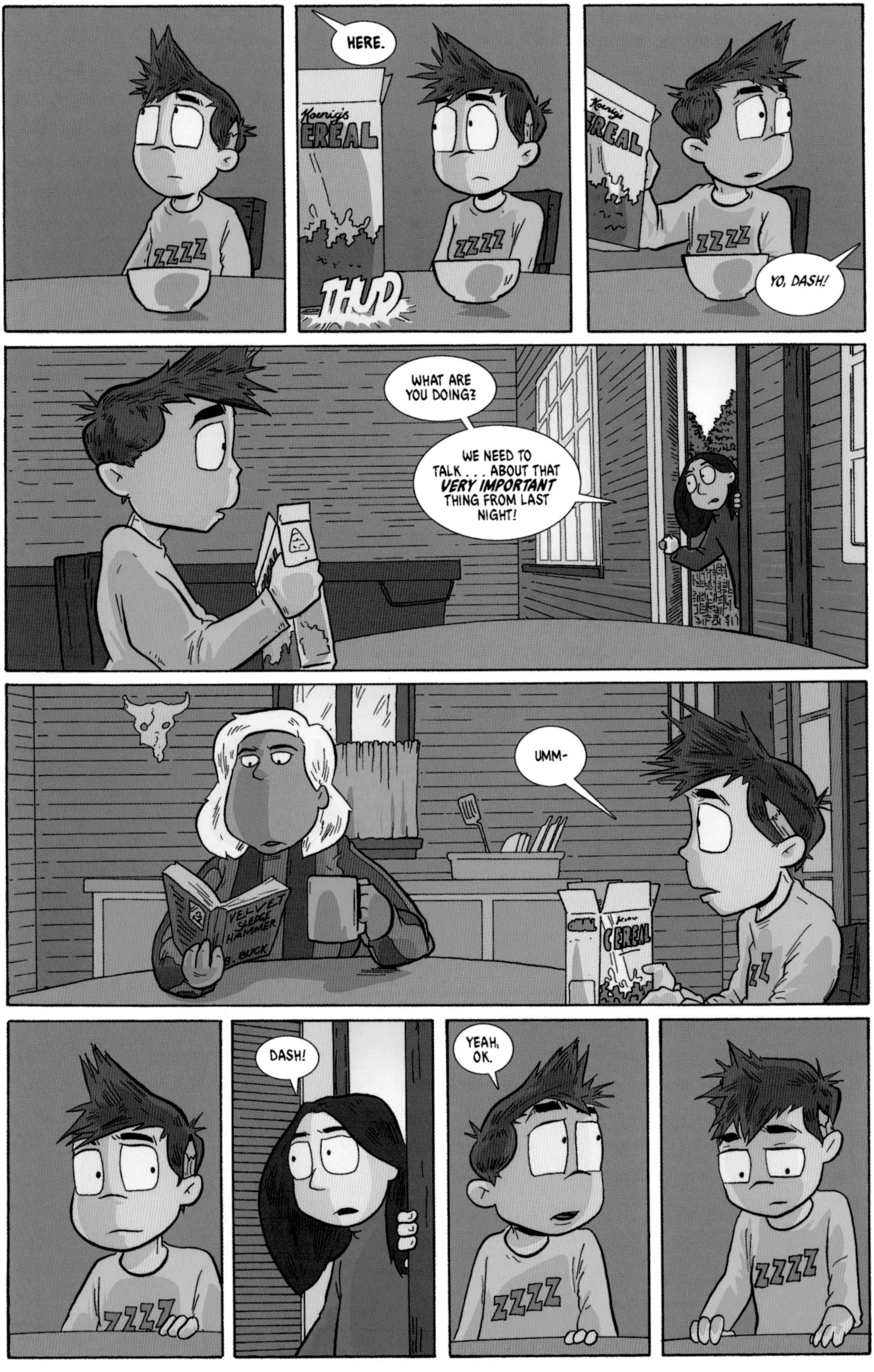
HERE.
Koenig's CEREAL
THUD
YO, DASH!
WHAT ARE YOU DOING?
WE NEED TO TALK . . . ABOUT THAT *VERY IMPORTANT* THING FROM LAST NIGHT!
VELVET SLEDGE HAMMER
B. BUCK
UMM-
DASH!
YEAH, OK.

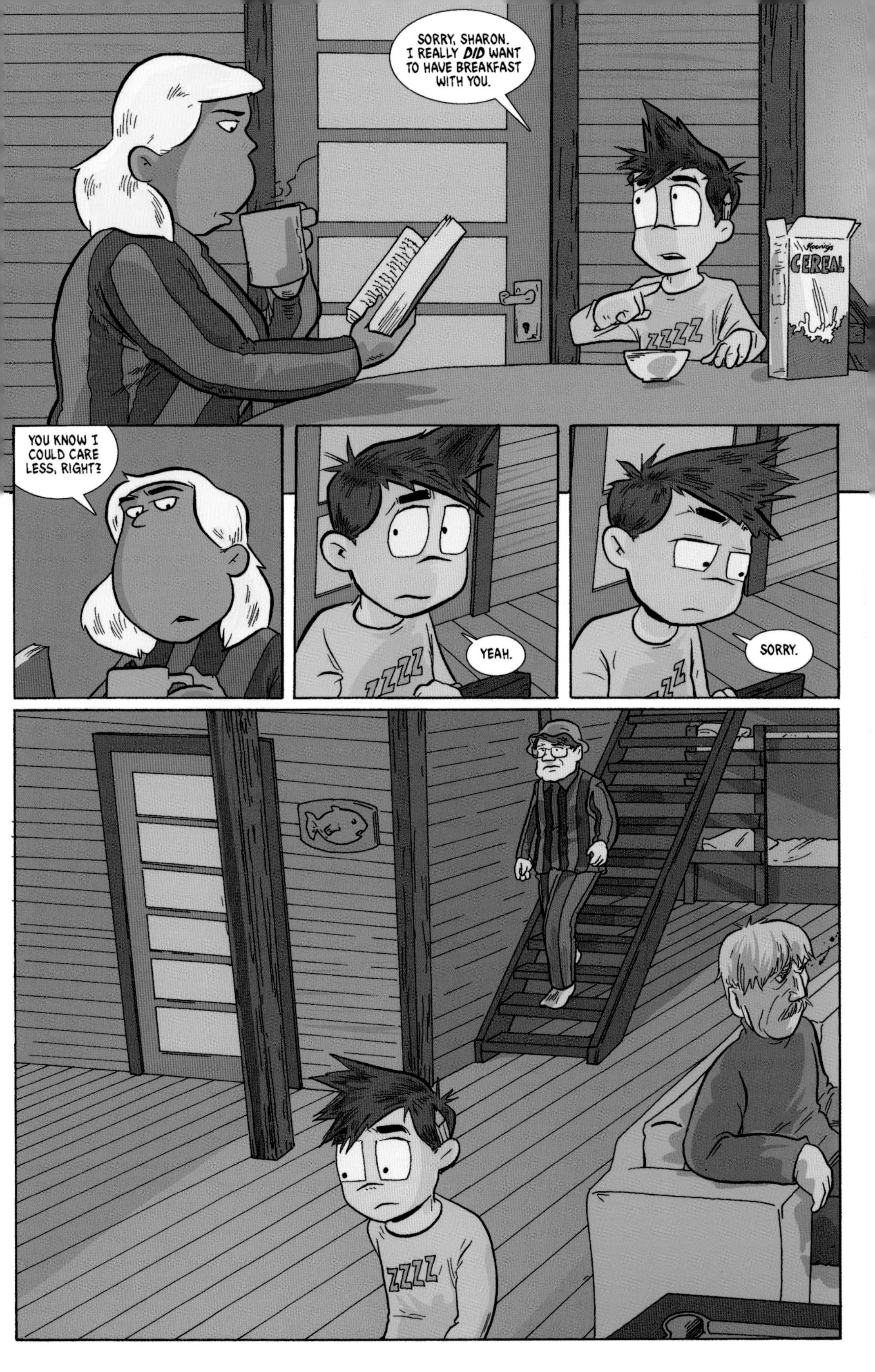
SORRY, SHARON. I REALLY *DID* WANT TO HAVE BREAKFAST WITH YOU.
CEREAL
YOU KNOW I COULD CARE LESS, RIGHT?
YEAH.
SORRY.

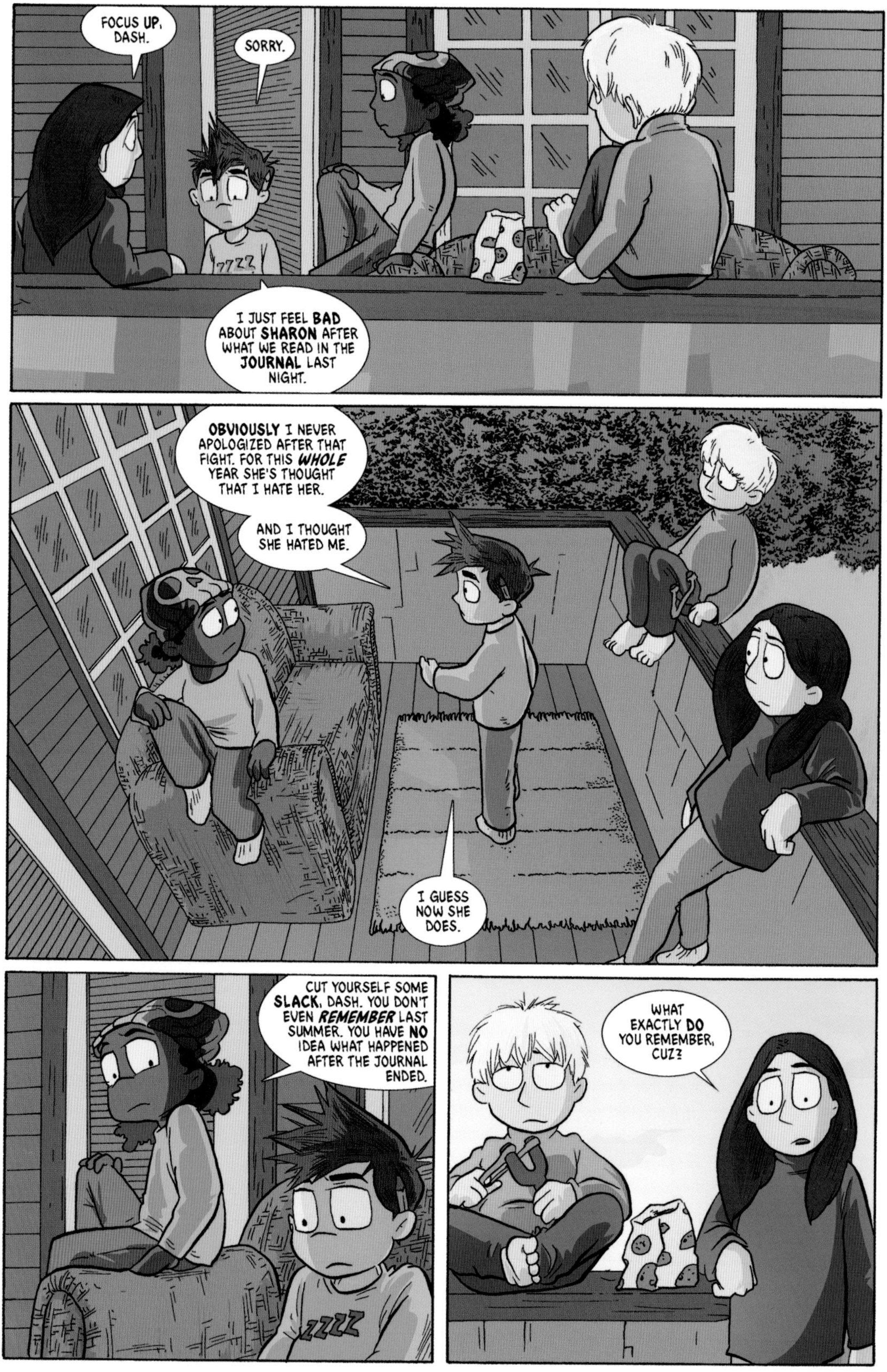
FOCUS UP, DASH.
SORRY.
I JUST FEEL BAD ABOUT SHARON AFTER WHAT WE READ IN THE JOURNAL LAST NIGHT.
OBVIOUSLY I NEVER APOLOGIZED AFTER THAT FIGHT. FOR THIS WHOLE YEAR SHE'S THOUGHT THAT I HATE HER.
AND I THOUGHT SHE HATED ME.
I GUESS NOW SHE DOES.
CUT YOURSELF SOME SLACK, DASH. YOU DON'T EVEN REMEMBER LAST SUMMER. YOU HAVE NO IDEA WHAT HAPPENED AFTER THE JOURNAL ENDED.
WHAT EXACTLY DO YOU REMEMBER, CUZ?

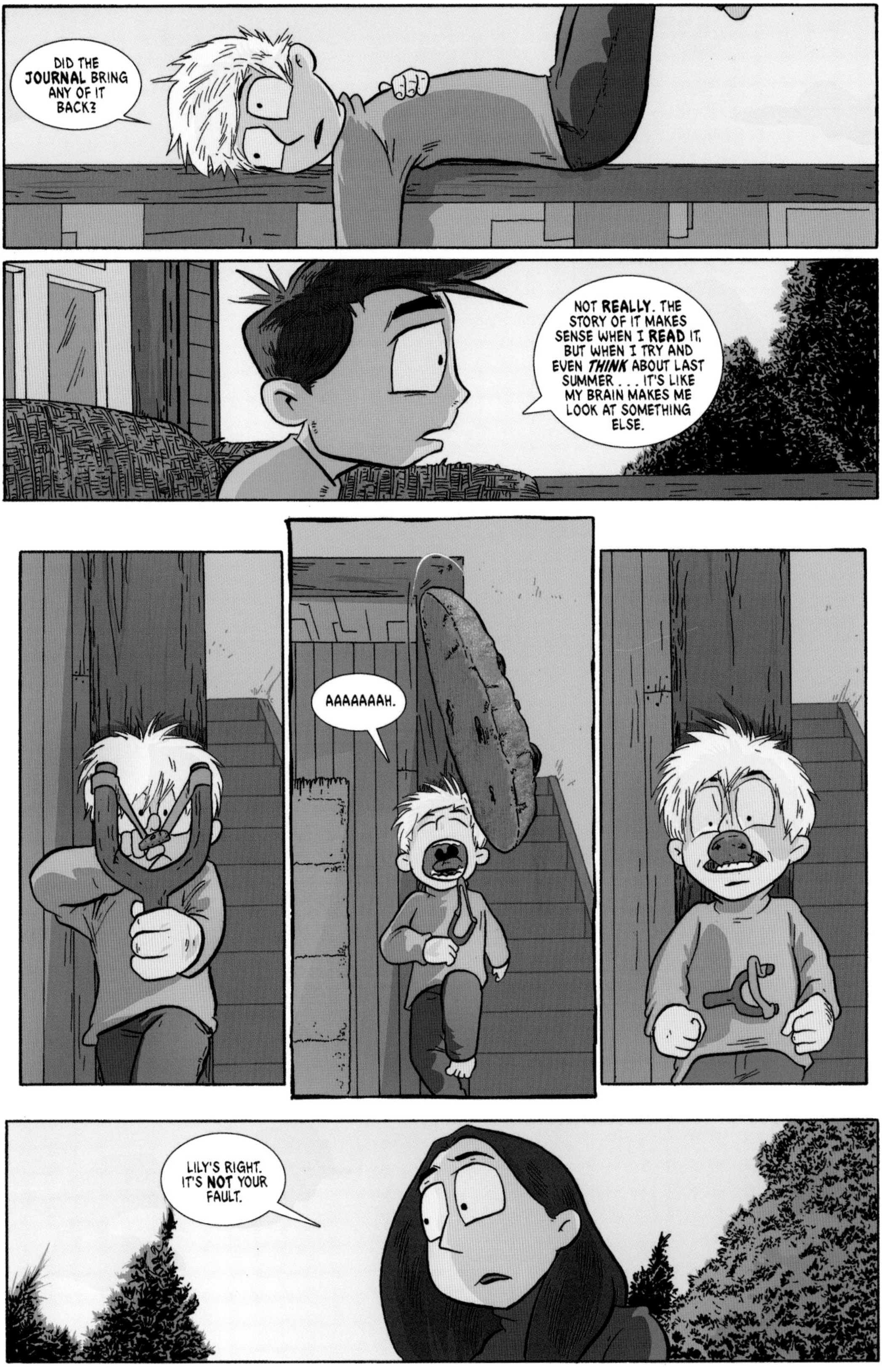
DID THE **JOURNAL** BRING ANY OF IT BACK?
NOT **REALLY**. THE STORY OF IT MAKES SENSE WHEN I **READ** IT, BUT WHEN I TRY AND EVEN ***THINK*** ABOUT LAST SUMMER . . . IT'S LIKE MY BRAIN MAKES ME LOOK AT SOMETHING ELSE.
AAAAAAAH.
LILY'S RIGHT. IT'S **NOT** YOUR FAULT.

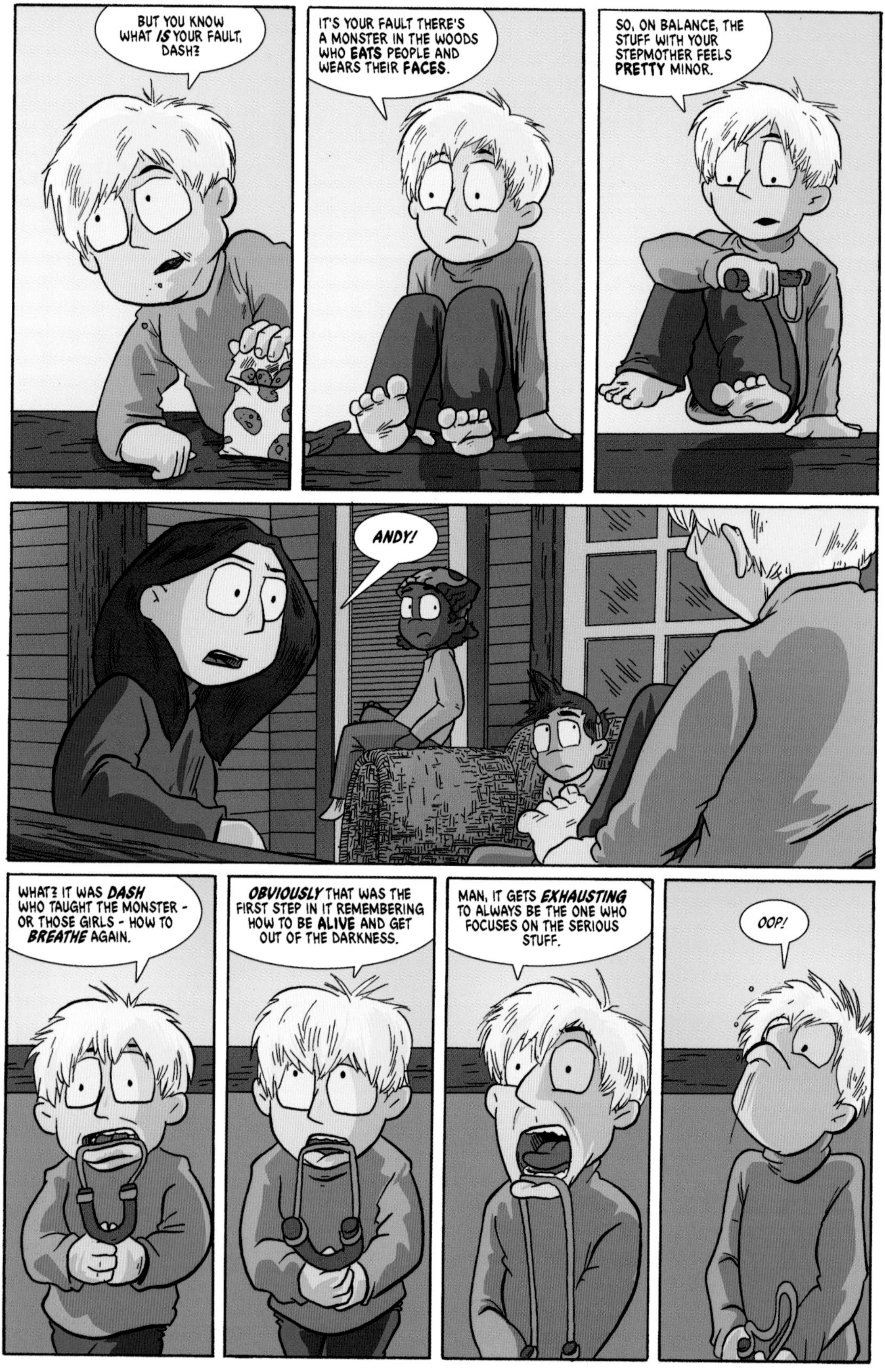
BUT YOU KNOW WHAT IS YOUR FAULT, DASH?
IT'S YOUR FAULT THERE'S A MONSTER IN THE WOODS WHO EATS PEOPLE AND WEARS THEIR FACES.
SO, ON BALANCE, THE STUFF WITH YOUR STEPMOTHER FEELS PRETTY MINOR.
ANDY!
WHAT? IT WAS DASH WHO TAUGHT THE MONSTER - OR THOSE GIRLS - HOW TO BREATHE AGAIN.
OBVIOUSLY THAT WAS THE FIRST STEP IN IT REMEMBERING HOW TO BE ALIVE AND GET OUT OF THE DARKNESS.
MAN, IT GETS EXHAUSTING TO ALWAYS BE THE ONE WHO FOCUSES ON THE SERIOUS STUFF.
OOP!

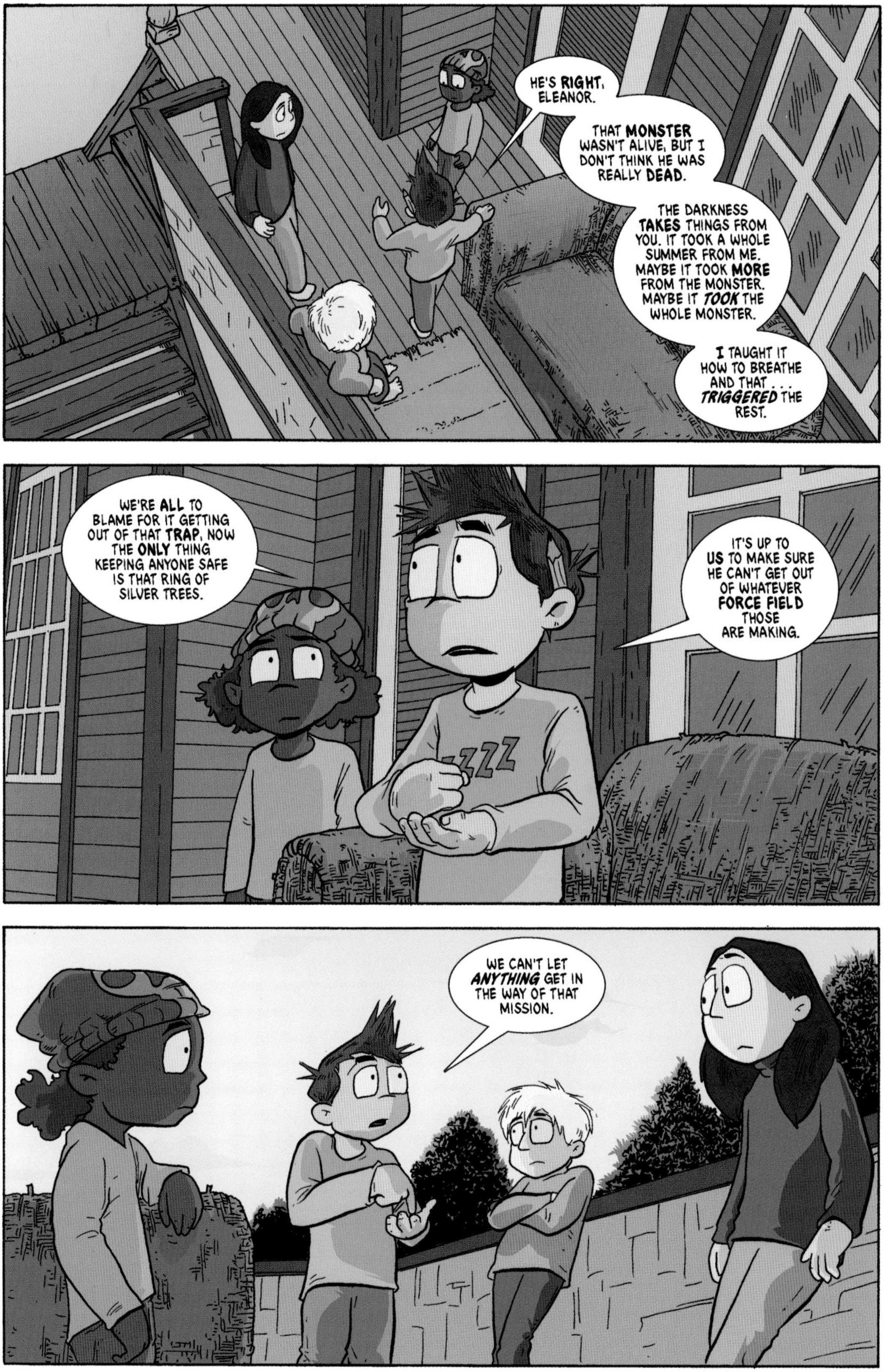
HE'S RIGHT, ELEANOR.
THAT MONSTER WASN'T ALIVE, BUT I DON'T THINK HE WAS REALLY DEAD.
THE DARKNESS TAKES THINGS FROM YOU. IT TOOK A WHOLE SUMMER FROM ME. MAYBE IT TOOK MORE FROM THE MONSTER. MAYBE IT TOOK THE WHOLE MONSTER.
I TAUGHT IT HOW TO BREATHE AND THAT . . . TRIGGERED THE REST.
WE'RE ALL TO BLAME FOR IT GETTING OUT OF THAT TRAP, NOW THE ONLY THING KEEPING ANYONE SAFE IS THAT RING OF SILVER TREES.
IT'S UP TO US TO MAKE SURE HE CAN'T GET OUT OF WHATEVER FORCE FIELD THOSE ARE MAKING.
WE CAN'T LET ANYTHING GET IN THE WAY OF THAT MISSION.

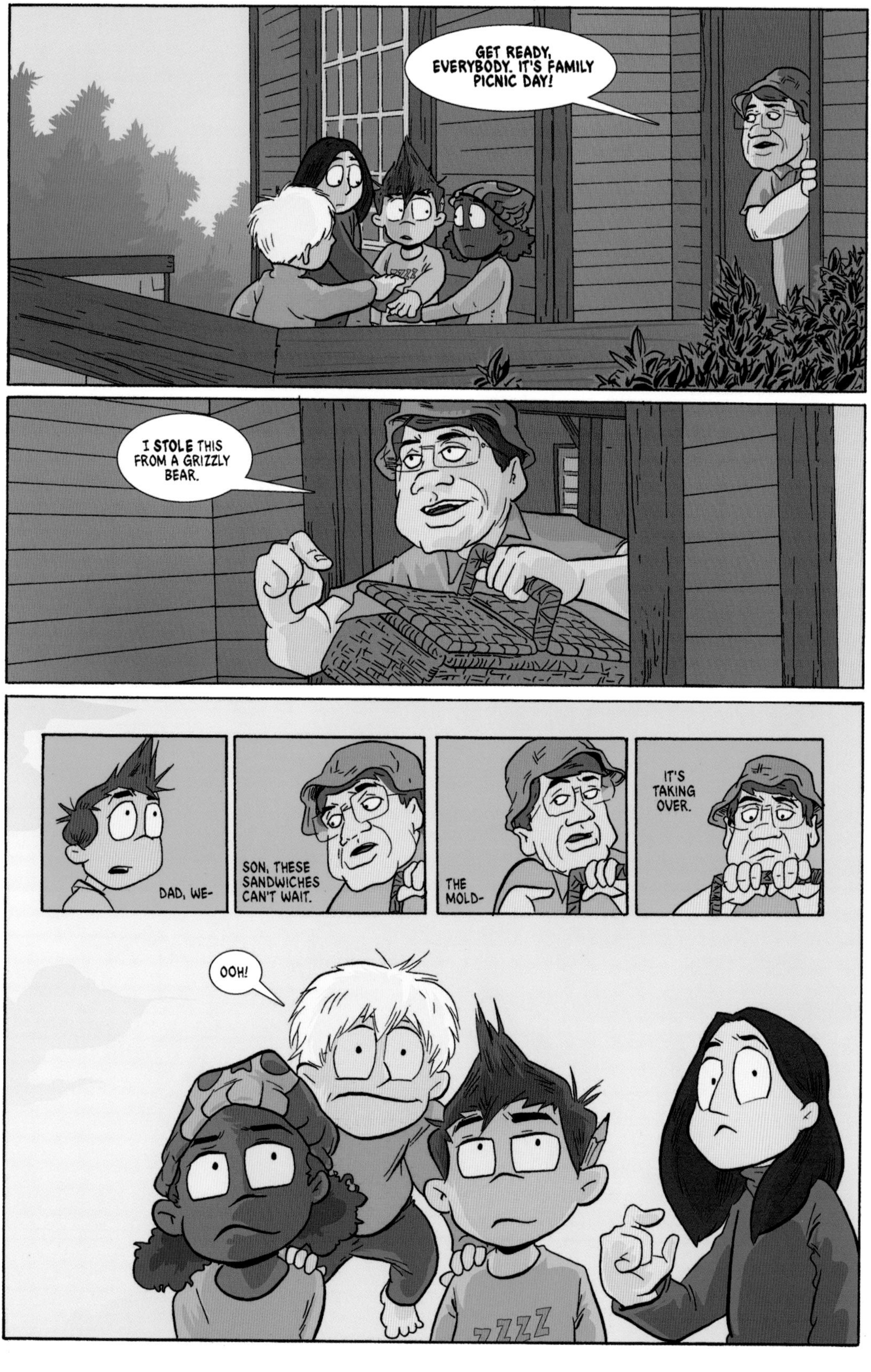
GET READY, EVERYBODY. IT'S FAMILY PICNIC DAY!
I STOLE THIS FROM A GRIZZLY BEAR.
DAD, WE-
SON, THESE SANDWICHES CAN'T WAIT.
THE MOLD-
IT'S TAKING OVER.
OOH!

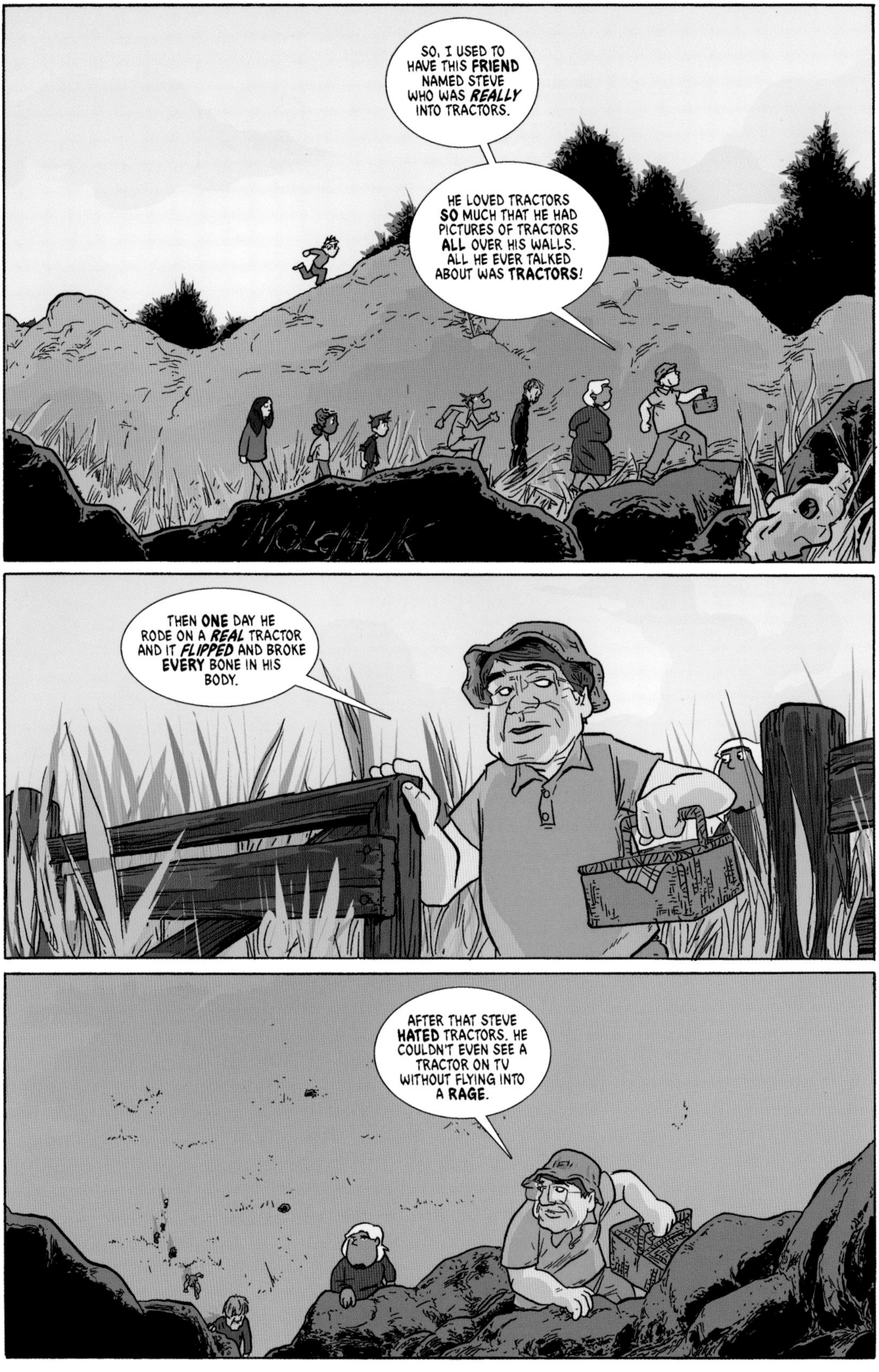
SO, I USED TO HAVE THIS **FRIEND** NAMED STEVE WHO WAS ***REALLY*** INTO TRACTORS.
HE LOVED TRACTORS **SO** MUCH THAT HE HAD PICTURES OF TRACTORS **ALL** OVER HIS WALLS. ALL HE EVER TALKED ABOUT WAS **TRACTORS**!
THEN **ONE** DAY HE RODE ON A ***REAL*** TRACTOR AND IT ***FLIPPED*** AND BROKE **EVERY** BONE IN HIS BODY.
AFTER THAT STEVE **HATED** TRACTORS. HE COULDN'T EVEN SEE A TRACTOR ON TV WITHOUT FLYING INTO A **RAGE**.

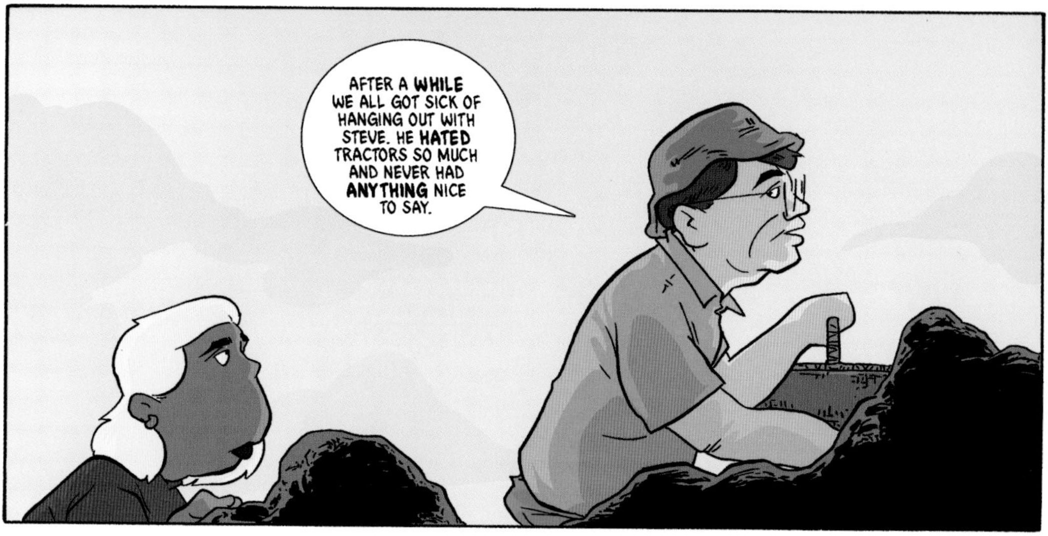
AFTER A **WHILE** WE ALL GOT SICK OF HANGING OUT WITH STEVE. HE **HATED** TRACTORS SO MUCH AND NEVER HAD **ANYTHING** NICE TO SAY.

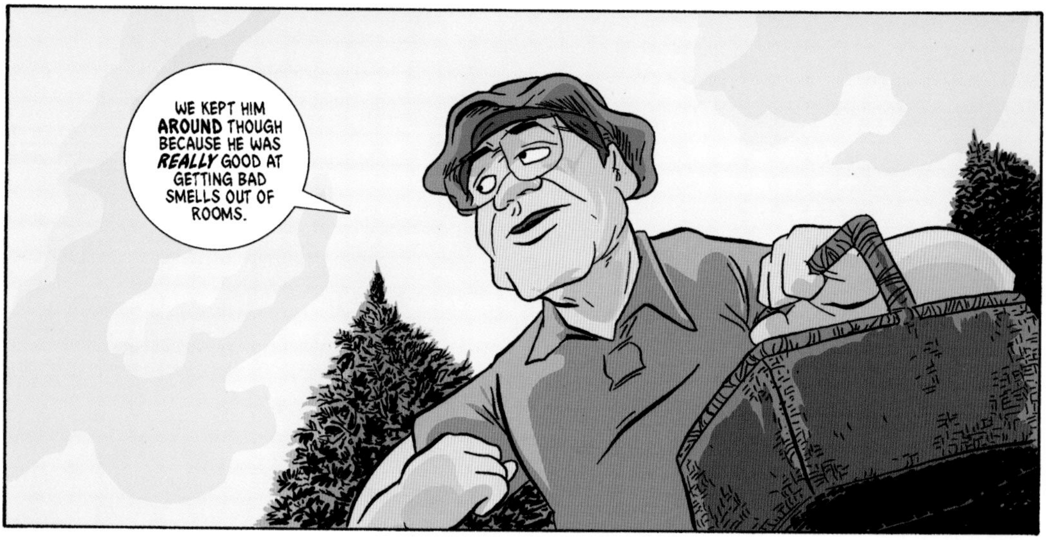
WE KEPT HIM **AROUND** THOUGH BECAUSE HE WAS ***REALLY*** GOOD AT GETTING BAD SMELLS OUT OF ROOMS.

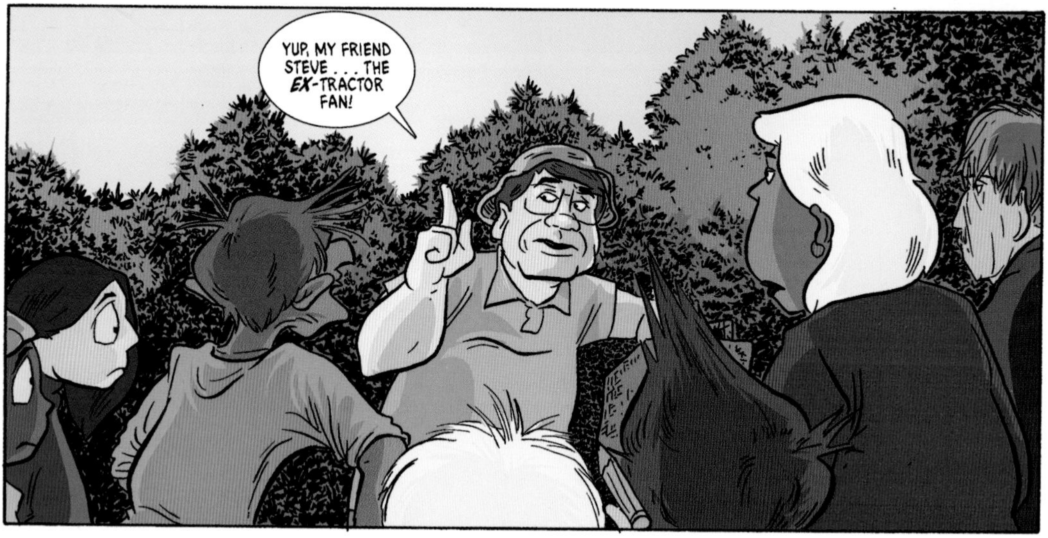
YUP, MY FRIEND STEVE . . . THE ***EX***-TRACTOR FAN!

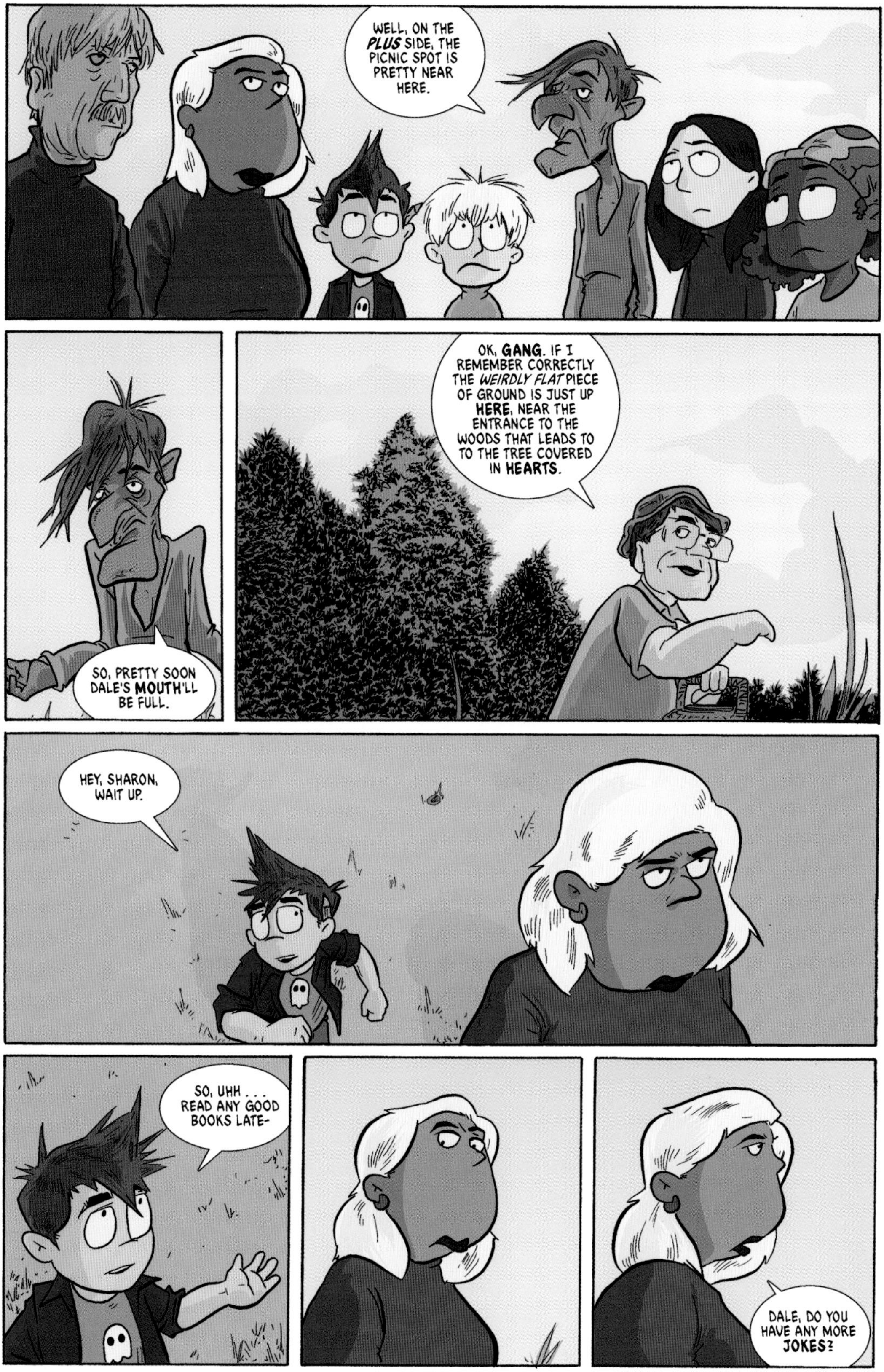
WELL, ON THE PLUS SIDE, THE PICNIC SPOT IS PRETTY NEAR HERE.
SO, PRETTY SOON DALE'S MOUTH'LL BE FULL.
OK, GANG. IF I REMEMBER CORRECTLY THE WEIRDLY FLAT PIECE OF GROUND IS JUST UP HERE, NEAR THE ENTRANCE TO THE WOODS THAT LEADS TO TO THE TREE COVERED IN HEARTS.
HEY, SHARON, WAIT UP.
SO, UHH . . . READ ANY GOOD BOOKS LATE-
DALE, DO YOU HAVE ANY MORE JOKES?

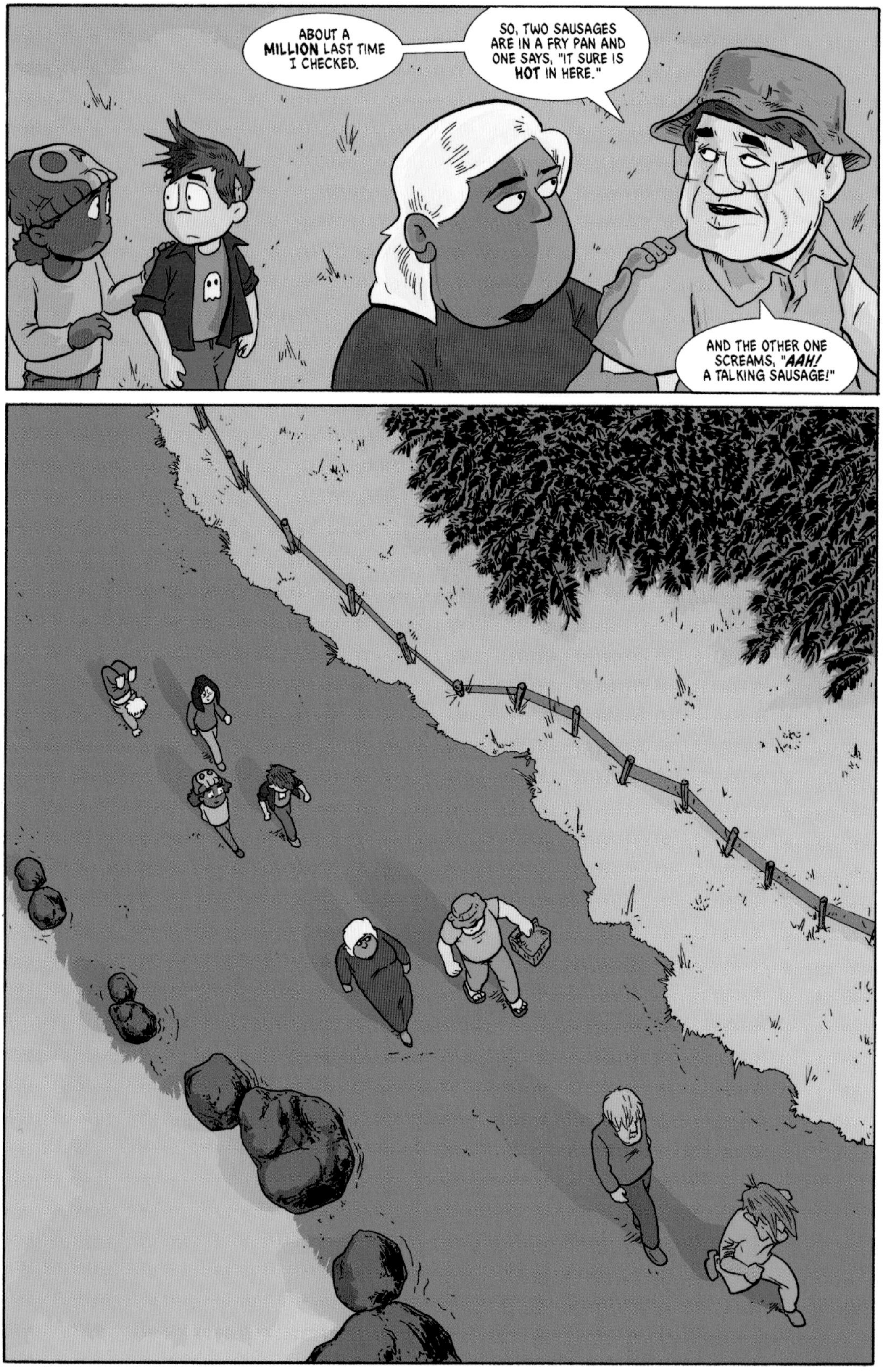
ABOUT A **MILLION** LAST TIME I CHECKED.
SO, TWO SAUSAGES ARE IN A FRY PAN AND ONE SAYS, "IT SURE IS **HOT** IN HERE."
AND THE OTHER ONE SCREAMS, "***AAH!*** A TALKING SAUSAGE!"

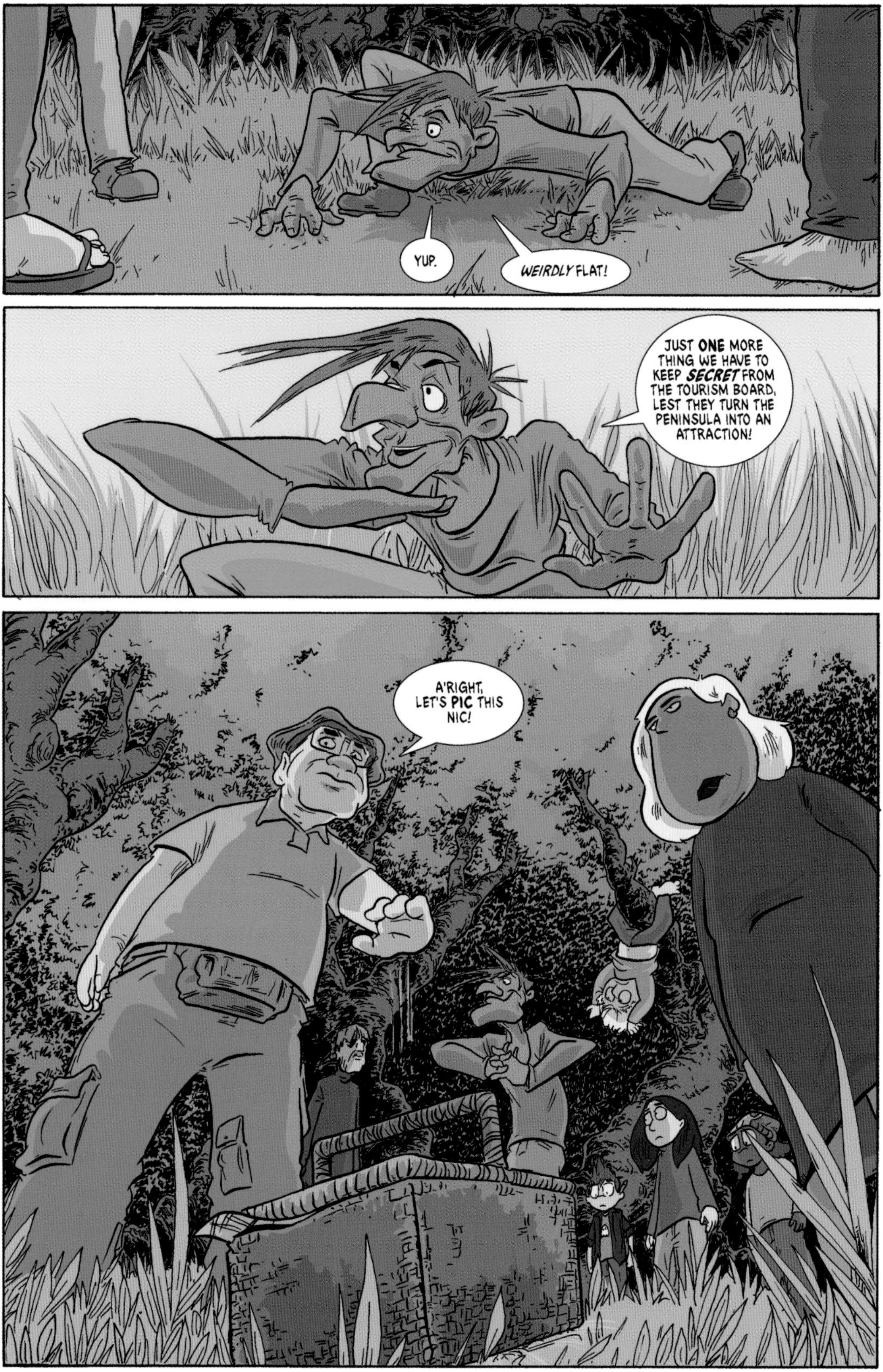
YUP.
WEIRDLY FLAT!
JUST ONE MORE THING WE HAVE TO KEEP SECRET FROM THE TOURISM BOARD, LEST THEY TURN THE PENINSULA INTO AN ATTRACTION!
A'RIGHT, LET'S PIC THIS NIC!

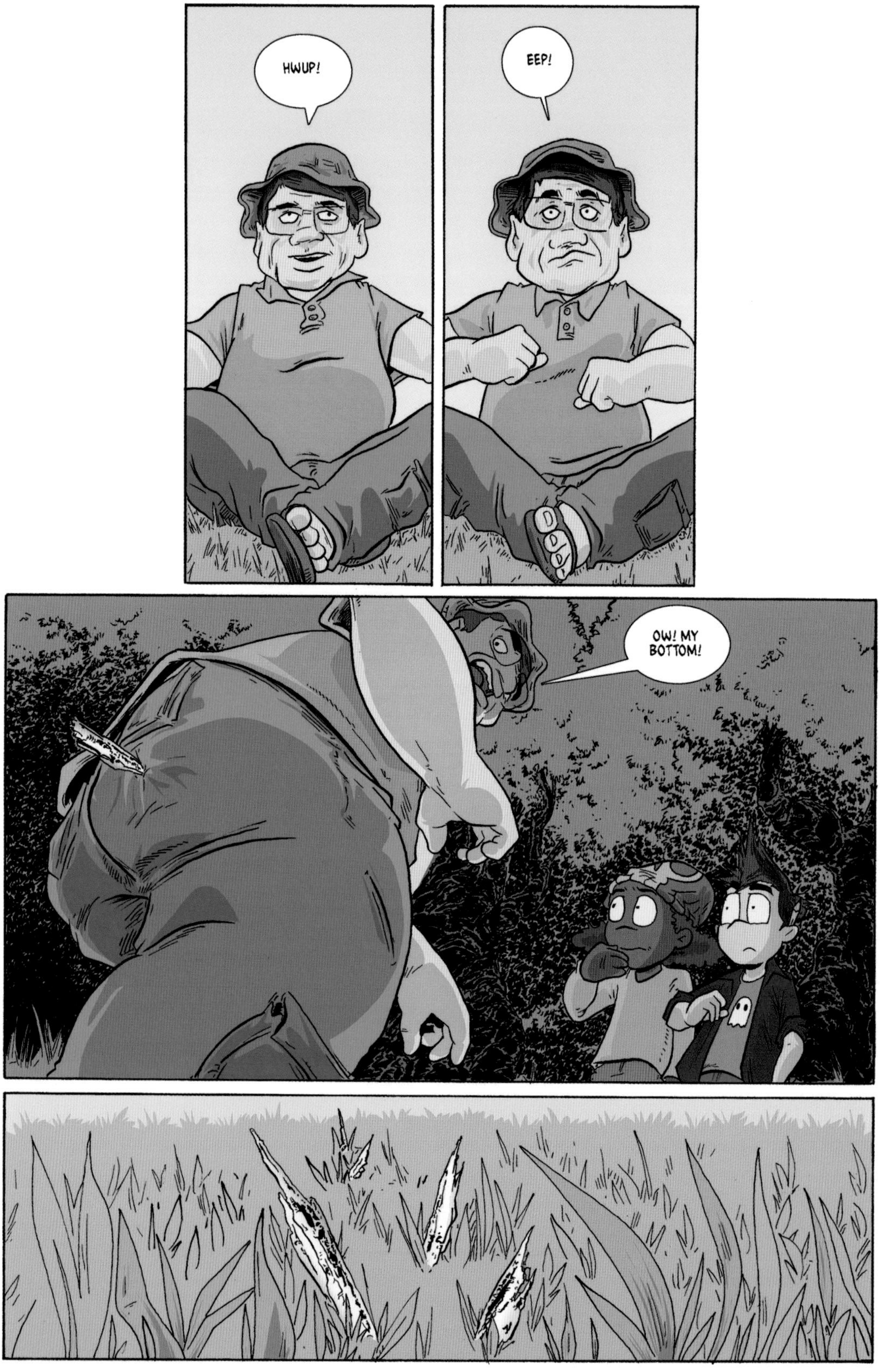
HWUP!
EEP!
OW! MY BOTTOM!

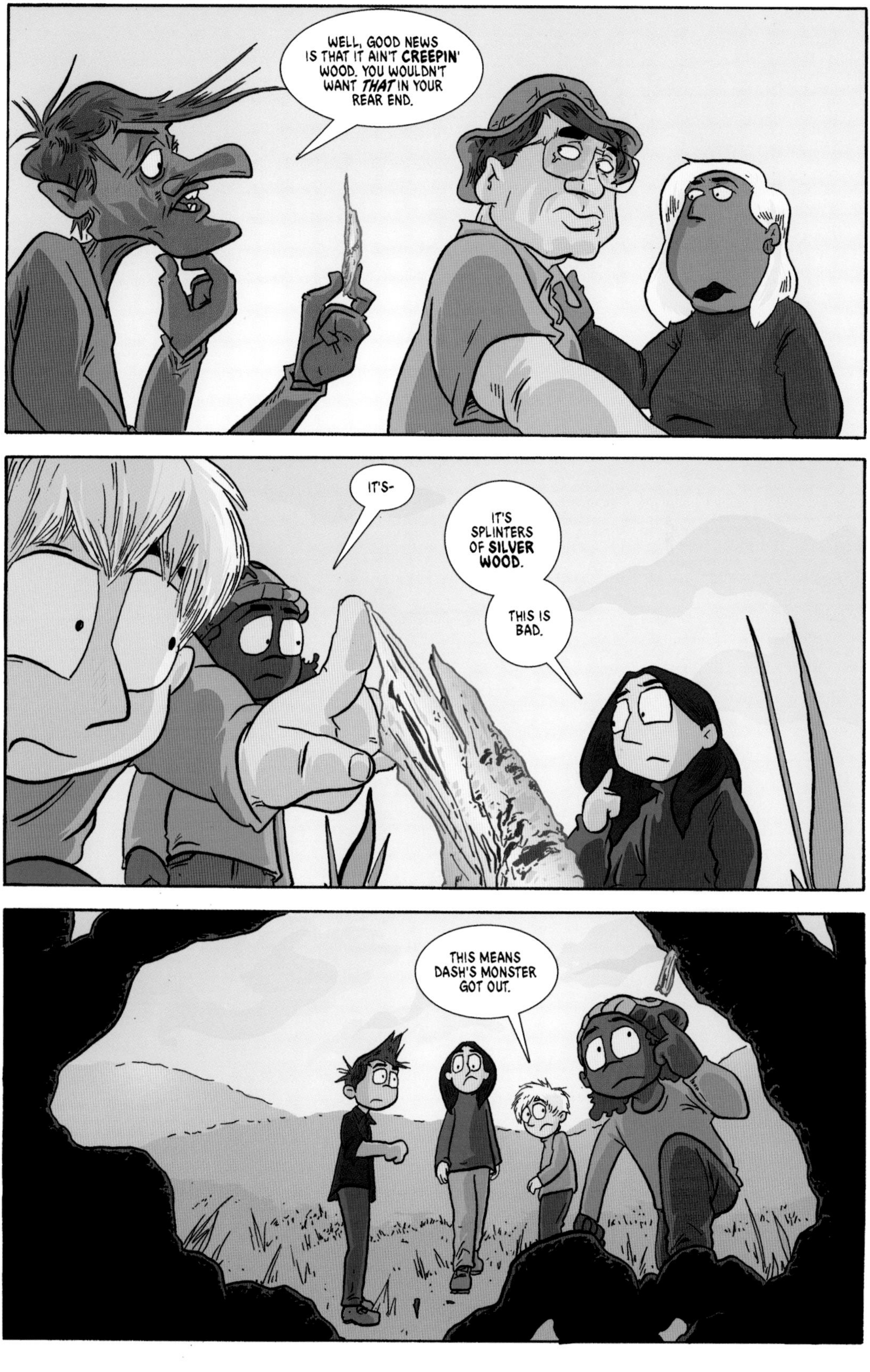
WELL, GOOD NEWS IS THAT IT AIN'T **CREEPIN'** WOOD. YOU WOULDN'T WANT ***THAT*** IN YOUR REAR END.
IT'S-
IT'S SPLINTERS OF **SILVER WOOD.**
THIS IS BAD.
THIS MEANS DASH'S MONSTER GOT OUT.

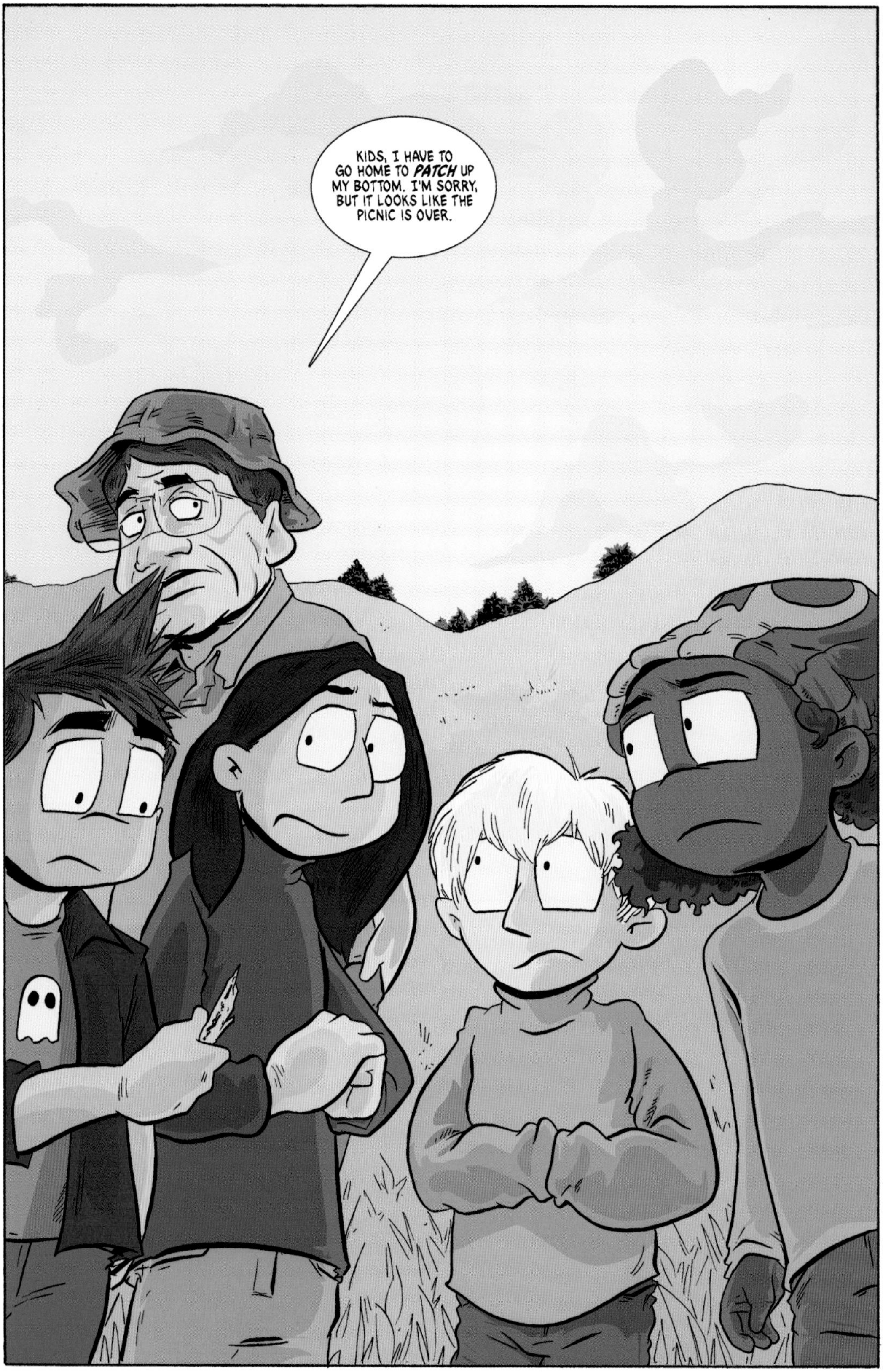
KIDS, I HAVE TO GO HOME TO PATCH UP MY BOTTOM. I'M SORRY, BUT IT LOOKS LIKE THE PICNIC IS OVER.

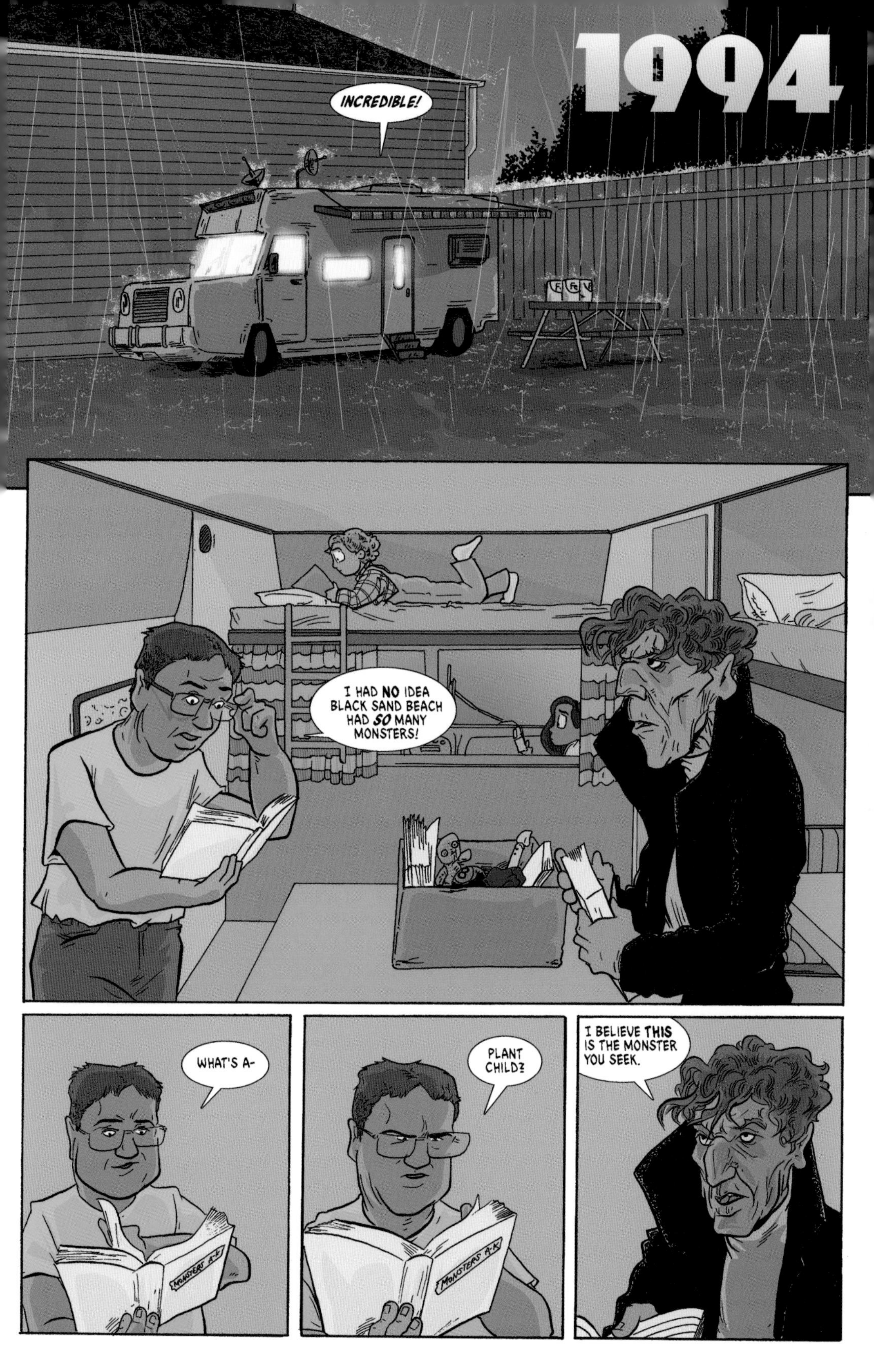
1994
INCREDIBLE!
I HAD NO IDEA BLACK SAND BEACH HAD SO MANY MONSTERS!
WHAT'S A-
PLANT CHILD?
I BELIEVE THIS IS THE MONSTER YOU SEEK.
MONSTERS A-K
MONSTERS A-K

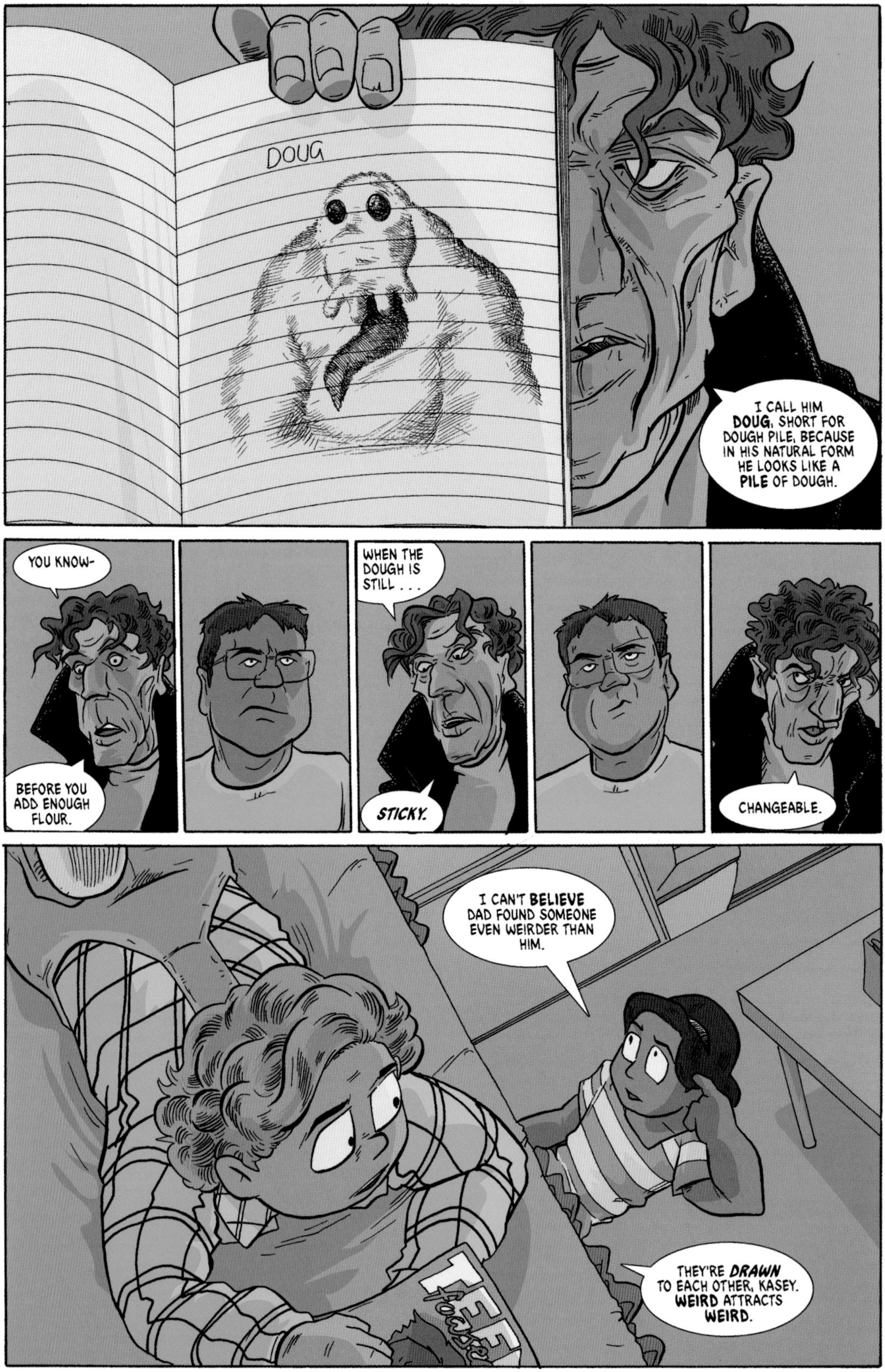
DOUG
I CALL HIM DOUG, SHORT FOR DOUGH PILE, BECAUSE IN HIS NATURAL FORM HE LOOKS LIKE A PILE OF DOUGH.
YOU KNOW-
BEFORE YOU ADD ENOUGH FLOUR.
WHEN THE DOUGH IS STILL . . .
STICKY.
CHANGEABLE.
I CAN'T BELIEVE DAD FOUND SOMEONE EVEN WEIRDER THAN HIM.
THEY'RE DRAWN TO EACH OTHER, KASEY. WEIRD ATTRACTS WEIRD.

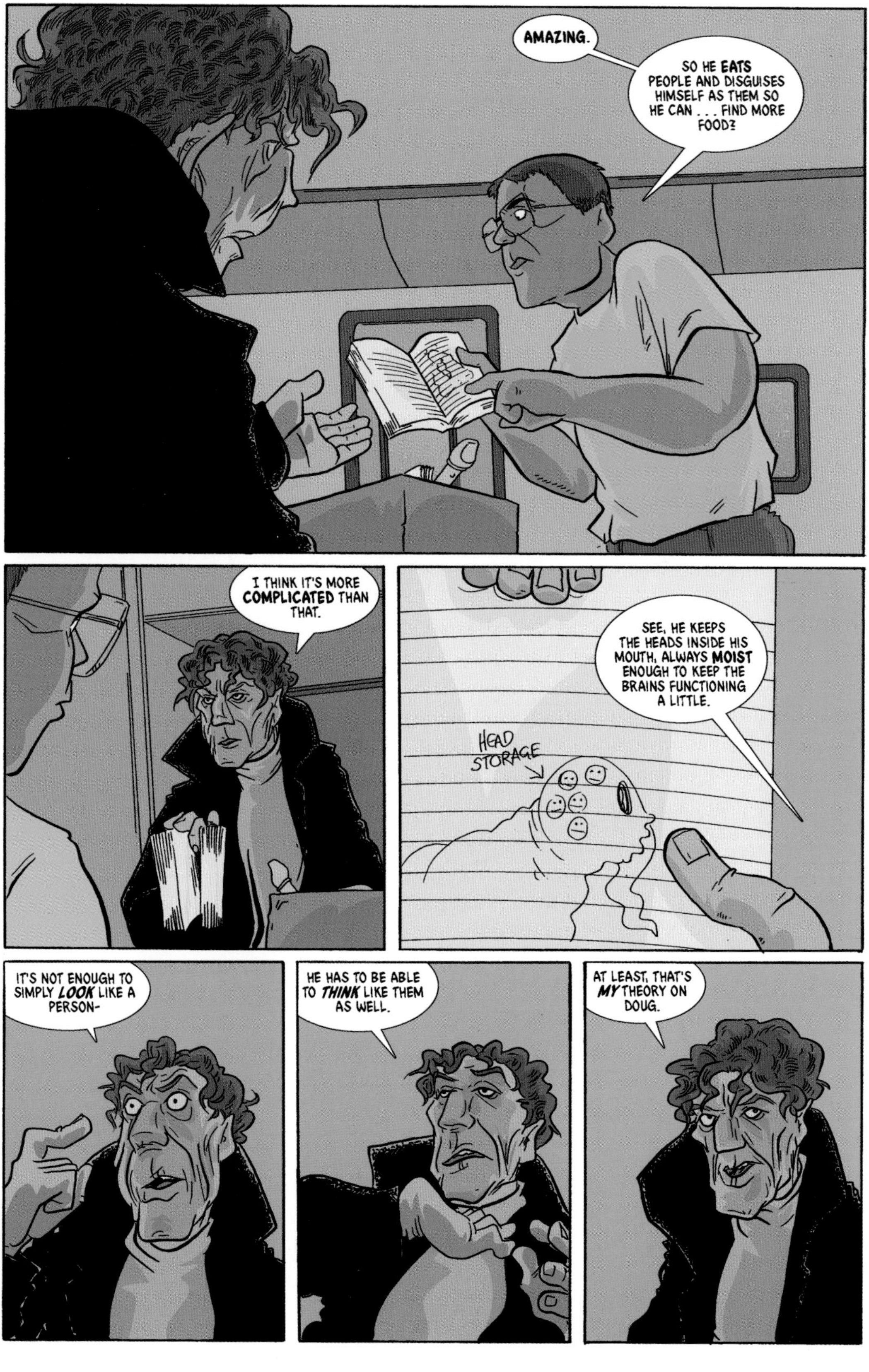
AMAZING.
SO HE EATS PEOPLE AND DISGUISES HIMSELF AS THEM SO HE CAN . . . FIND MORE FOOD?
I THINK IT'S MORE COMPLICATED THAN THAT.
SEE, HE KEEPS THE HEADS INSIDE HIS MOUTH, ALWAYS MOIST ENOUGH TO KEEP THE BRAINS FUNCTIONING A LITTLE.
HEAD STORAGE
IT'S NOT ENOUGH TO SIMPLY LOOK LIKE A PERSON-
HE HAS TO BE ABLE TO THINK LIKE THEM AS WELL.
AT LEAST, THAT'S MY THEORY ON DOUG.

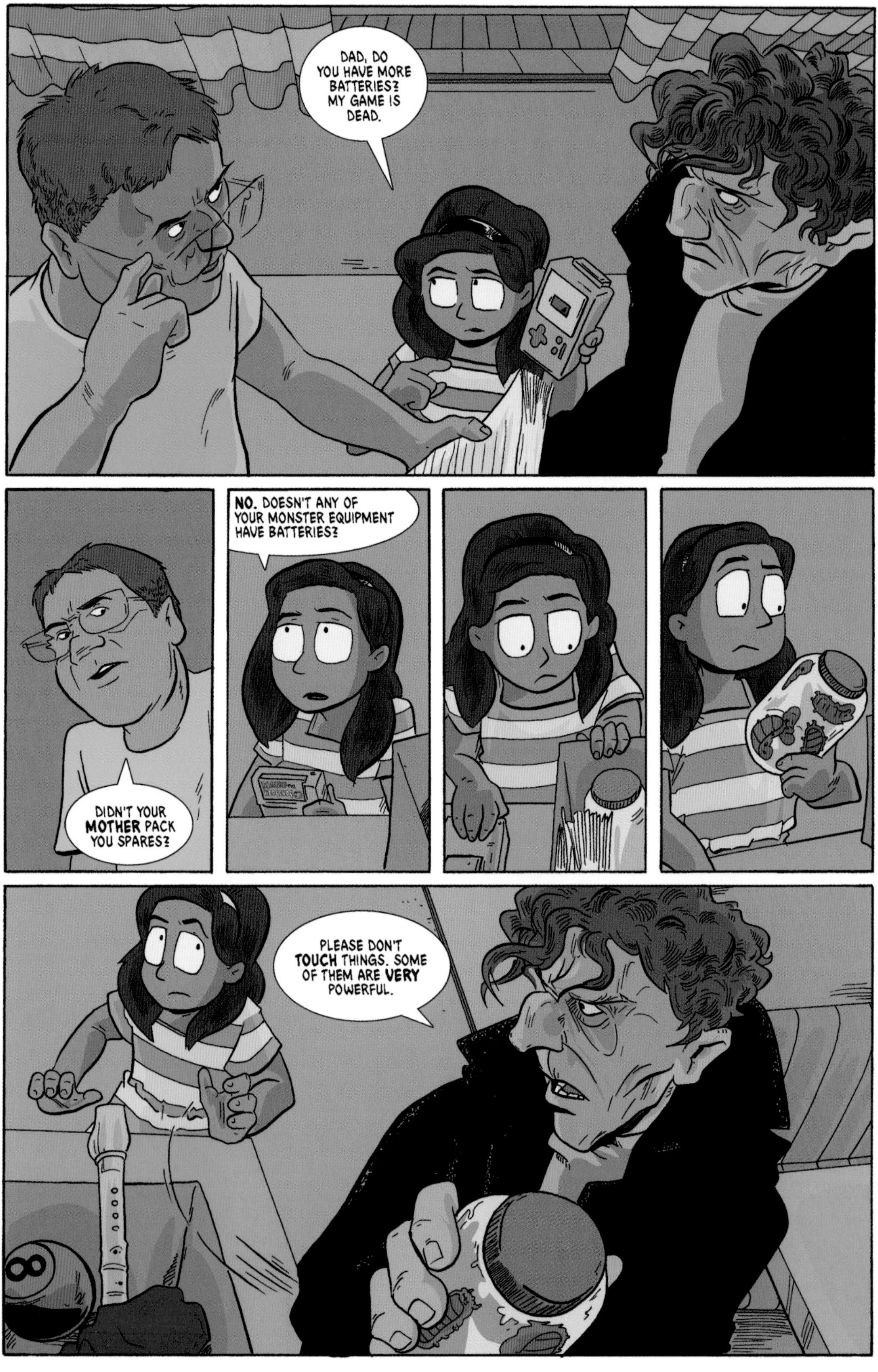
DAD, DO YOU HAVE MORE BATTERIES? MY GAME IS DEAD.
DIDN'T YOUR **MOTHER** PACK YOU SPARES?
NO. DOESN'T ANY OF YOUR MONSTER EQUIPMENT HAVE BATTERIES?
PLEASE DON'T **TOUCH** THINGS. SOME OF THEM ARE **VERY** POWERFUL.

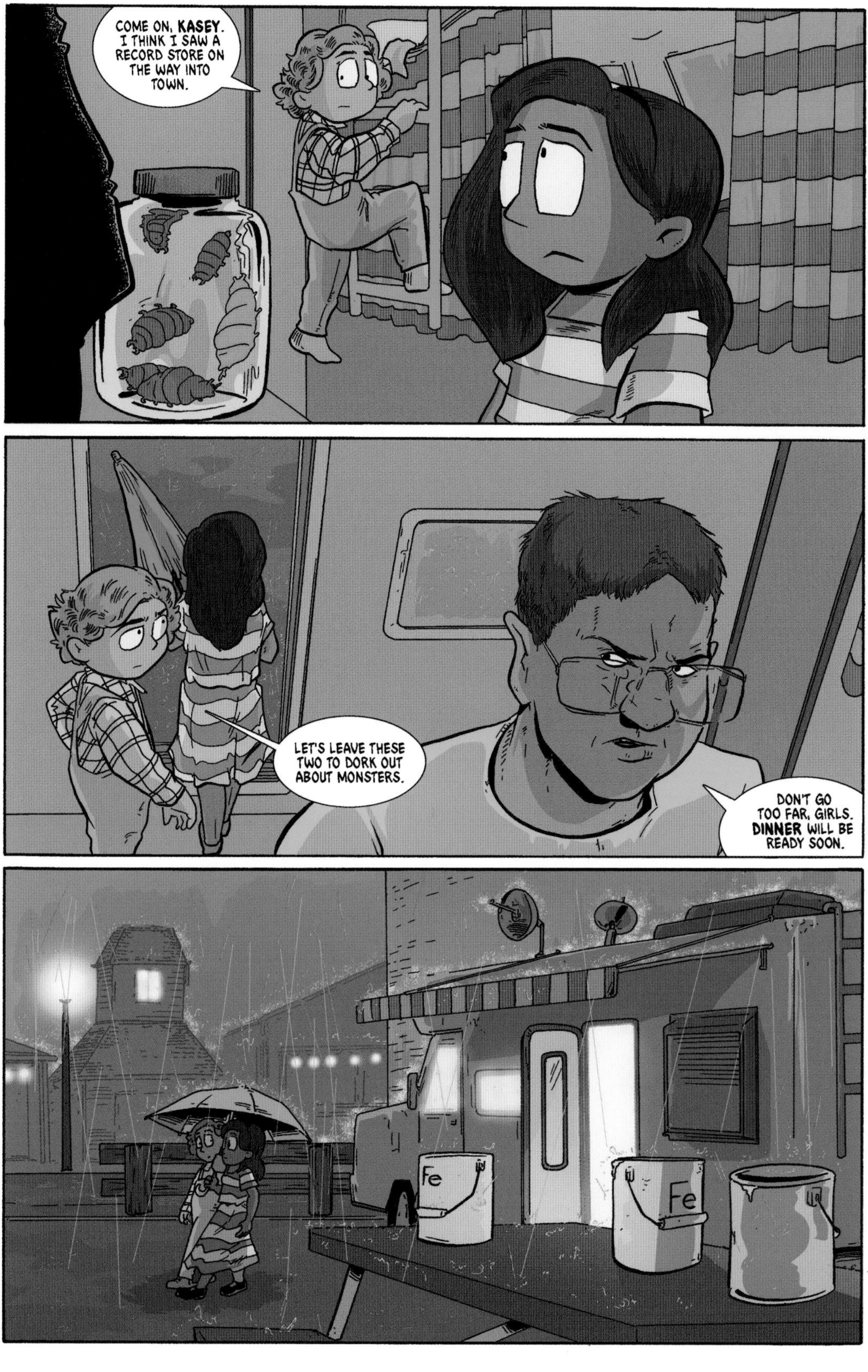
COME ON, KASEY. I THINK I SAW A RECORD STORE ON THE WAY INTO TOWN.
LET'S LEAVE THESE TWO TO DORK OUT ABOUT MONSTERS.
DON'T GO TOO FAR, GIRLS. DINNER WILL BE READY SOON.
Fe
Fe

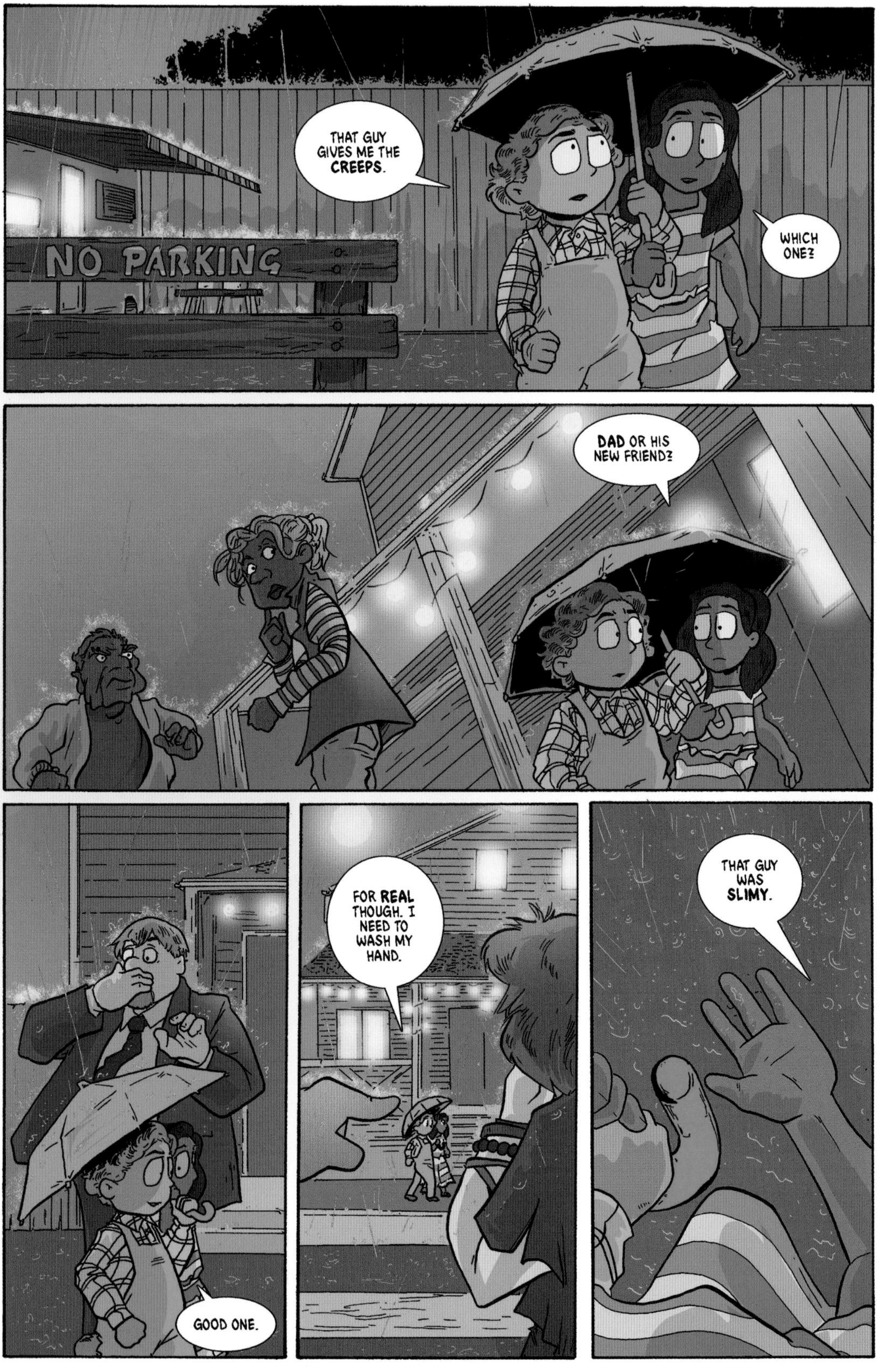
THAT GUY GIVES ME THE CREEPS.
WHICH ONE?
DAD OR HIS NEW FRIEND?
NO PARKING
GOOD ONE.
FOR REAL THOUGH. I NEED TO WASH MY HAND.
THAT GUY WAS SLIMY.

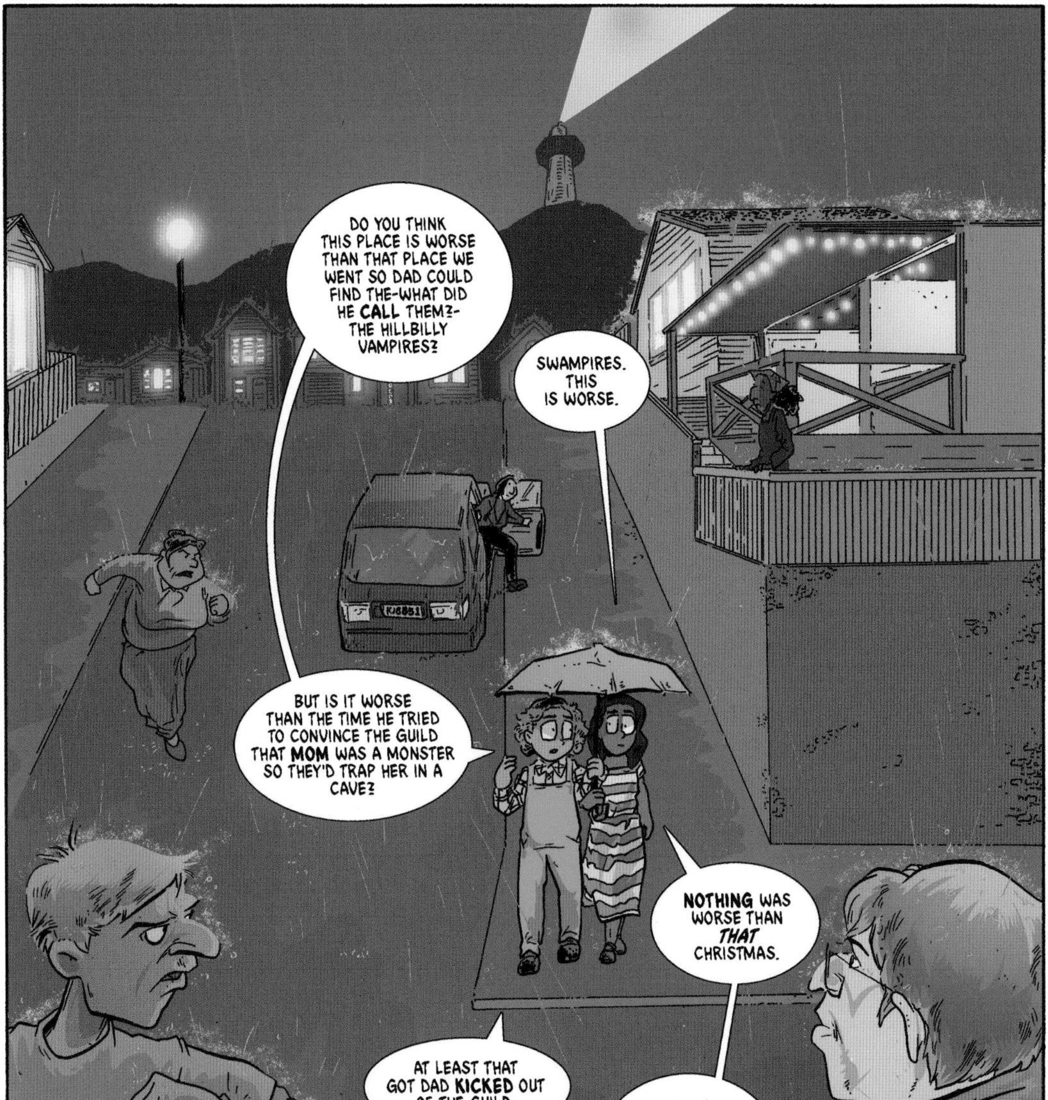
DO YOU THINK THIS PLACE IS WORSE THAN THAT PLACE WE WENT SO DAD COULD FIND THE-WHAT DID HE CALL THEM?- THE HILLBILLY VAMPIRES?
SWAMPIRES. THIS IS WORSE.
BUT IS IT WORSE THAN THE TIME HE TRIED TO CONVINCE THE GUILD THAT MOM WAS A MONSTER SO THEY'D TRAP HER IN A CAVE?
NOTHING WAS WORSE THAN THAT CHRISTMAS.
AT LEAST THAT GOT DAD KICKED OUT OF THE GUILD.
I MISS WHEN DAD JUST FIXED FAX MACHINES AND DID THE MONSTER STUFF ON WEEKENDS.

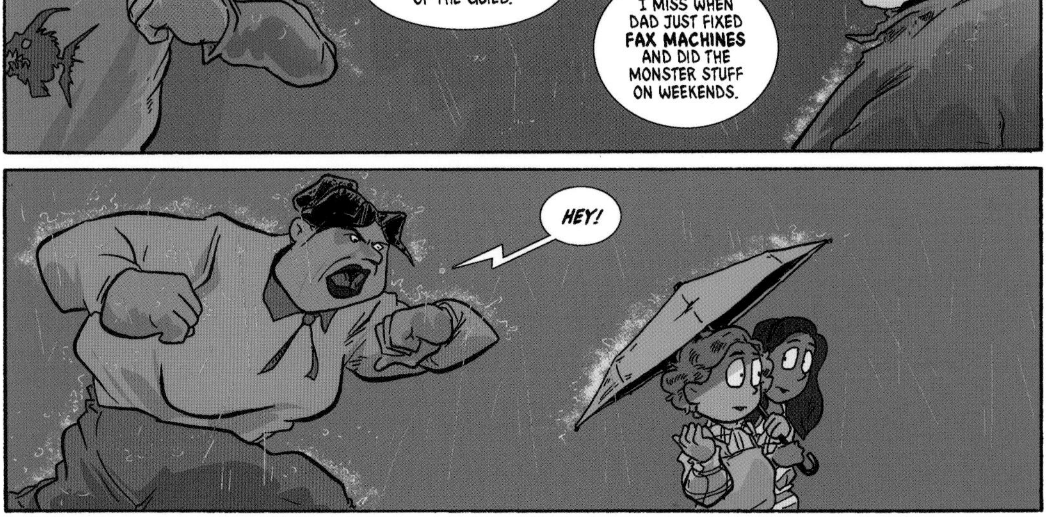
HEY!

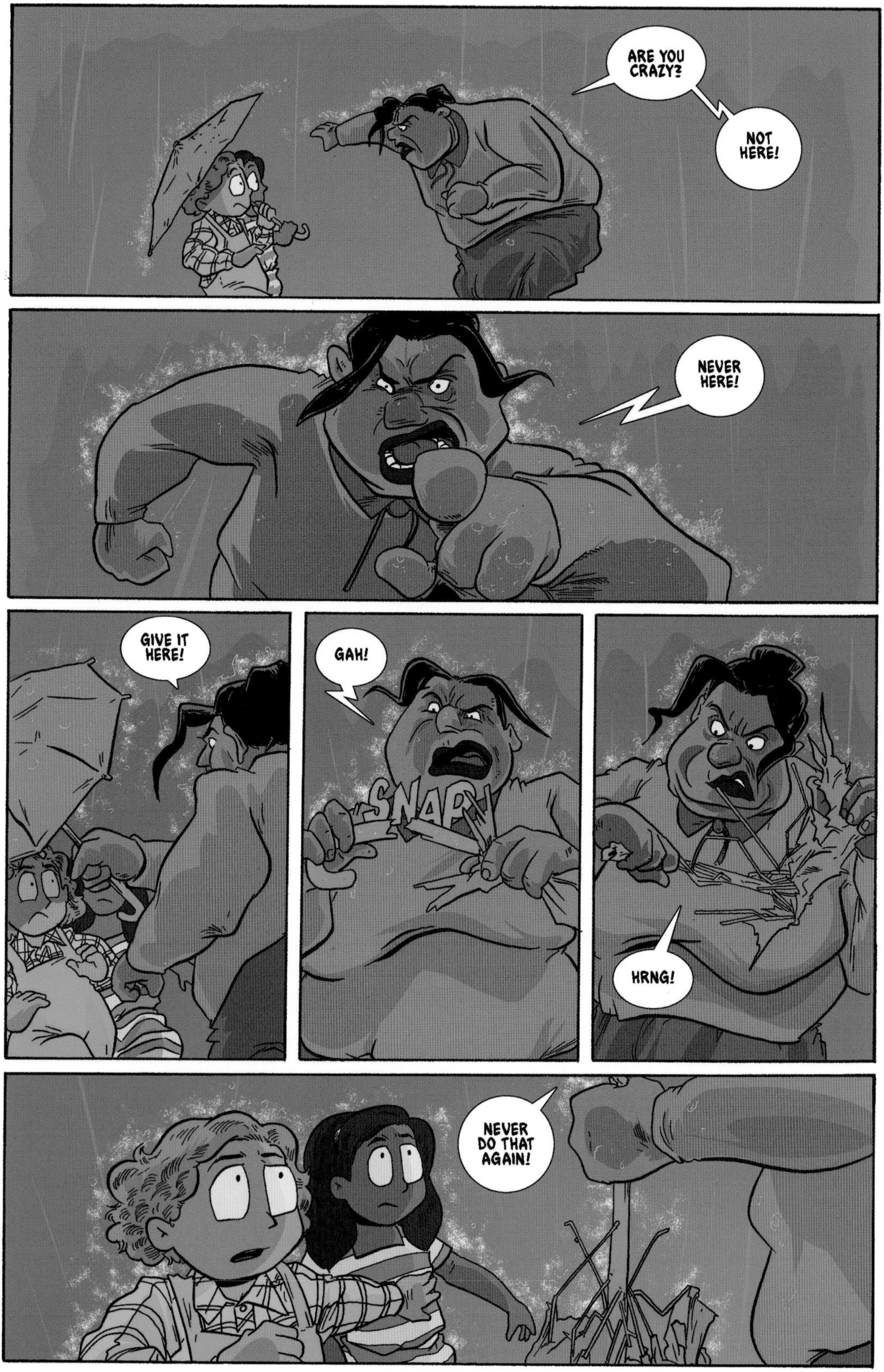
ARE YOU CRAZY?
NOT HERE!
NEVER HERE!
GIVE IT HERE!
GAH!
SNAP!
HRNG!
NEVER DO THAT AGAIN!

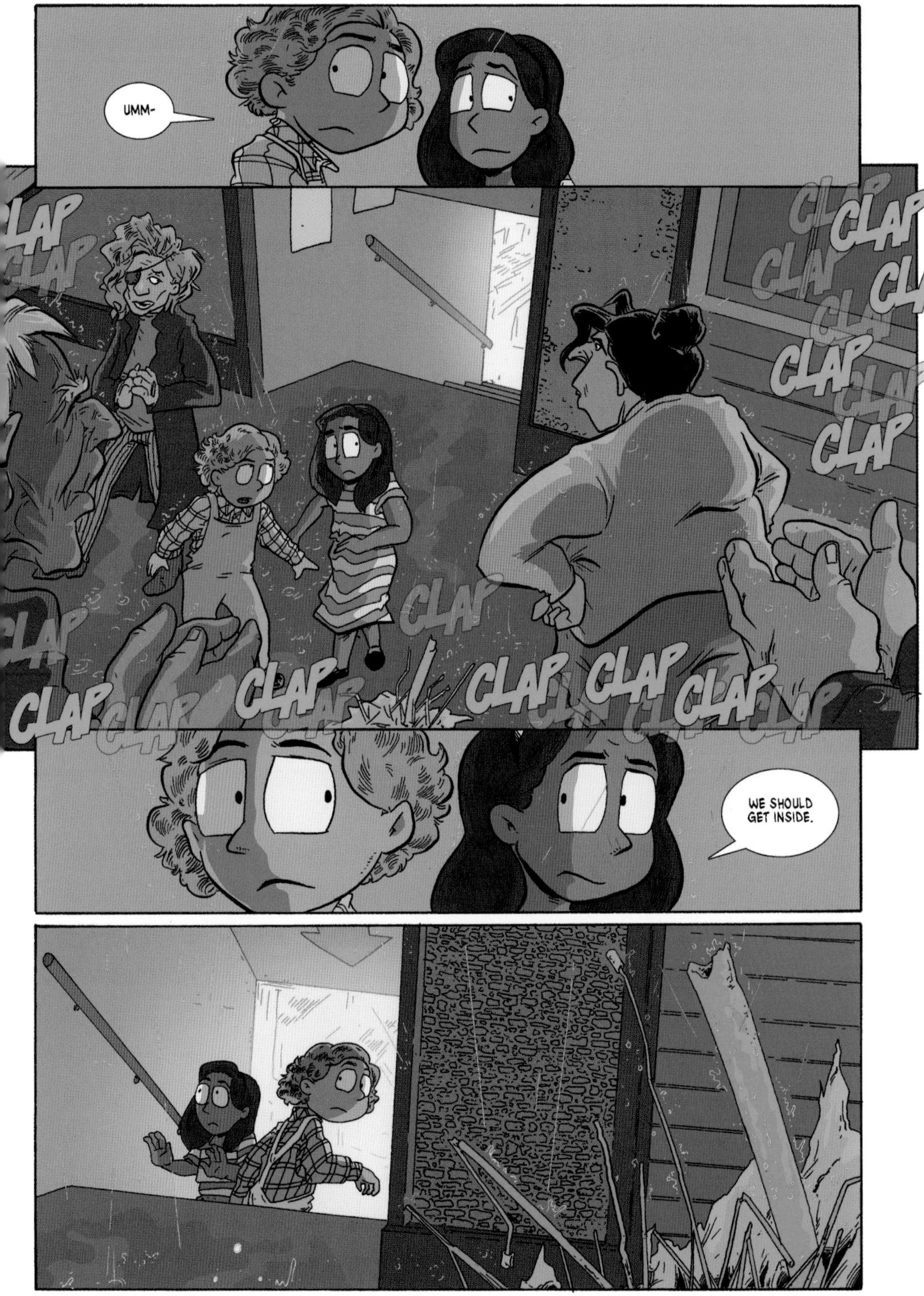
UMM-
CLAP CLAP CLAP CLAP CLAP CLAP CLAP CLAP CLAP CLAP CLAP CLAP
WE SHOULD GET INSIDE.

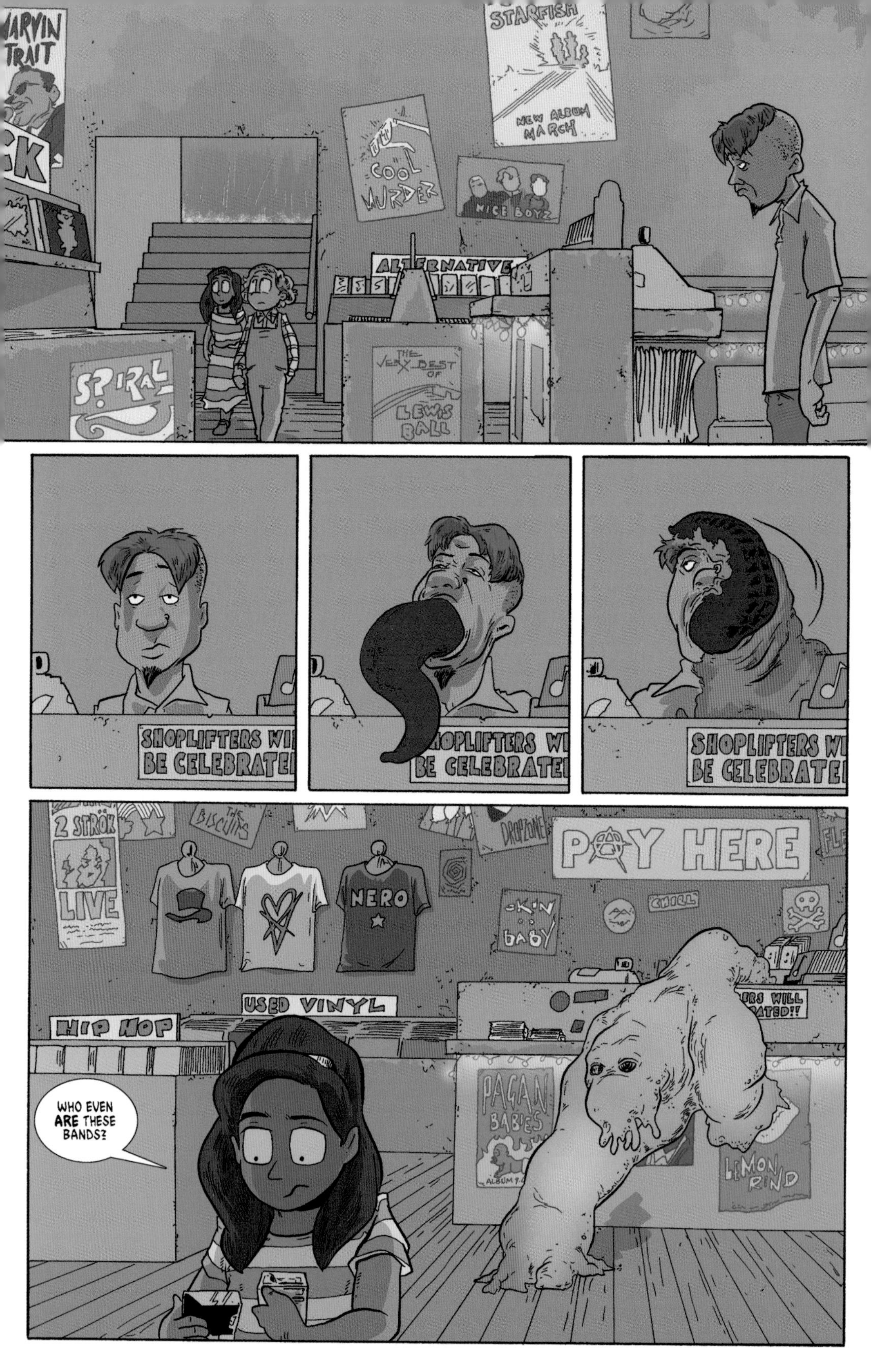

MARVIN TRAIT
STARFISH
NEW ALBUM MARCH
COOL MURDER
NICE BOYZ
ALTERNATIVE
S?IRAL
THE VERY BEST OF LEWIS BALL
SHOPLIFTERS WI
BE CELEBRATE
SHOPLIFTERS WI
BE CELEBRATE
SHOPLIFTERS WI
BE CELEBRATE
2 STRÖK
LIVE
THE BISCUITS
DROPZONE
PAY HERE
NERO
SKIN BABY
CHILL
USED VINYL
HIP HOP
PAGAN BABIES
LEMON RIND
WHO EVEN **ARE** THESE BANDS?

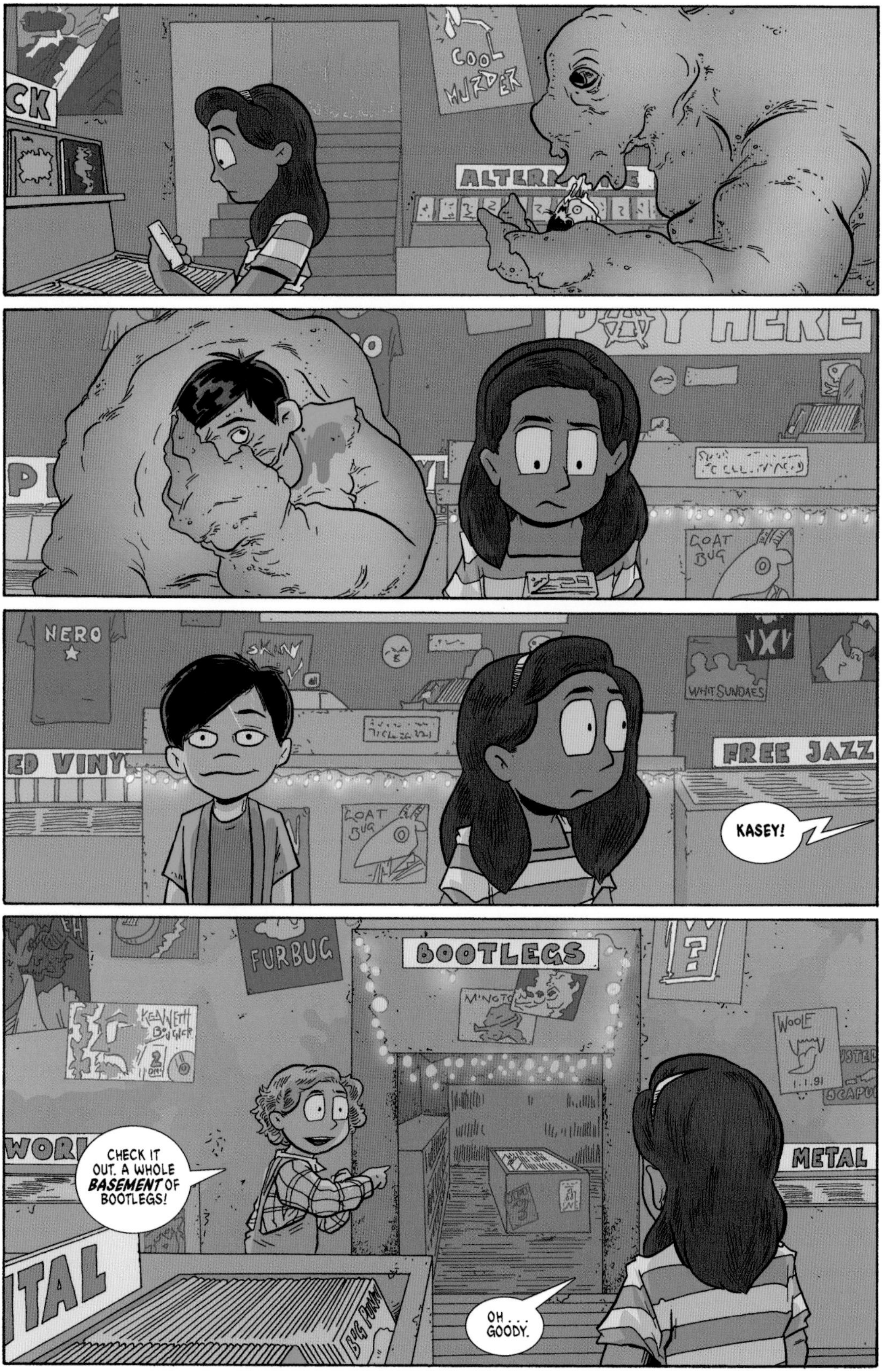
COOL MURDER
PAY HERE
GOAT BUG
NERO
WHITSUNDAES
FREE JAZZ
KASEY!
FURBUG
BOOTLEGS
WOOLF
1.1.91
METAL
CHECK IT OUT. A WHOLE *BASEMENT* OF BOOTLEGS!
OH . . . GOODY.

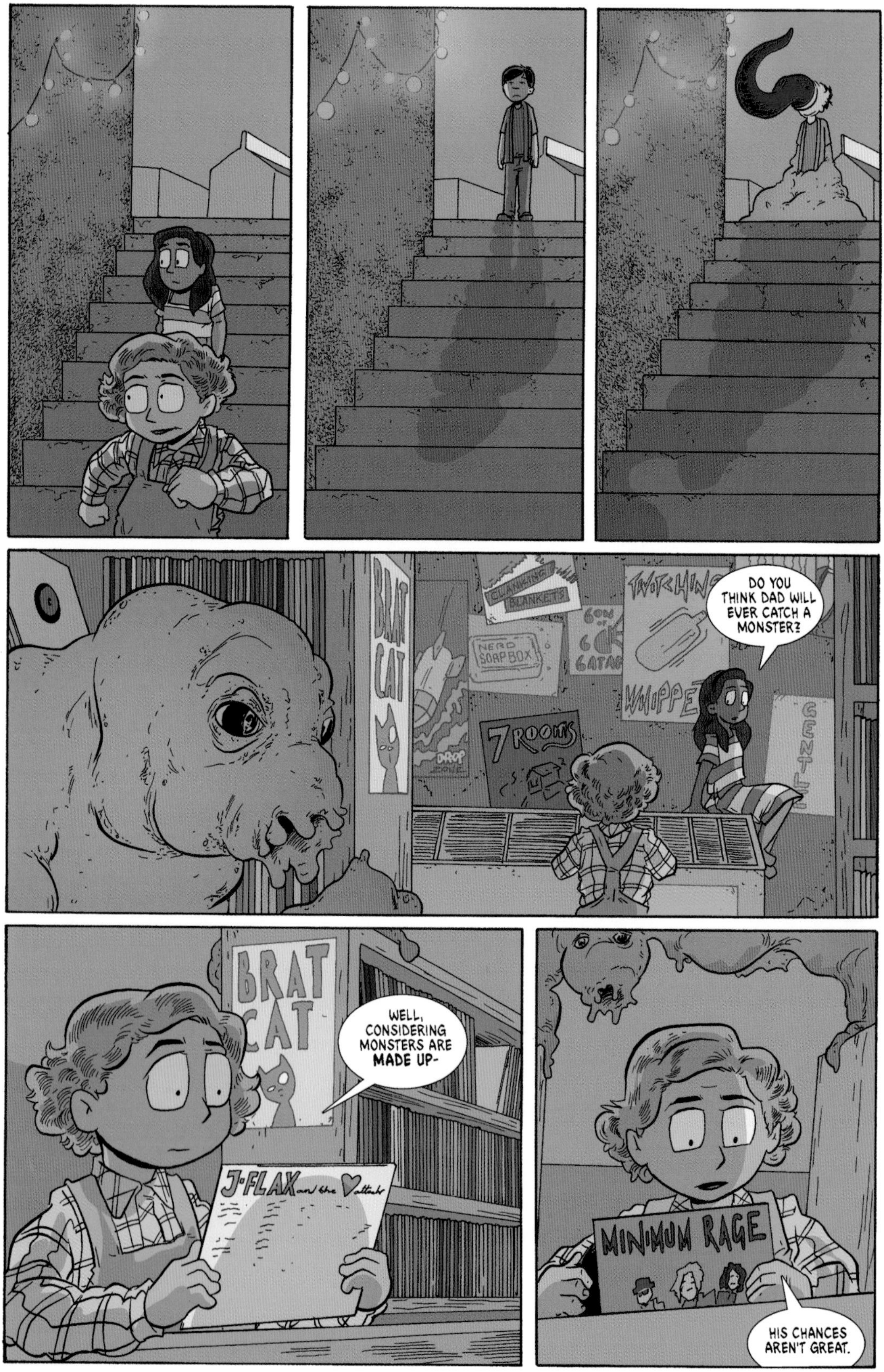
BRAT CAT
CLANKING BLANKETS
NERD SOAPBOX
7 ROOMS
DO YOU THINK DAD WILL EVER CATCH A MONSTER?
BRAT CAT
WELL, CONSIDERING MONSTERS ARE **MADE UP**-
MINIMUM RAGE
HIS CHANCES AREN'T GREAT.

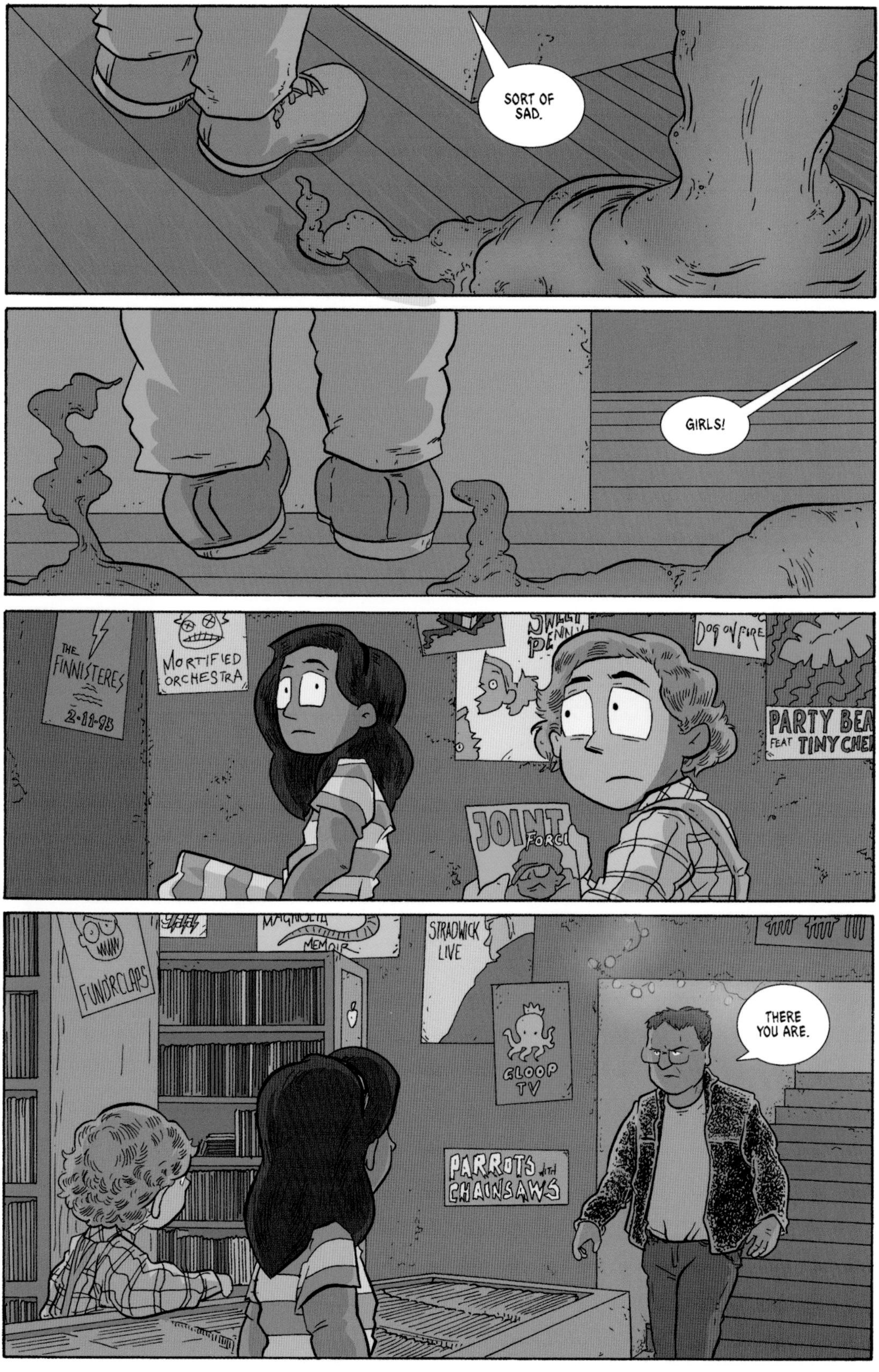
SORT OF SAD.
GIRLS!
THE FINNISTERES 2-11-93
MORTIFIED ORCHESTRA
DOG ON FIRE
FUND'RCLAPS
STRADWICK LIVE
GLOOP TV
PARROTS with CHAINSAWS
THERE YOU ARE.

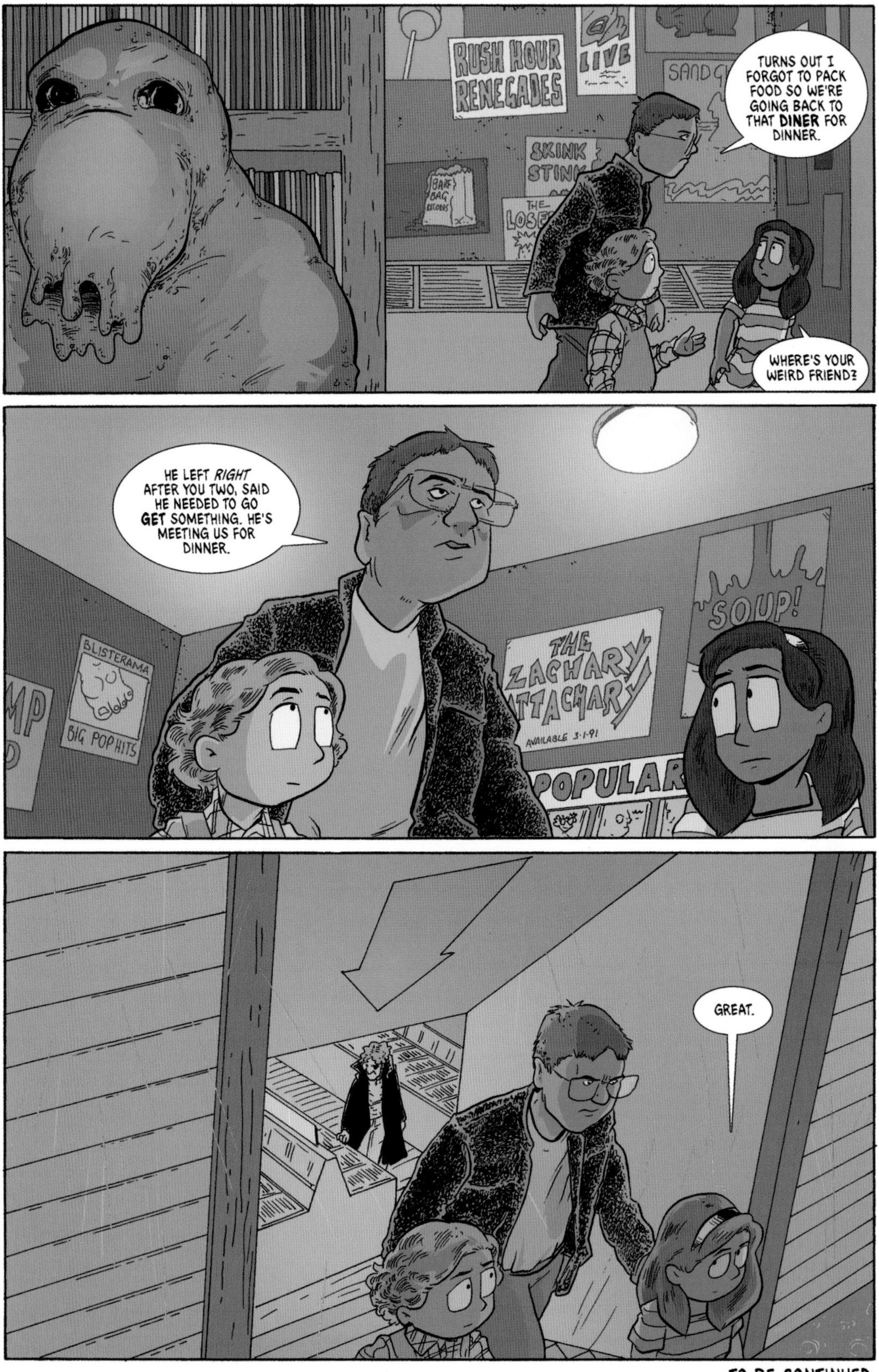

RUSH HOUR RENEGADES
LIVE
SKINK STINK
TURNS OUT I FORGOT TO PACK FOOD SO WE'RE GOING BACK TO THAT **DINER** FOR DINNER.
WHERE'S YOUR WEIRD FRIEND?
HE LEFT *RIGHT* AFTER YOU TWO, SAID HE NEEDED TO GO **GET** SOMETHING. HE'S MEETING US FOR DINNER.
BLISTERAMA
BIG POP HITS
THE ZACHARY ATTACHARY
AVAILABLE 3·1·91
SOUP!
GREAT.

TO BE CONTINUED.

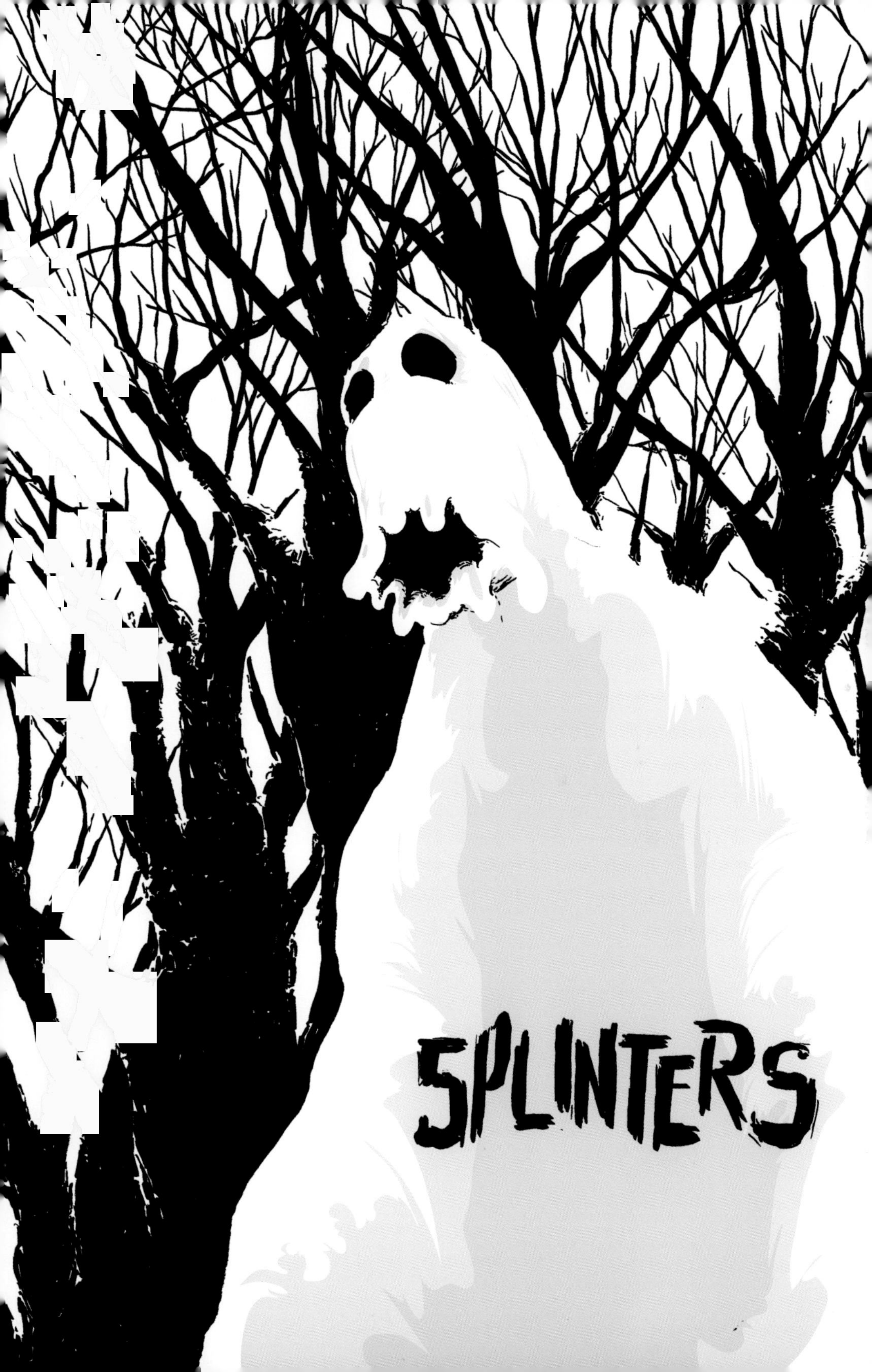
SPLINTERS

SPLINTERS

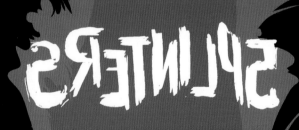

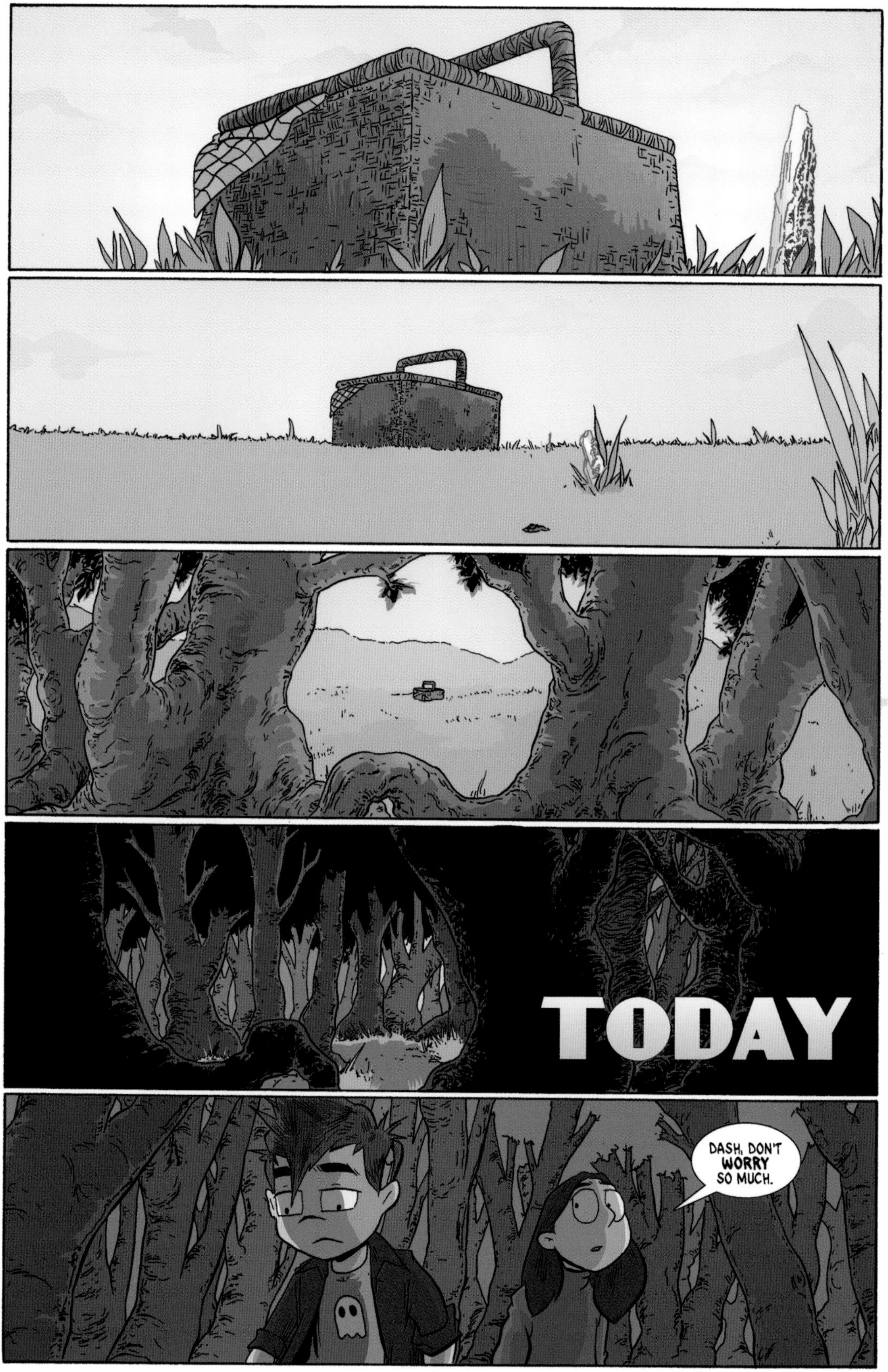
TODAY
DASH, DON'T WORRY SO MUCH.

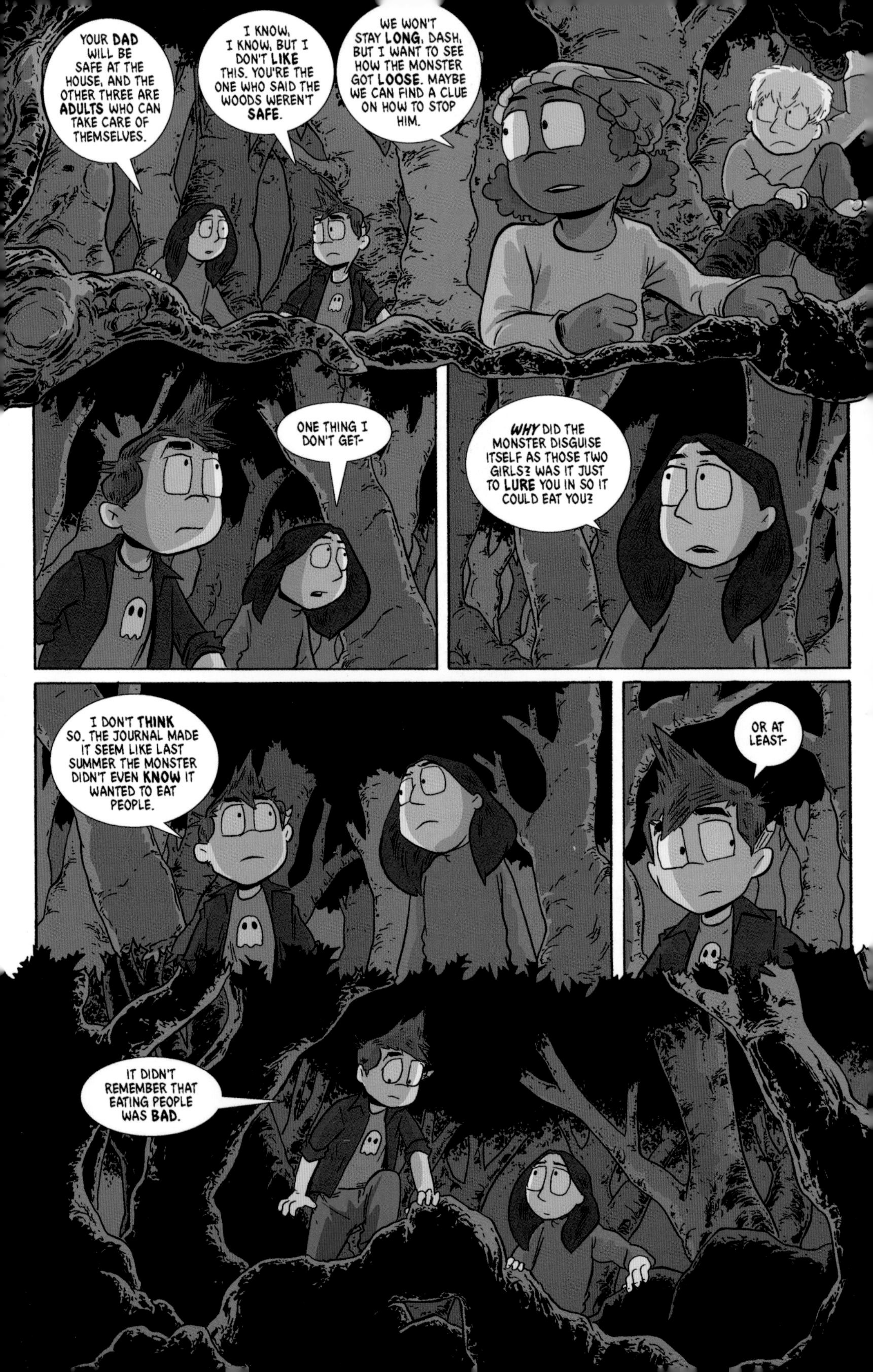

YOUR DAD WILL BE SAFE AT THE HOUSE, AND THE OTHER THREE ARE ADULTS WHO CAN TAKE CARE OF THEMSELVES.
I KNOW, I KNOW, BUT I DON'T LIKE THIS. YOU'RE THE ONE WHO SAID THE WOODS WEREN'T SAFE.
WE WON'T STAY LONG, DASH, BUT I WANT TO SEE HOW THE MONSTER GOT LOOSE. MAYBE WE CAN FIND A CLUE ON HOW TO STOP HIM.
ONE THING I DON'T GET-
WHY DID THE MONSTER DISGUISE ITSELF AS THOSE TWO GIRLS? WAS IT JUST TO LURE YOU IN SO IT COULD EAT YOU?
I DON'T THINK SO. THE JOURNAL MADE IT SEEM LIKE LAST SUMMER THE MONSTER DIDN'T EVEN KNOW IT WANTED TO EAT PEOPLE.
OR AT LEAST-
IT DIDN'T REMEMBER THAT EATING PEOPLE WAS BAD.

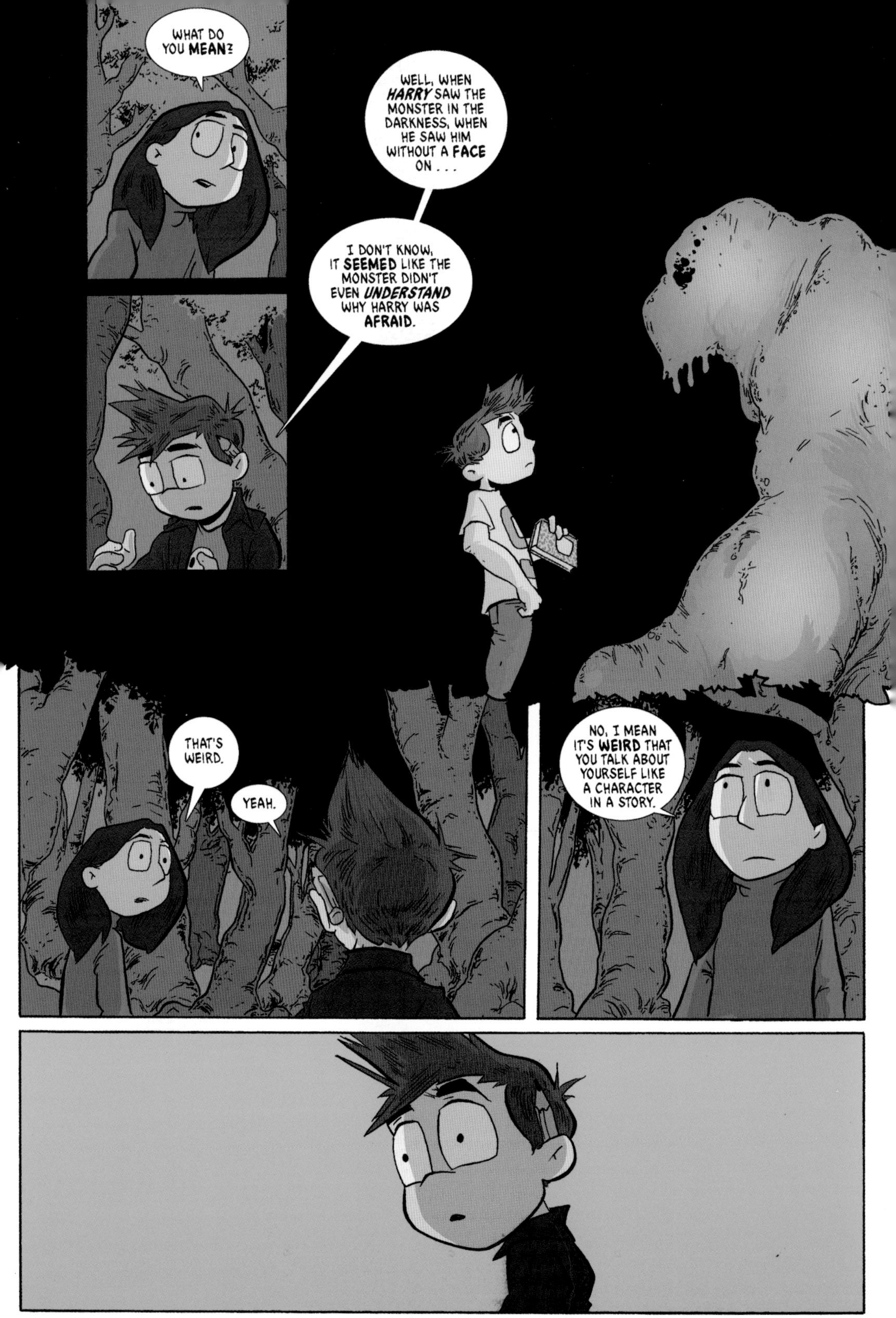
WHAT DO YOU MEAN?
WELL, WHEN HARRY SAW THE MONSTER IN THE DARKNESS, WHEN HE SAW HIM WITHOUT A FACE ON . . .
I DON'T KNOW, IT SEEMED LIKE THE MONSTER DIDN'T EVEN UNDERSTAND WHY HARRY WAS AFRAID.
THAT'S WEIRD.
YEAH.
NO, I MEAN IT'S WEIRD THAT YOU TALK ABOUT YOURSELF LIKE A CHARACTER IN A STORY.

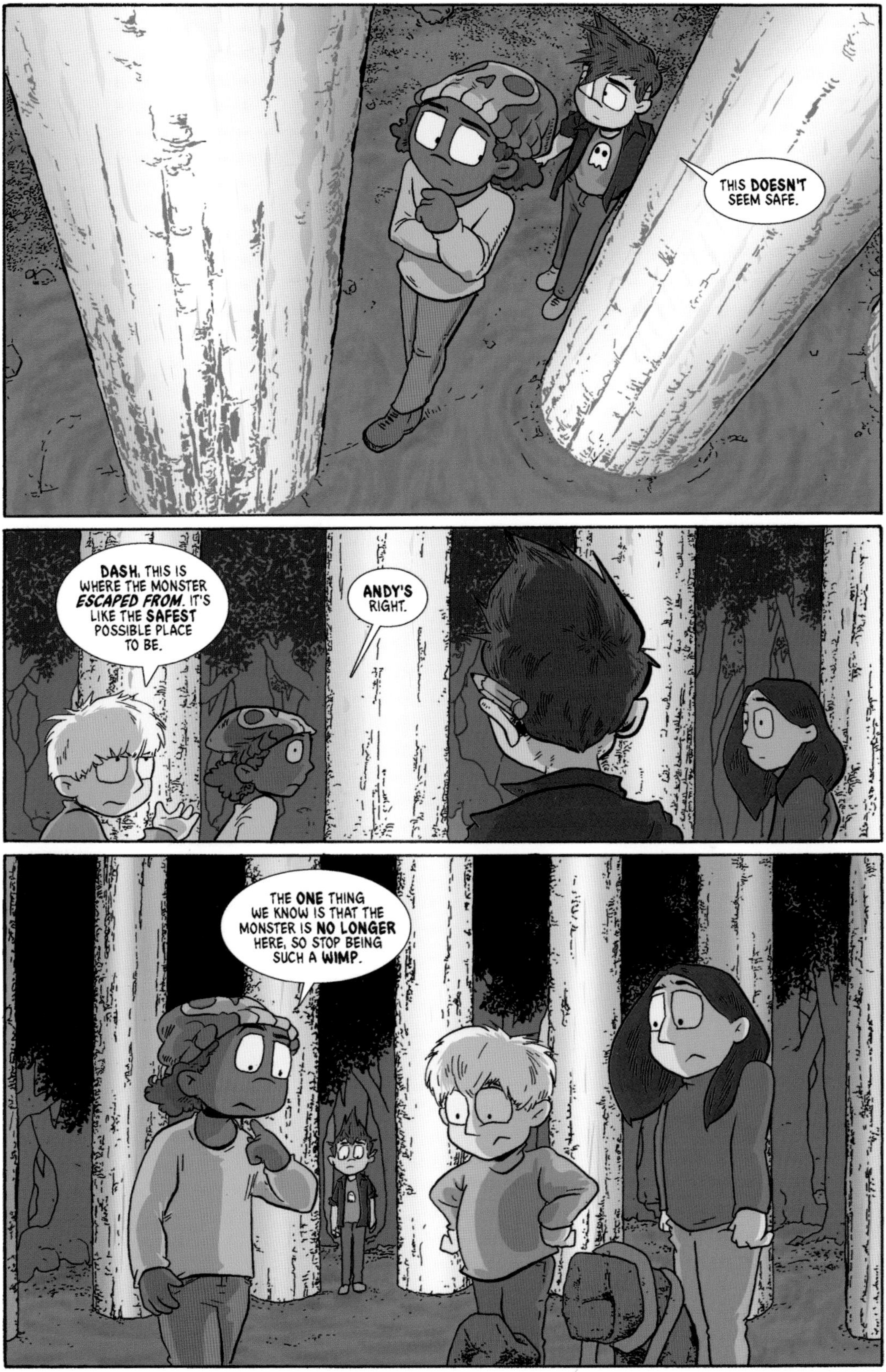
THIS **DOESN'T** SEEM SAFE.
DASH, THIS IS WHERE THE MONSTER ***ESCAPED FROM***. IT'S LIKE THE **SAFEST** POSSIBLE PLACE TO BE.
ANDY'S RIGHT.
THE **ONE** THING WE KNOW IS THAT THE MONSTER IS **NO LONGER** HERE, SO STOP BEING SUCH A **WIMP**.

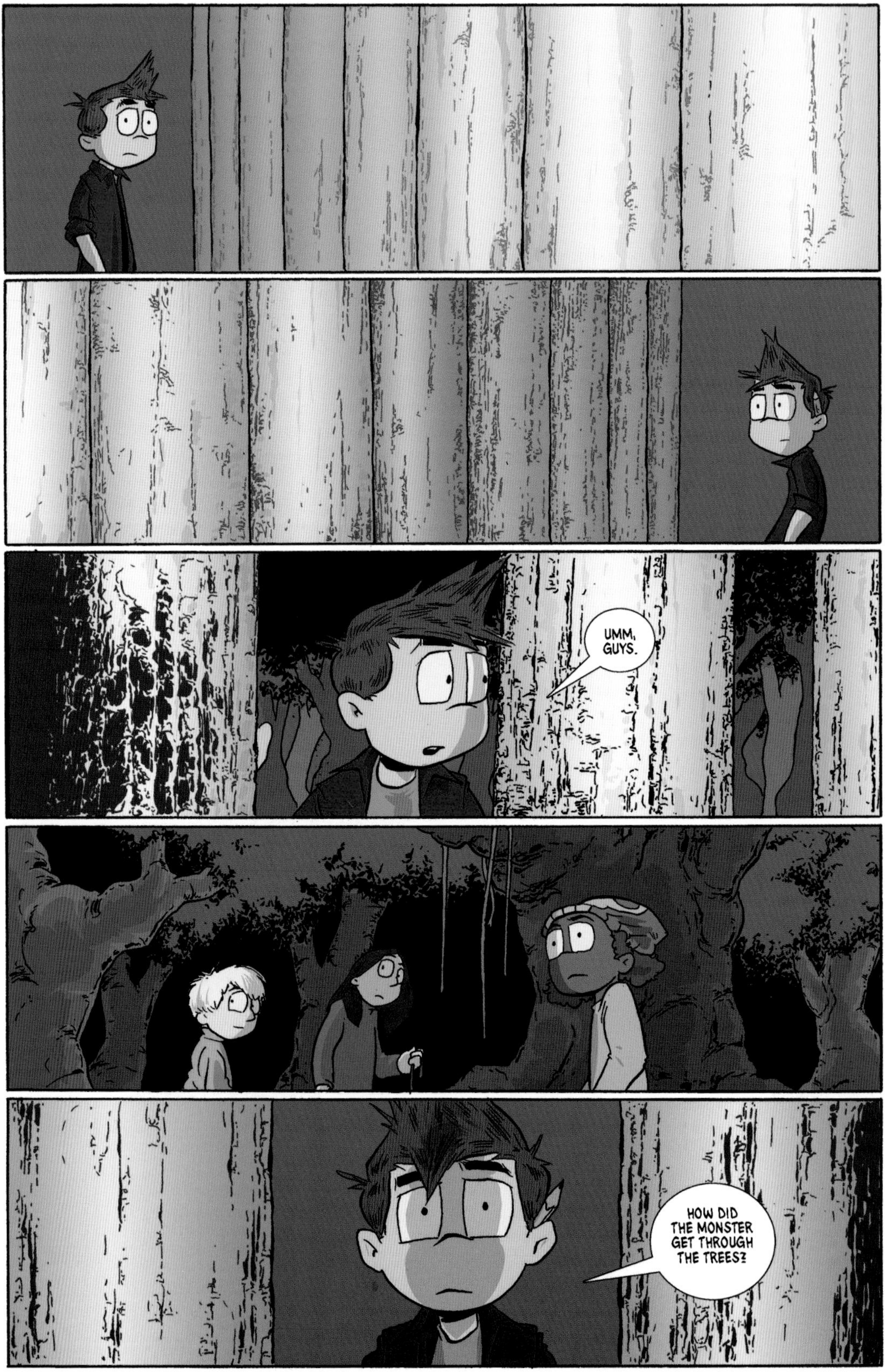
UMM, GUYS.
HOW DID THE MONSTER GET THROUGH THE TREES?

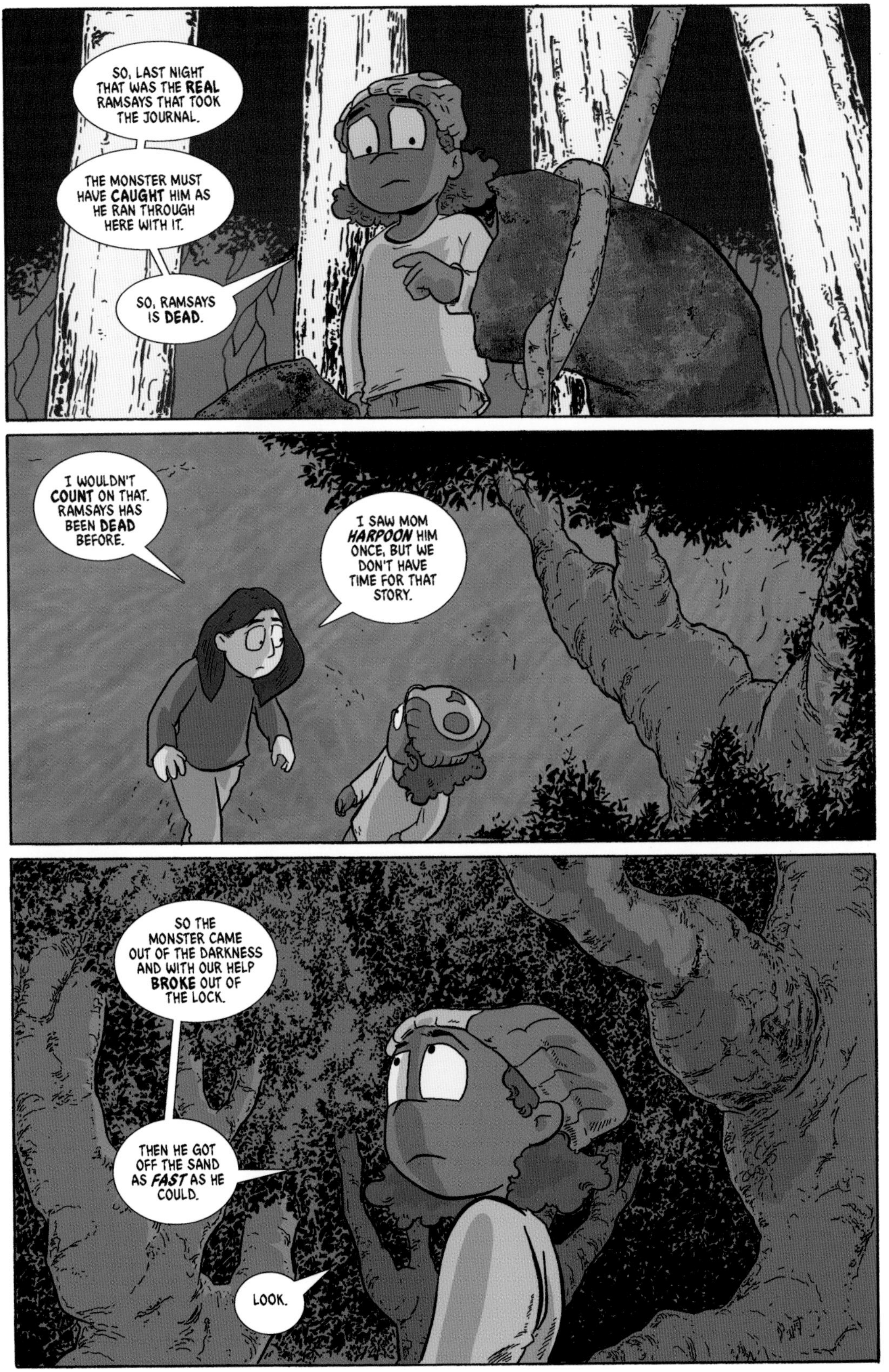
SO, LAST NIGHT THAT WAS THE **REAL** RAMSAYS THAT TOOK THE JOURNAL.
THE MONSTER MUST HAVE **CAUGHT** HIM AS HE RAN THROUGH HERE WITH IT.
SO, RAMSAYS IS **DEAD**.
I WOULDN'T **COUNT** ON THAT. RAMSAYS HAS BEEN **DEAD** BEFORE.
I SAW MOM ***HARPOON*** HIM ONCE, BUT WE DON'T HAVE TIME FOR THAT STORY.
SO THE MONSTER CAME OUT OF THE DARKNESS AND WITH OUR HELP **BROKE** OUT OF THE LOCK.
THEN HE GOT OFF THE SAND AS ***FAST*** AS HE COULD.
LOOK.

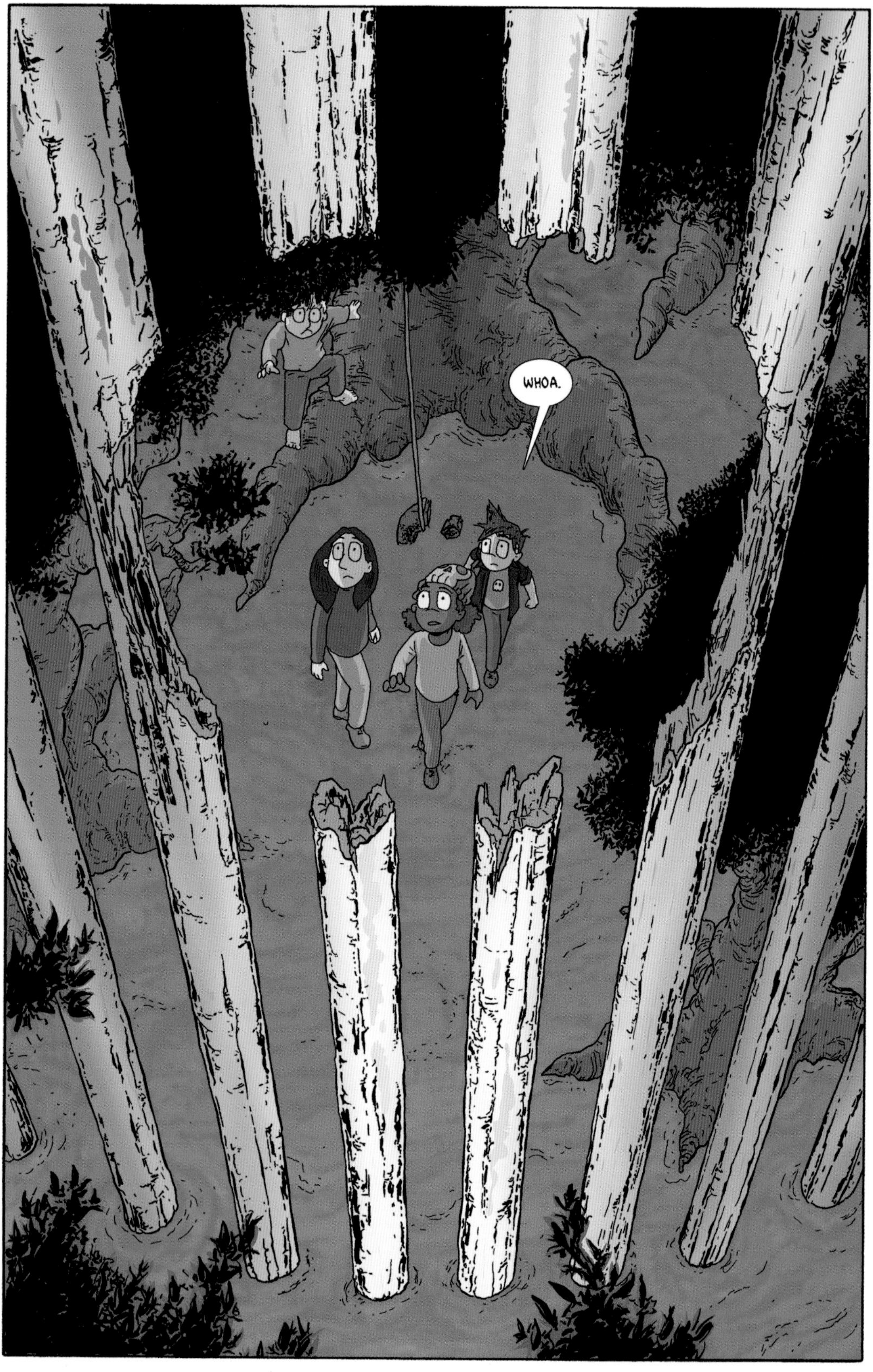
WHOA.

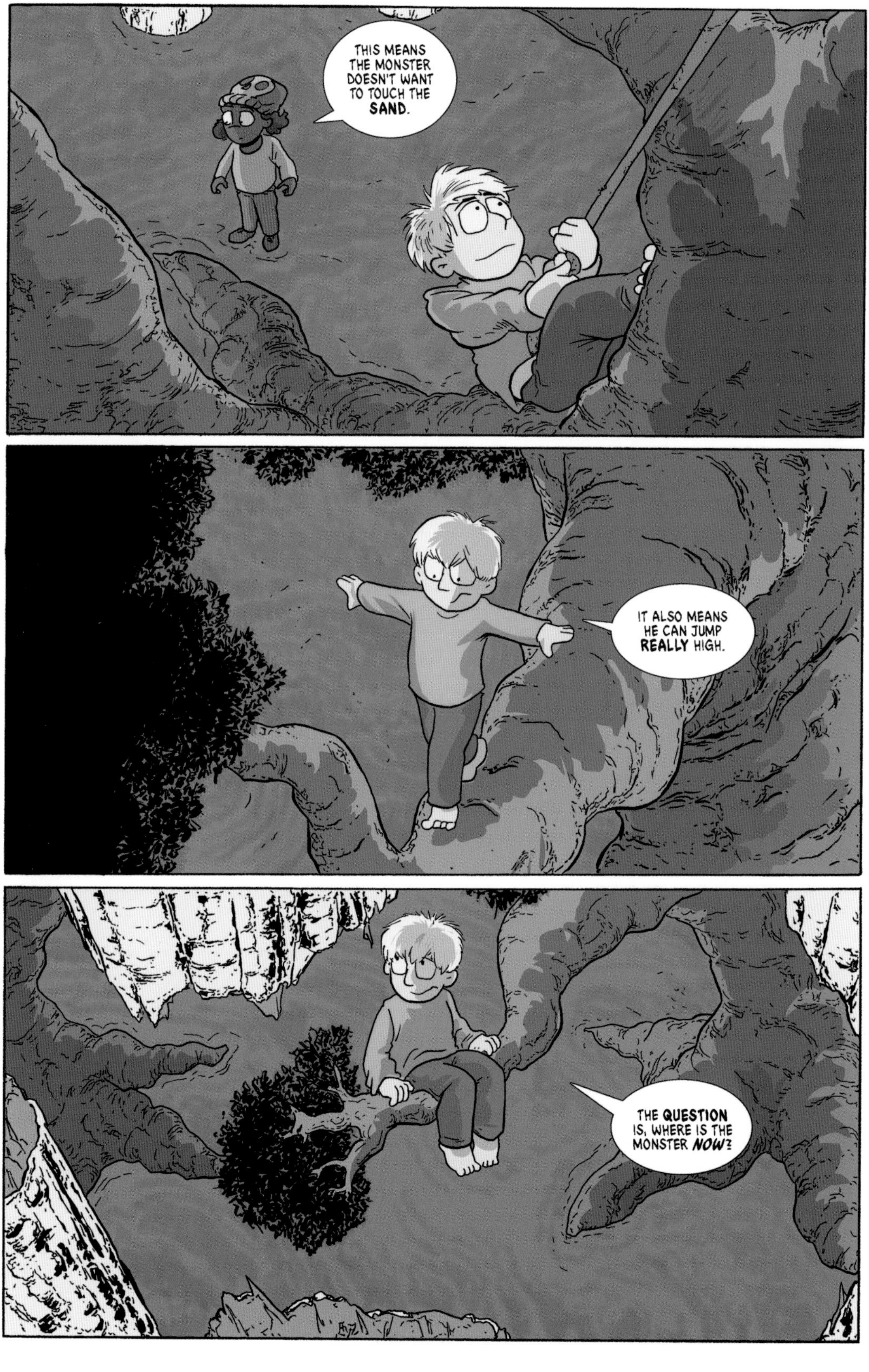
THIS MEANS THE MONSTER DOESN'T WANT TO TOUCH THE **SAND**.
IT ALSO MEANS HE CAN JUMP **REALLY** HIGH.
THE **QUESTION** IS, WHERE IS THE MONSTER ***NOW***?

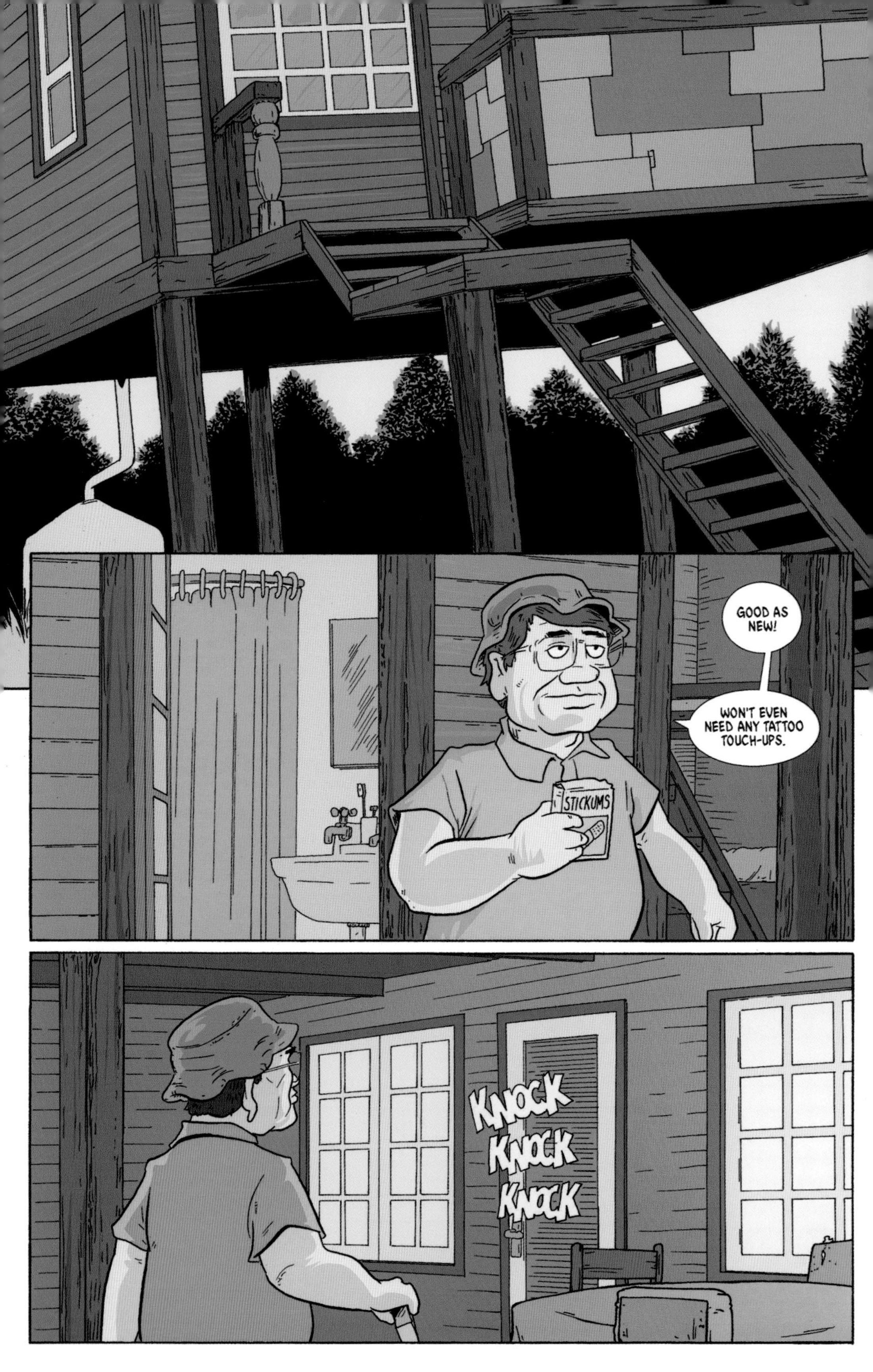
GOOD AS NEW!
WON'T EVEN NEED ANY TATTOO TOUCH-UPS.
STICKUMS
KNOCK
KNOCK
KNOCK

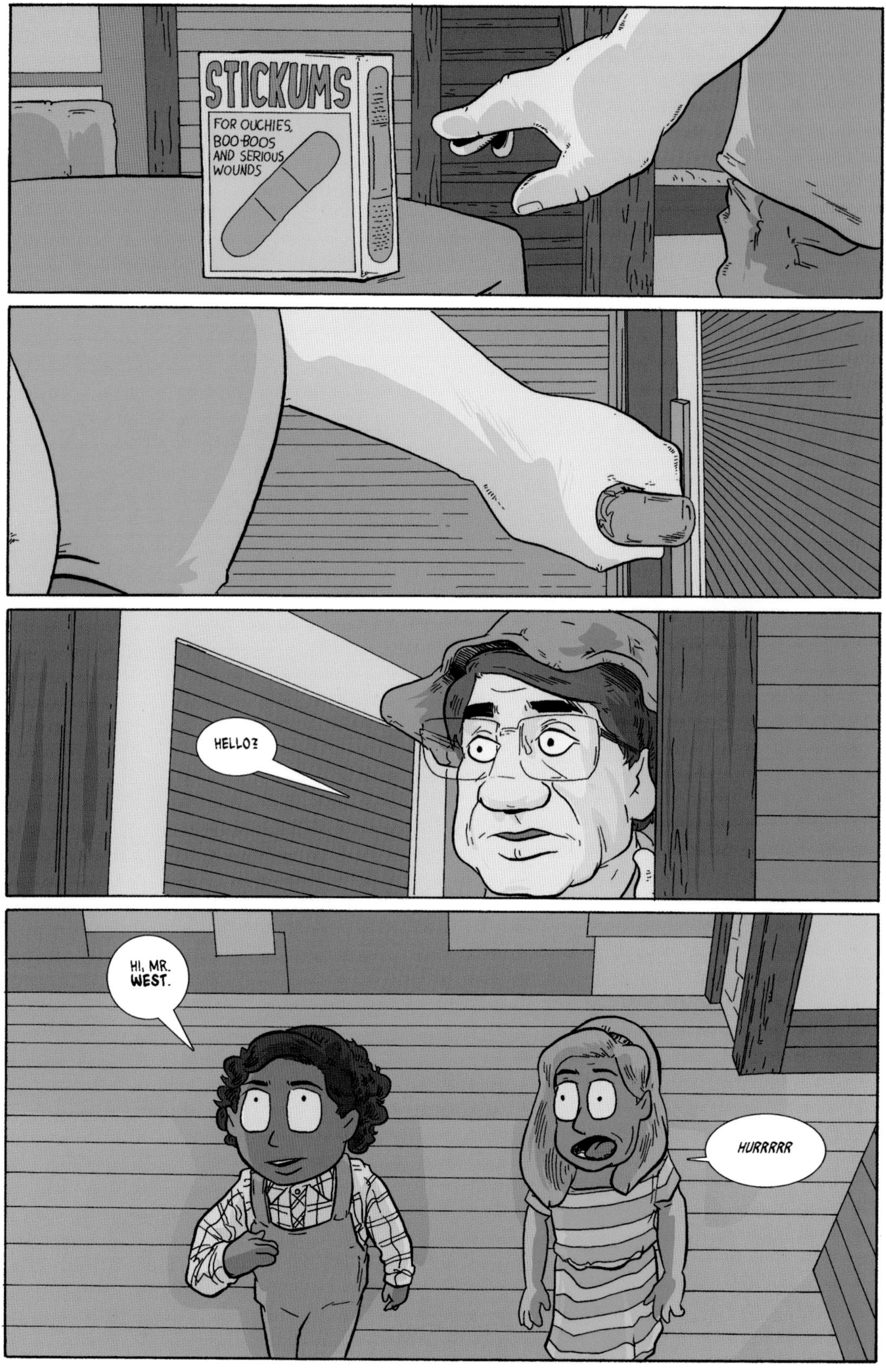
STICKUMS
FOR OUCHIES, BOO-BOOS AND SERIOUS WOUNDS
HELLO?
HI, MR. WEST.
HURRRRR

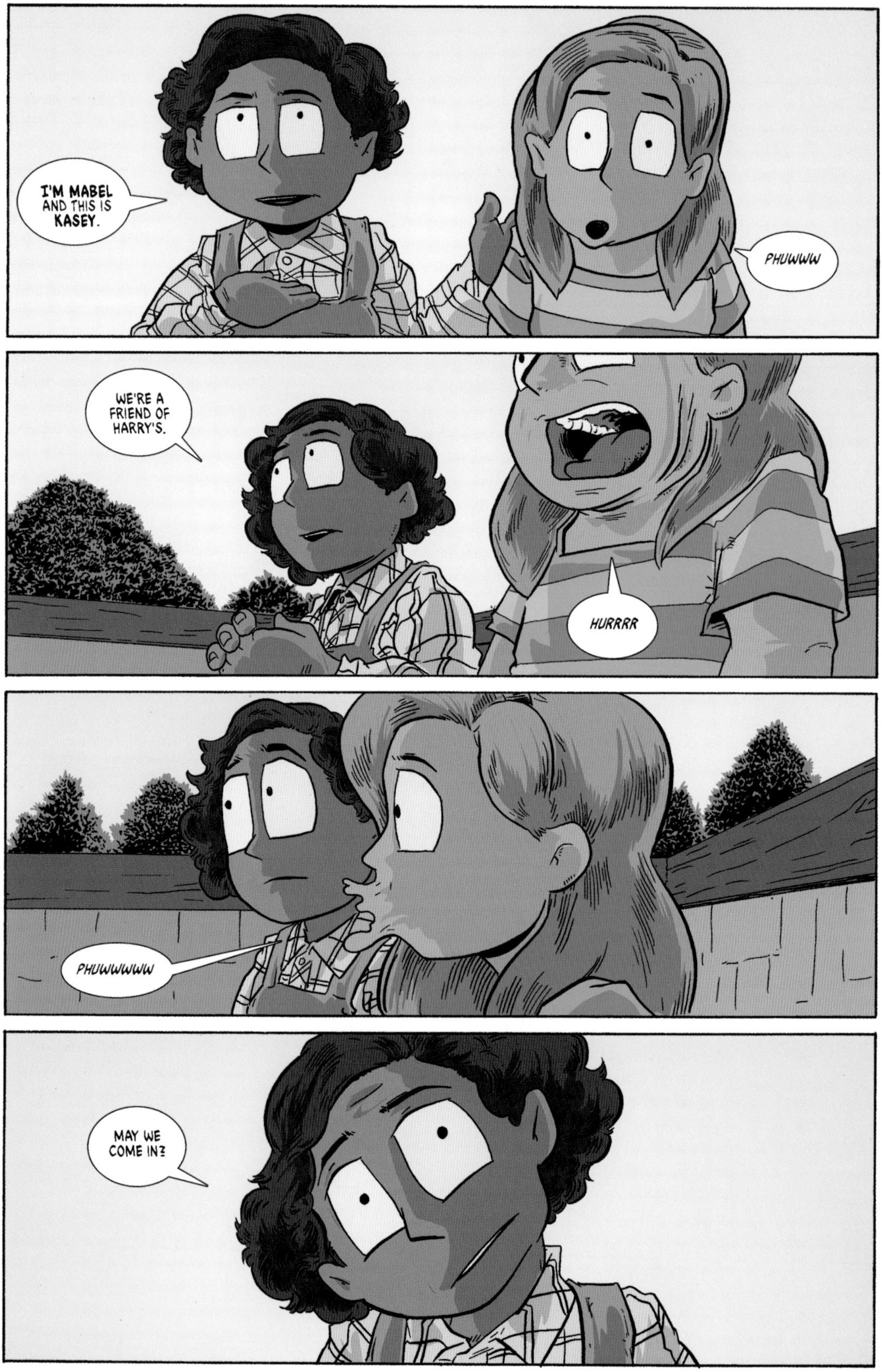
I'M MABEL AND THIS IS KASEY.
PHUWWW
WE'RE A FRIEND OF HARRY'S.
HURRRR
PHUWWWWW
MAY WE COME IN?

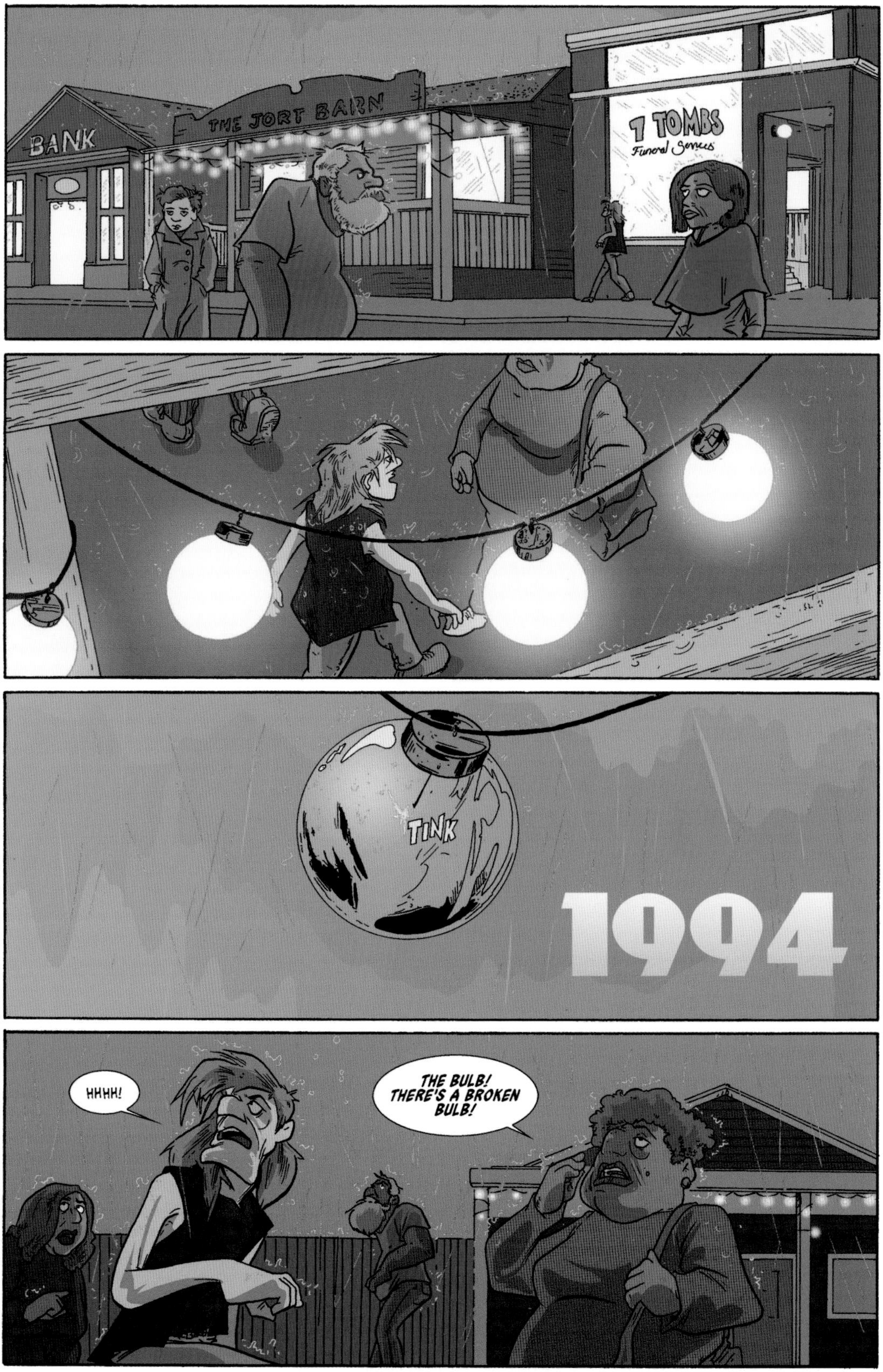
BANK
THE JORT BARN
7 TOMBS
Funeral Services
TINK
1994
HHHH!
THE BULB! THERE'S A BROKEN BULB!

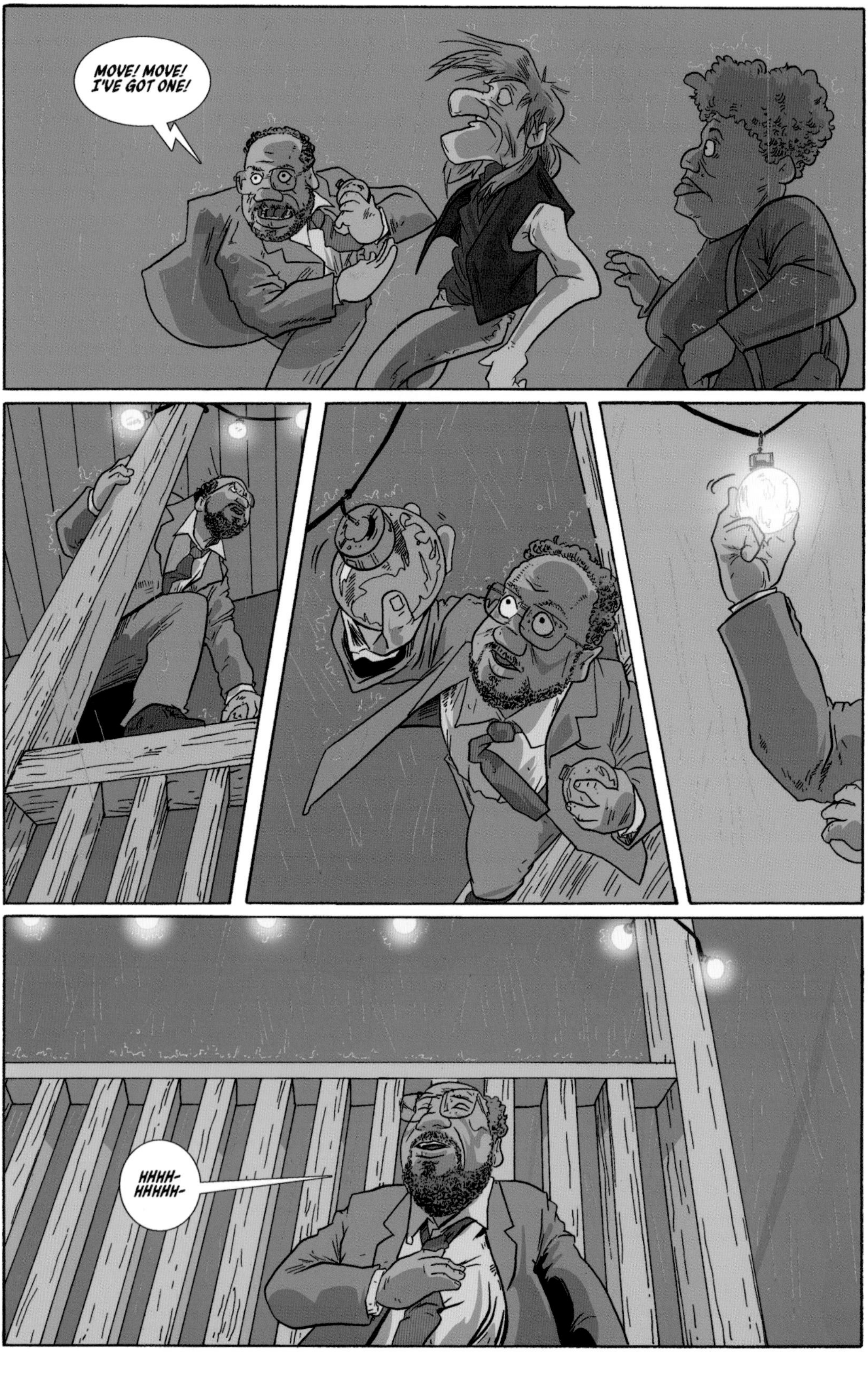
MOVE! MOVE! I'VE GOT ONE!
HHHH-HHHHH-

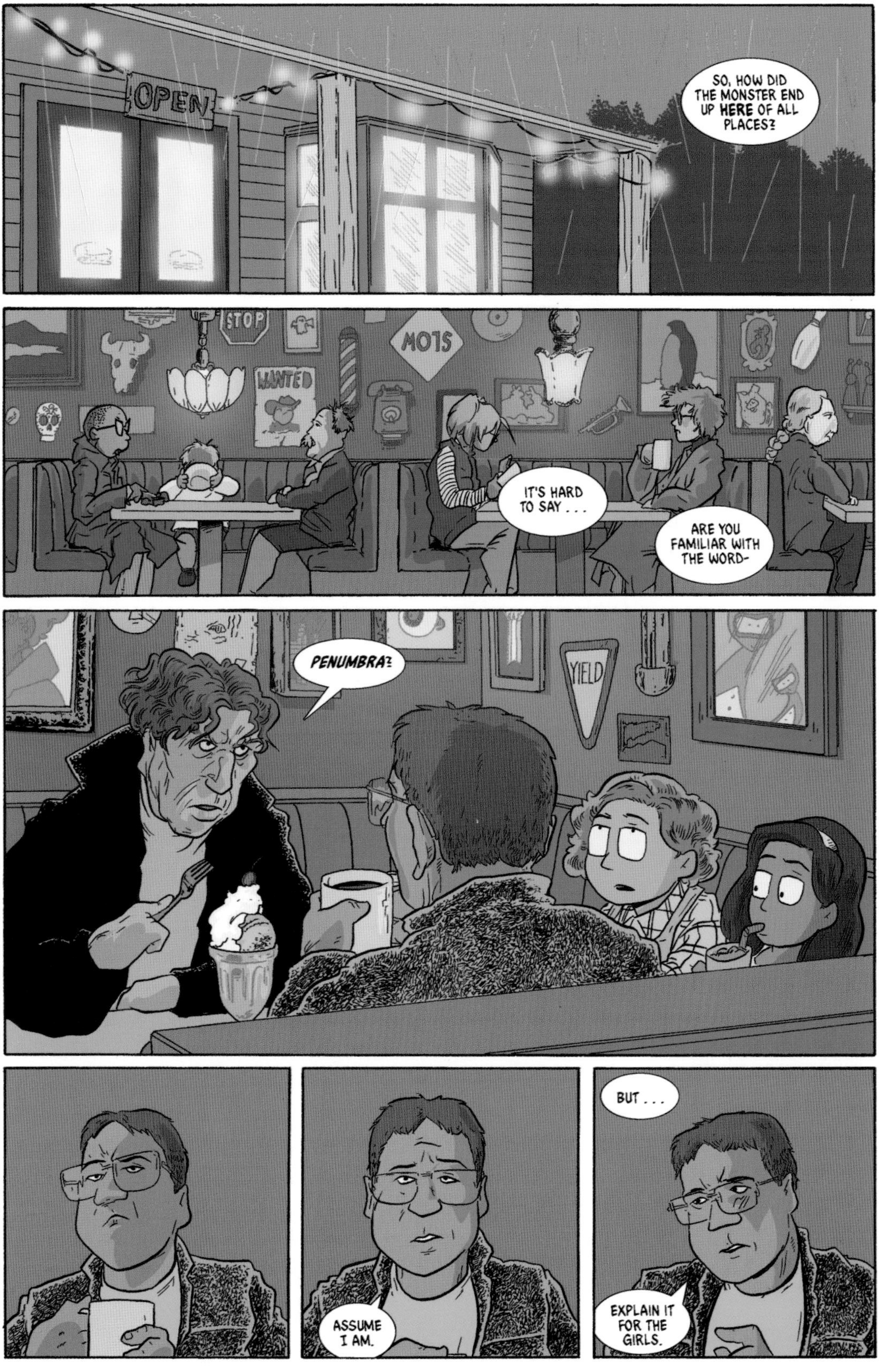
OPEN
SO, HOW DID THE MONSTER END UP HERE OF ALL PLACES?
STOP
STOP
WANTED
IT'S HARD TO SAY . . .
ARE YOU FAMILIAR WITH THE WORD-
PENUMBRA?
YIELD
ASSUME I AM.
BUT . . .
EXPLAIN IT FOR THE GIRLS.

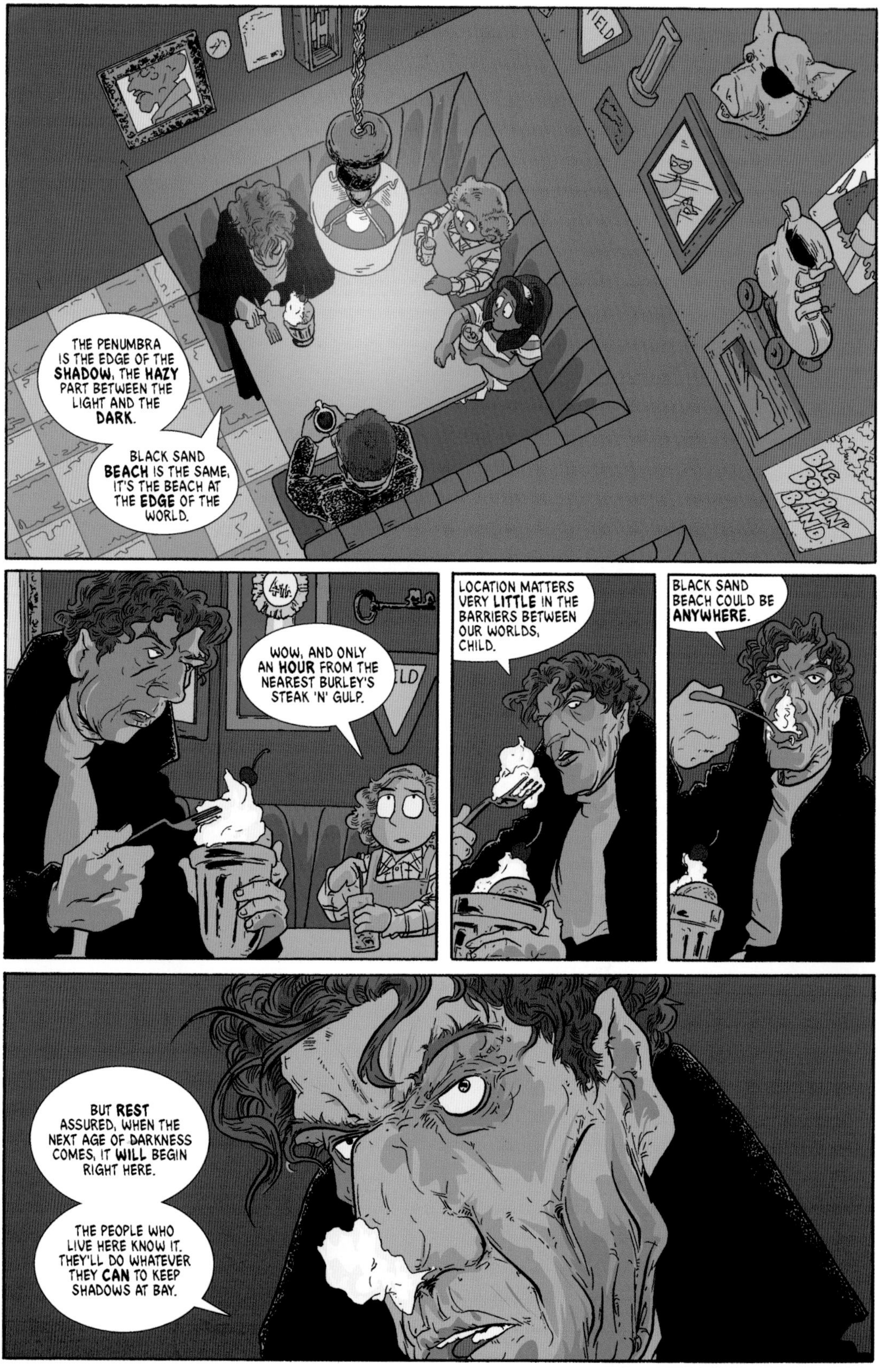
THE PENUMBRA IS THE EDGE OF THE **SHADOW**, THE **HAZY** PART BETWEEN THE LIGHT AND THE **DARK**.
BLACK SAND **BEACH** IS THE SAME, IT'S THE BEACH AT THE **EDGE** OF THE WORLD.
BIG BOPPIN' BAND
WOW, AND ONLY AN **HOUR** FROM THE NEAREST BURLEY'S STEAK 'N' GULP.
LOCATION MATTERS VERY **LITTLE** IN THE BARRIERS BETWEEN OUR WORLDS, CHILD.
BLACK SAND BEACH COULD BE **ANYWHERE**.
BUT **REST** ASSURED, WHEN THE NEXT AGE OF DARKNESS COMES, IT **WILL** BEGIN RIGHT HERE.
THE PEOPLE WHO LIVE HERE KNOW IT. THEY'LL DO WHATEVER THEY **CAN** TO KEEP SHADOWS AT BAY.

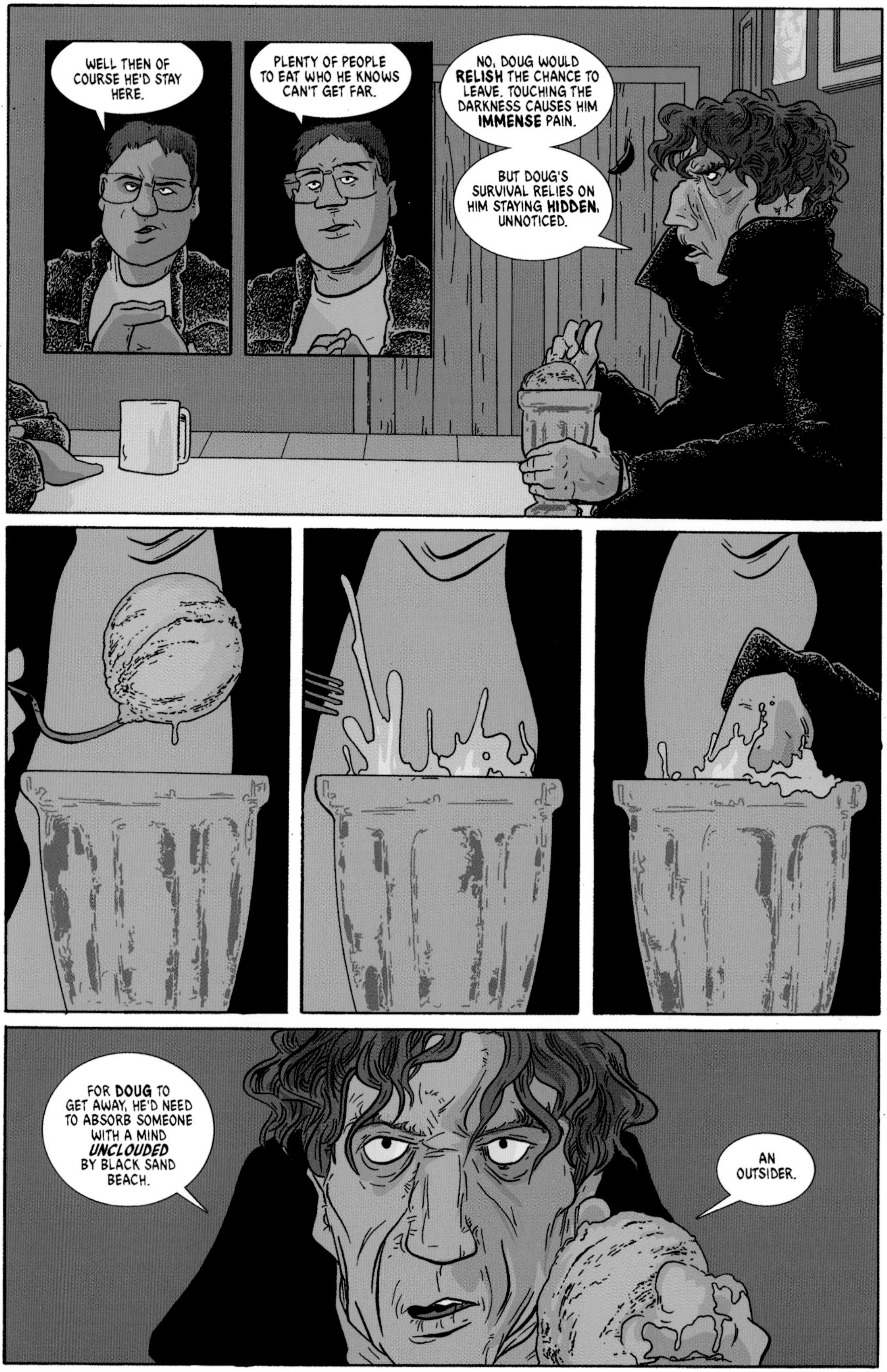
WELL THEN OF COURSE HE'D STAY HERE.
PLENTY OF PEOPLE TO EAT WHO HE KNOWS CAN'T GET FAR.
NO, DOUG WOULD **RELISH** THE CHANCE TO LEAVE. TOUCHING THE DARKNESS CAUSES HIM **IMMENSE** PAIN.
BUT DOUG'S SURVIVAL RELIES ON HIM STAYING **HIDDEN**, UNNOTICED.
FOR **DOUG** TO GET AWAY, HE'D NEED TO ABSORB SOMEONE WITH A MIND ***UNCLOUDED*** BY BLACK SAND BEACH.
AN OUTSIDER.

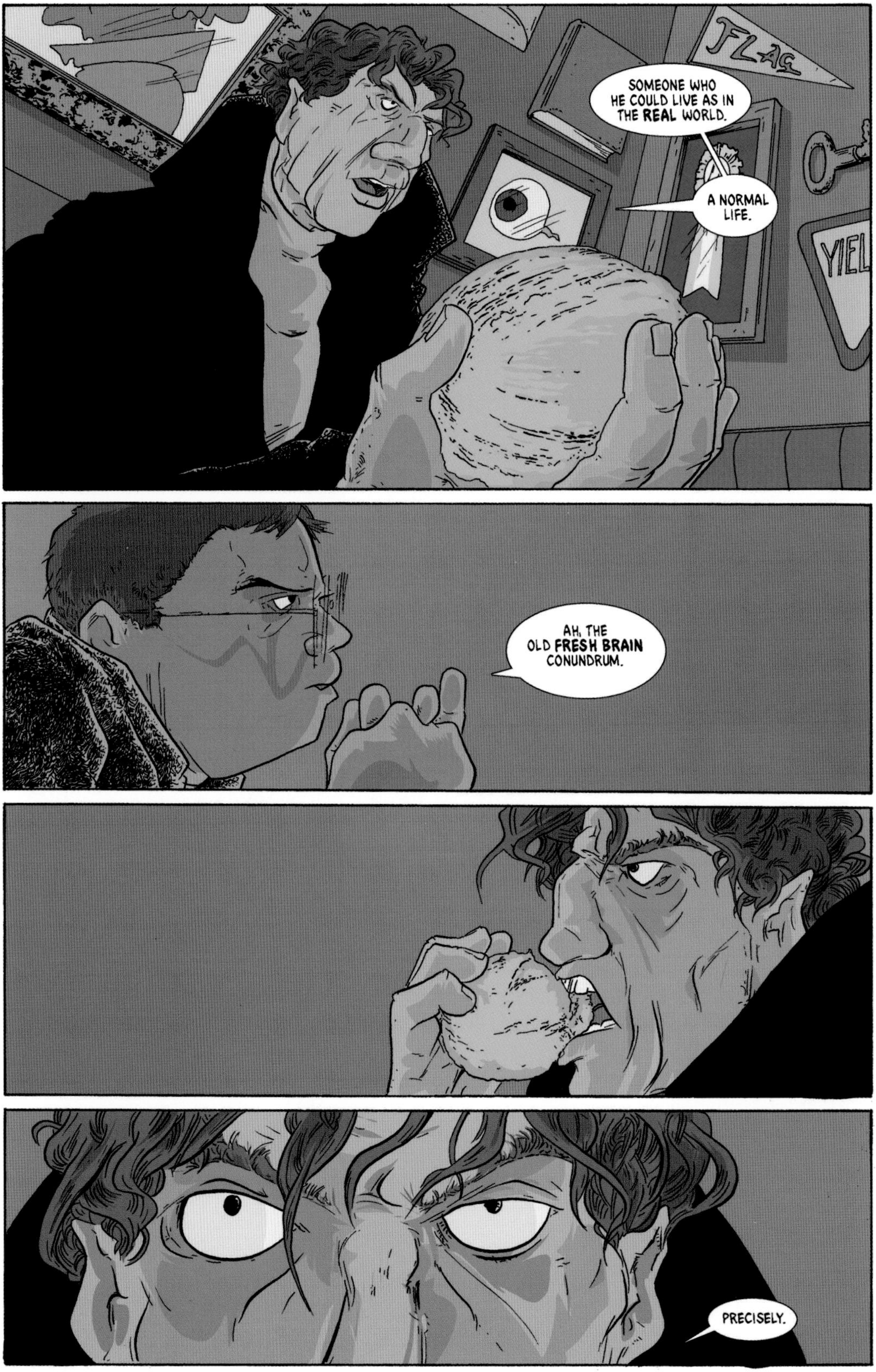
SOMEONE WHO HE COULD LIVE AS IN THE REAL WORLD.
A NORMAL LIFE.
AH, THE OLD FRESH BRAIN CONUNDRUM.
PRECISELY.

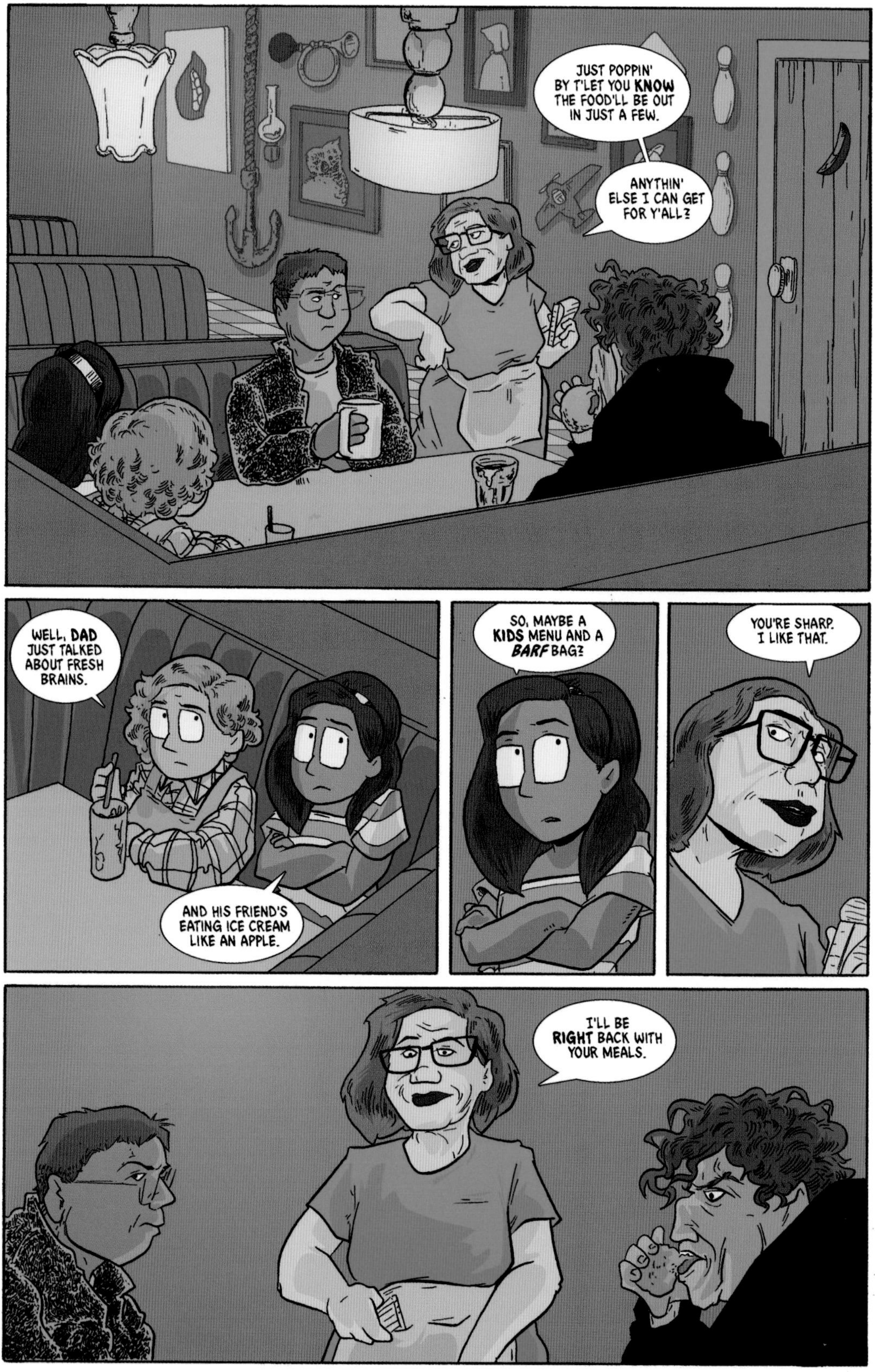

JUST POPPIN' BY T'LET YOU KNOW THE FOOD'LL BE OUT IN JUST A FEW.
ANYTHIN' ELSE I CAN GET FOR Y'ALL?
WELL, DAD JUST TALKED ABOUT FRESH BRAINS.
AND HIS FRIEND'S EATING ICE CREAM LIKE AN APPLE.
SO, MAYBE A KIDS MENU AND A BARF BAG?
YOU'RE SHARP. I LIKE THAT.
I'LL BE RIGHT BACK WITH YOUR MEALS.

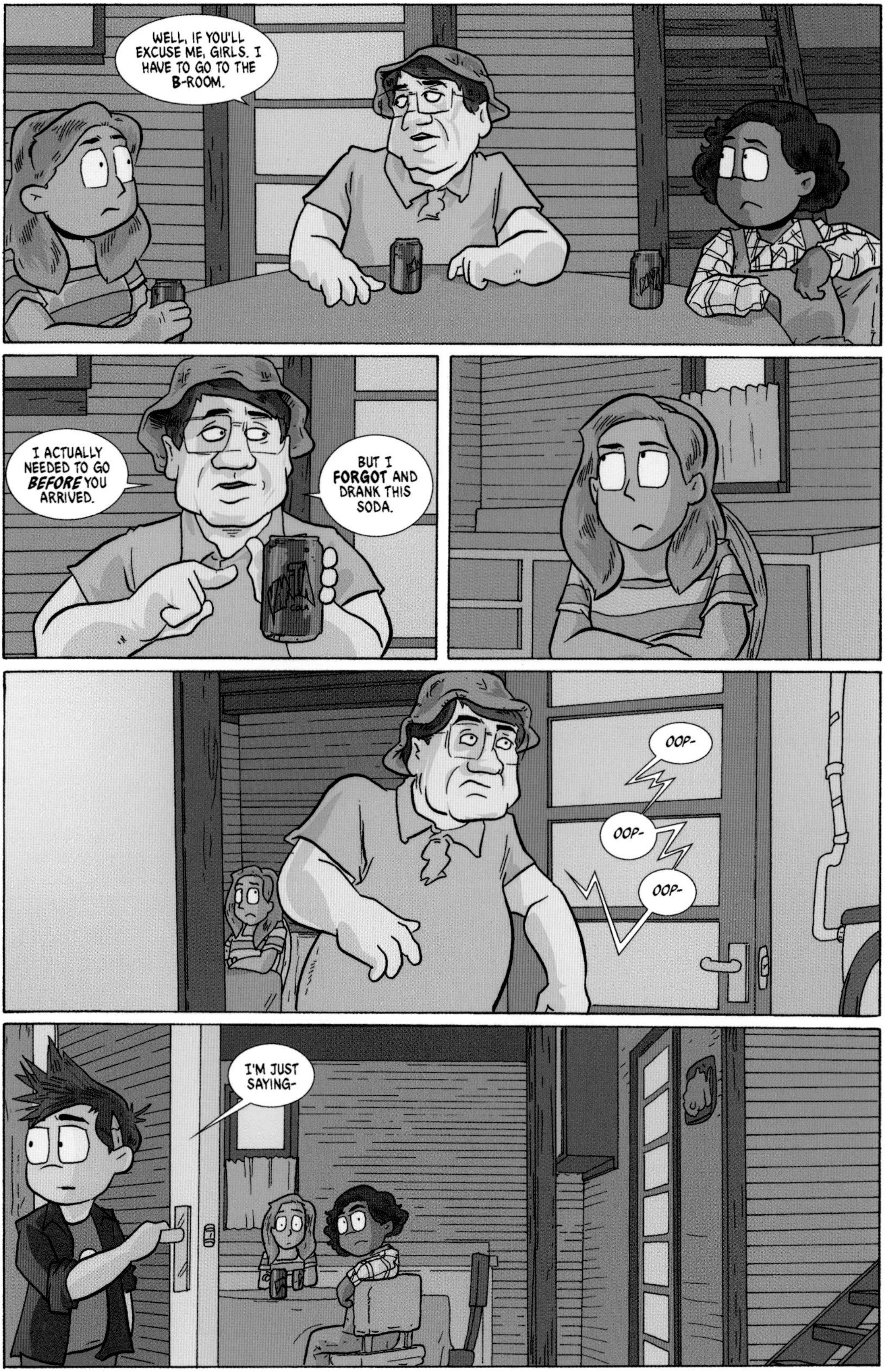
WELL, IF YOU'LL EXCUSE ME, GIRLS. I HAVE TO GO TO THE B-ROOM.
I ACTUALLY NEEDED TO GO BEFORE YOU ARRIVED.
BUT I FORGOT AND DRANK THIS SODA.
OOP-
OOP-
OOP-
I'M JUST SAYING-

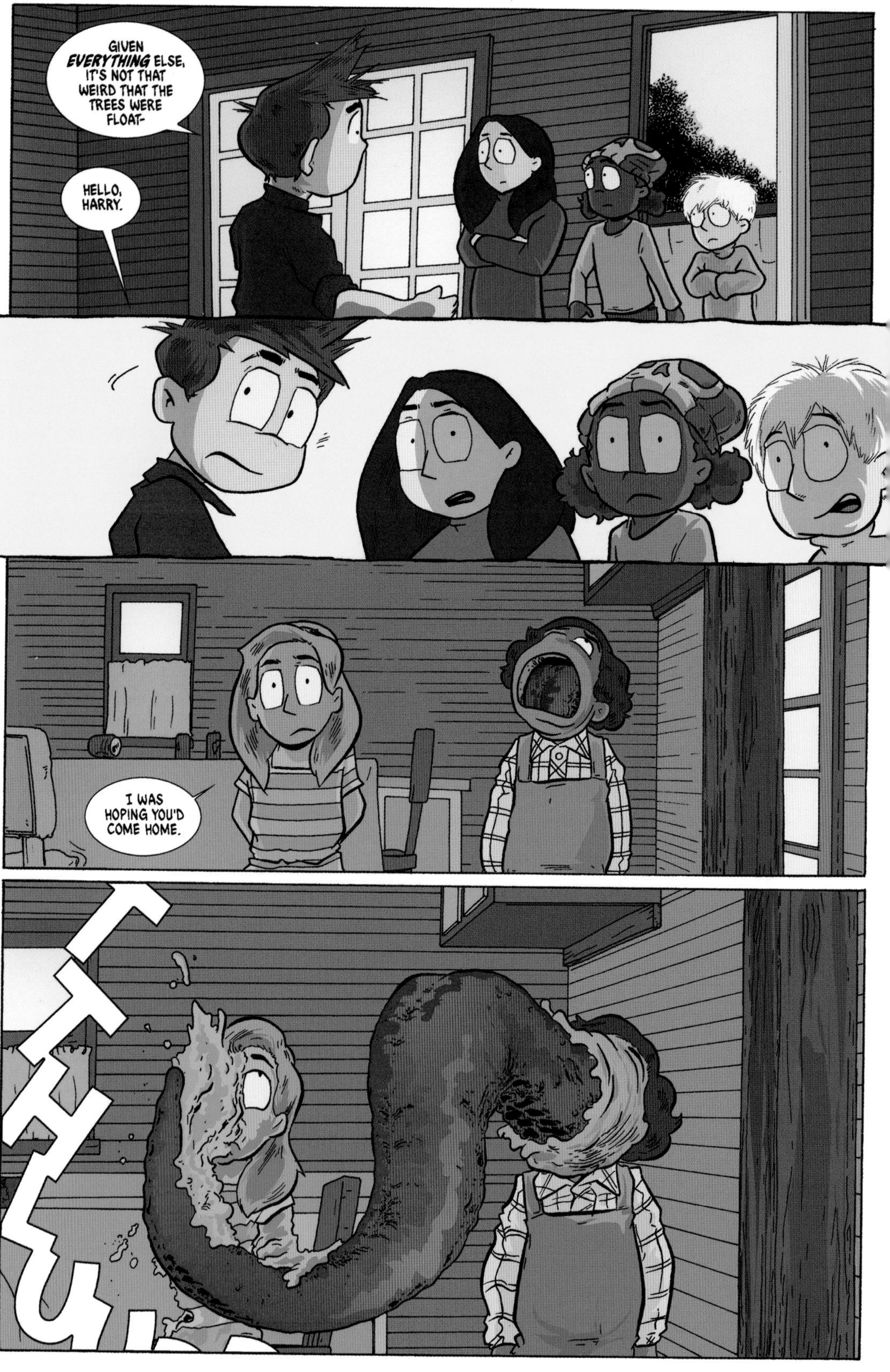

GIVEN *EVERYTHING* ELSE, IT'S NOT THAT WEIRD THAT THE TREES WERE FLOAT-
HELLO, HARRY.
I WAS HOPING YOU'D COME HOME.
THWU

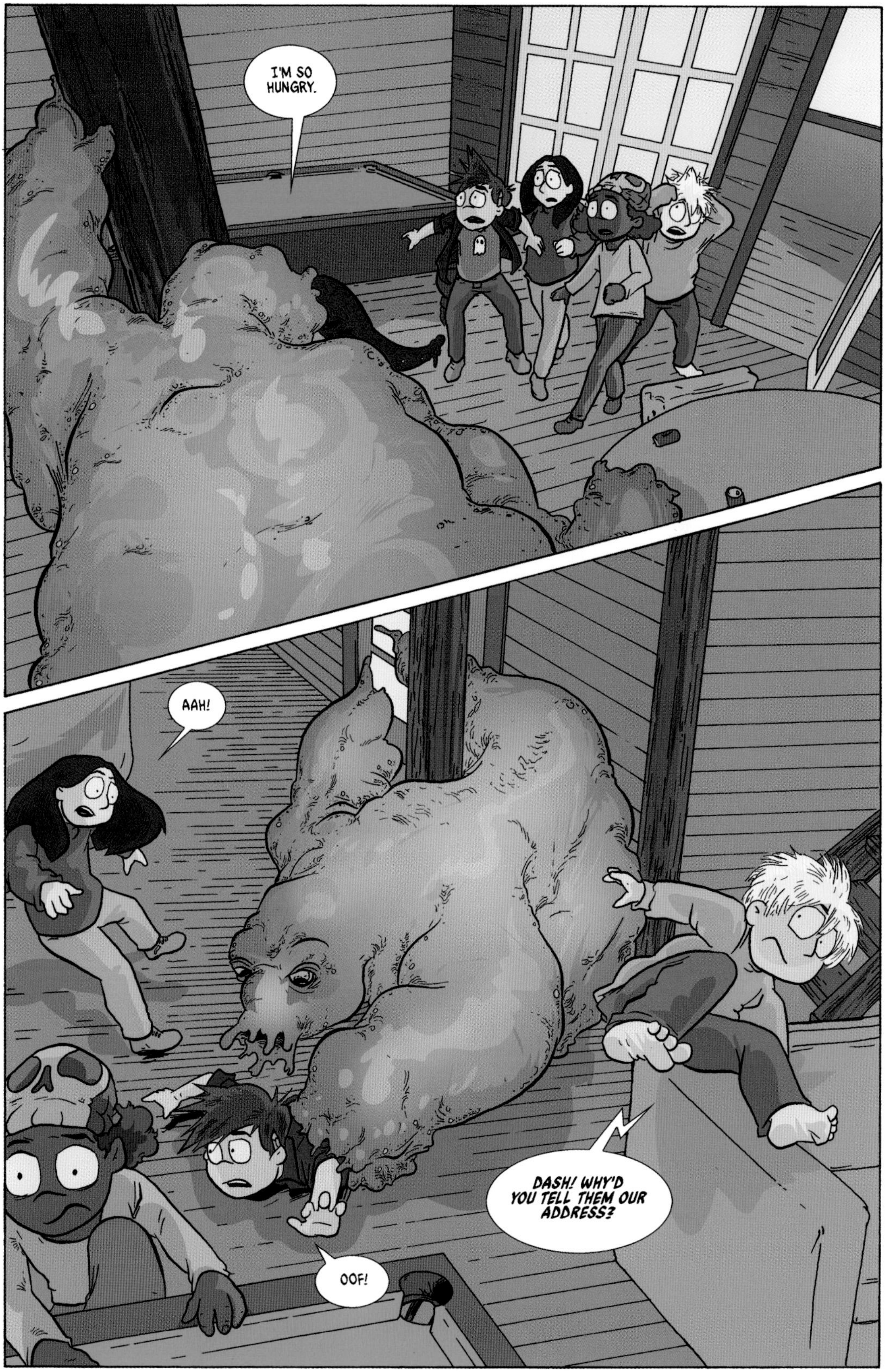
I'M SO HUNGRY.
AAH!
DASH! WHY'D YOU TELL THEM OUR ADDRESS?
OOF!

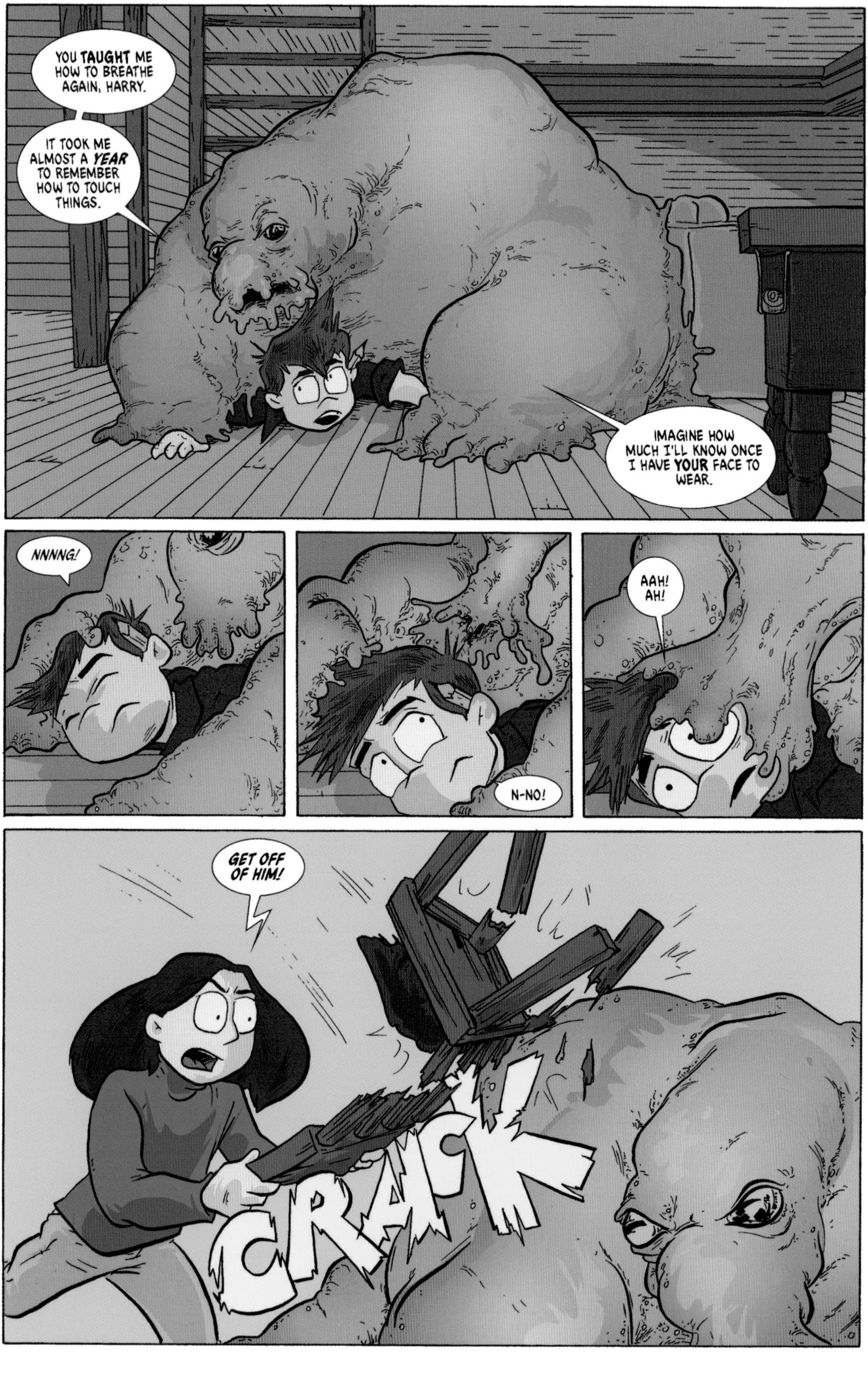
YOU TAUGHT ME HOW TO BREATHE AGAIN, HARRY.
IT TOOK ME ALMOST A YEAR TO REMEMBER HOW TO TOUCH THINGS.
IMAGINE HOW MUCH I'LL KNOW ONCE I HAVE YOUR FACE TO WEAR.
NNNNG!
N-NO!
AAH! AH!
GET OFF OF HIM!
CRACK

A'RIGHT-
LET'S SEET HOW YOU LIKE-
BLUP
OOP!
STHLUP

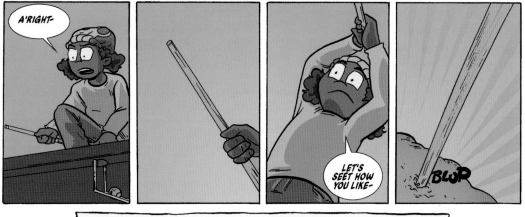

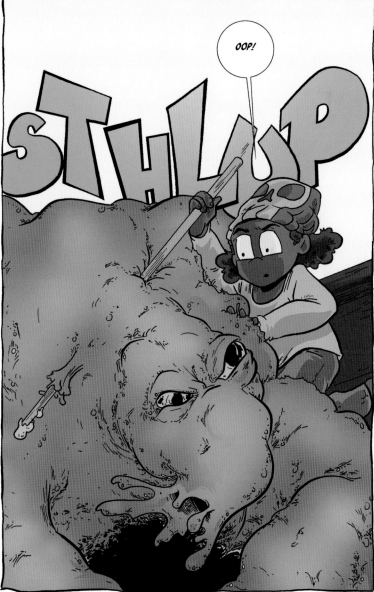

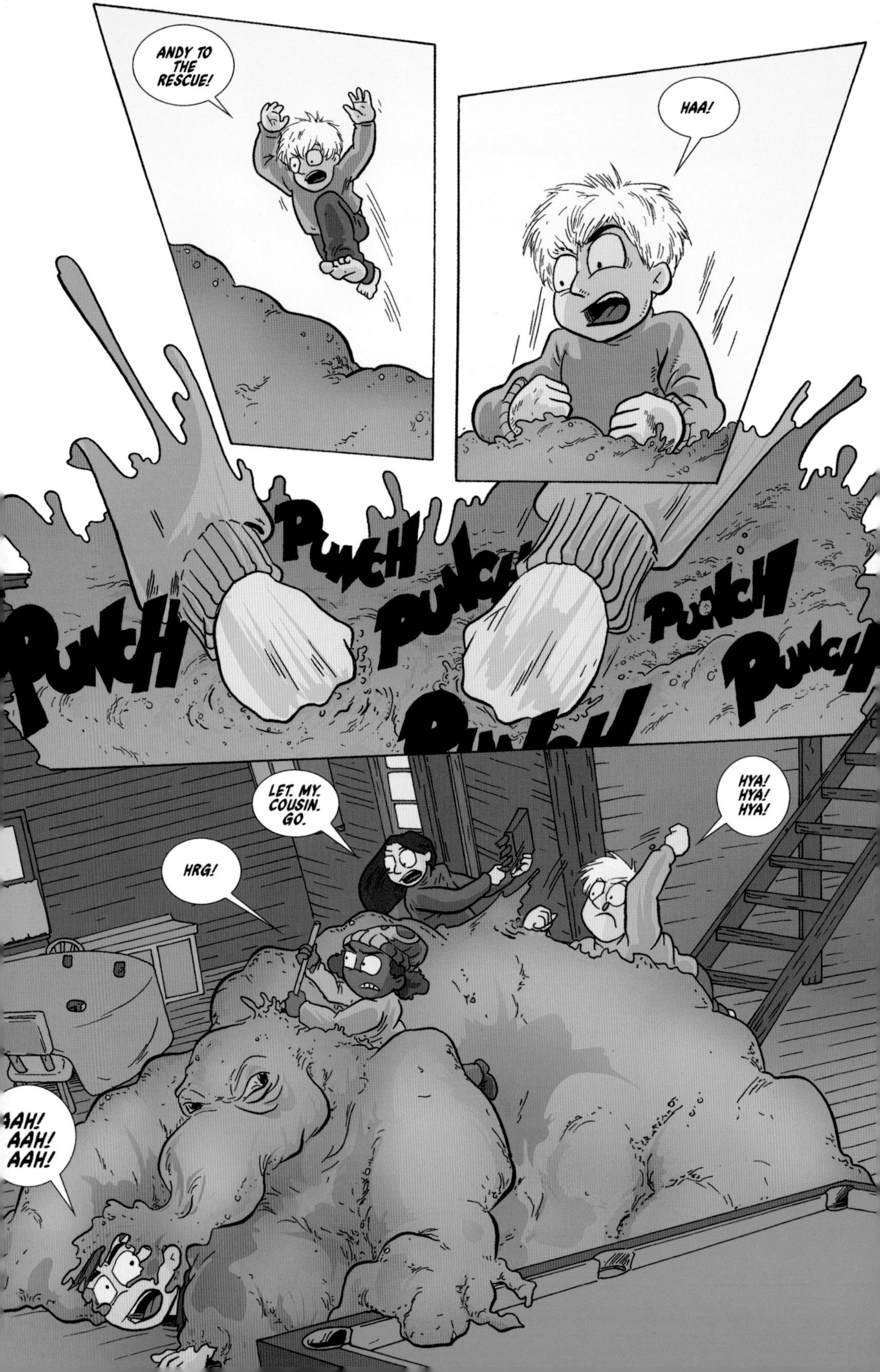
ANDY TO THE RESCUE!
HAA!
PUNCH
PUNCH
PUNCH
PUNCH
PUNCH
PUNCH
LET. MY. COUSIN. GO.
HYA! HYA! HYA!
HRG!
AAH! AAH! AAH!

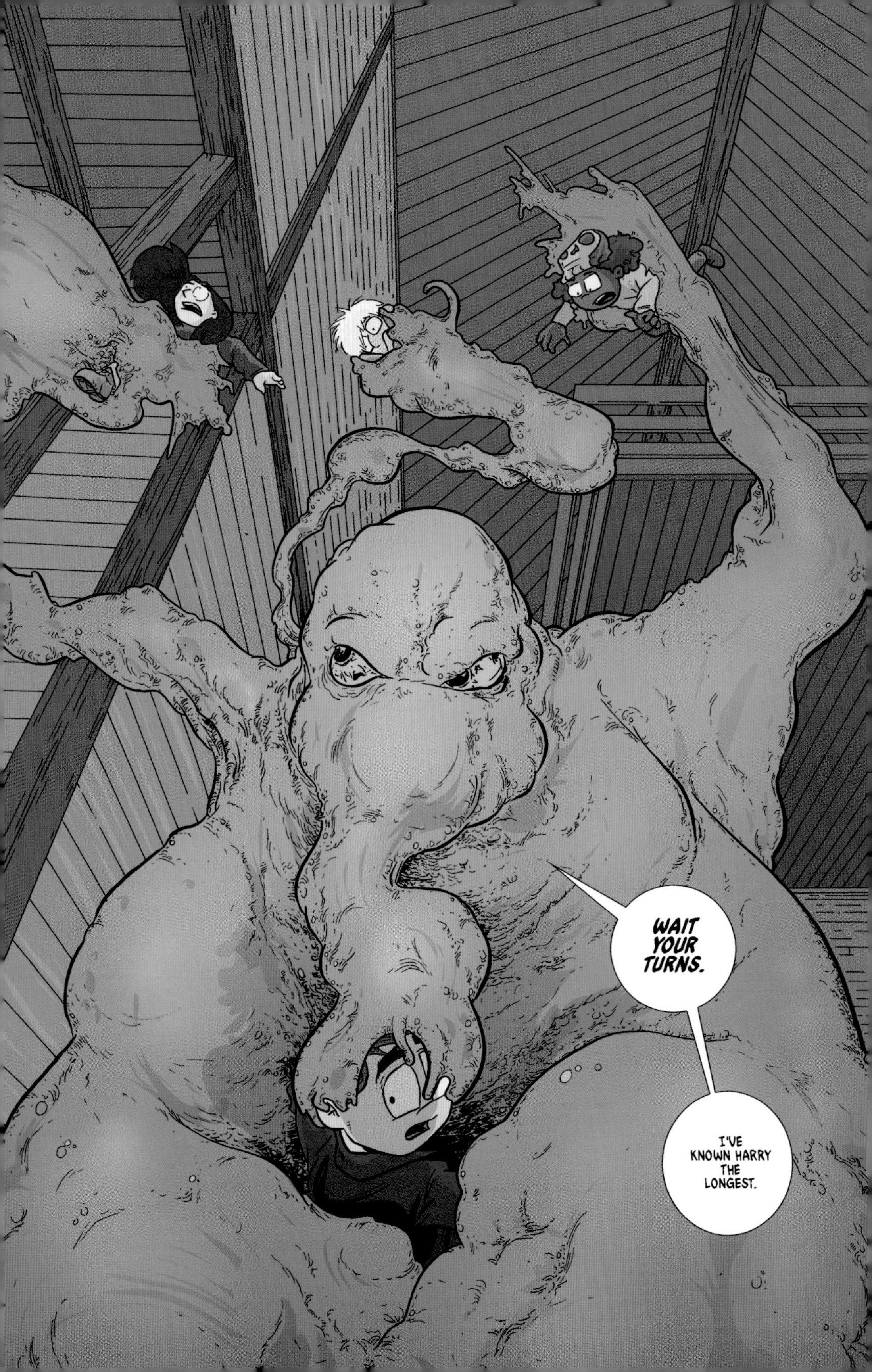
WAIT YOUR TURNS.
I'VE KNOWN HARRY THE LONGEST.

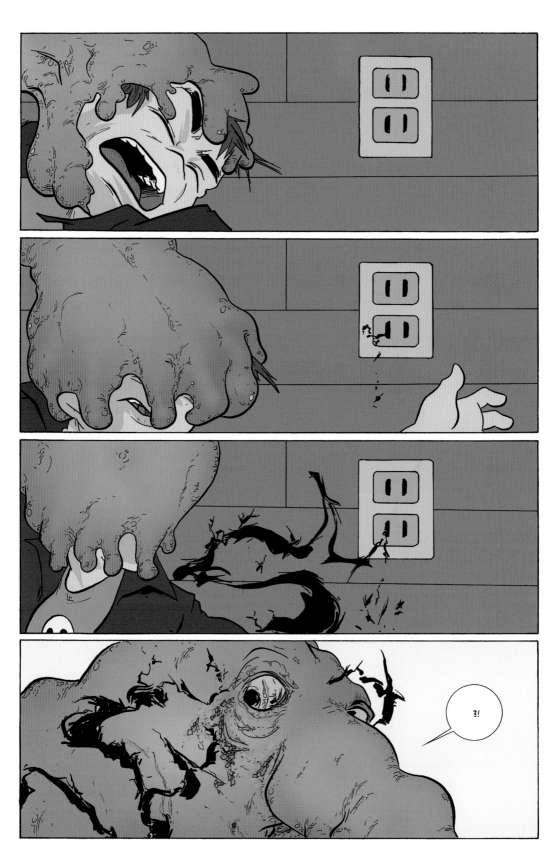

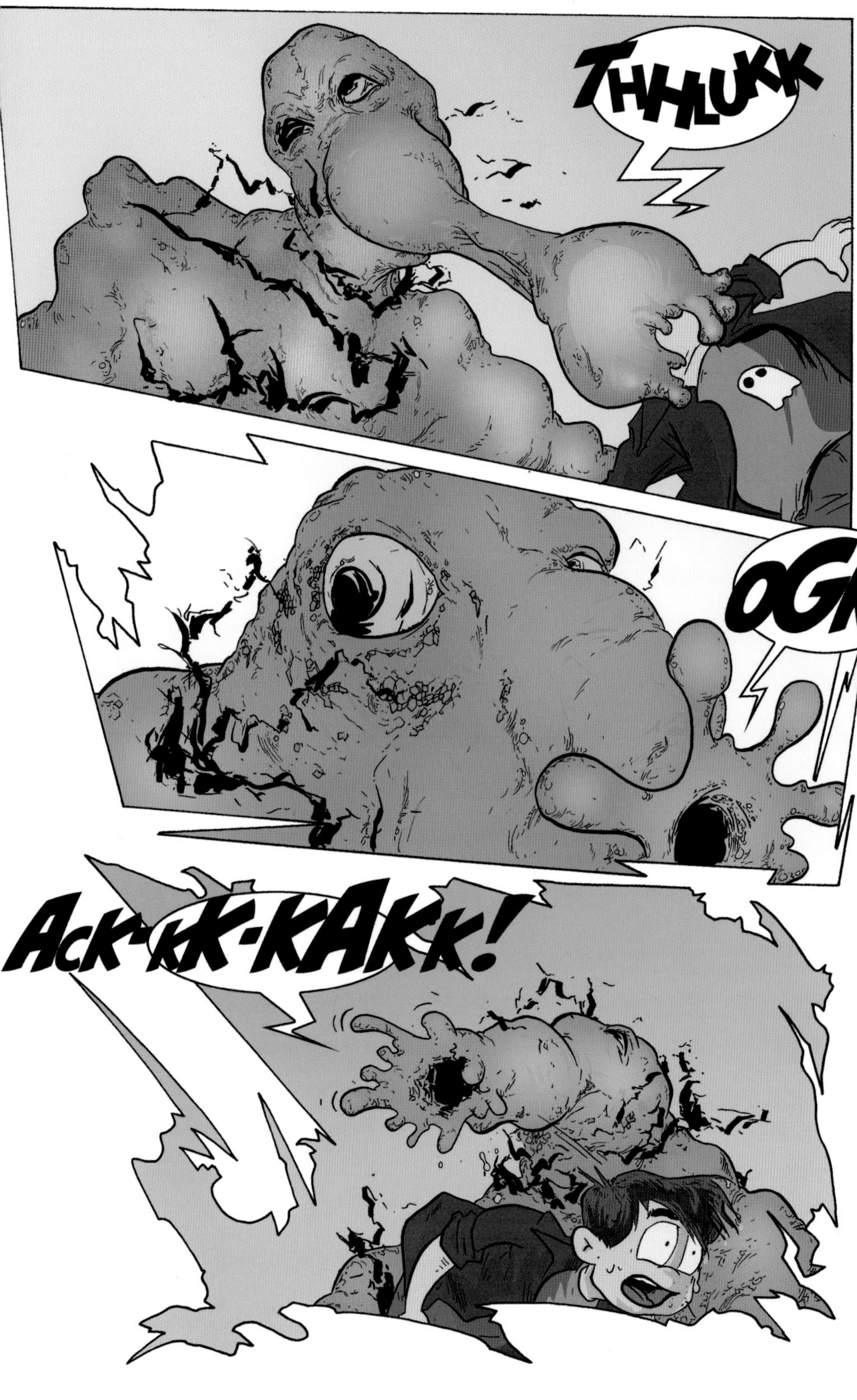
THHLUKK
OGK!
ACK-KK-KAKK!

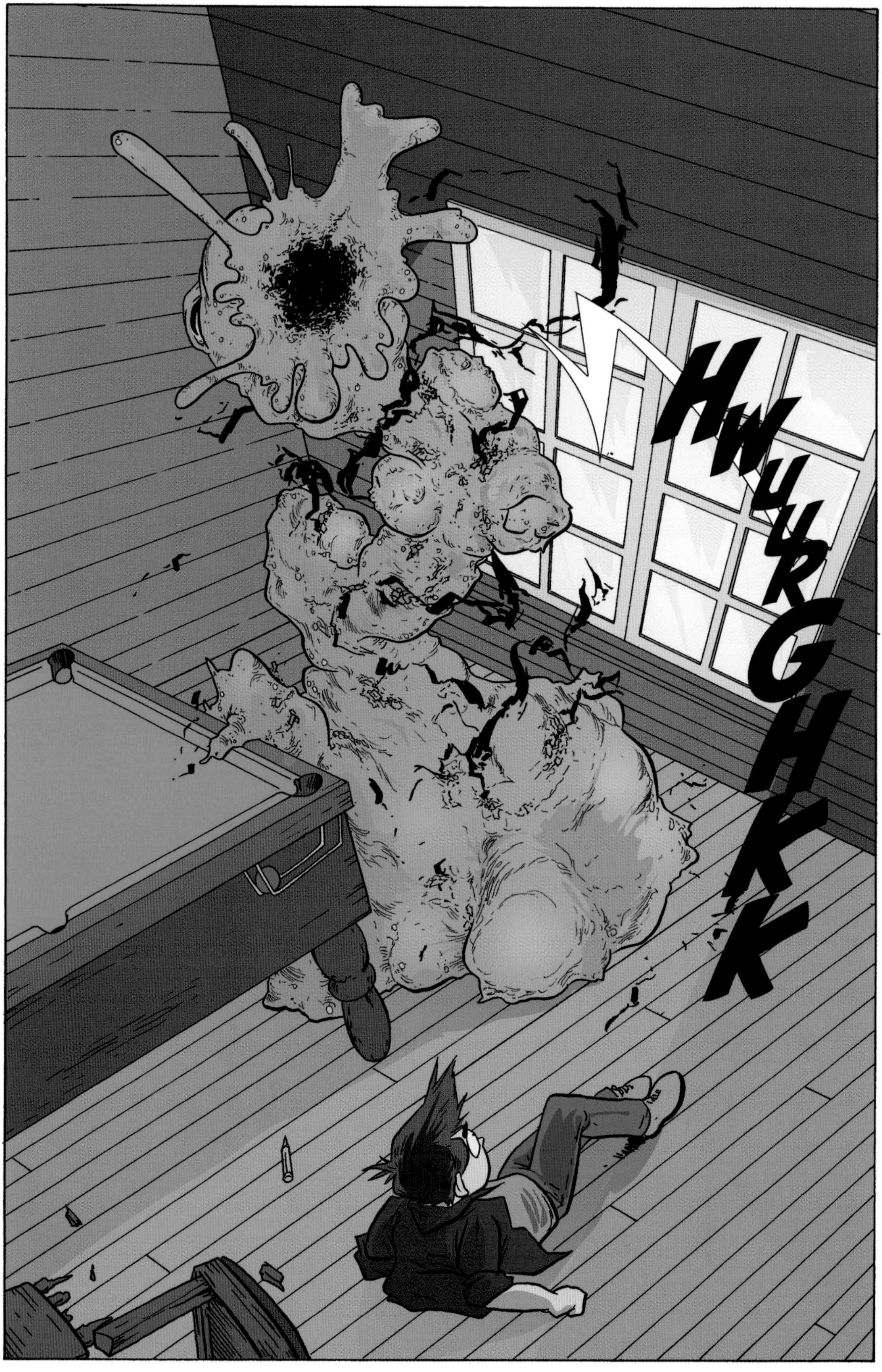
HWURRGHKK

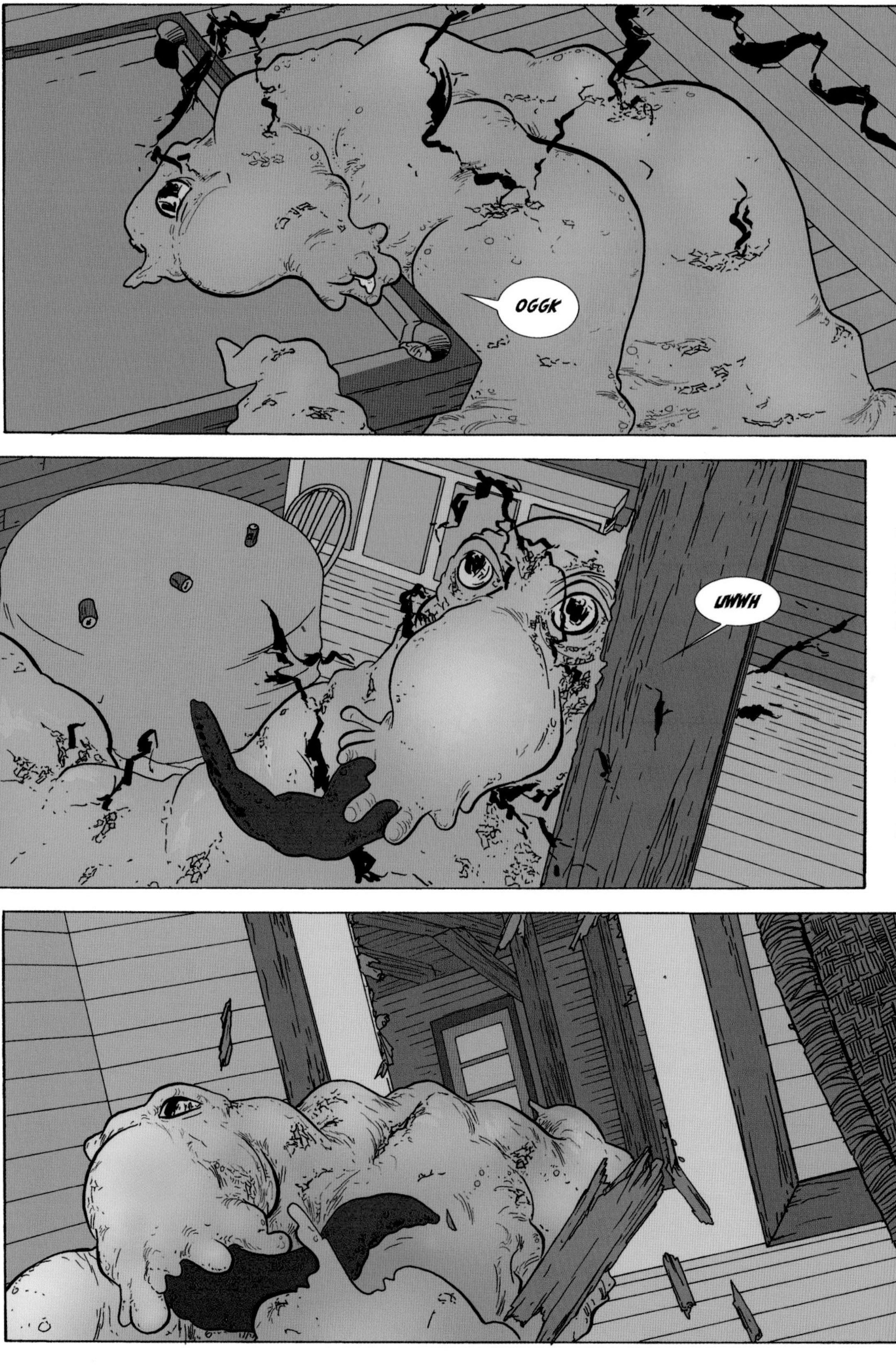
OGGK
UWWH

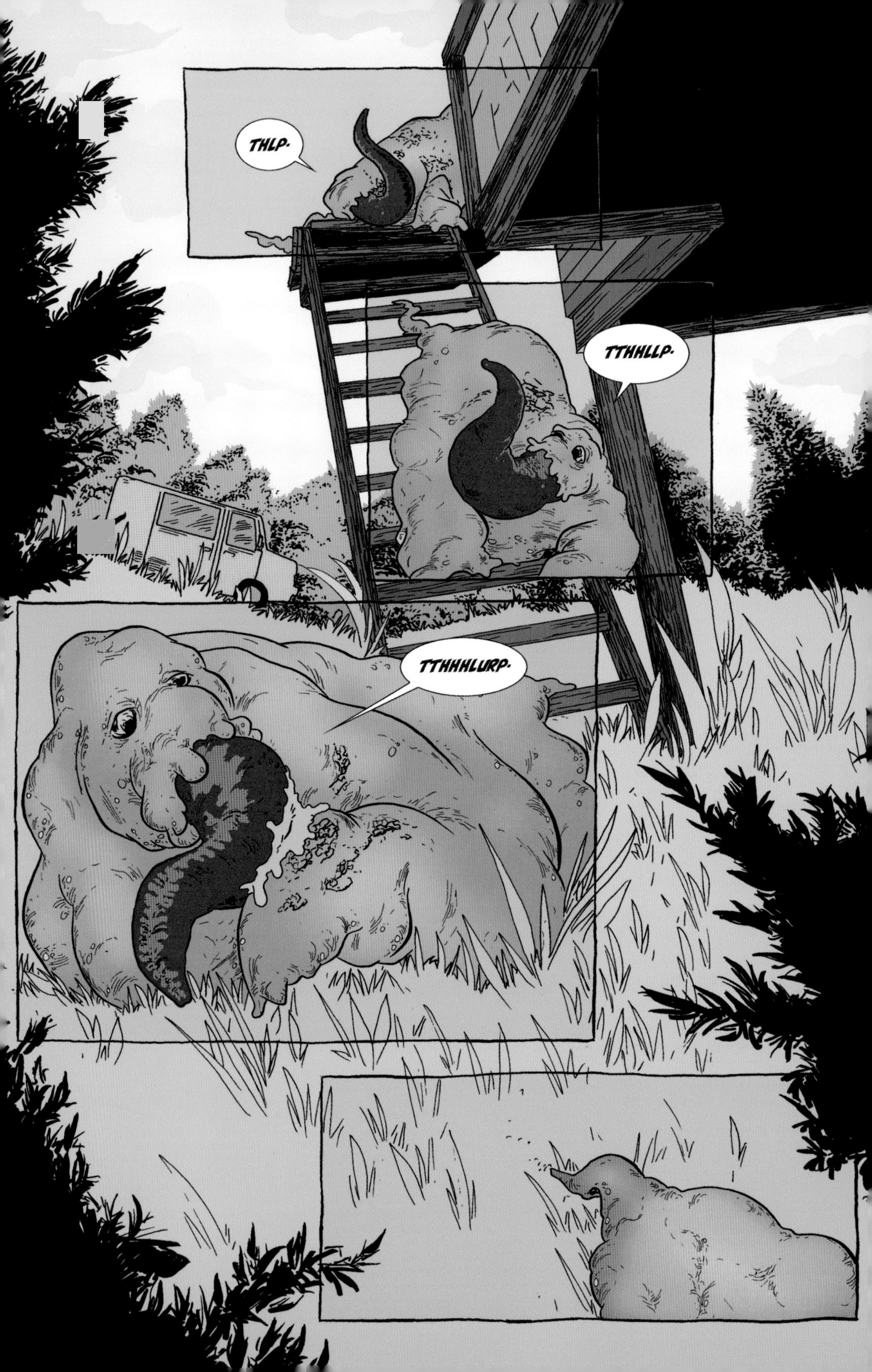
THLP.
TTHHLLP.
TTHHHLURP.

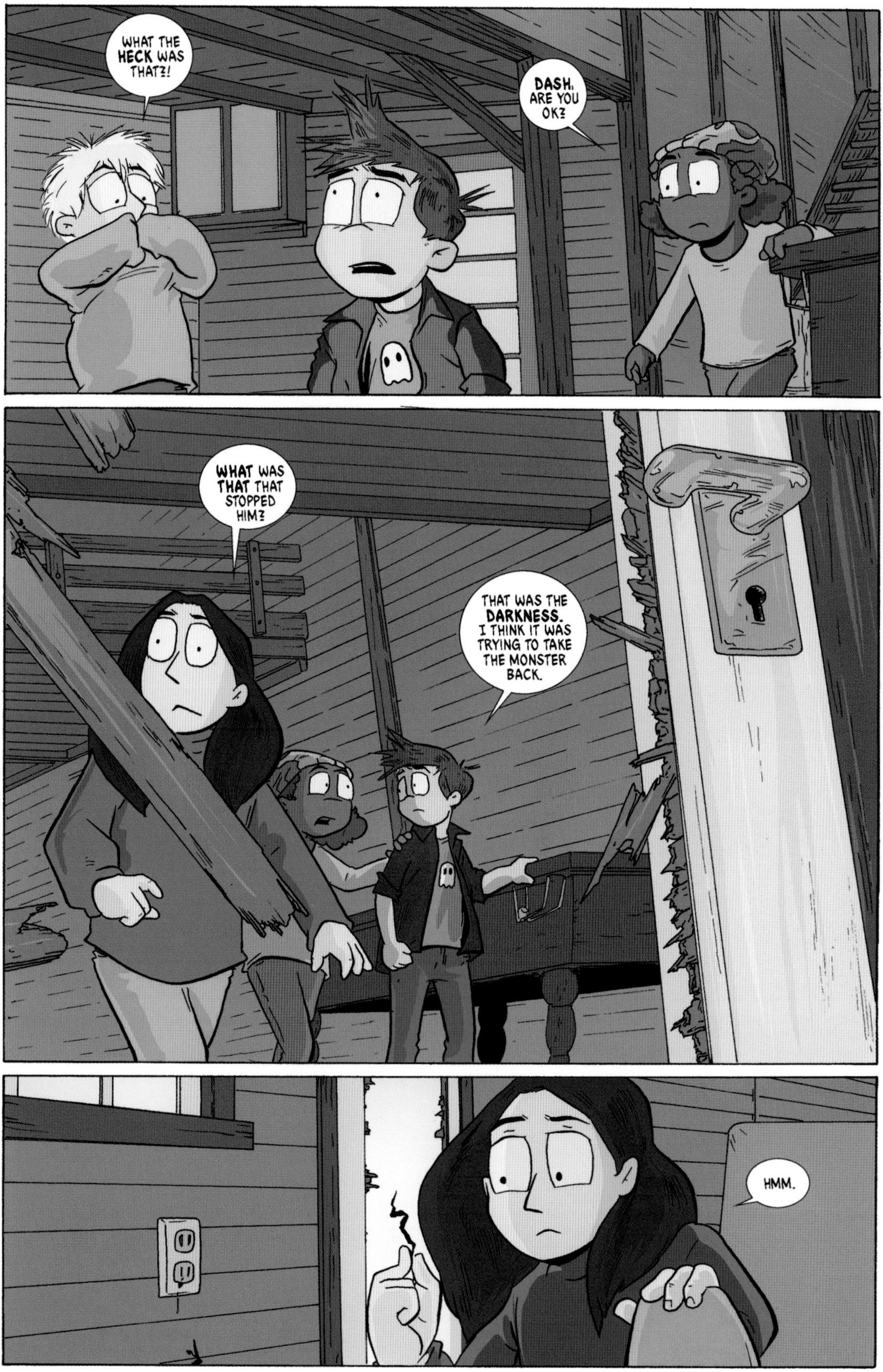
WHAT THE HECK WAS THAT?!
DASH, ARE YOU OK?
WHAT WAS THAT THAT STOPPED HIM?
THAT WAS THE DARKNESS. I THINK IT WAS TRYING TO TAKE THE MONSTER BACK.
HMM.

TO BE CONTINUED.

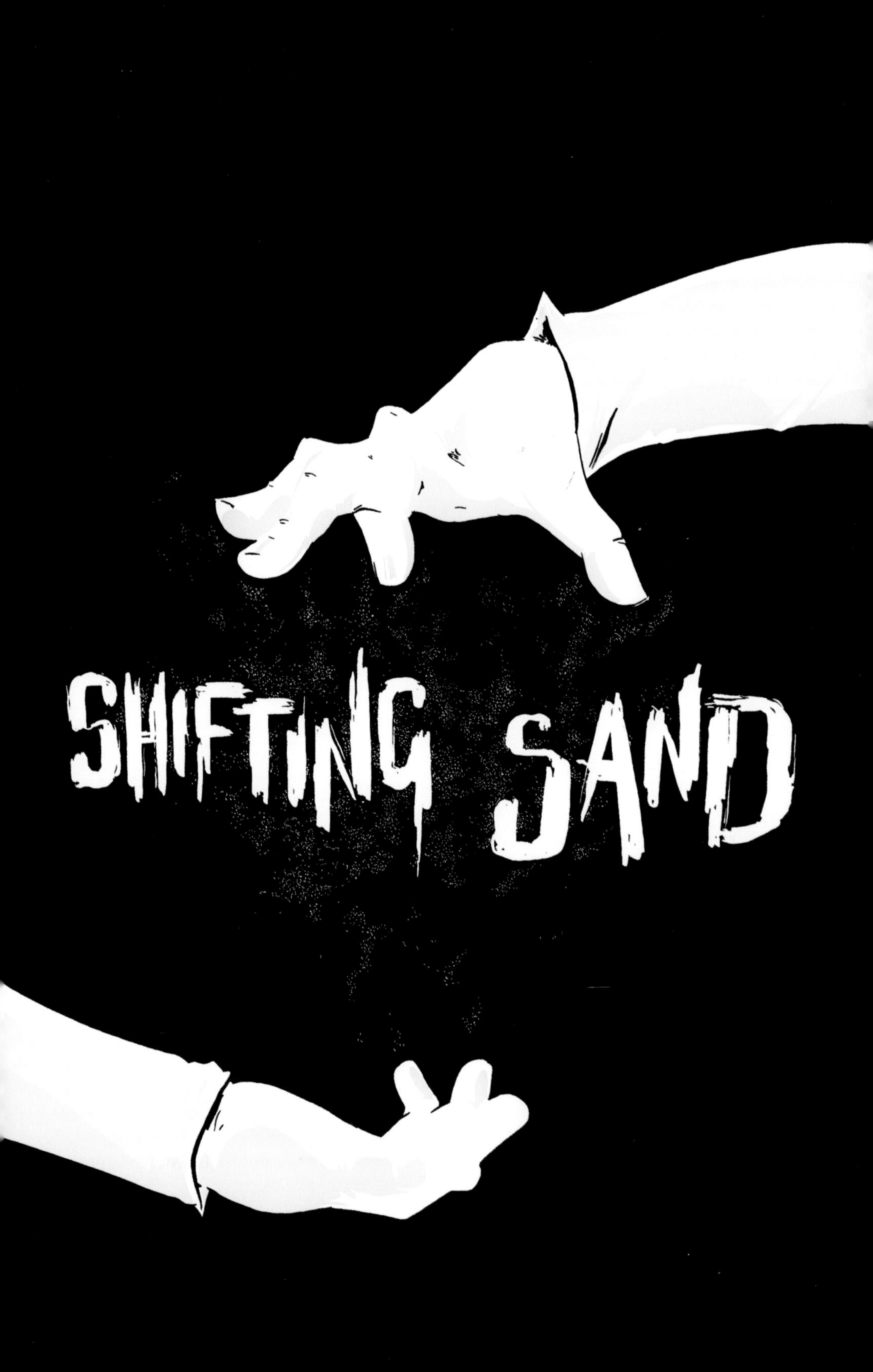
SHIFTING SAND

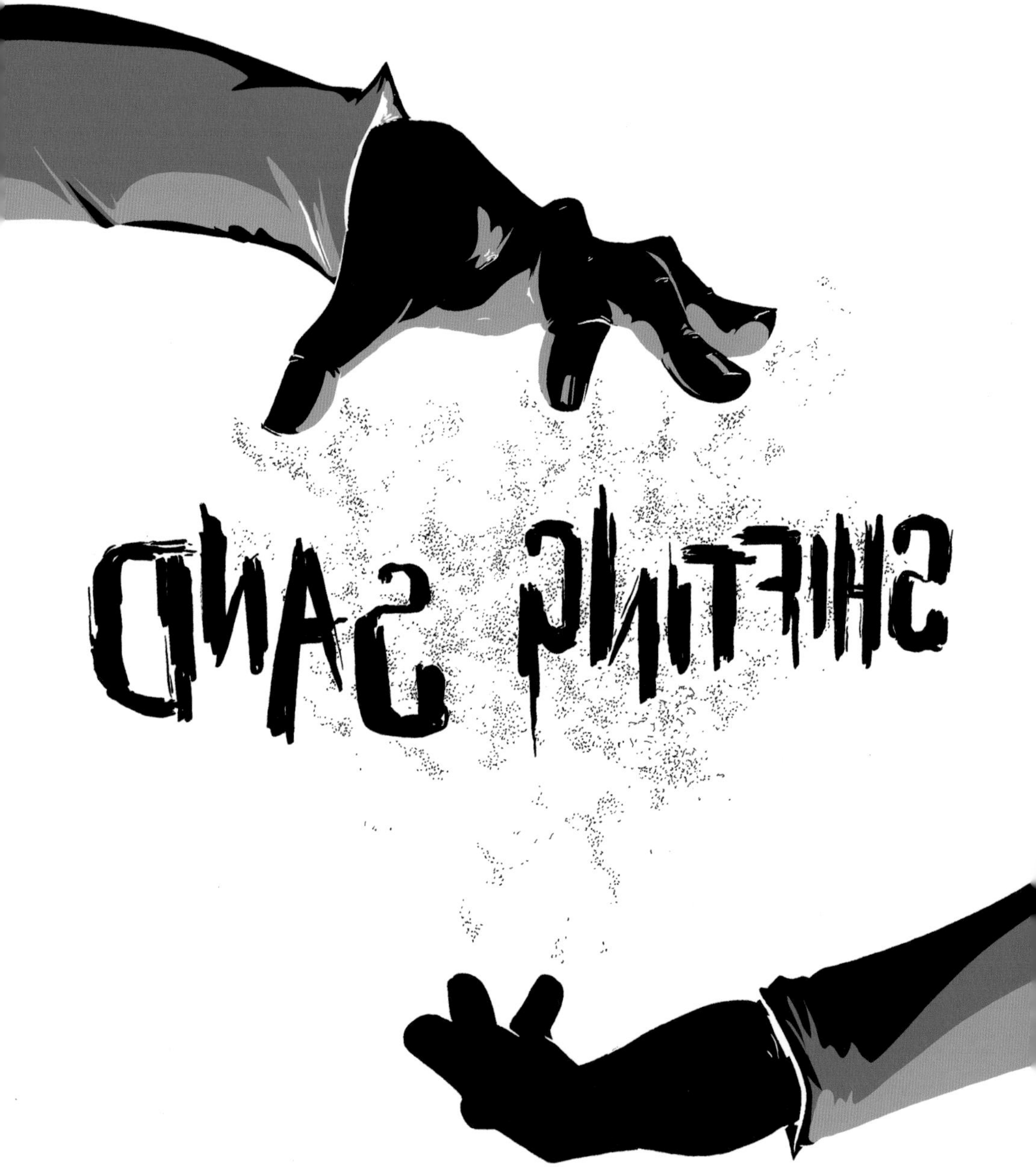
SHIFTING SAND

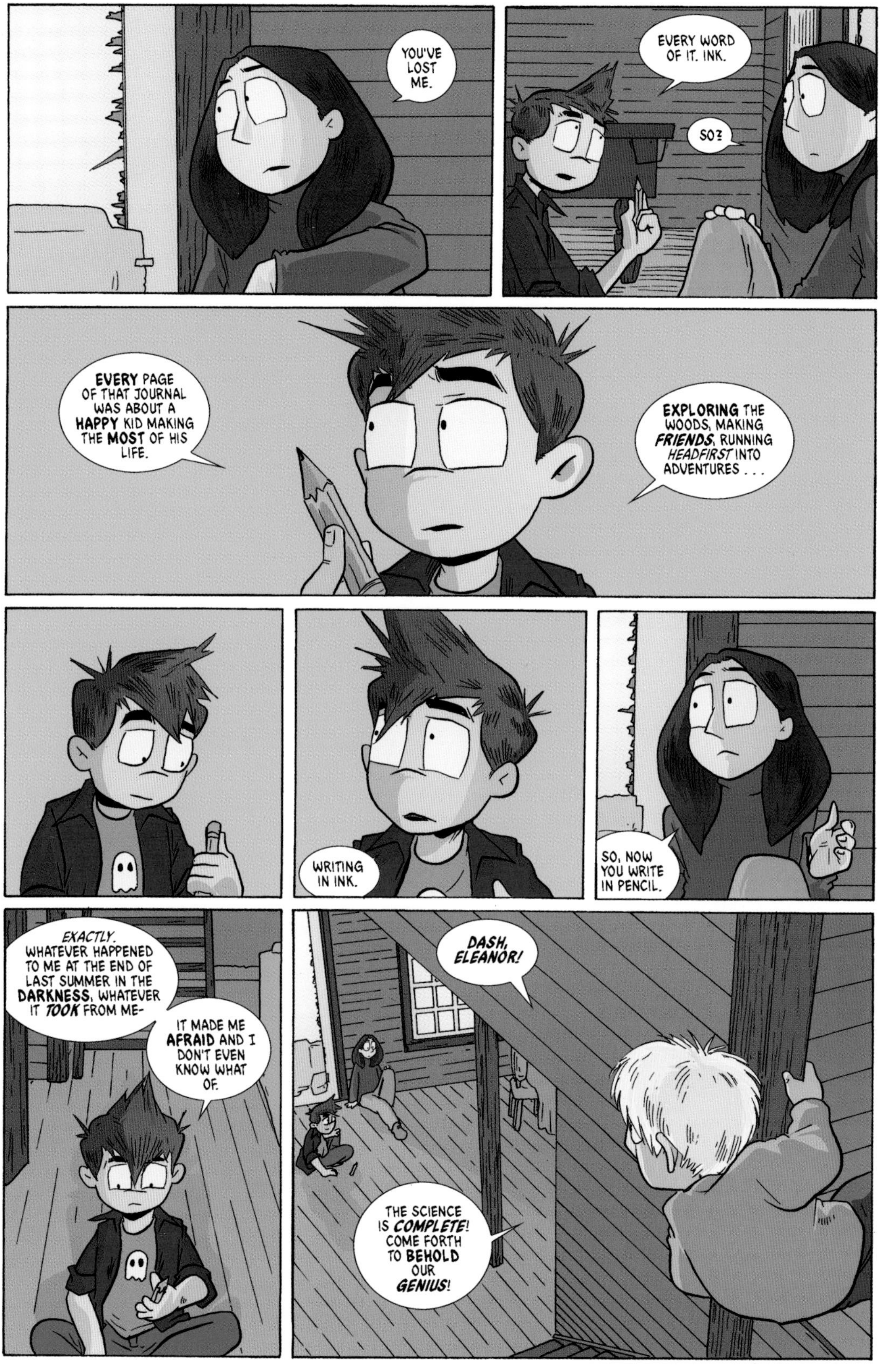
YOU'VE LOST ME.
EVERY WORD OF IT. INK.
SO?
EVERY PAGE OF THAT JOURNAL WAS ABOUT A **HAPPY** KID MAKING THE **MOST** OF HIS LIFE.
EXPLORING THE WOODS, MAKING ***FRIENDS***, RUNNING *HEADFIRST* INTO ADVENTURES . . .
WRITING IN INK.
SO, NOW YOU WRITE IN PENCIL.
EXACTLY. WHATEVER HAPPENED TO ME AT THE END OF LAST SUMMER IN THE **DARKNESS**, WHATEVER IT ***TOOK*** FROM ME-
IT MADE ME **AFRAID** AND I DON'T EVEN KNOW WHAT OF.
DASH, ELEANOR!
THE SCIENCE IS ***COMPLETE***! COME FORTH TO **BEHOLD** OUR ***GENIUS***!

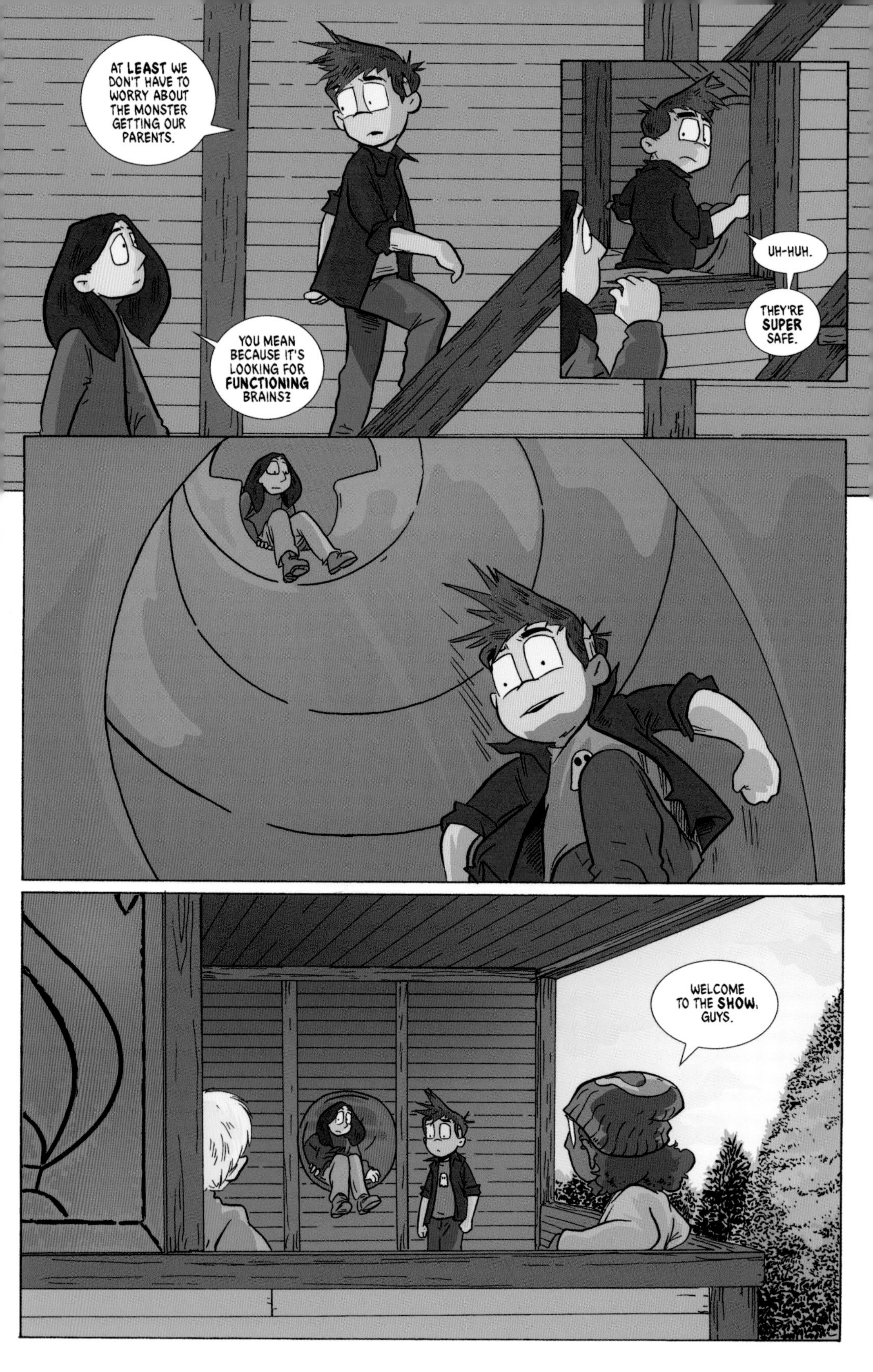
AT LEAST WE DON'T HAVE TO WORRY ABOUT THE MONSTER GETTING OUR PARENTS.
YOU MEAN BECAUSE IT'S LOOKING FOR FUNCTIONING BRAINS?
UH-HUH.
THEY'RE SUPER SAFE.
WELCOME TO THE SHOW, GUYS.

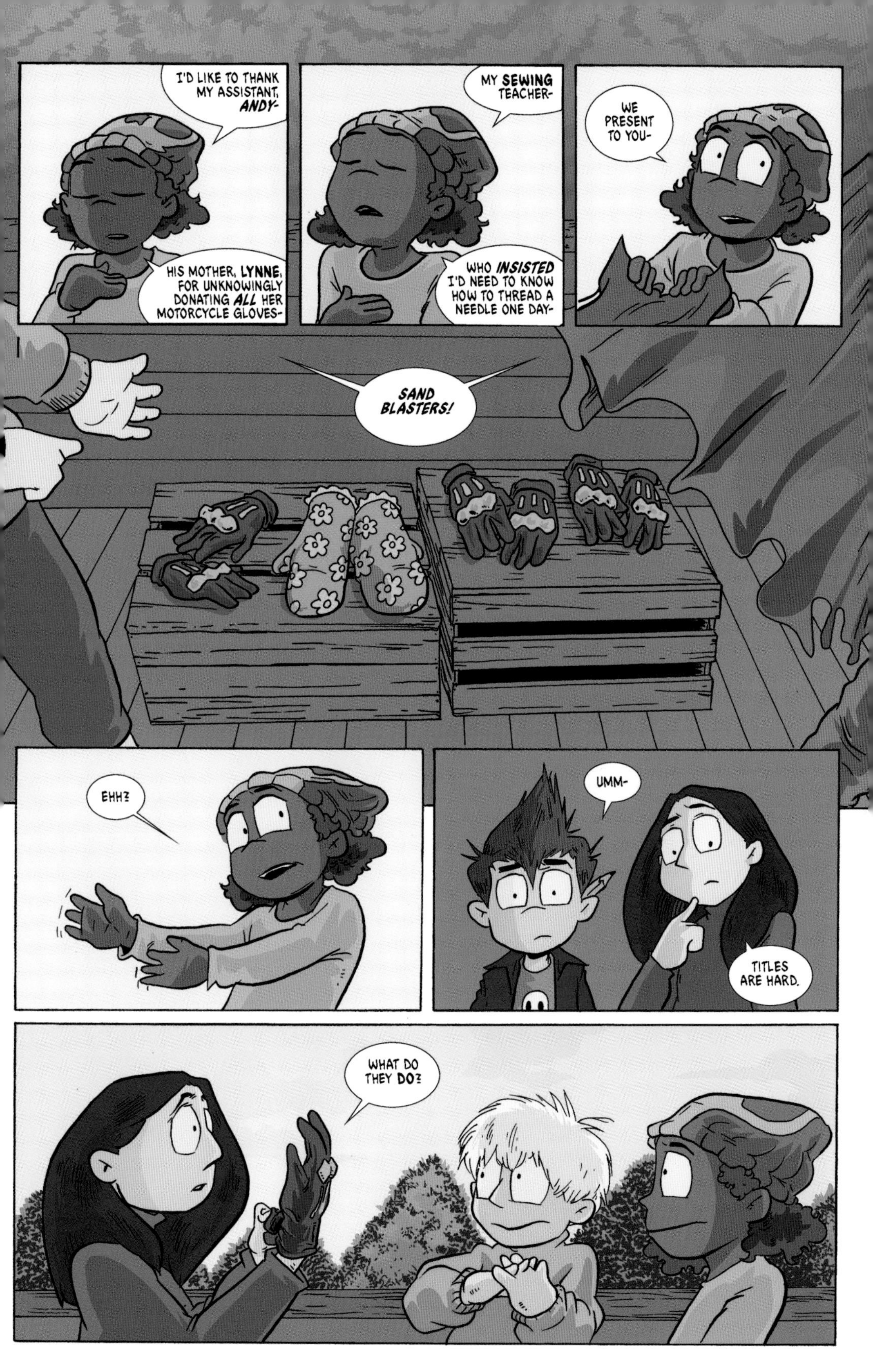
I'D LIKE TO THANK MY ASSISTANT, ANDY-
HIS MOTHER, LYNNE, FOR UNKNOWINGLY DONATING ALL HER MOTORCYCLE GLOVES-
MY SEWING TEACHER-
WHO INSISTED I'D NEED TO KNOW HOW TO THREAD A NEEDLE ONE DAY-
WE PRESENT TO YOU-
SAND BLASTERS!
EHH?
UMM-
TITLES ARE HARD.
WHAT DO THEY DO?

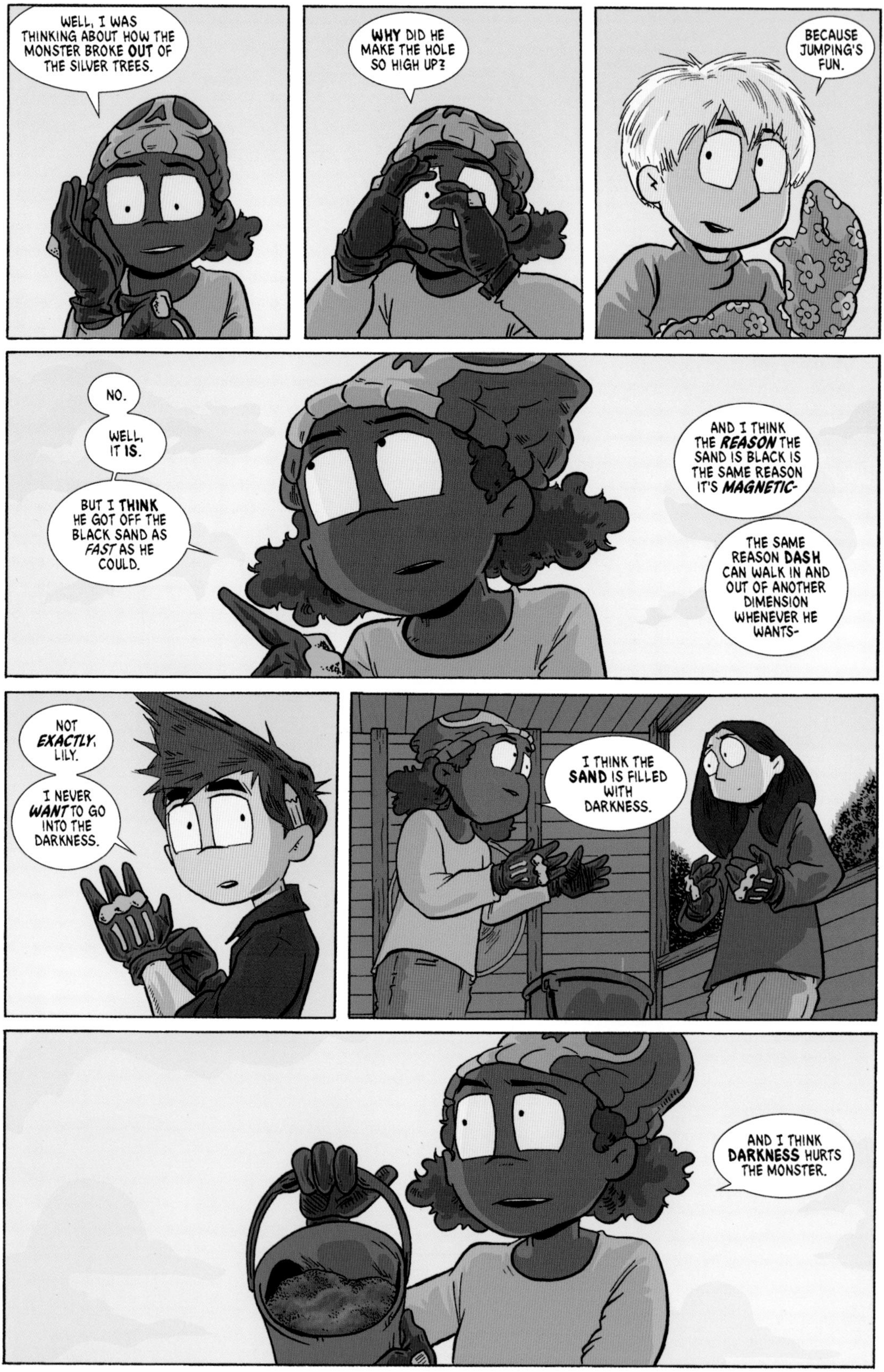
WELL, I WAS THINKING ABOUT HOW THE MONSTER BROKE **OUT** OF THE SILVER TREES.
WHY DID HE MAKE THE HOLE SO HIGH UP?
BECAUSE JUMPING'S FUN.
NO.
WELL, IT **IS**.
BUT I **THINK** HE GOT OFF THE BLACK SAND AS *FAST* AS HE COULD.
AND I THINK THE ***REASON*** THE SAND IS BLACK IS THE SAME REASON IT'S ***MAGNETIC***-
THE SAME REASON **DASH** CAN WALK IN AND OUT OF ANOTHER DIMENSION WHENEVER HE WANTS-
NOT ***EXACTLY***, LILY.
I NEVER ***WANT*** TO GO INTO THE DARKNESS.
I THINK THE **SAND** IS FILLED WITH DARKNESS.
AND I THINK **DARKNESS** HURTS THE MONSTER.

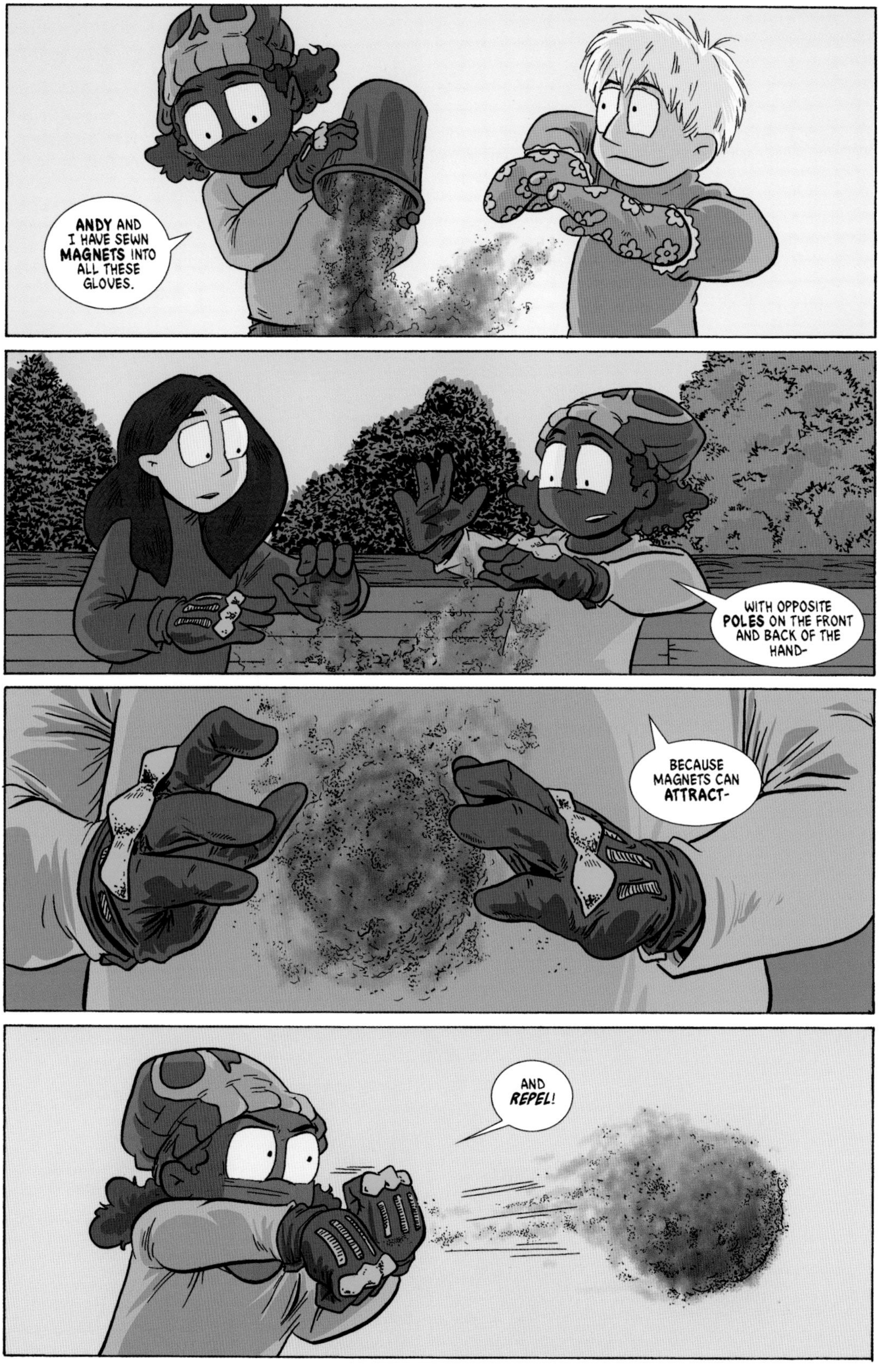
ANDY AND I HAVE SEWN MAGNETS INTO ALL THESE GLOVES.
WITH OPPOSITE POLES ON THE FRONT AND BACK OF THE HAND-
BECAUSE MAGNETS CAN ATTRACT-
AND REPEL!

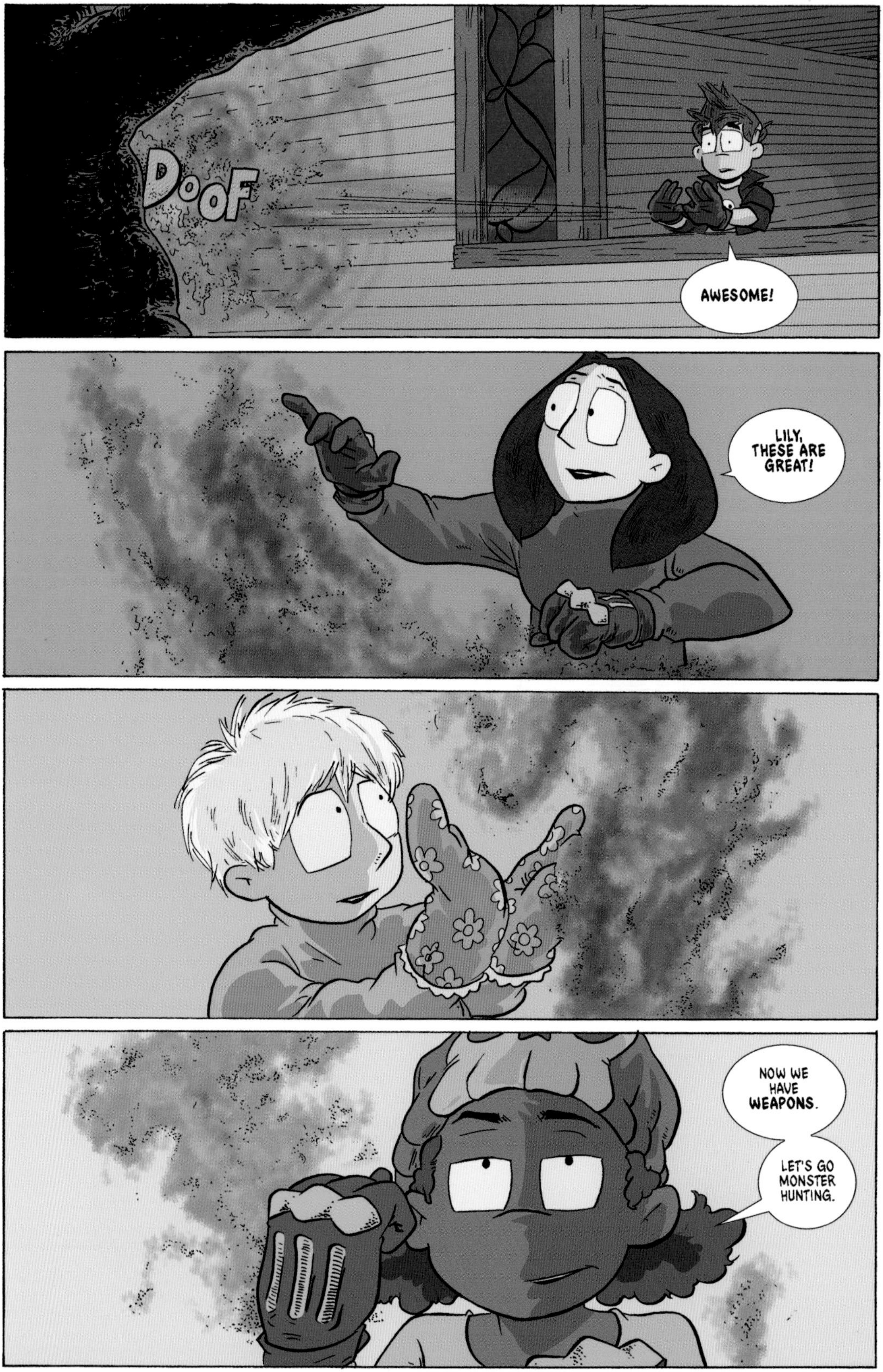
DOOF
AWESOME!
LILY, THESE ARE GREAT!
NOW WE HAVE WEAPONS.
LET'S GO MONSTER HUNTING.

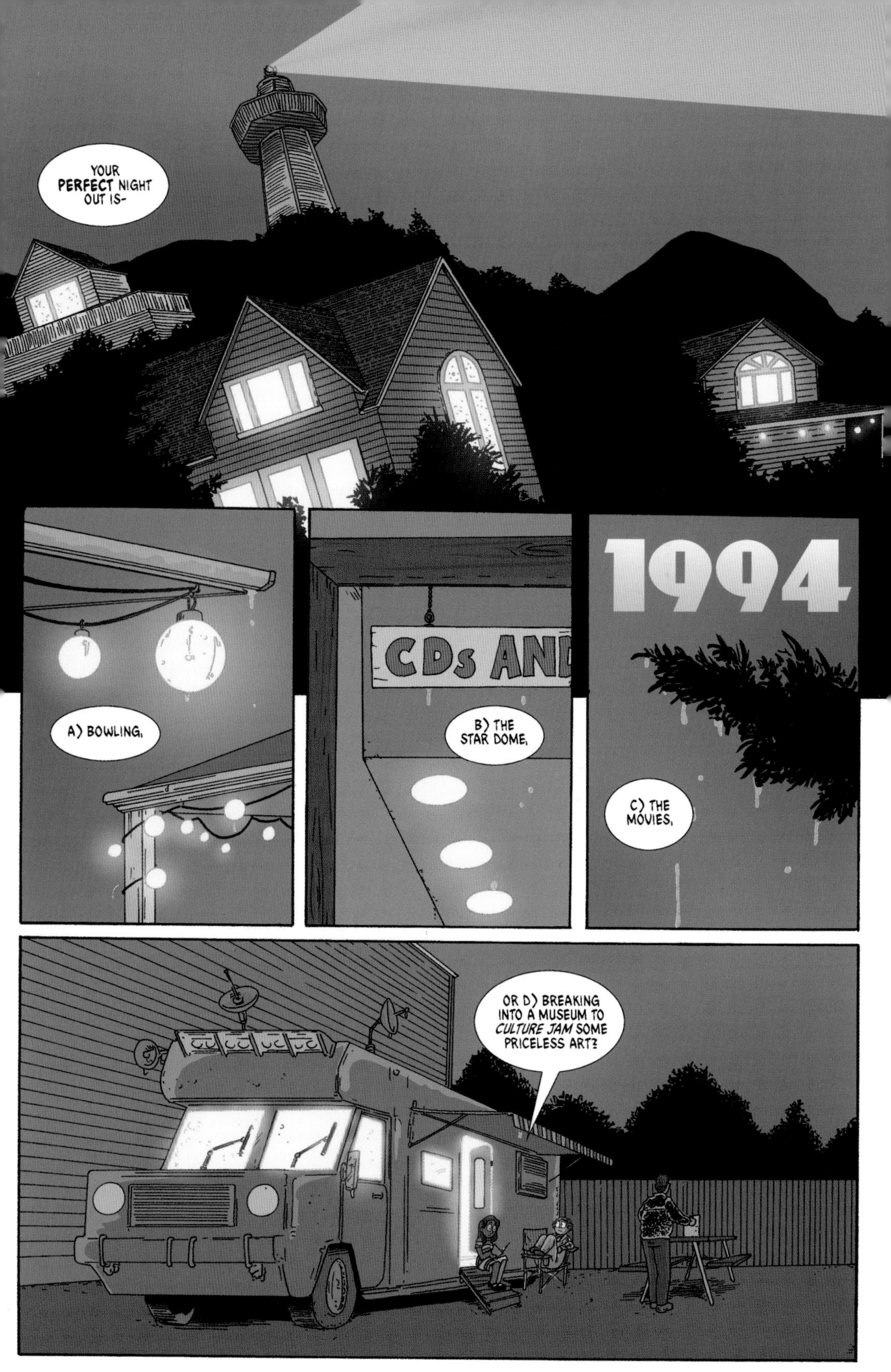
YOUR PERFECT NIGHT OUT IS-
A) BOWLING,
CDs AND
B) THE STAR DOME,
1994
C) THE MOVIES,
OR D) BREAKING INTO A MUSEUM TO *CULTURE JAM* SOME PRICELESS ART?

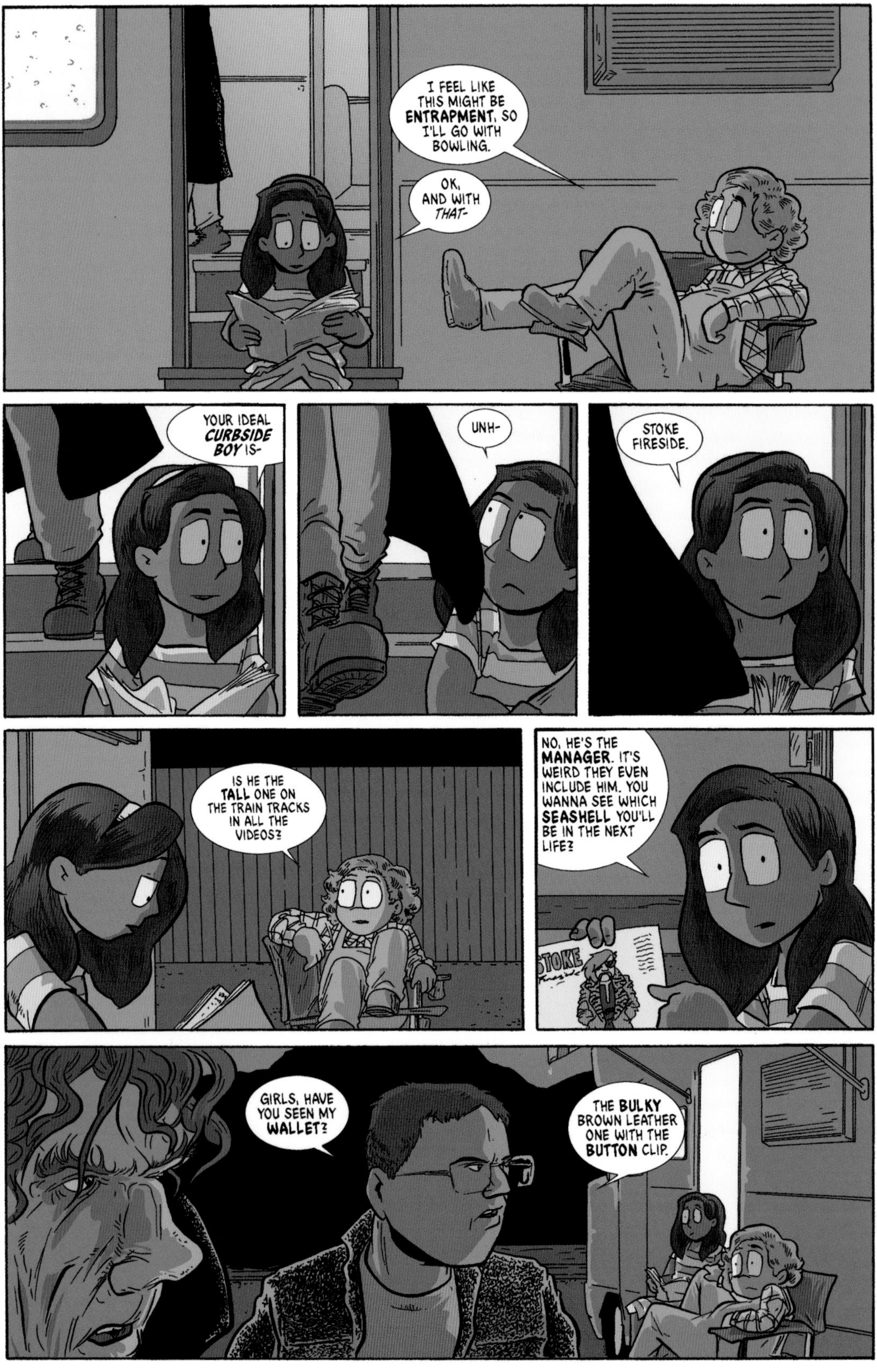
I FEEL LIKE THIS MIGHT BE **ENTRAPMENT**, SO I'LL GO WITH BOWLING.
OK, AND WITH *THAT*-
YOUR IDEAL ***CURBSIDE BOY*** IS-
UNH-
STOKE FIRESIDE.
IS HE THE **TALL** ONE ON THE TRAIN TRACKS IN ALL THE VIDEOS?
NO, HE'S THE **MANAGER**. IT'S WEIRD THEY EVEN INCLUDE HIM. YOU WANNA SEE WHICH **SEASHELL** YOU'LL BE IN THE NEXT LIFE?
STOKE
GIRLS, HAVE YOU SEEN MY **WALLET**?
THE **BULKY** BROWN LEATHER ONE WITH THE **BUTTON** CLIP.

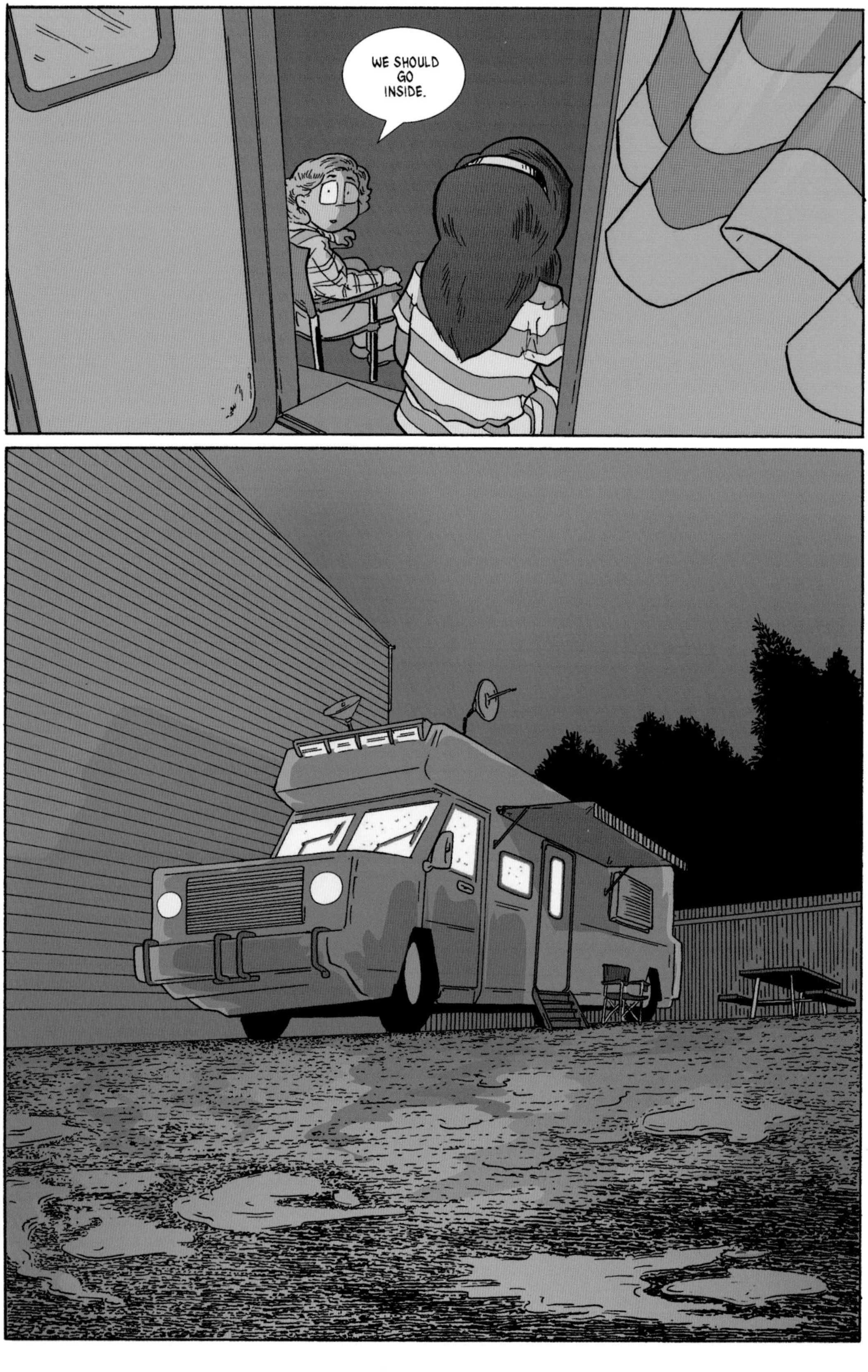
WE SHOULD GO INSIDE.

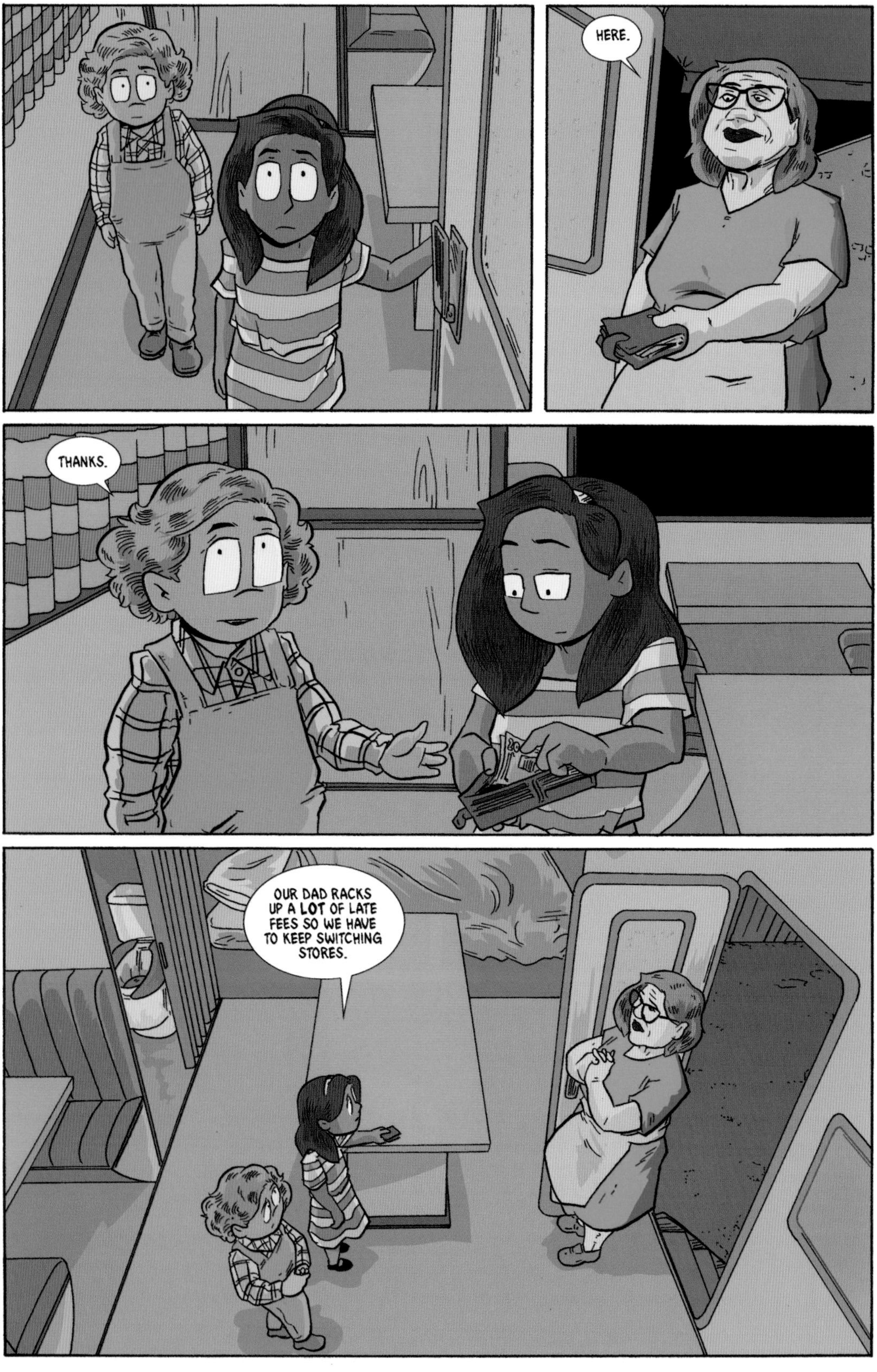
HERE.
THANKS.
OUR DAD RACKS UP A LOT OF LATE FEES SO WE HAVE TO KEEP SWITCHING STORES.

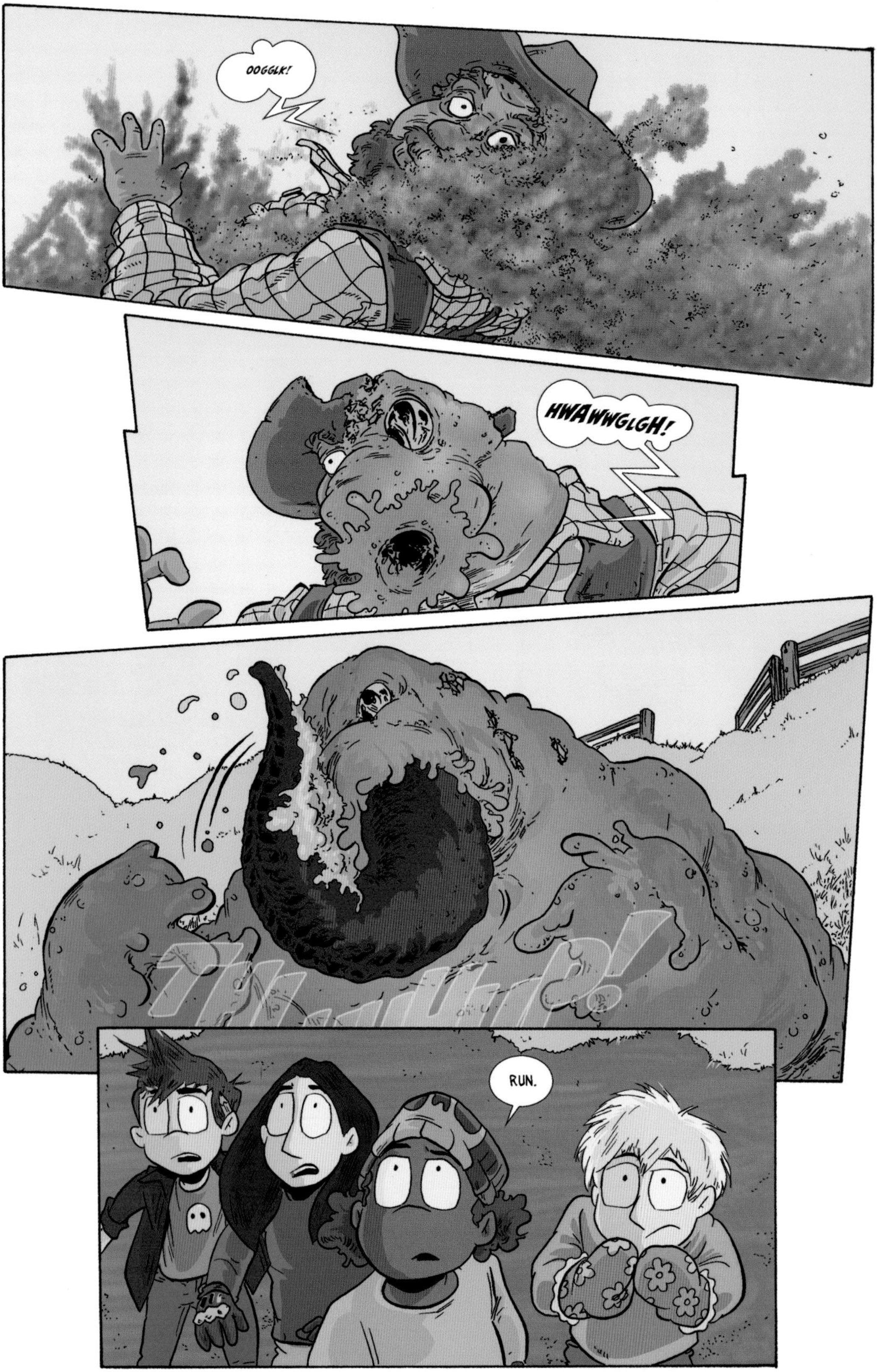
OOGGLK!
HWAWWGLGH!
RUN.

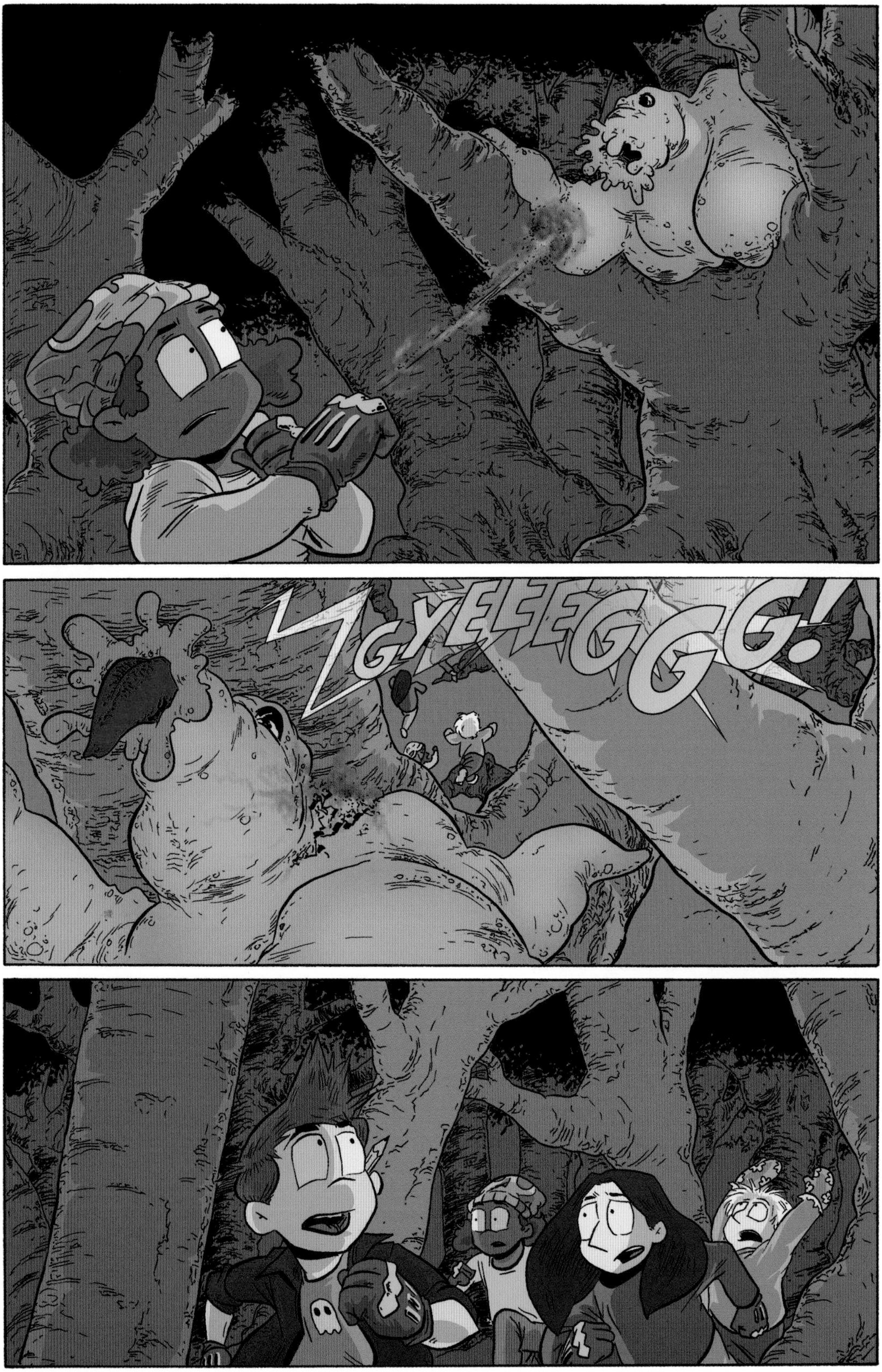
GYEEEGGG!

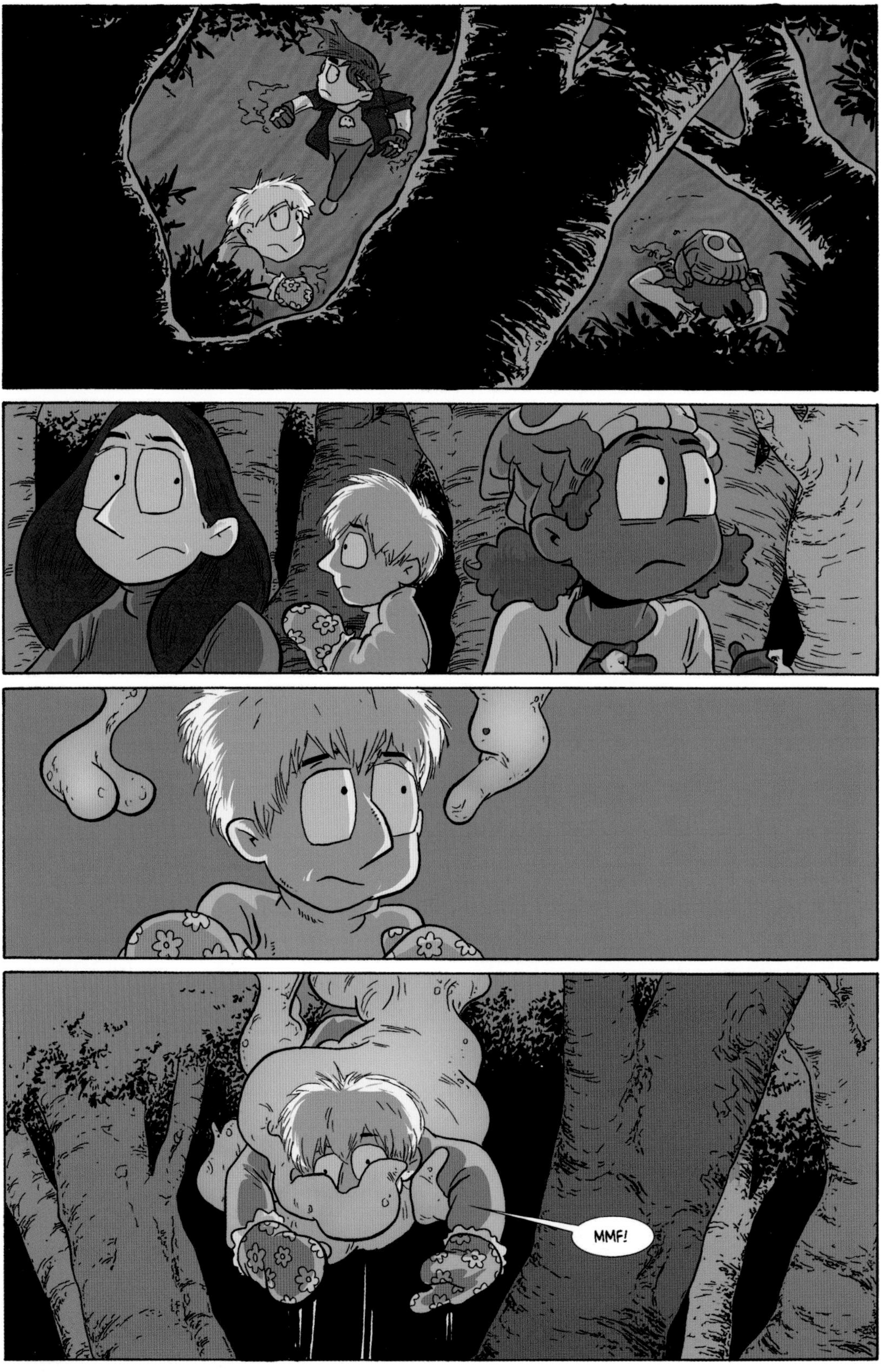
MMF!

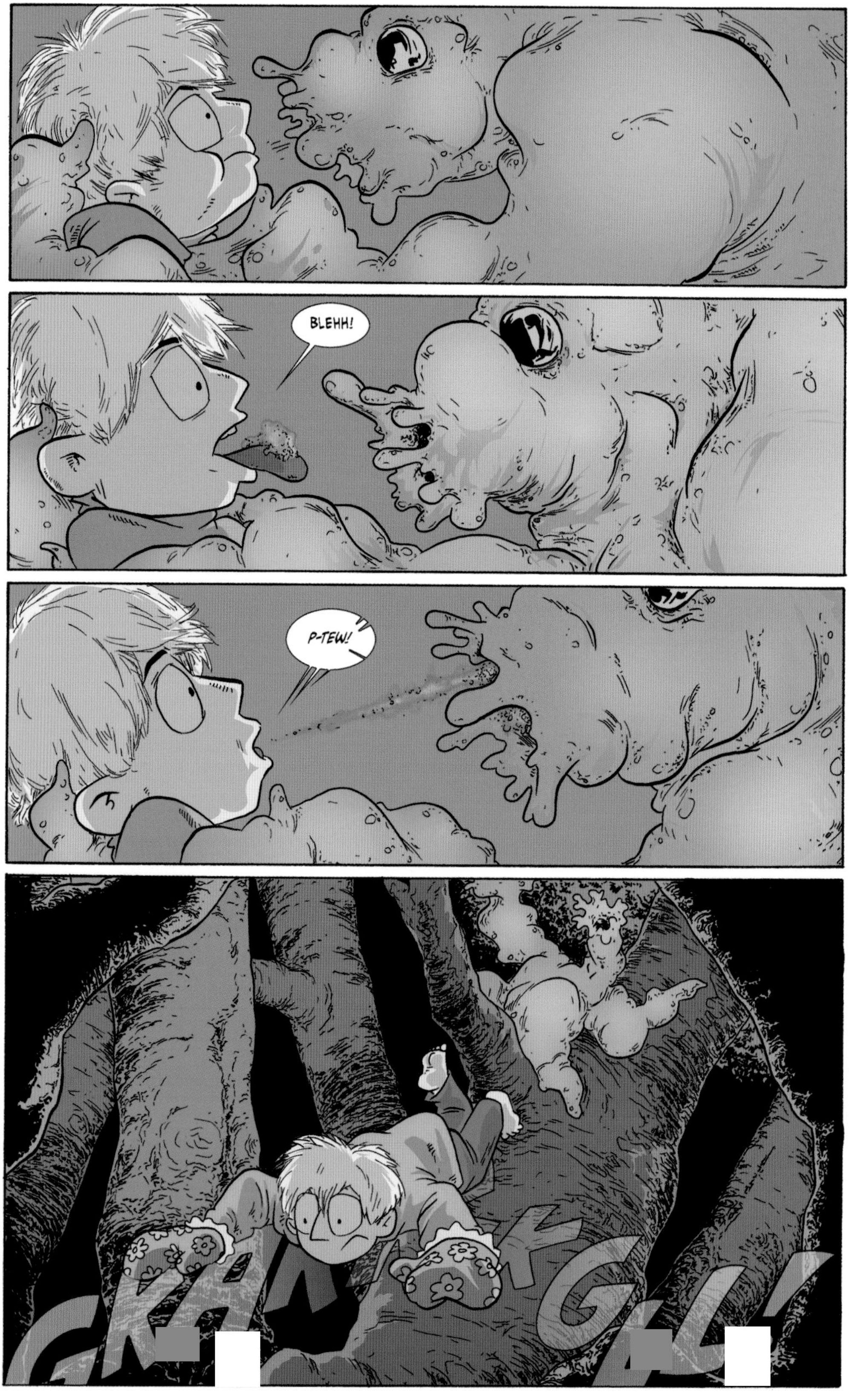
BLEHH!
P-TEW!

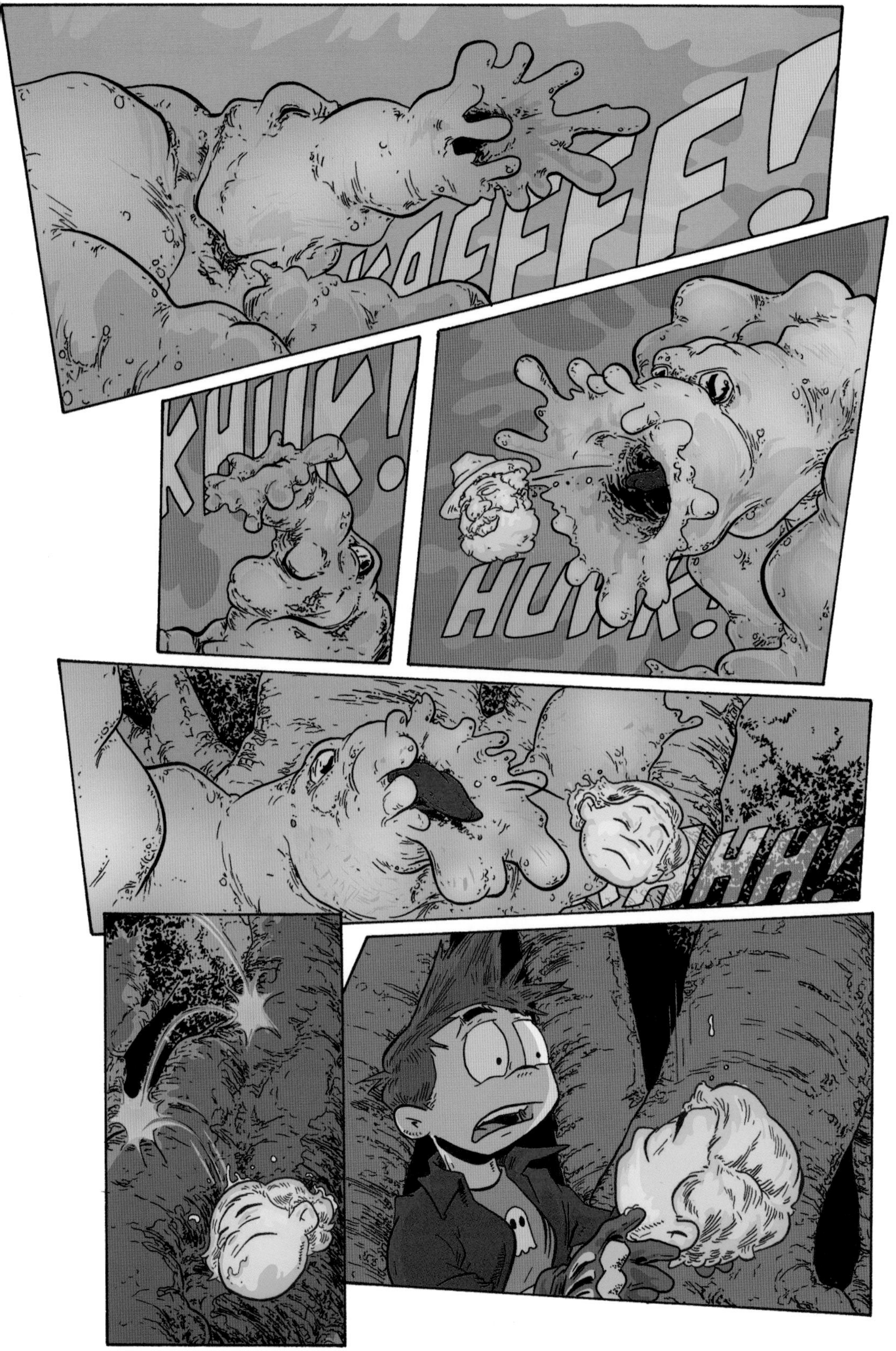
KHUK!

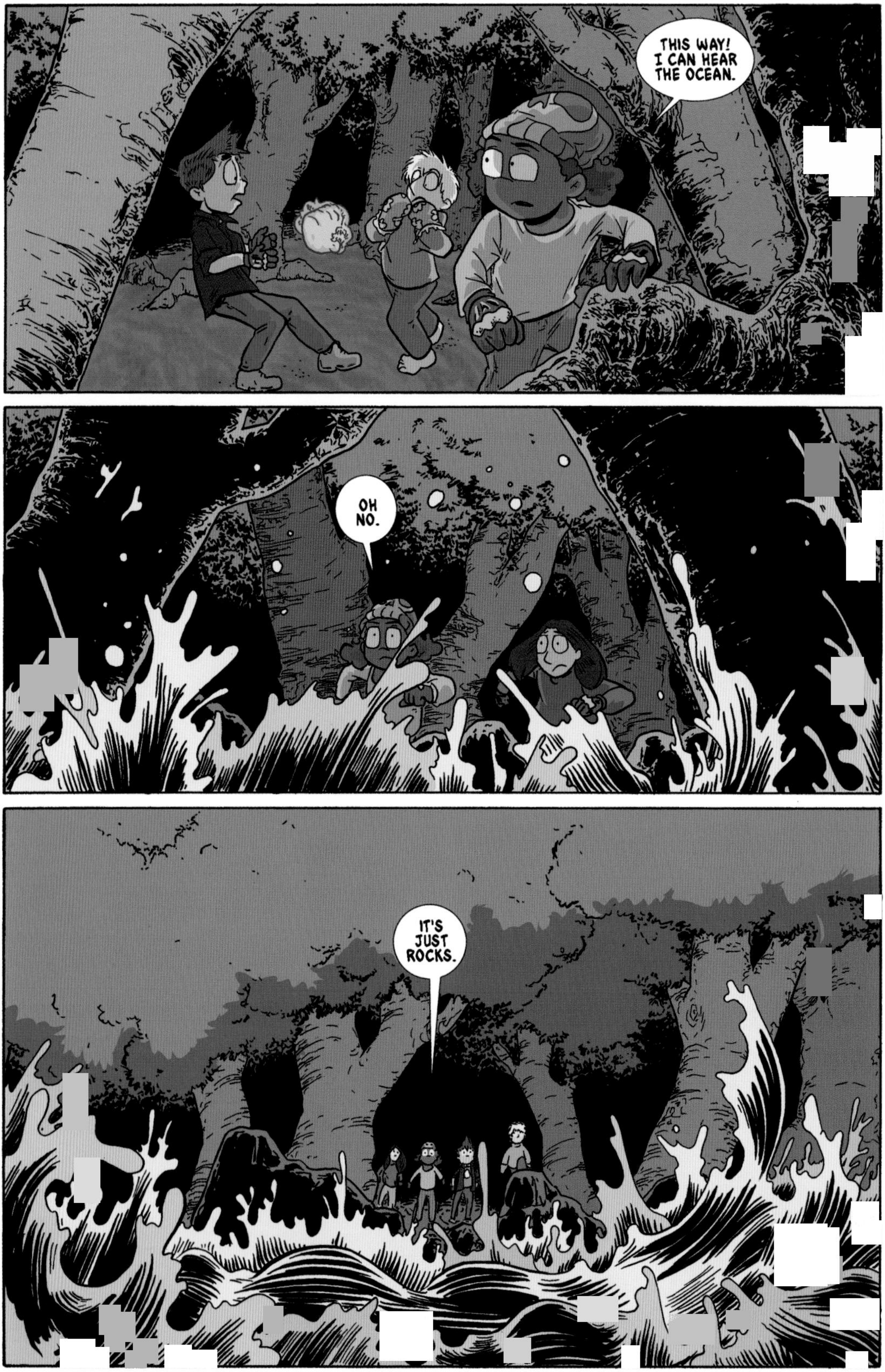
THIS WAY! I CAN HEAR THE OCEAN.
OH NO.
IT'S JUST ROCKS.

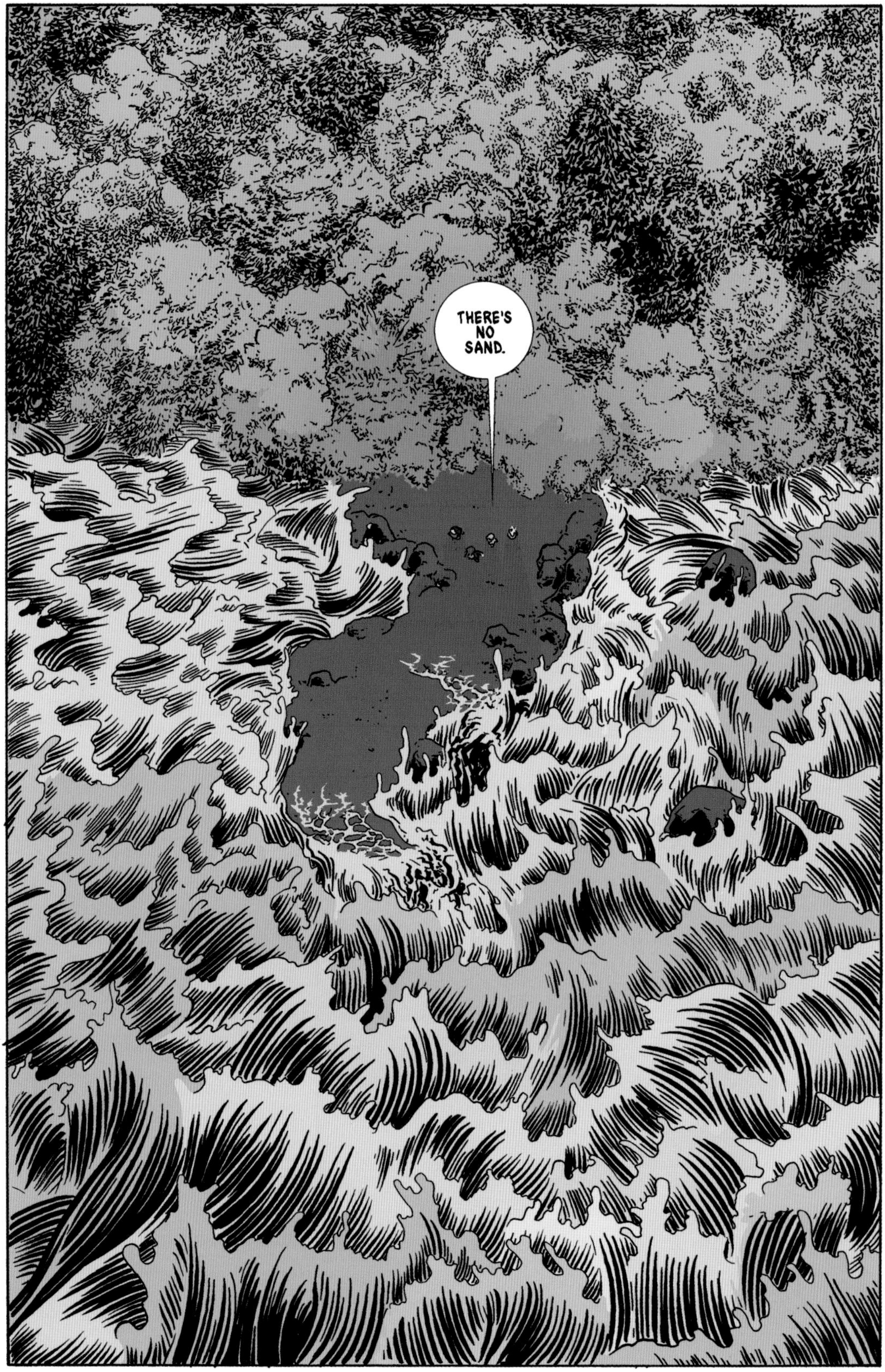
THERE'S NO SAND.

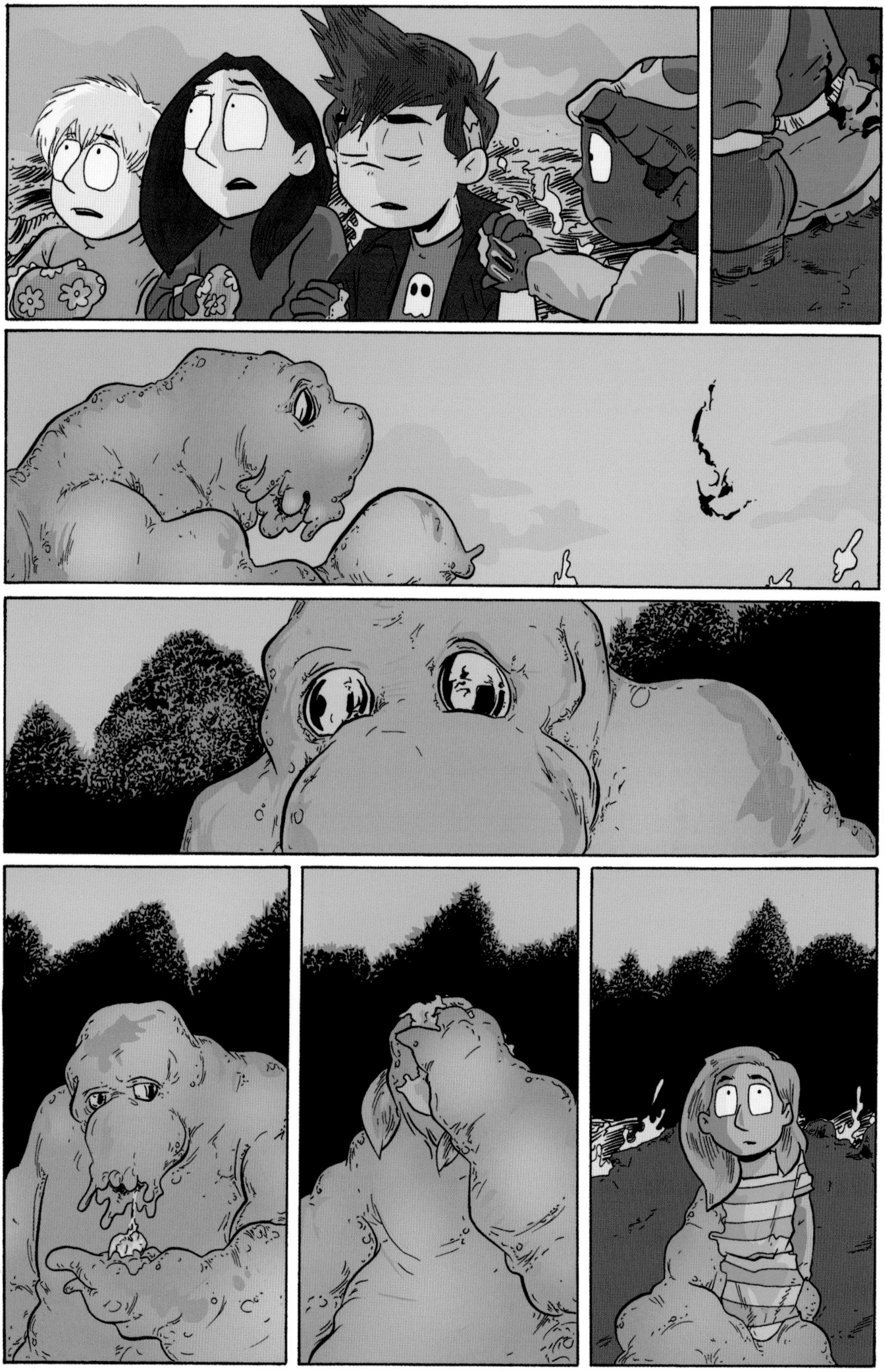

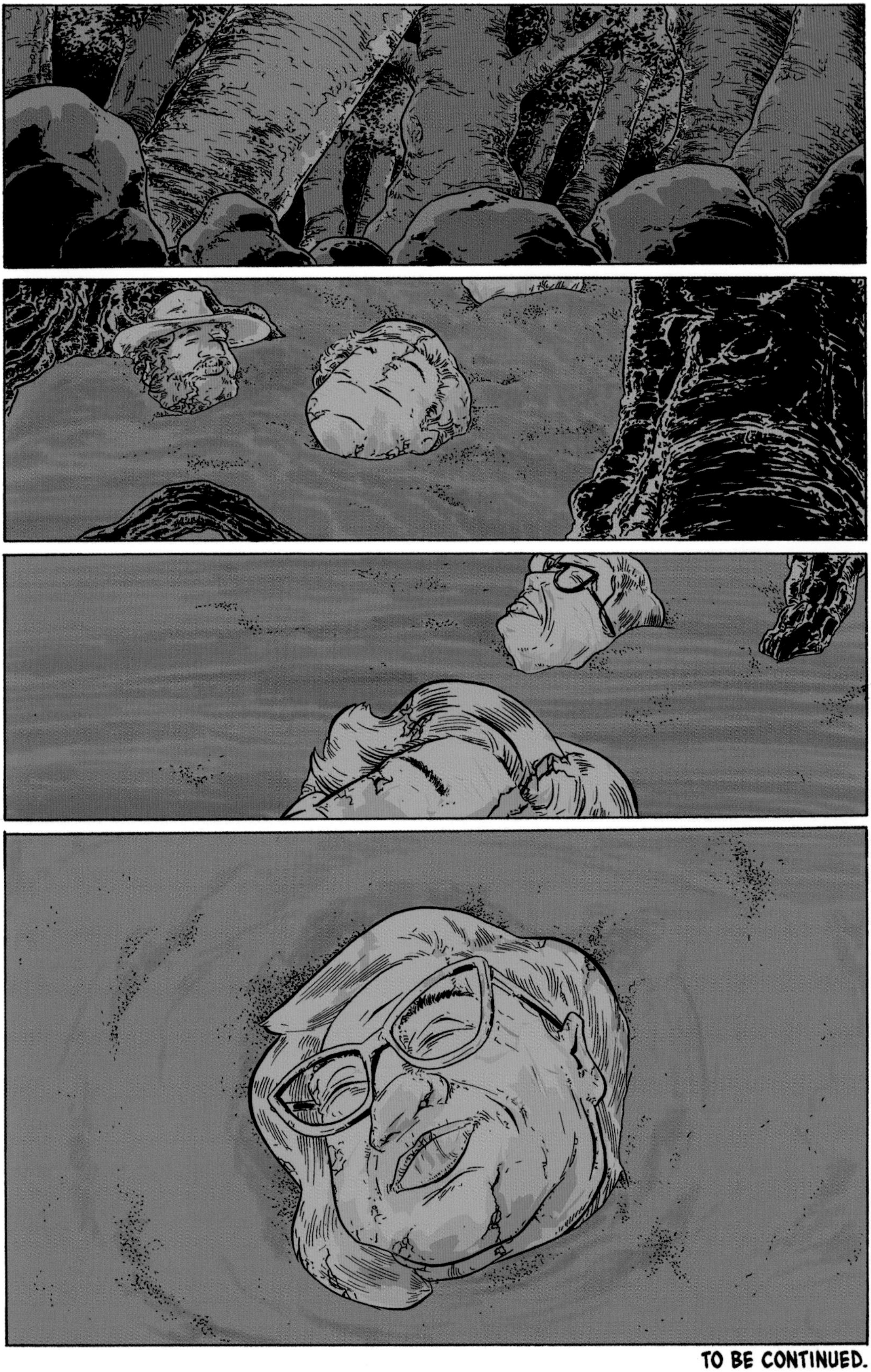

TO BE CONTINUED.

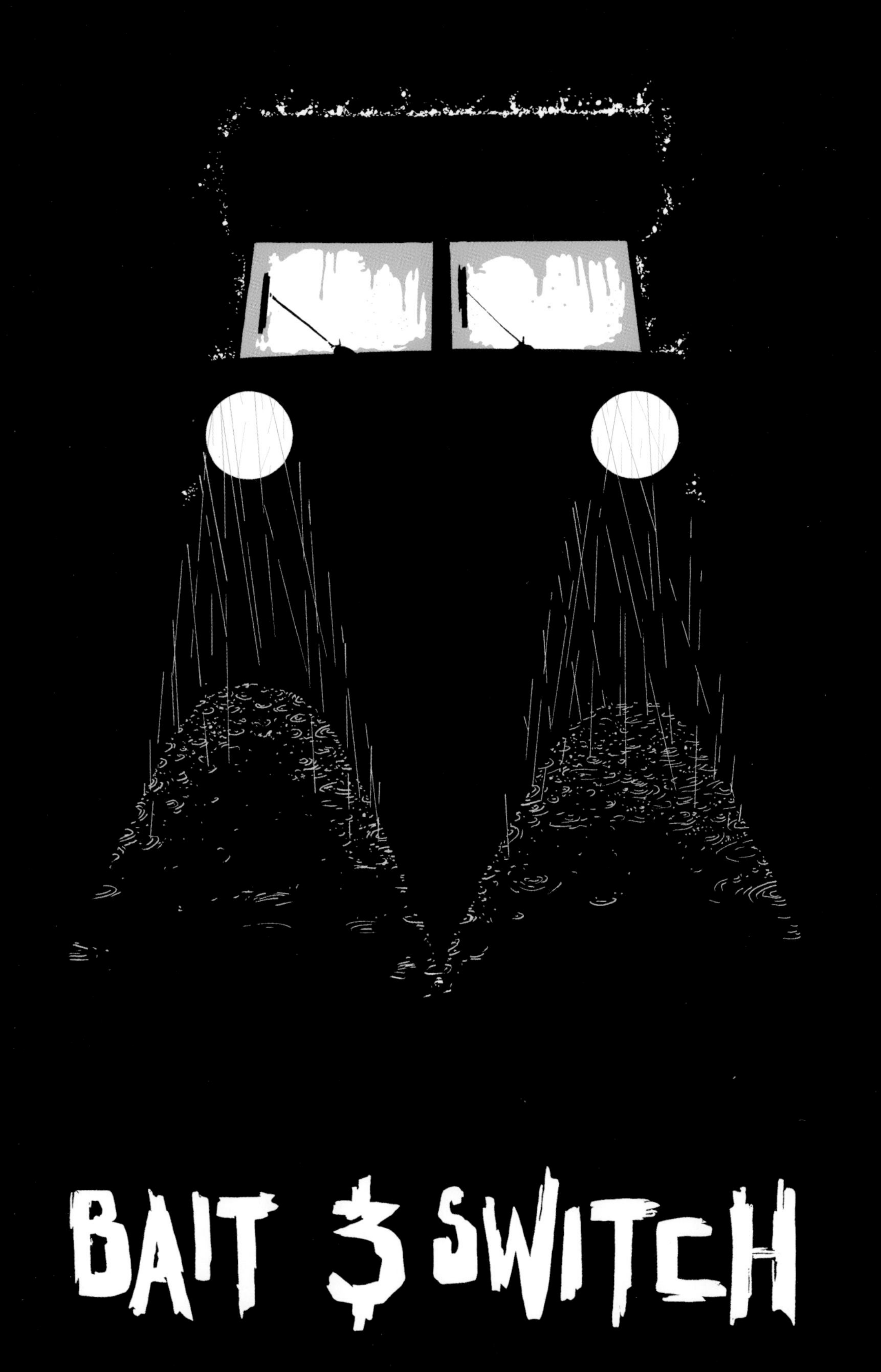
BAIT $ SWITCH

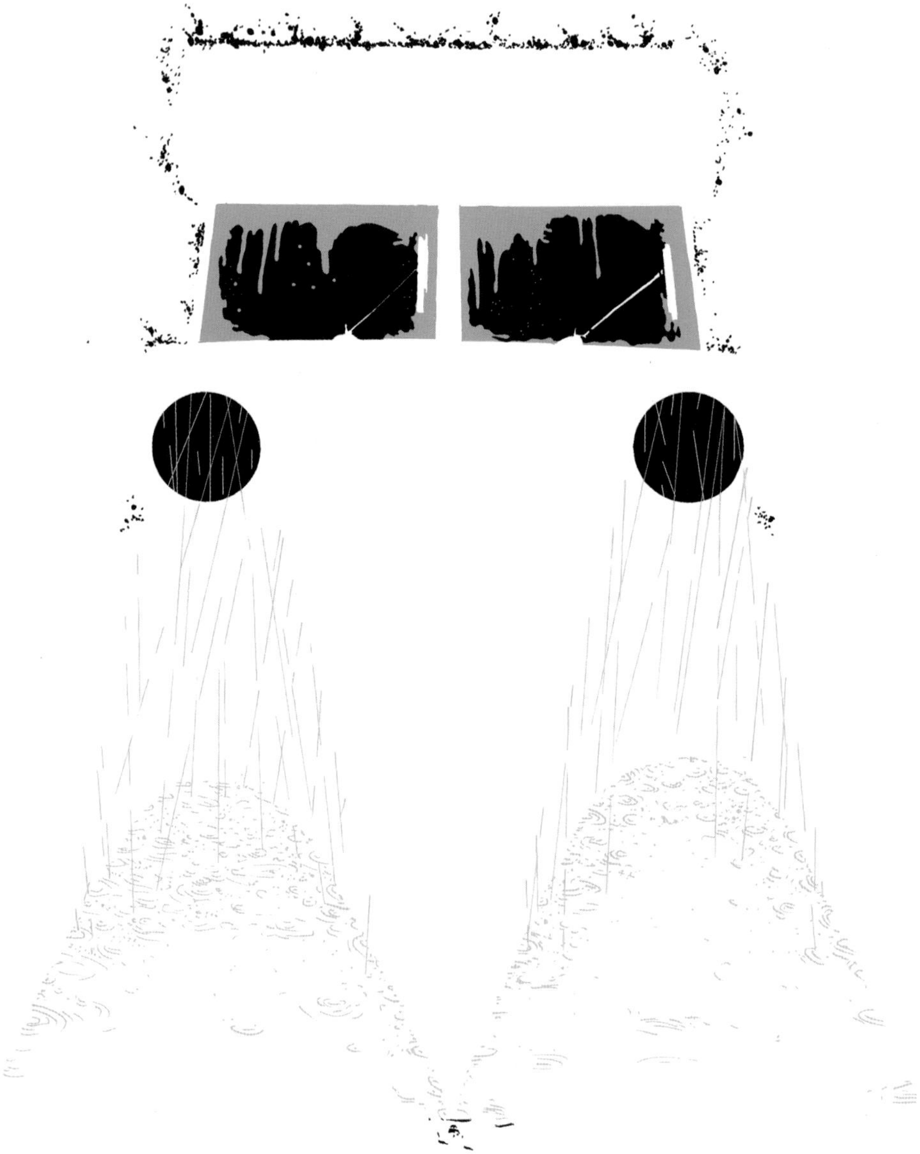

BAIT & SWITCH

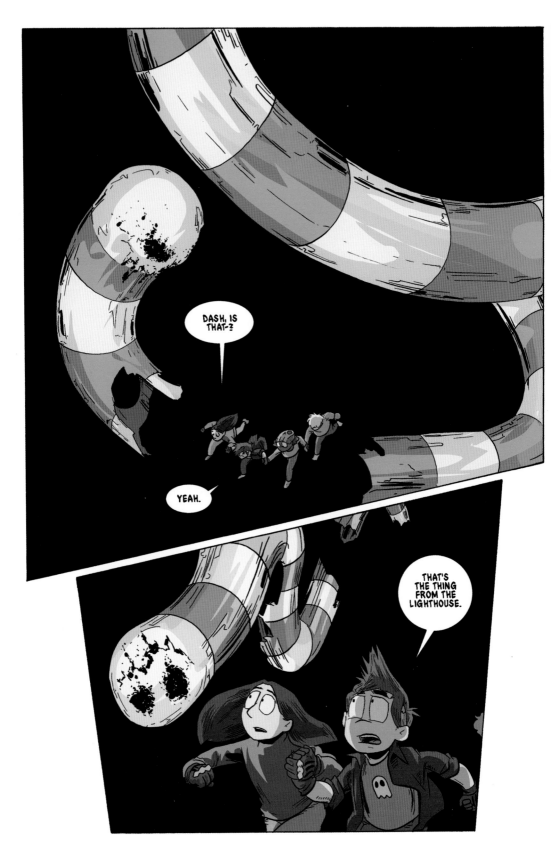

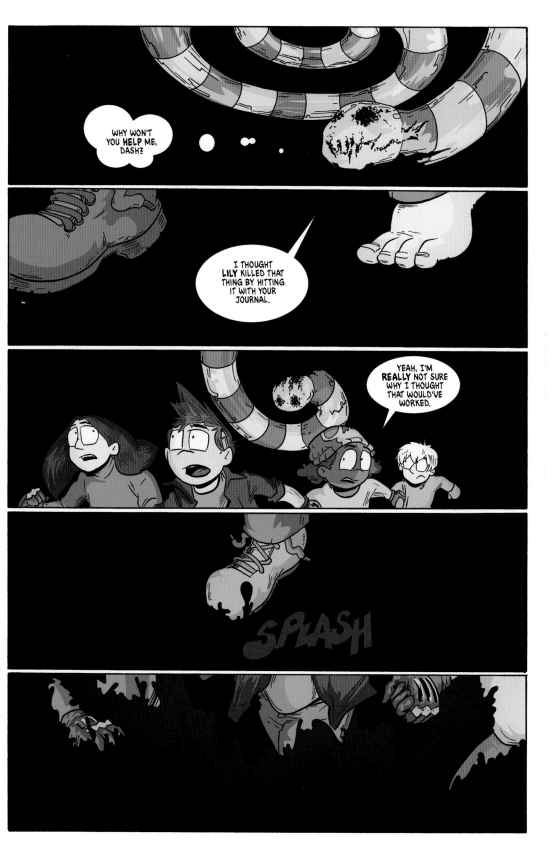

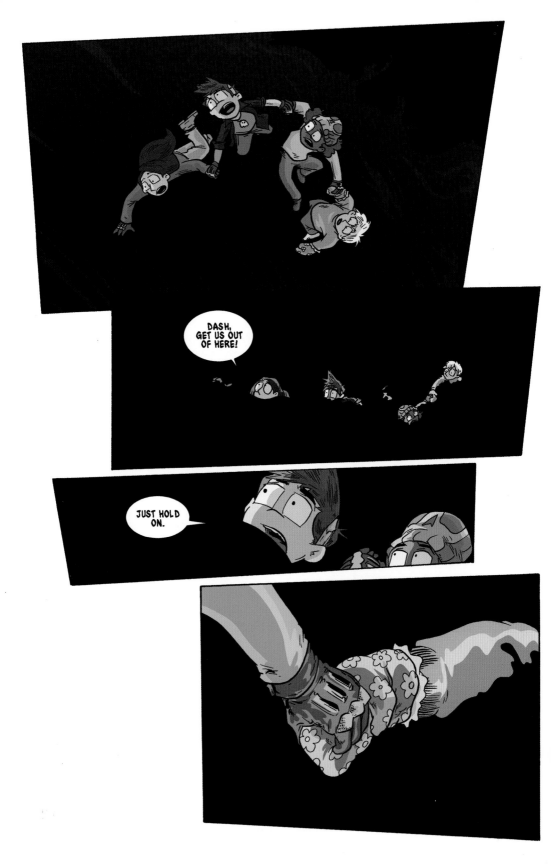

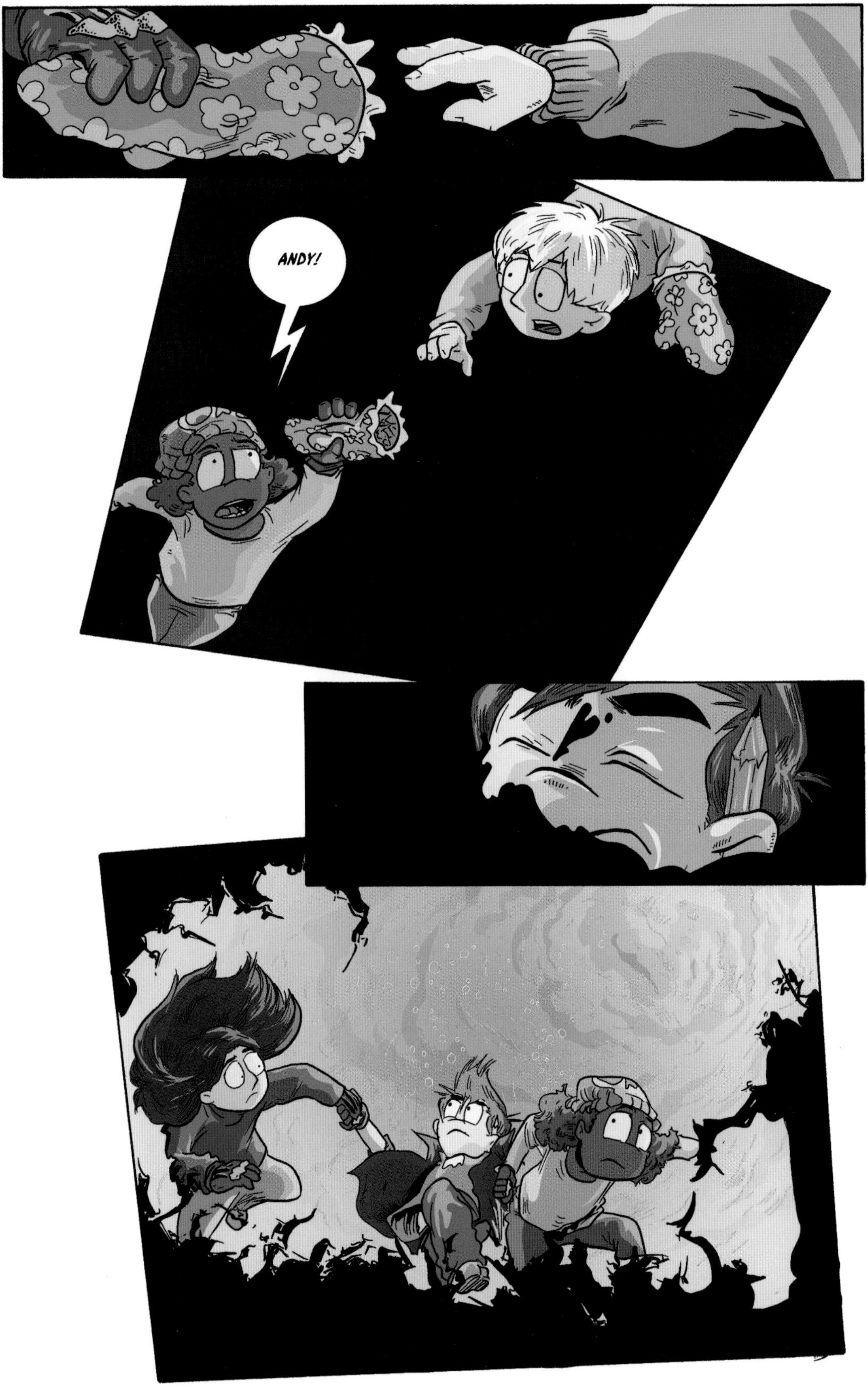
ANDY!

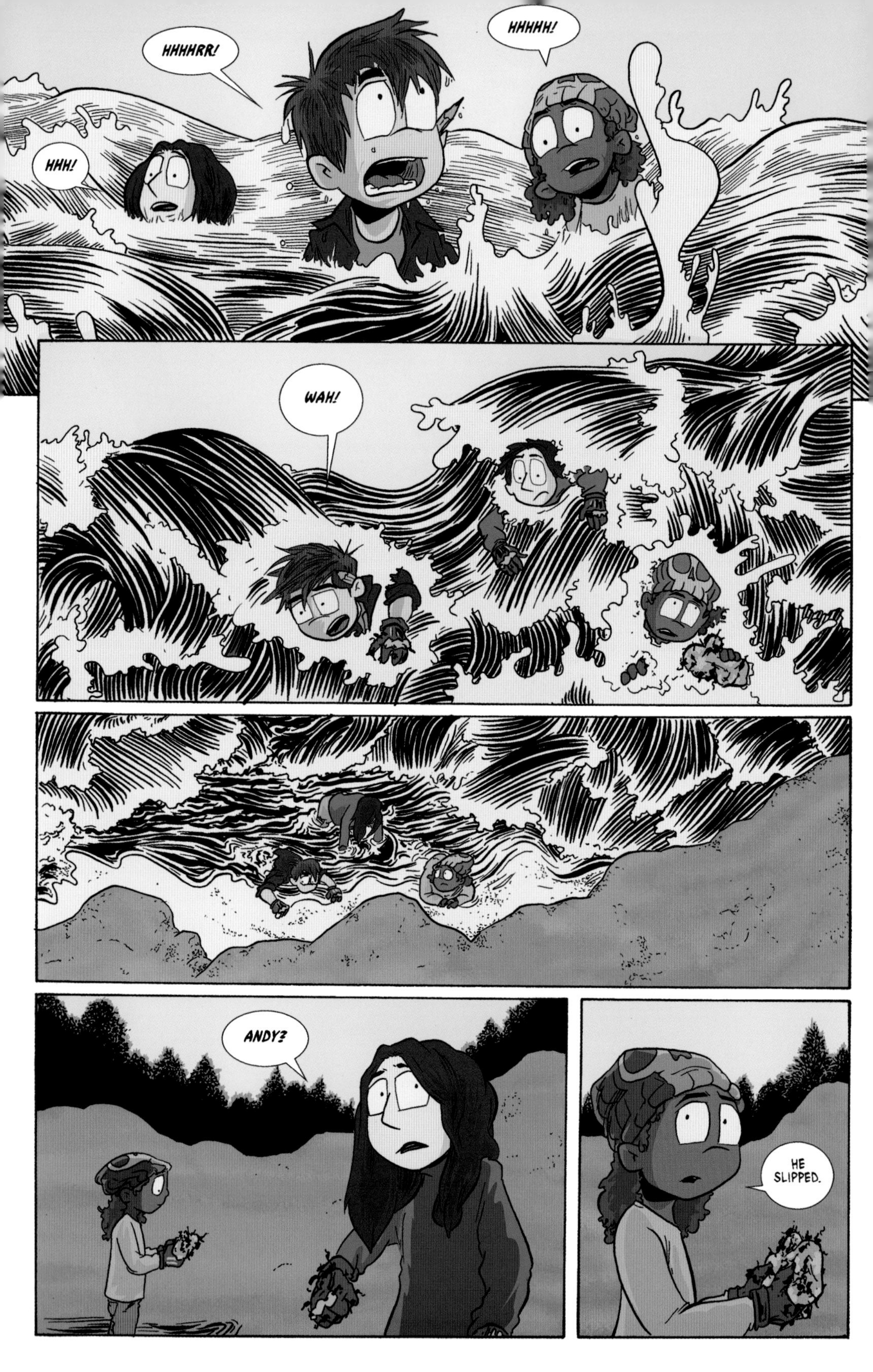
HHHHRR!
HHHHH!
HHH!
WAH!
ANDY?
HE SLIPPED.

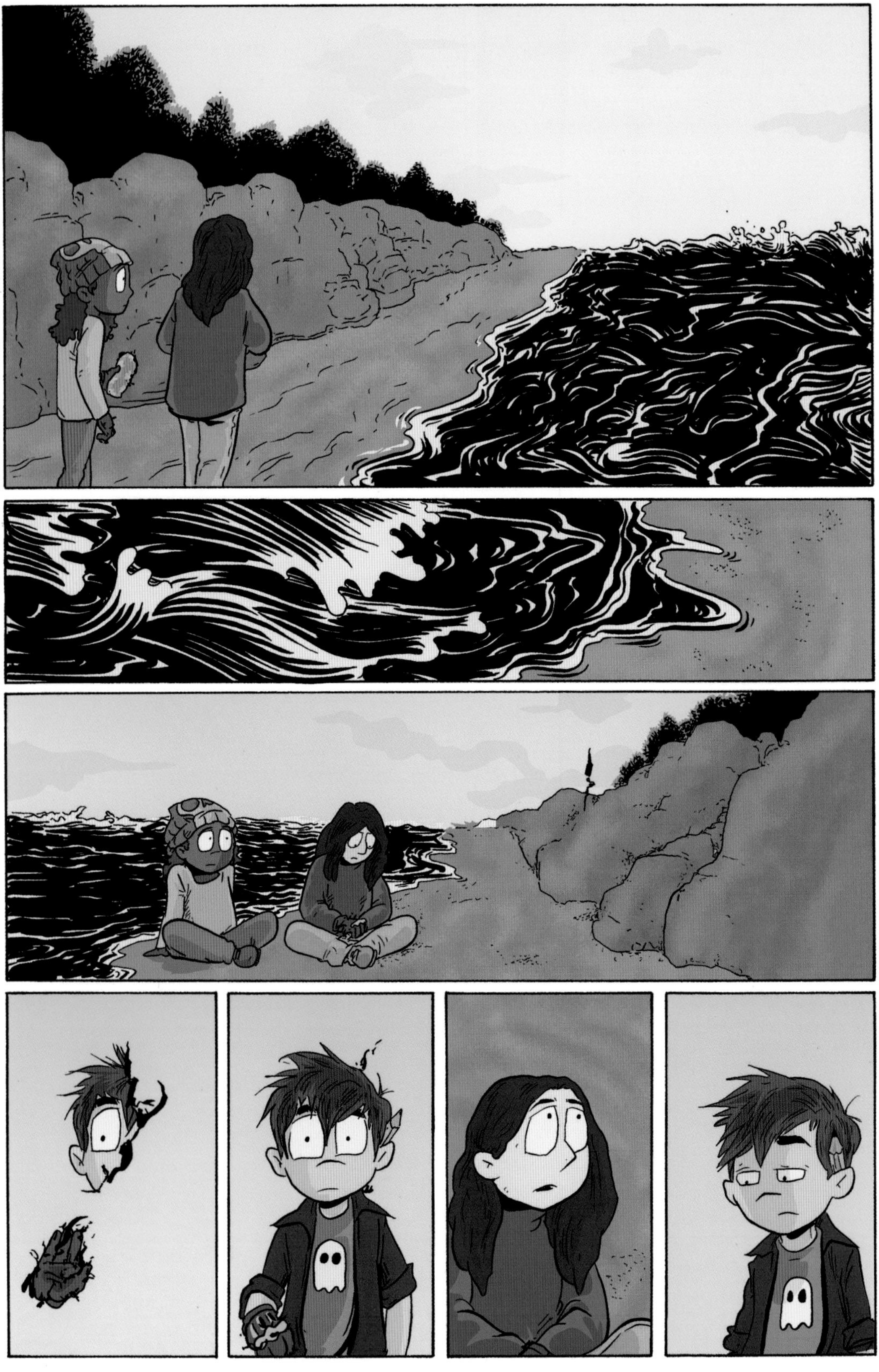

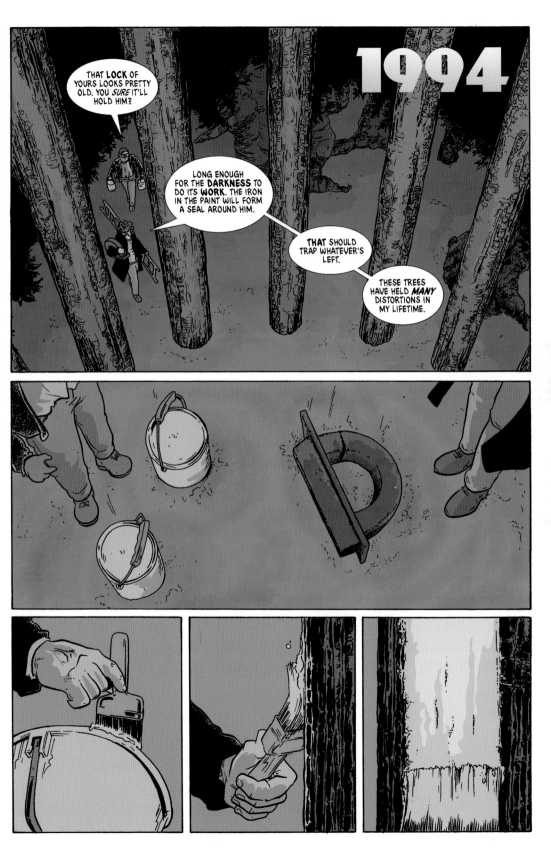

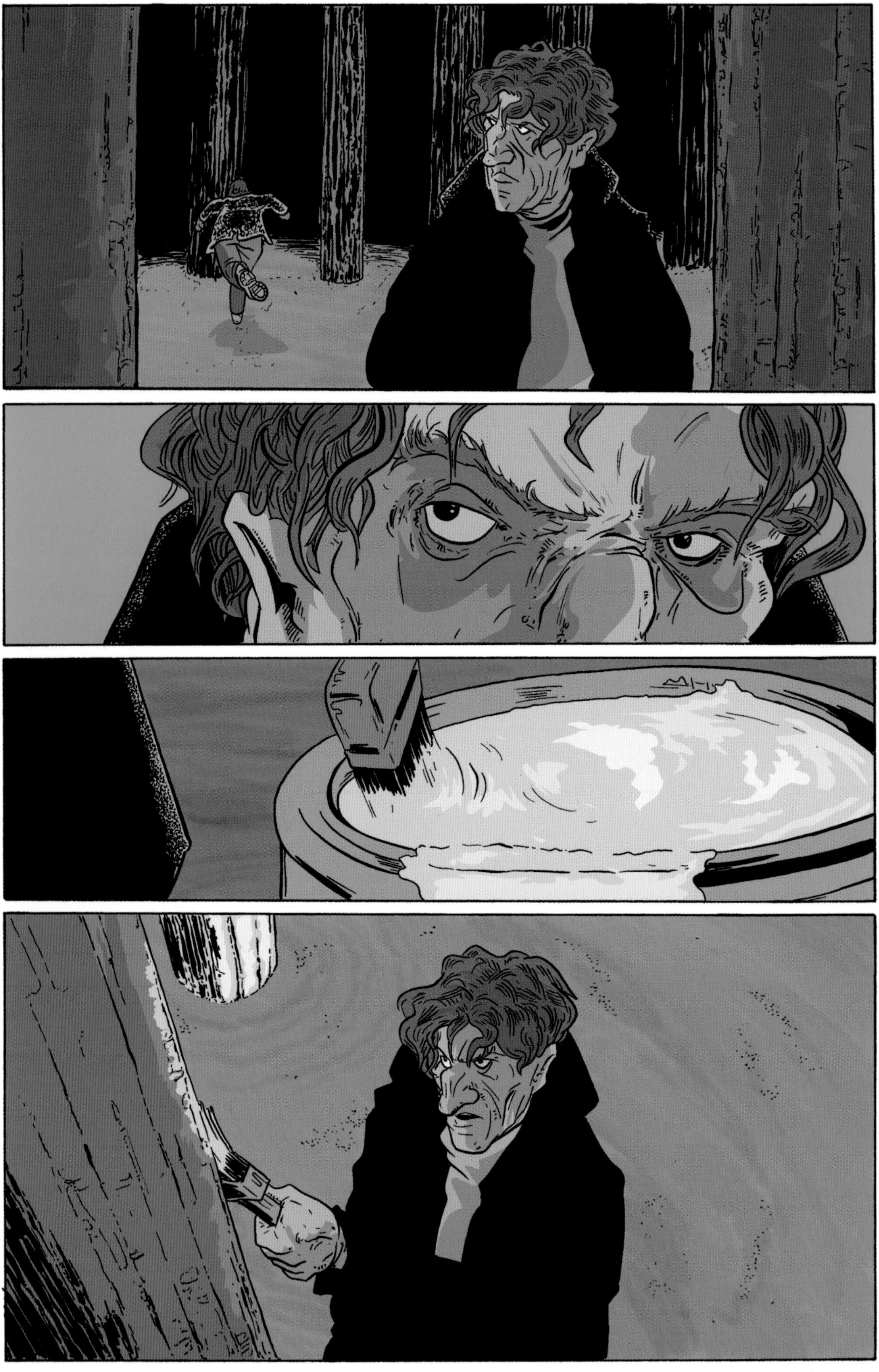

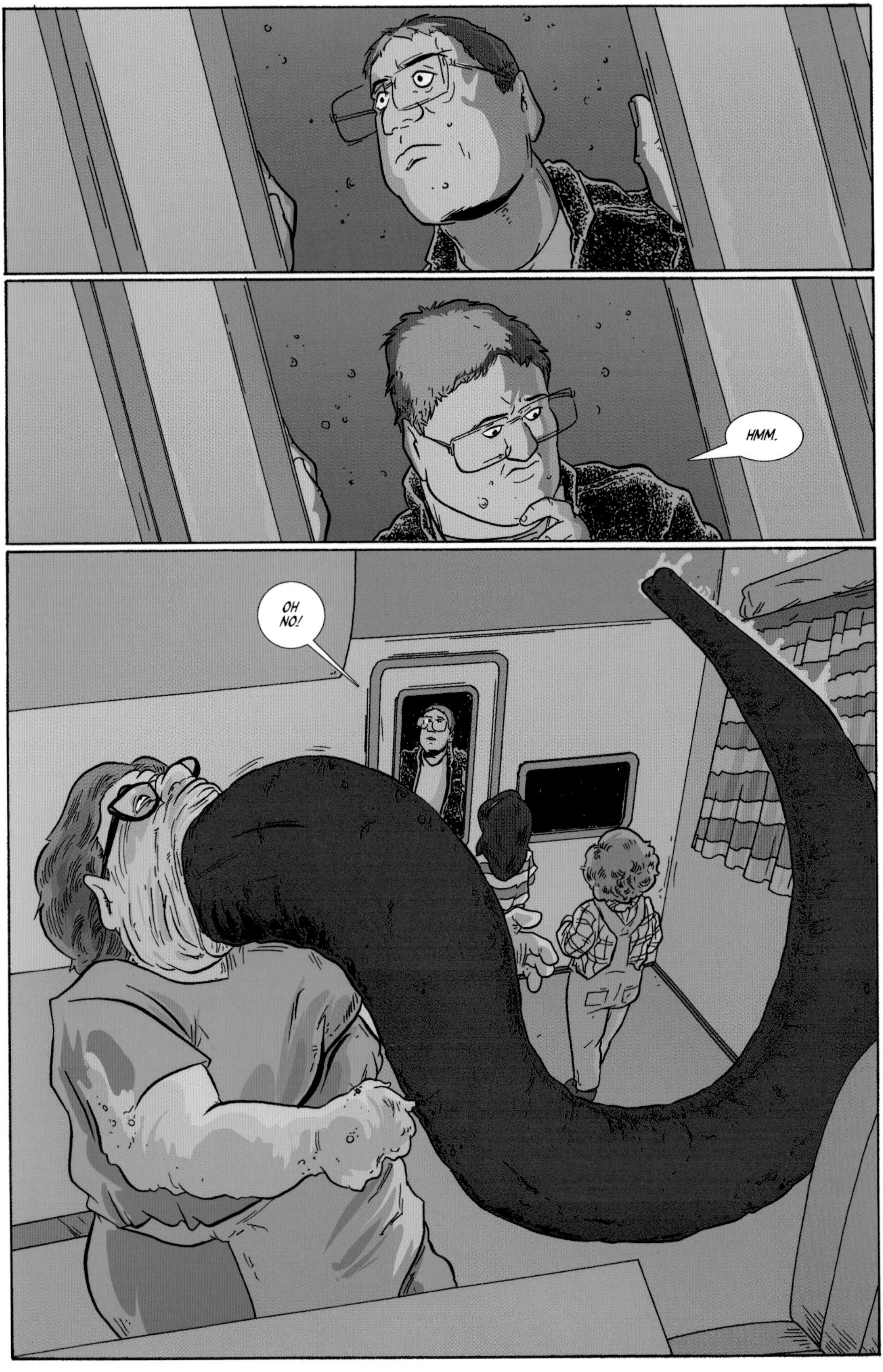
HMM.
OH NO!

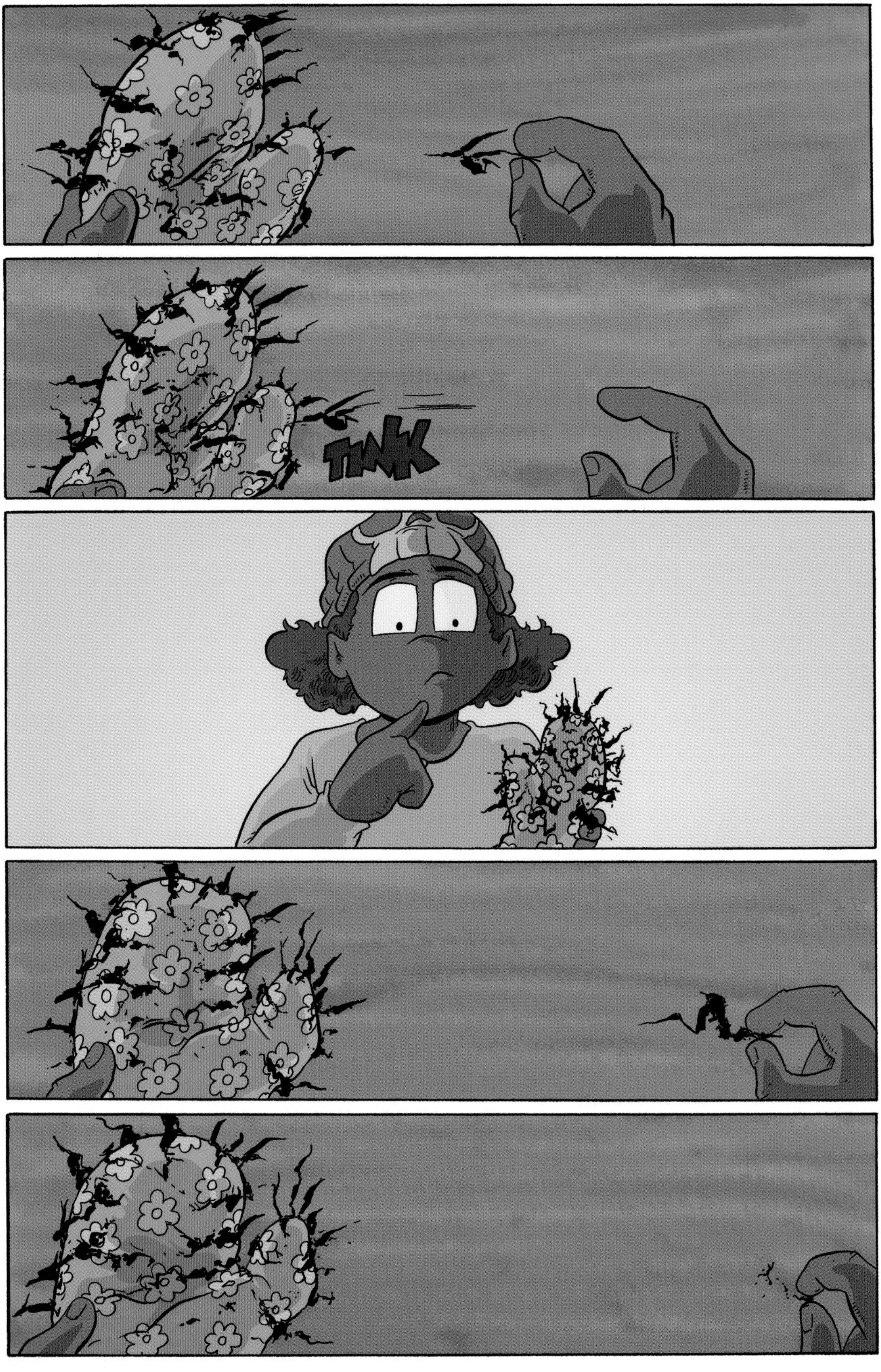
TINK

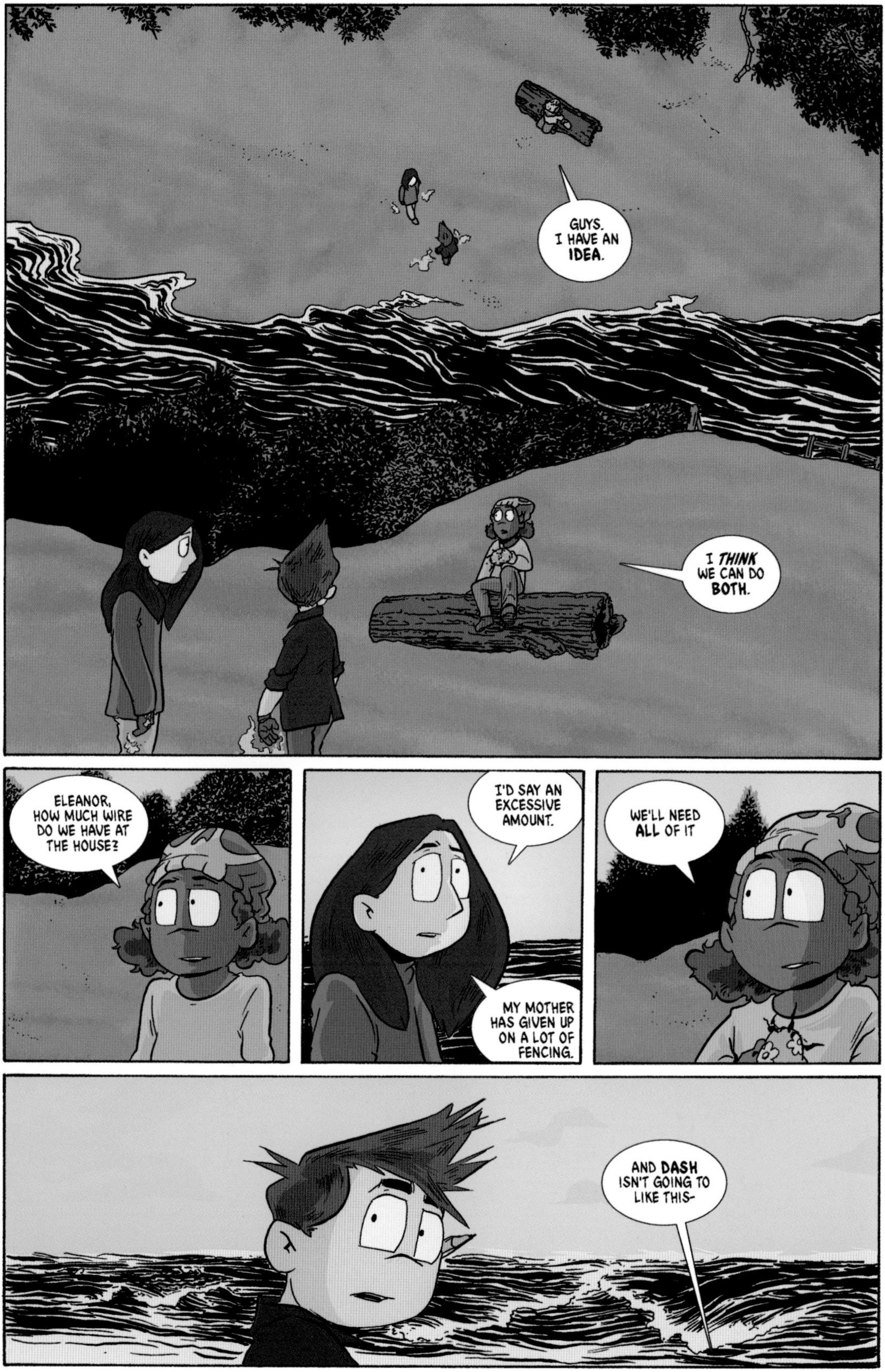
GUYS. I HAVE AN IDEA.
I THINK WE CAN DO BOTH.
ELEANOR, HOW MUCH WIRE DO WE HAVE AT THE HOUSE?
I'D SAY AN EXCESSIVE AMOUNT.
MY MOTHER HAS GIVEN UP ON A LOT OF FENCING.
WE'LL NEED ALL OF IT
AND DASH ISN'T GOING TO LIKE THIS-

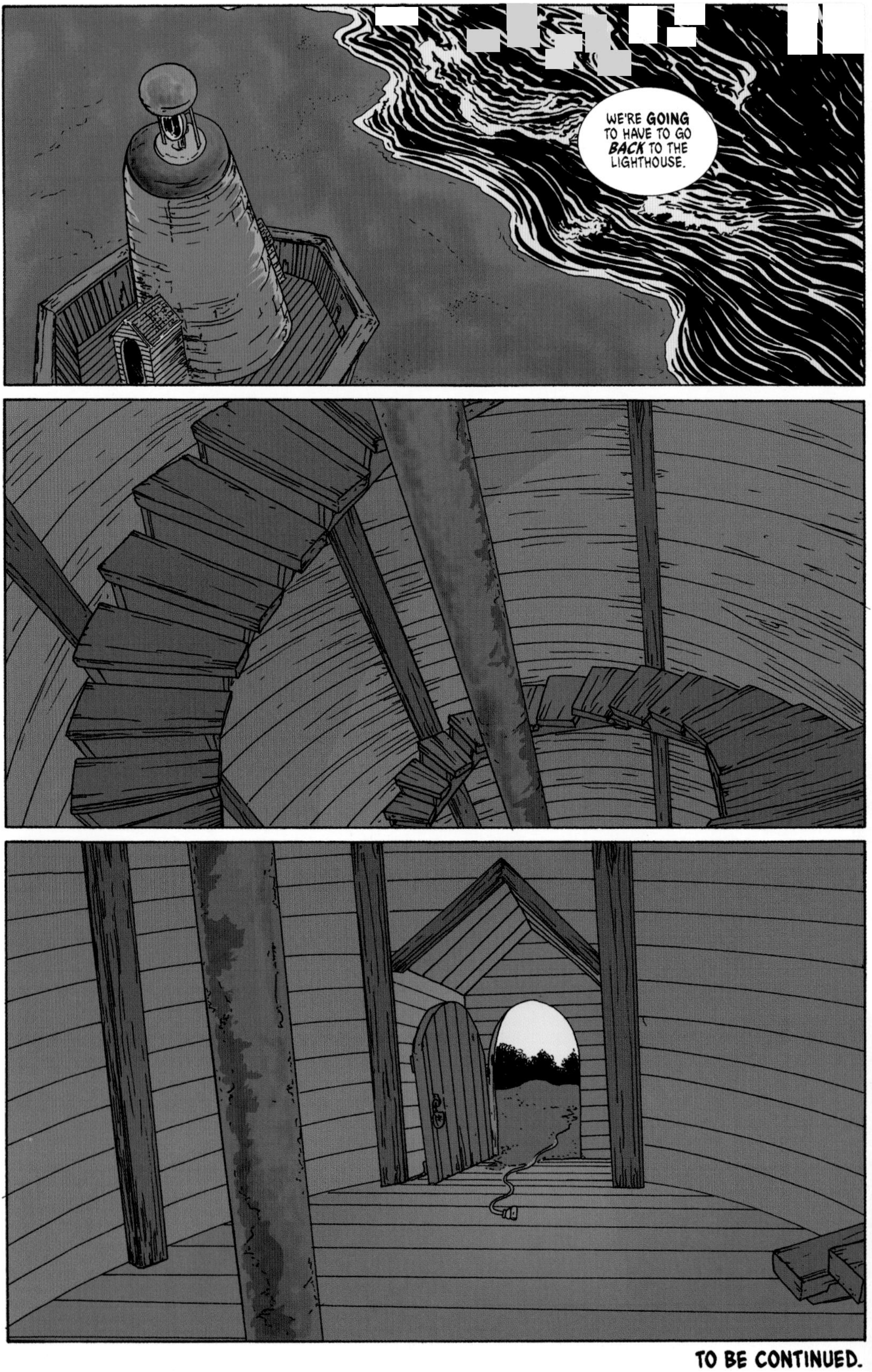
WE'RE **GOING** TO HAVE TO GO ***BACK*** TO THE LIGHTHOUSE.

TO BE CONTINUED.

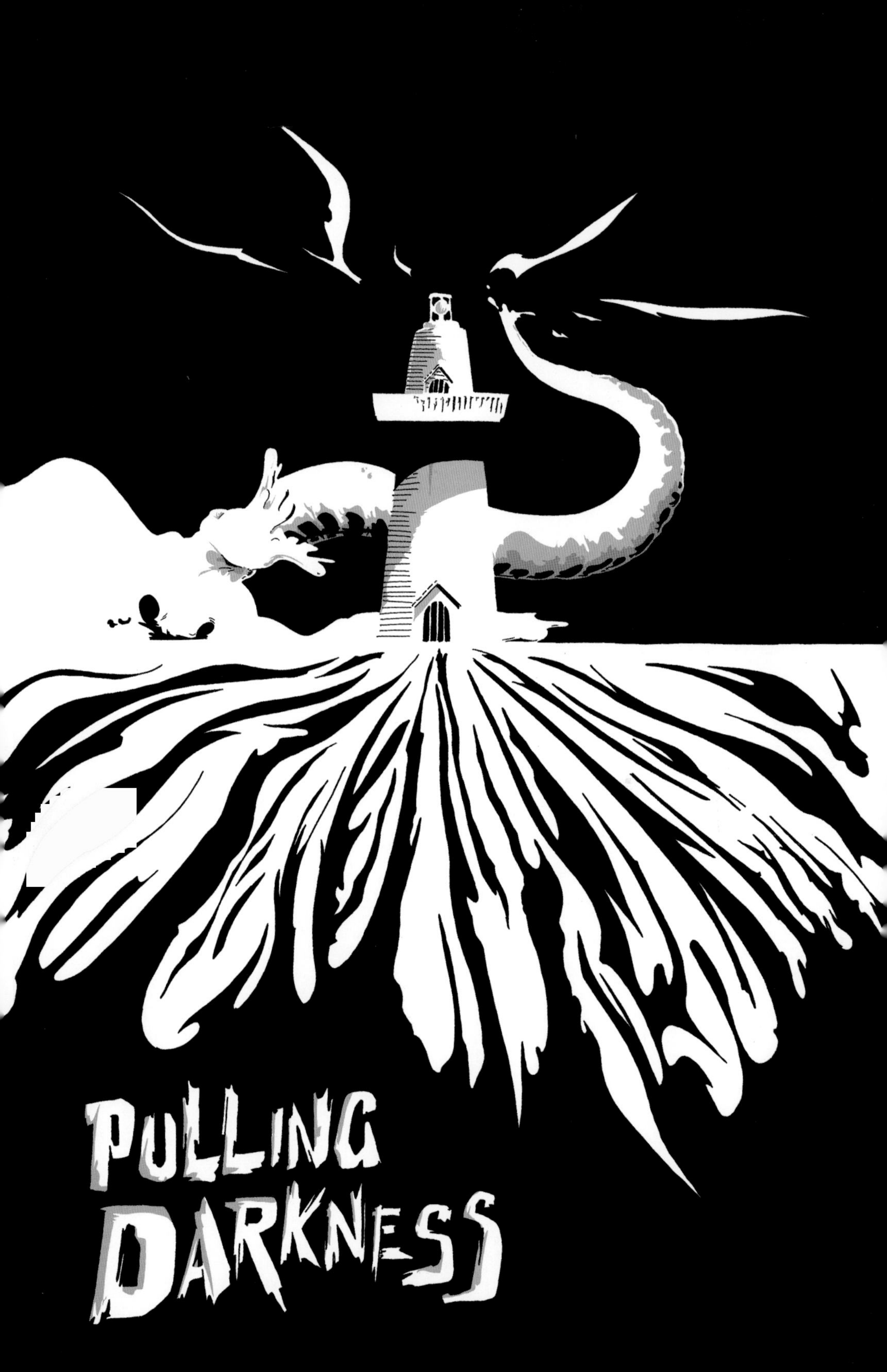
PULLING
DARKNESS

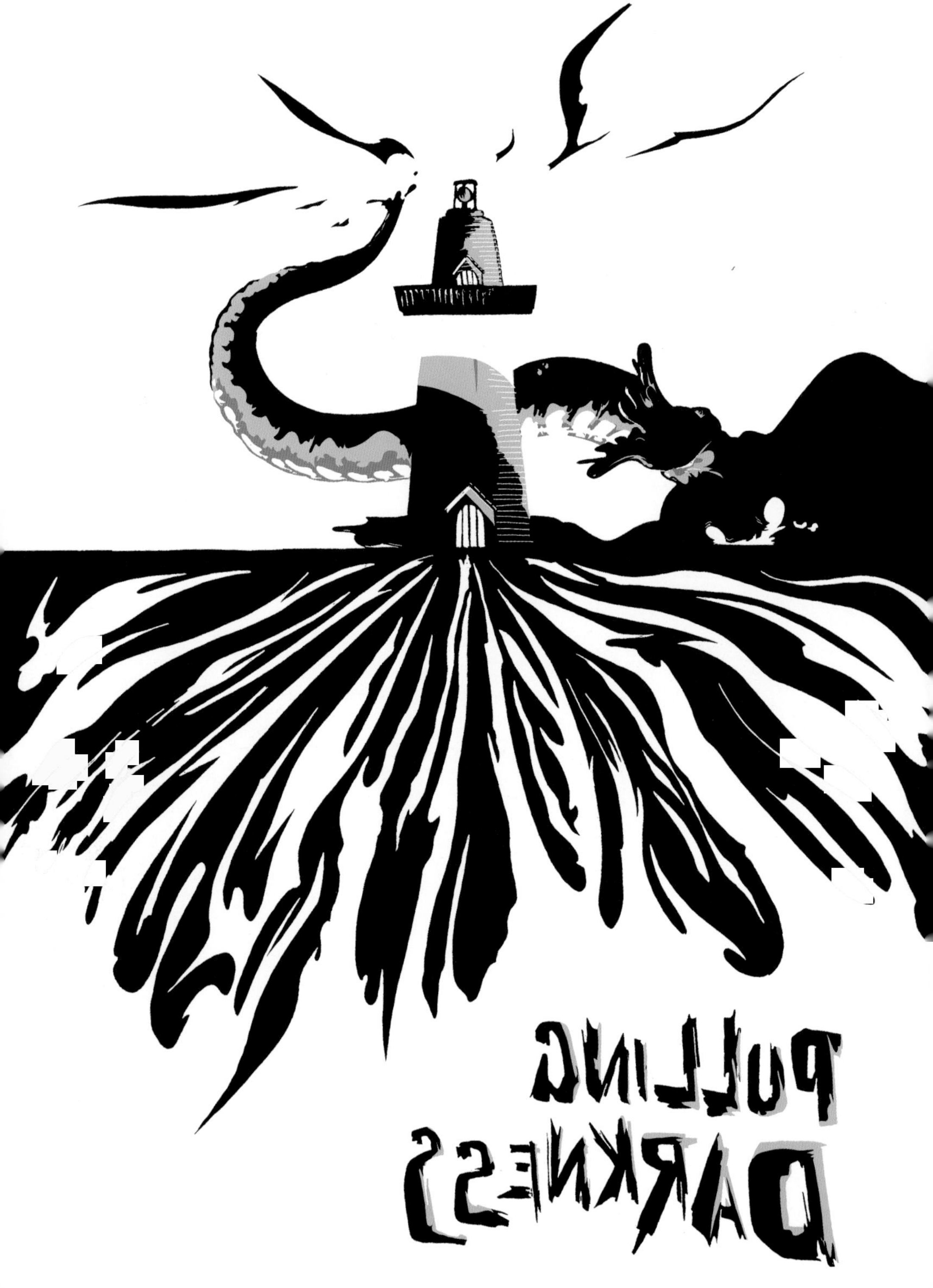
PULLING
DARKNESS

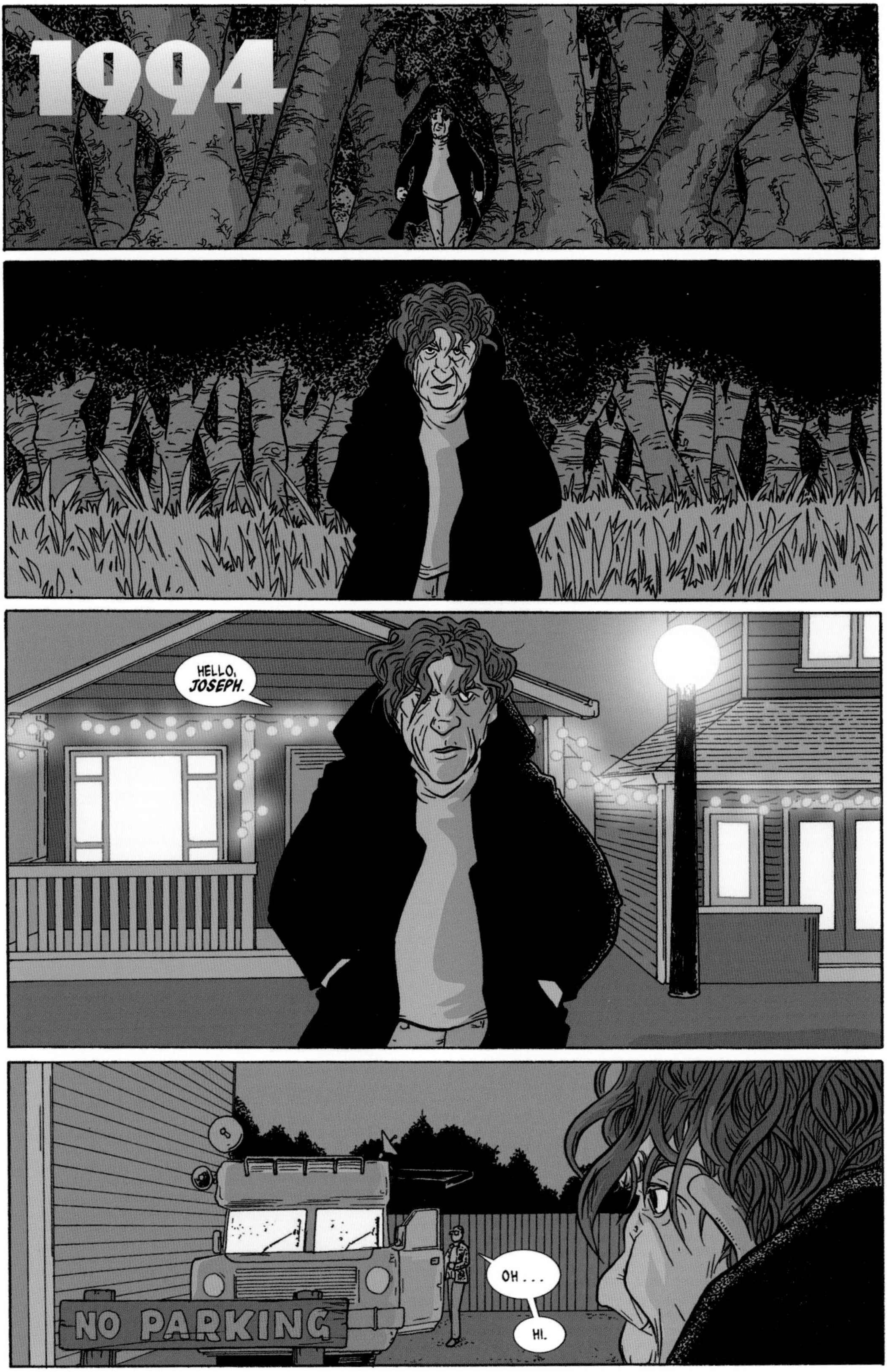
1994
HELLO, JOSEPH.
OH . . .
HI.
NO PARKING

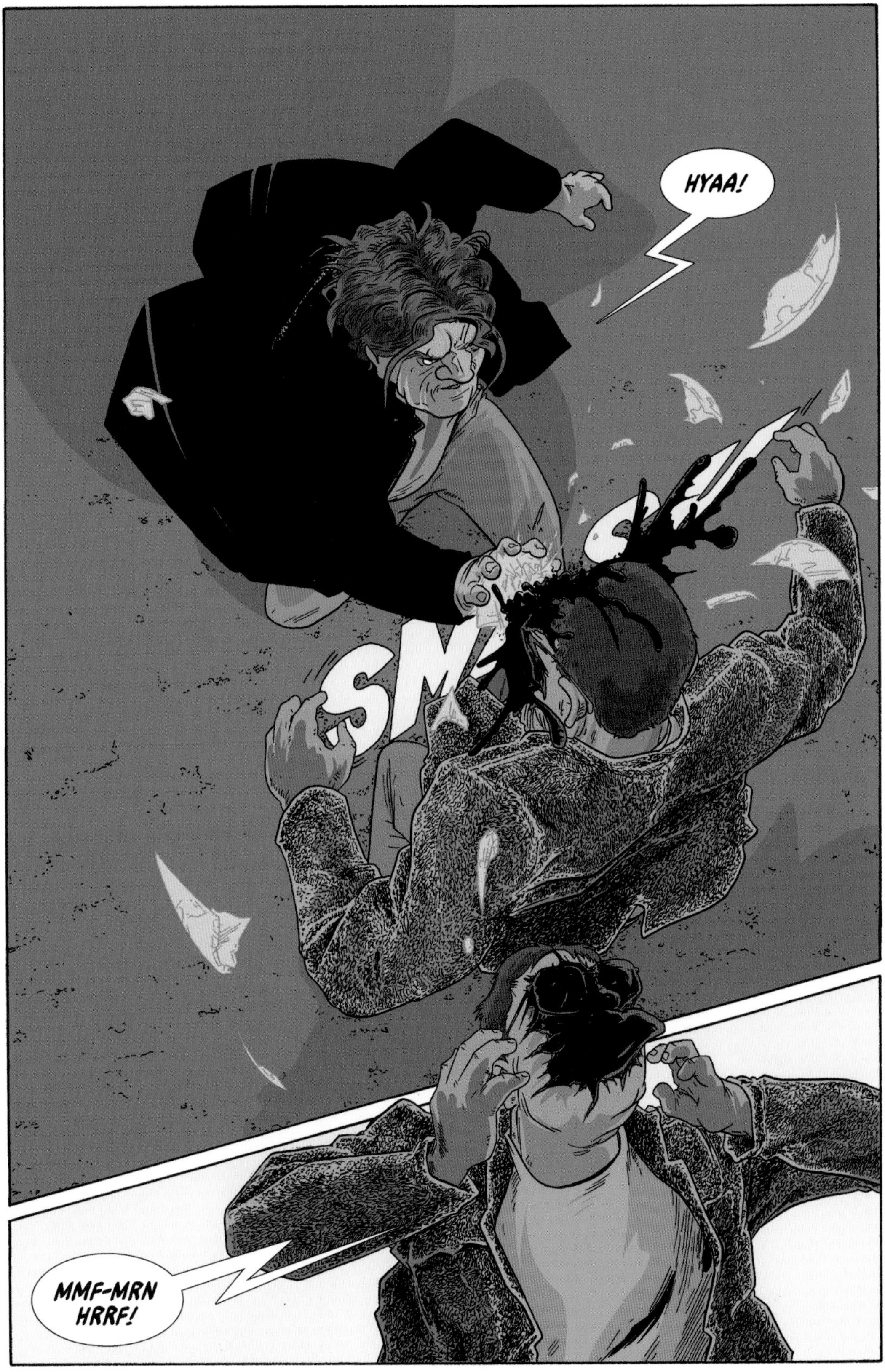
HYAA!
MMF-MRN HRRF!

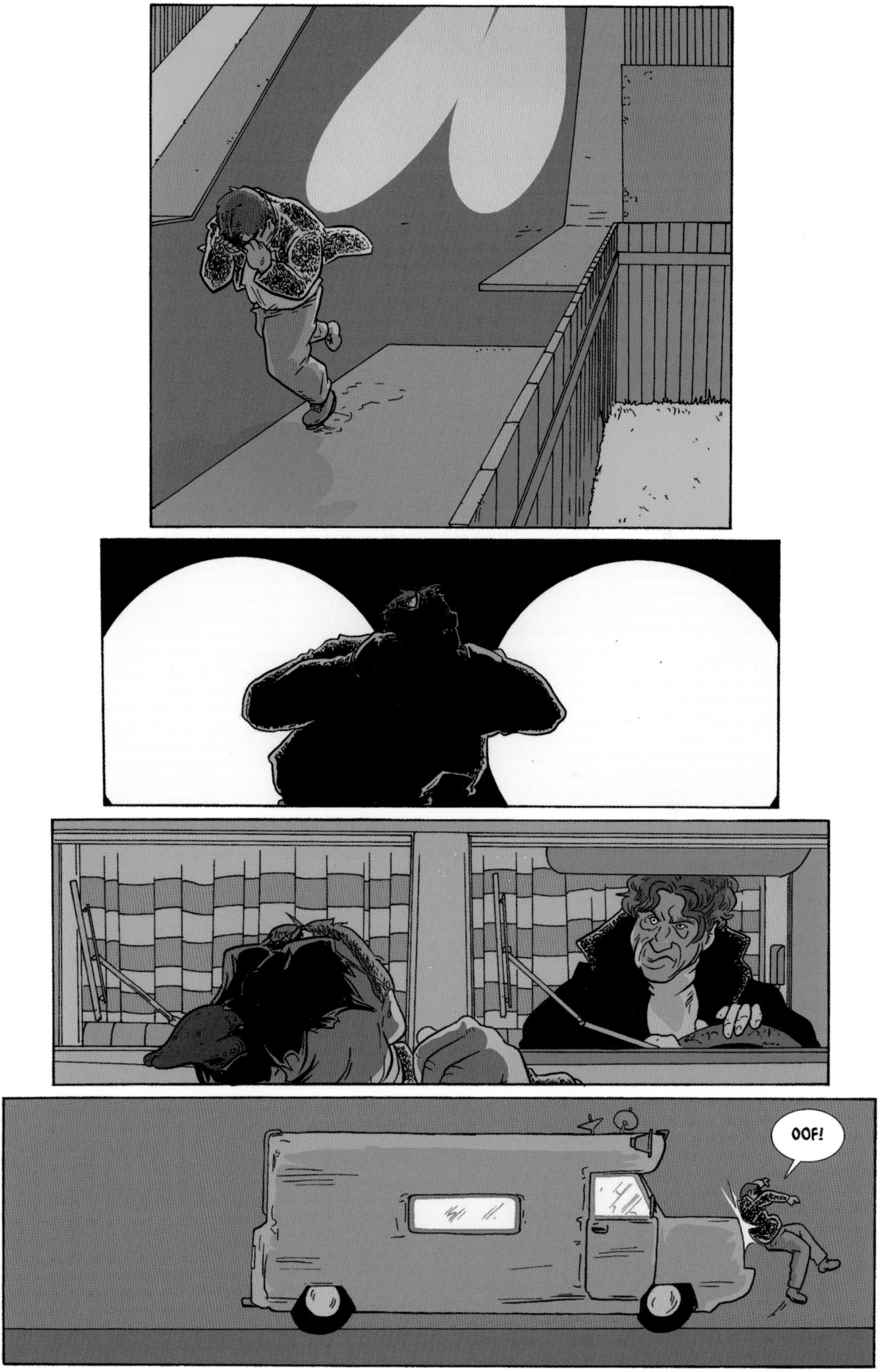
OOF!

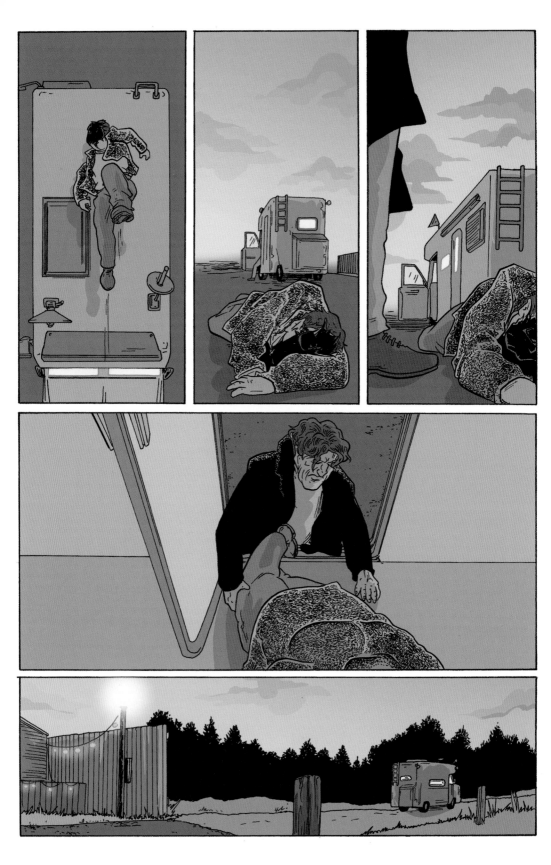

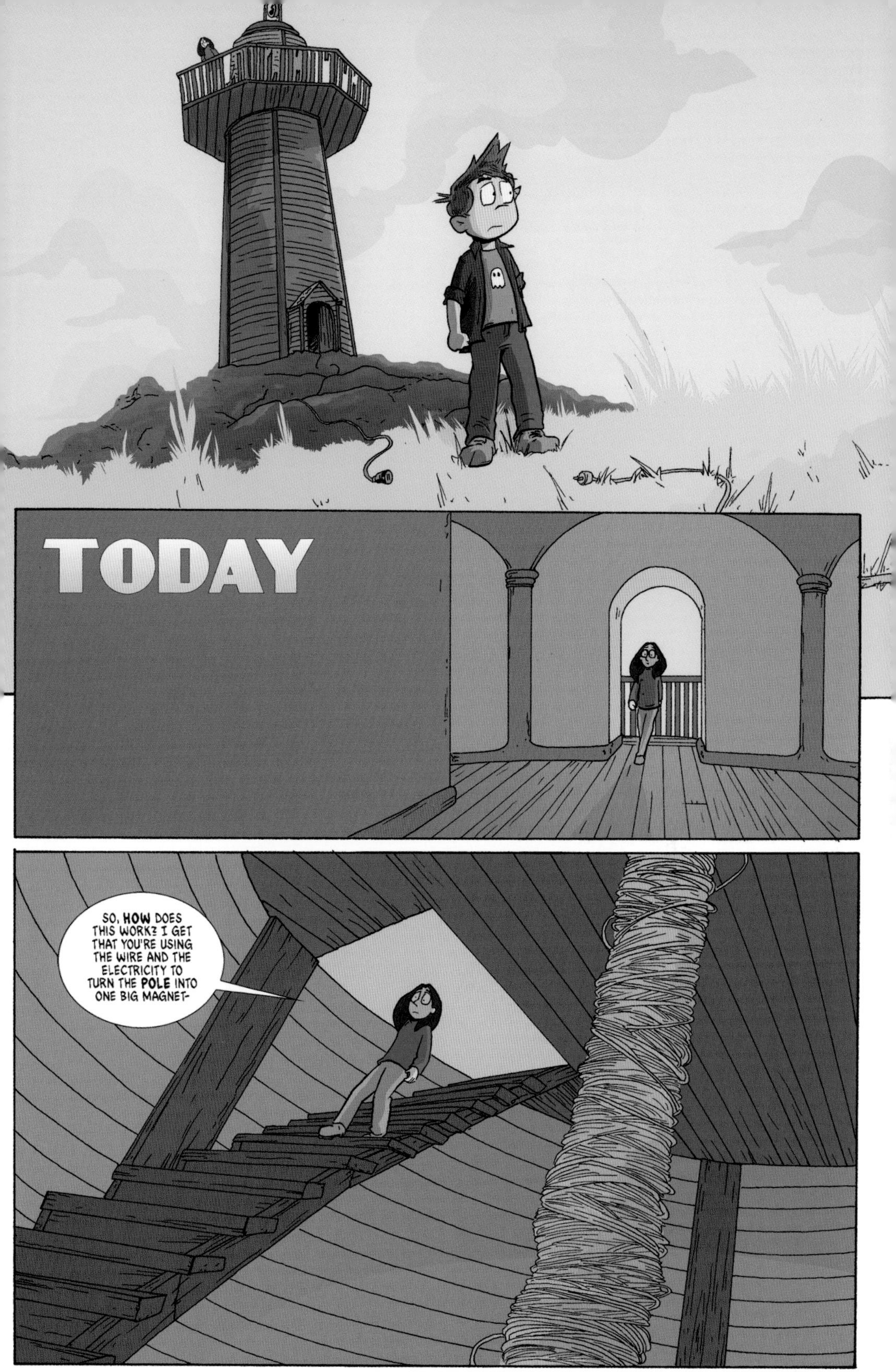
TODAY
SO, HOW DOES THIS WORK? I GET THAT YOU'RE USING THE WIRE AND THE ELECTRICITY TO TURN THE POLE INTO ONE BIG MAGNET-

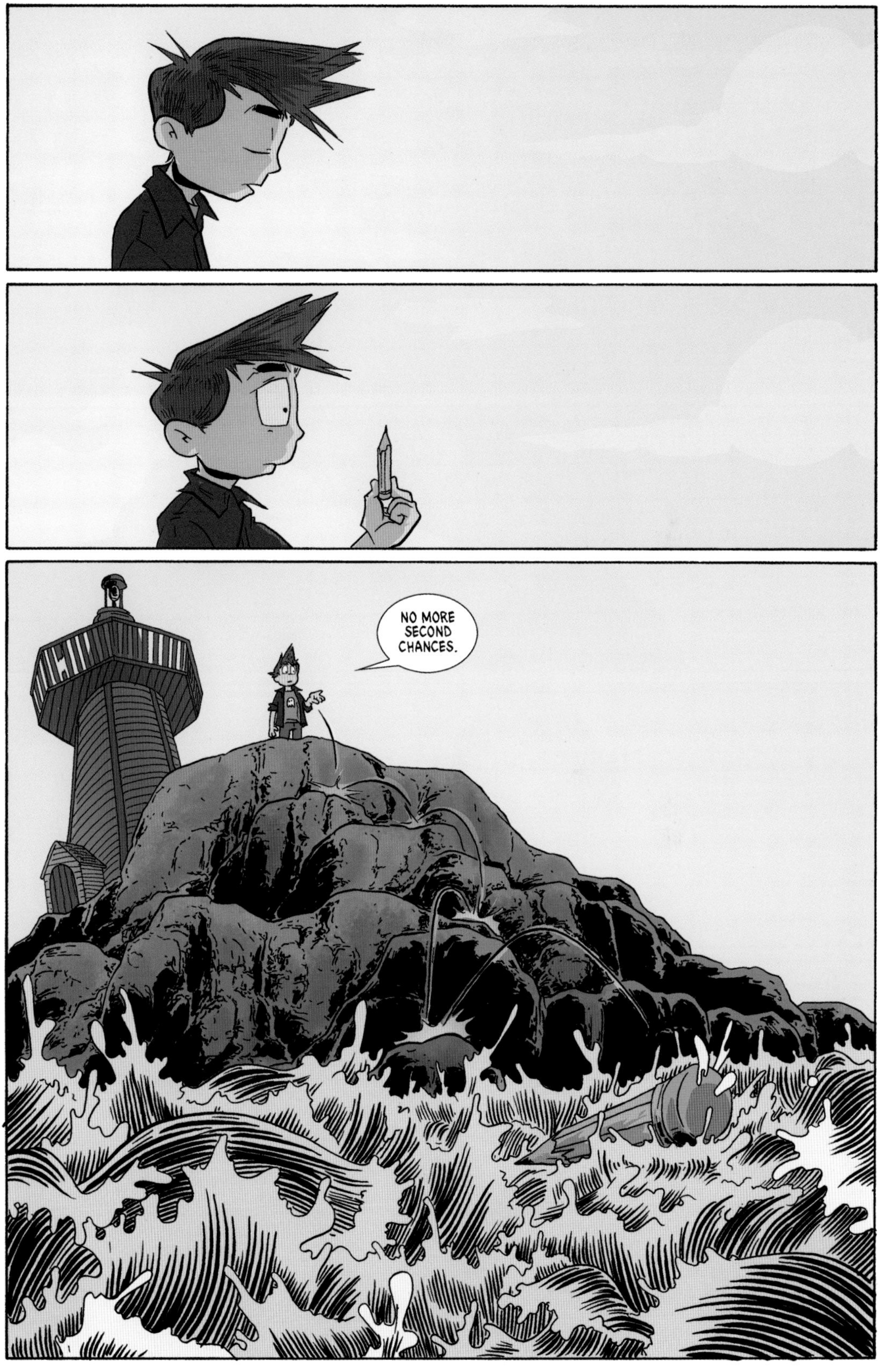
NO MORE SECOND CHANCES.

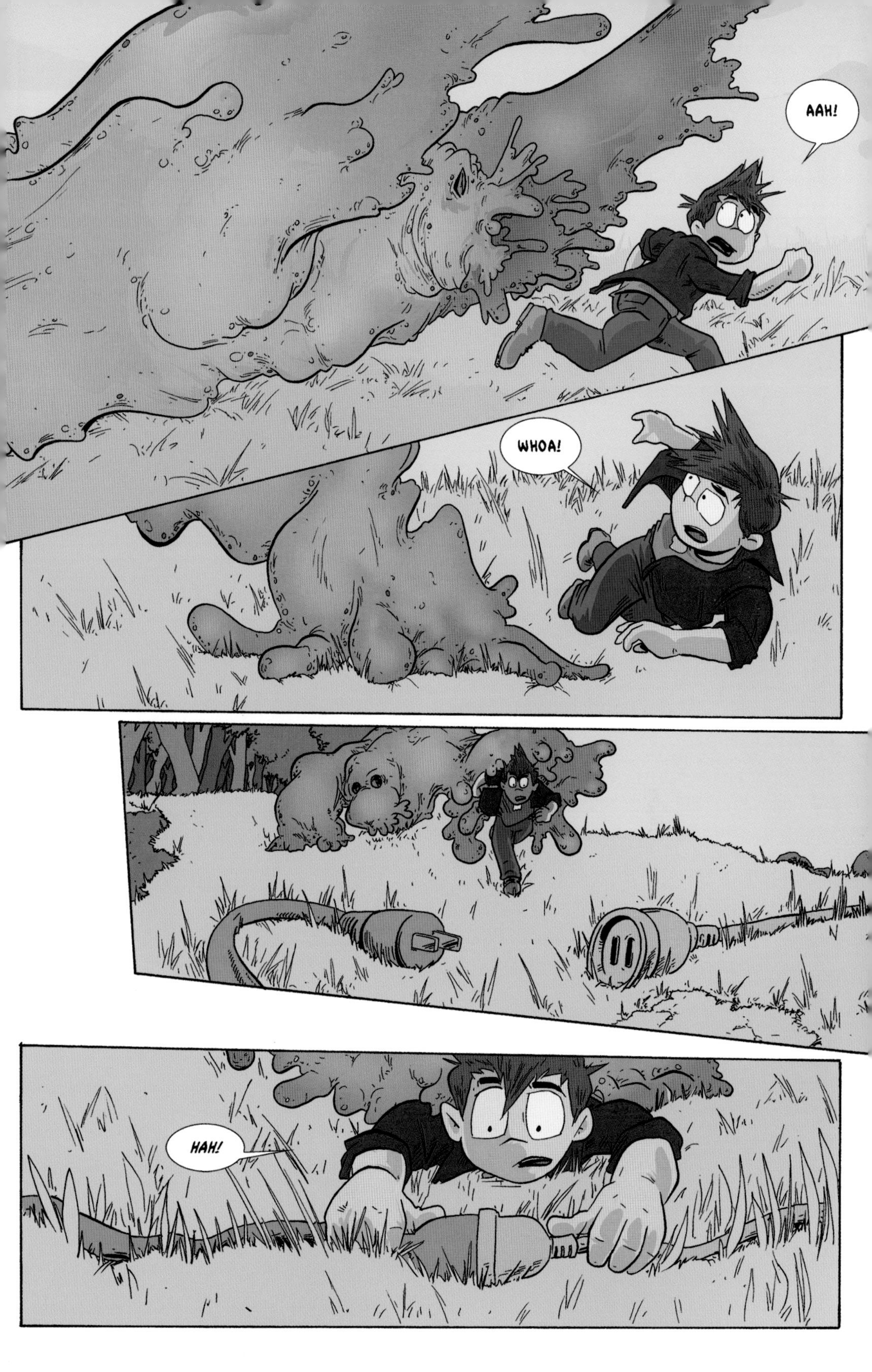
AAH!
WHOA!
HAH!

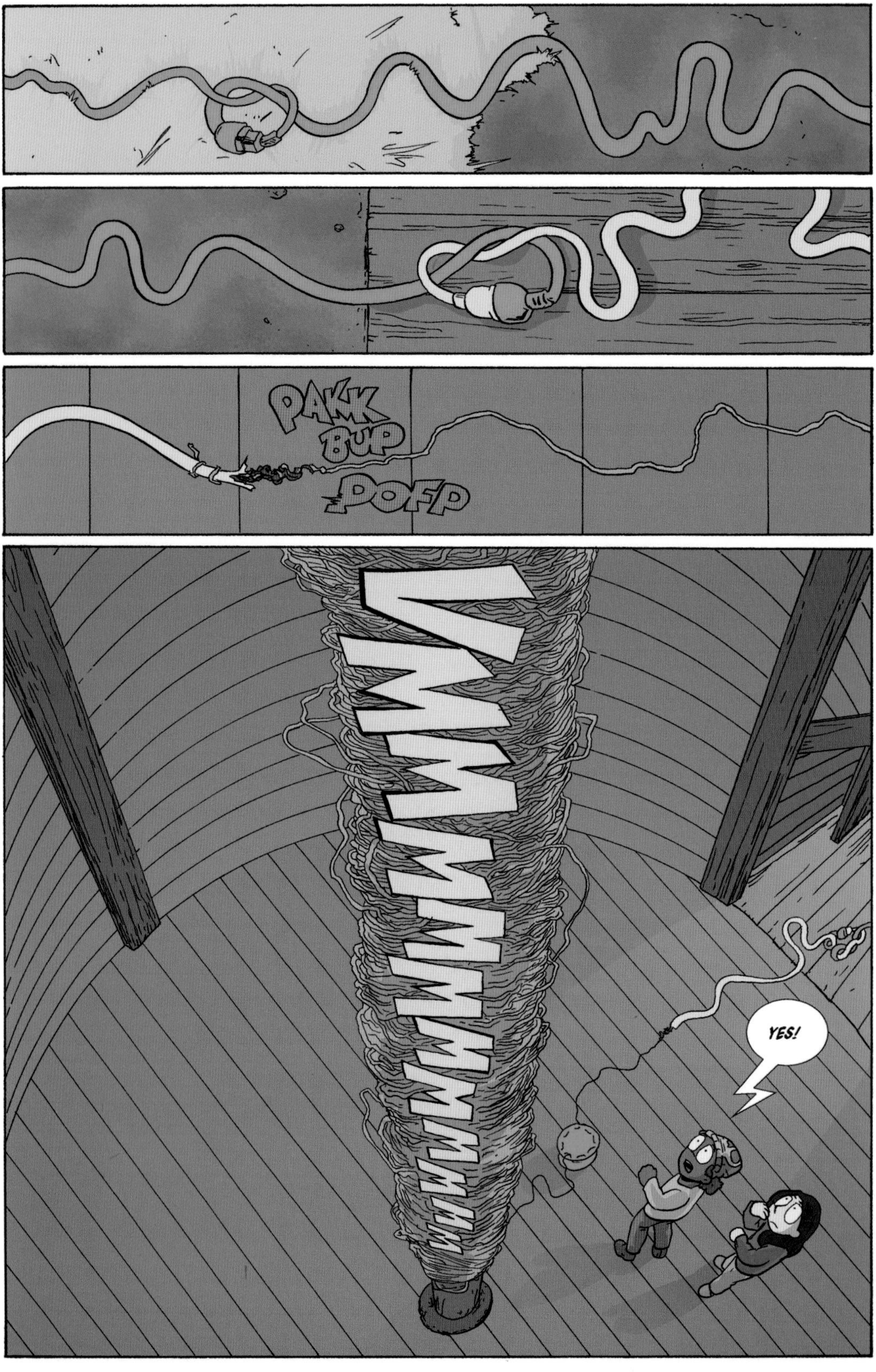
PAKK
BUP
POFP
VMMMMMMMMMMM
YES!

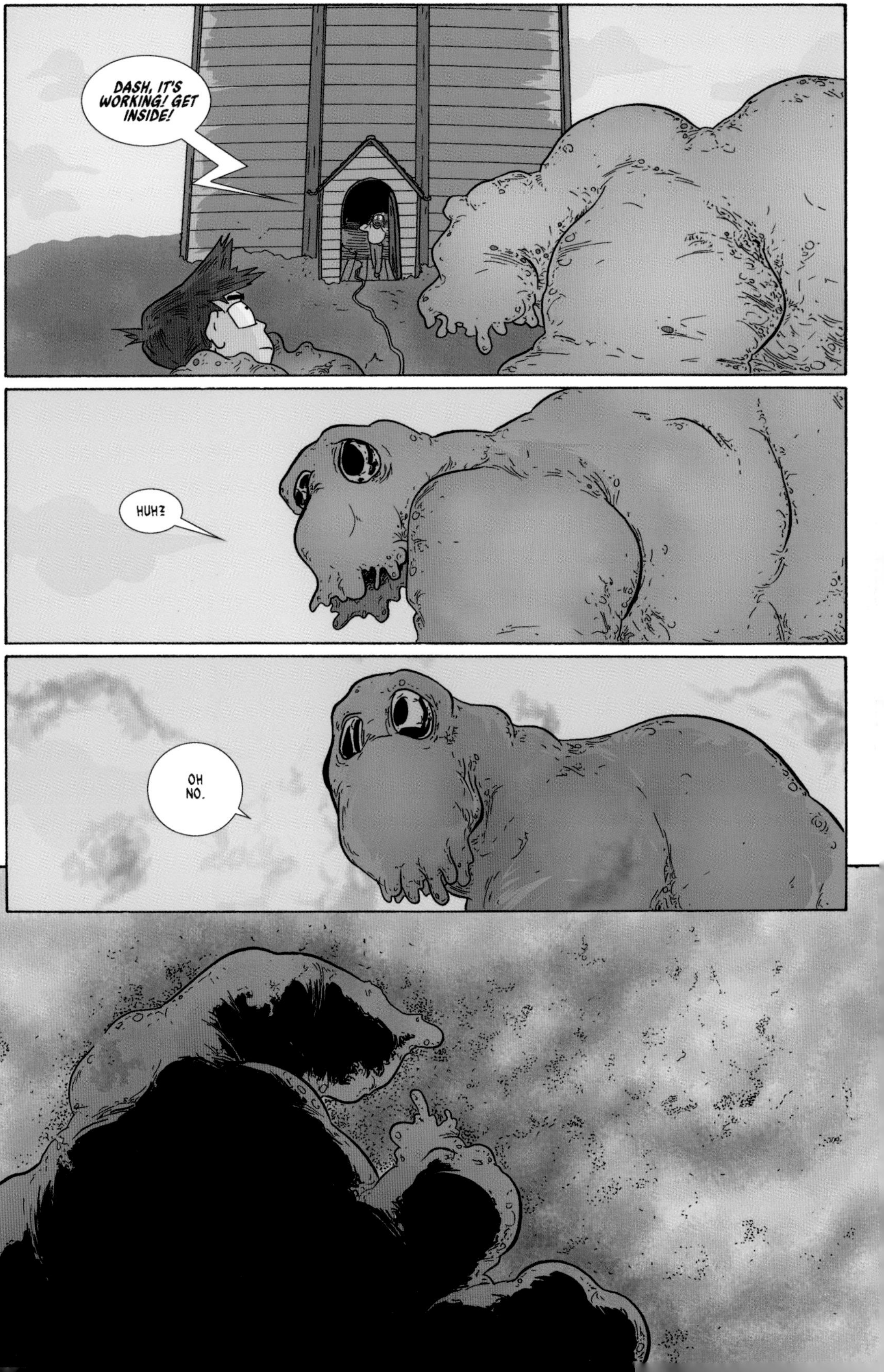
DASH, IT'S WORKING! GET INSIDE!
HUH?
OH NO.

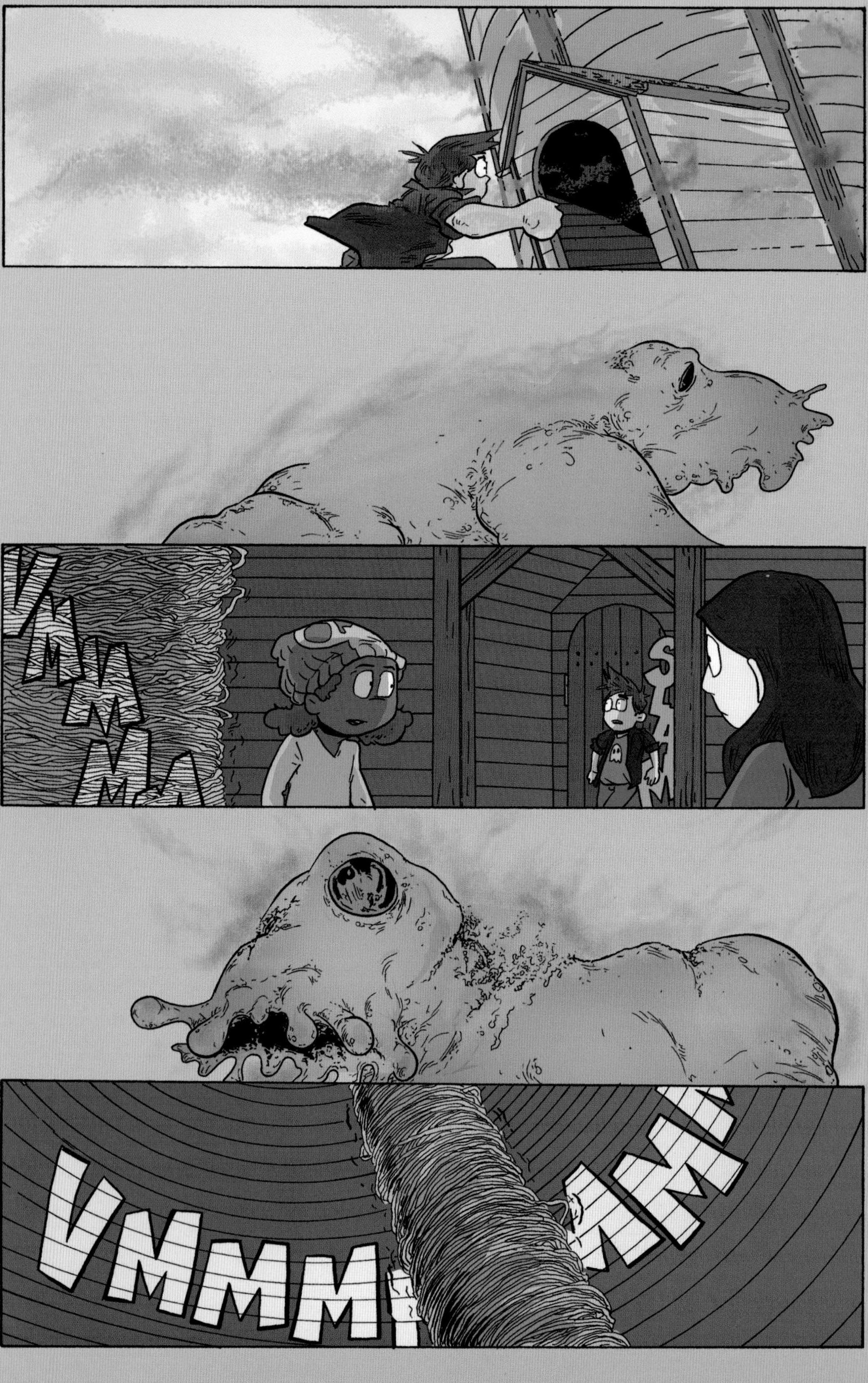
VMMMMMA
VMMMMMM

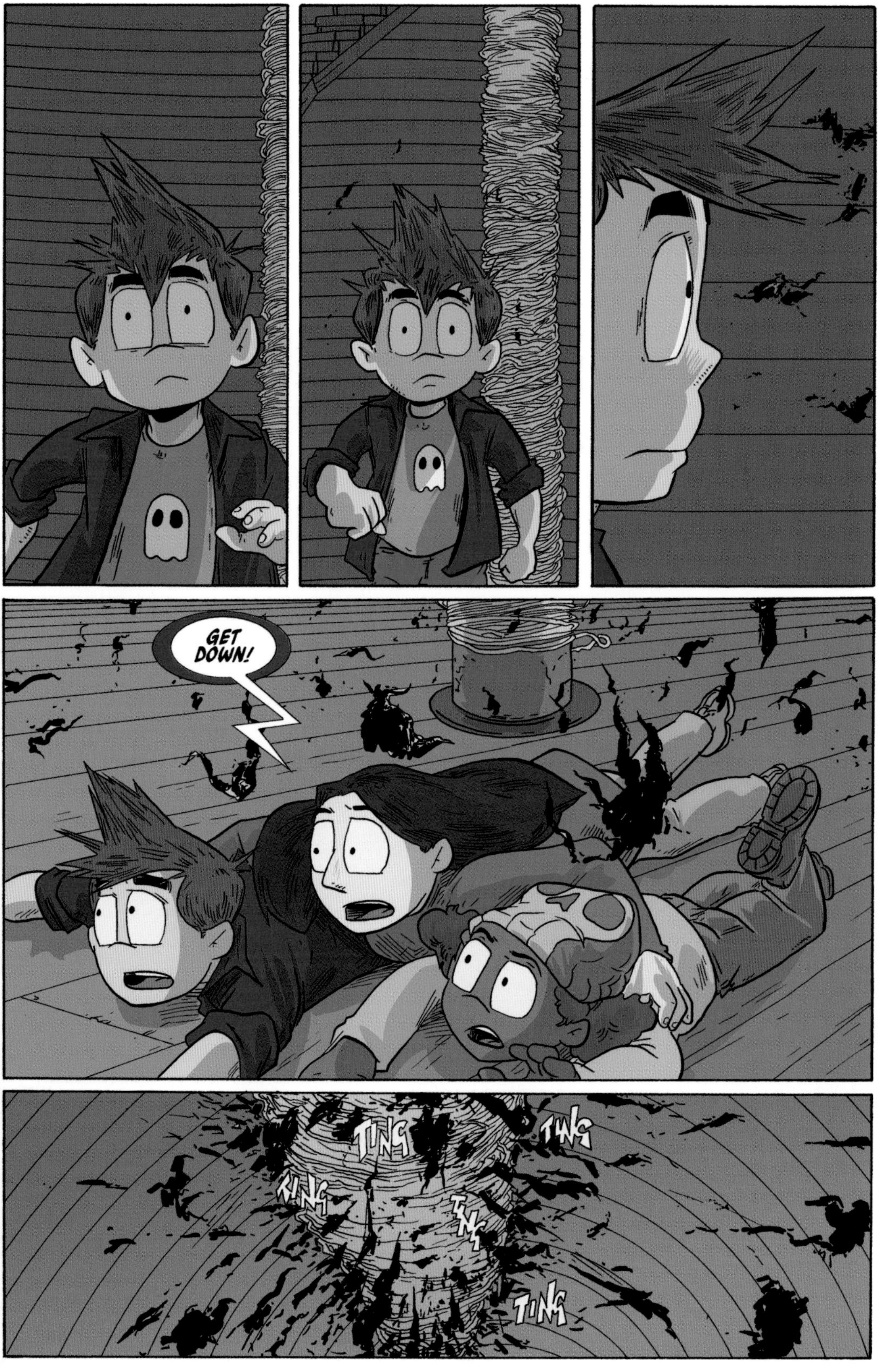
GET DOWN!
TING
TING
RING
TING
TING

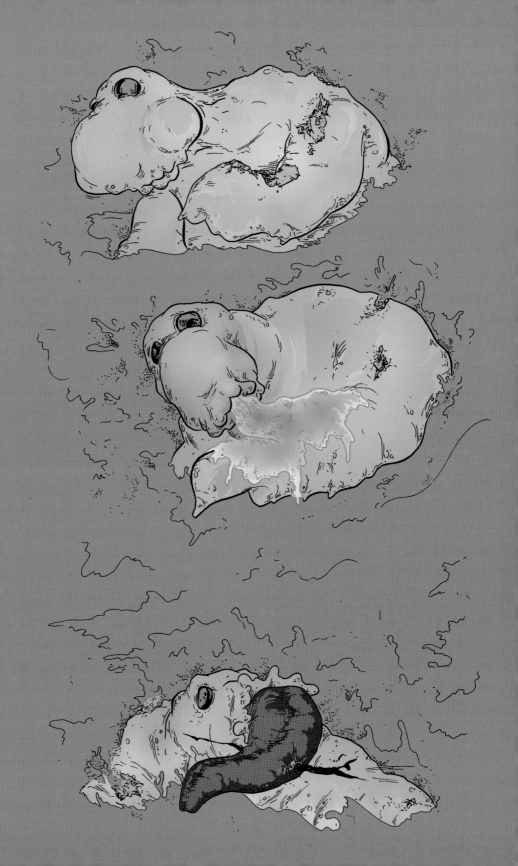

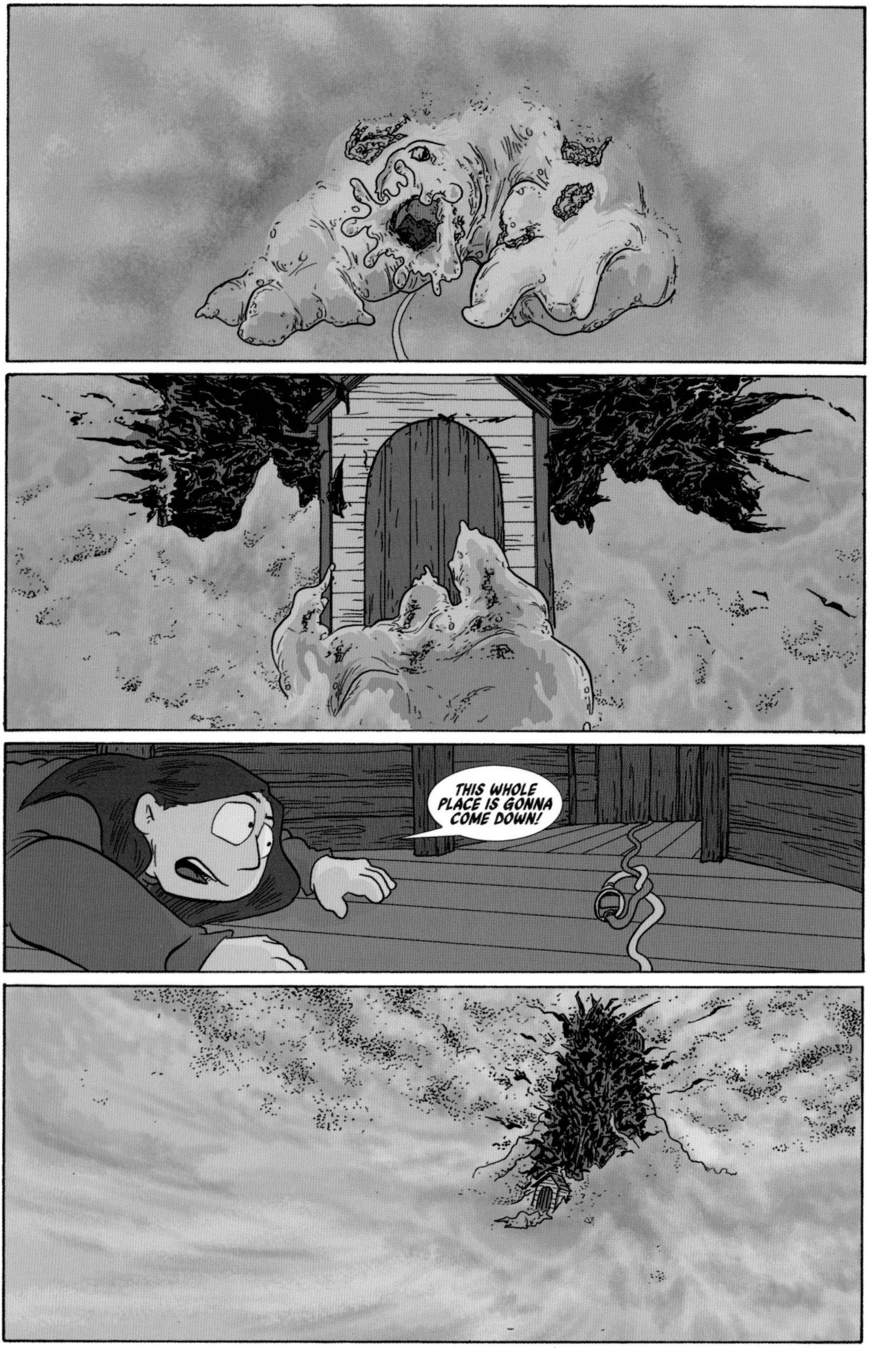
THIS WHOLE PLACE IS GONNA COME DOWN!

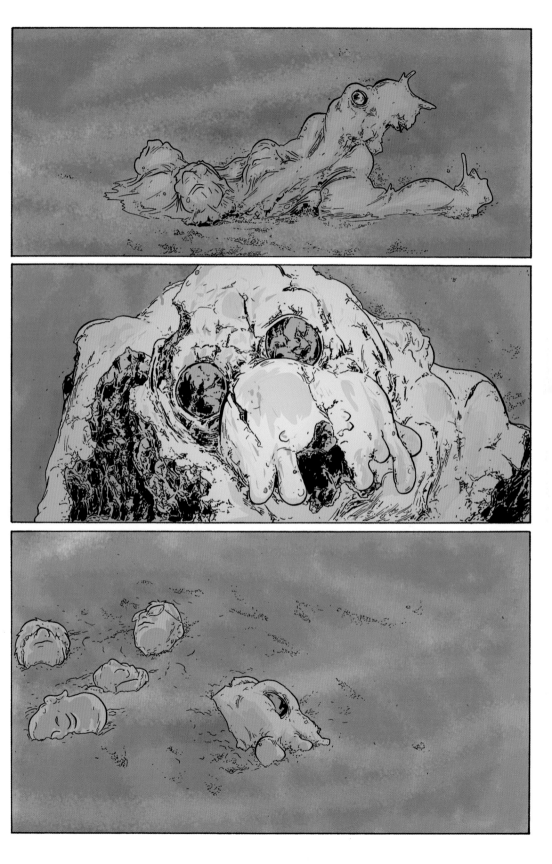

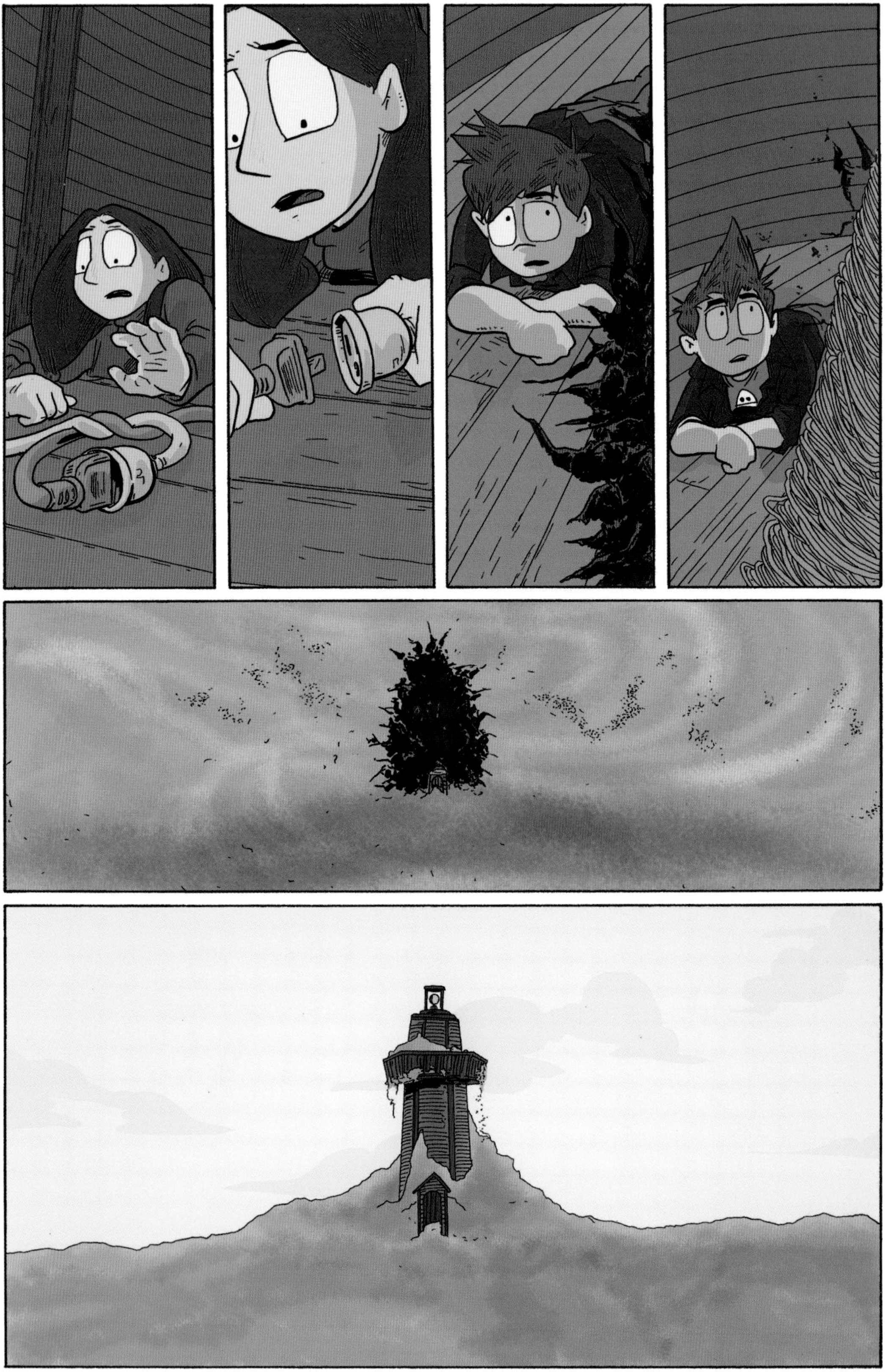

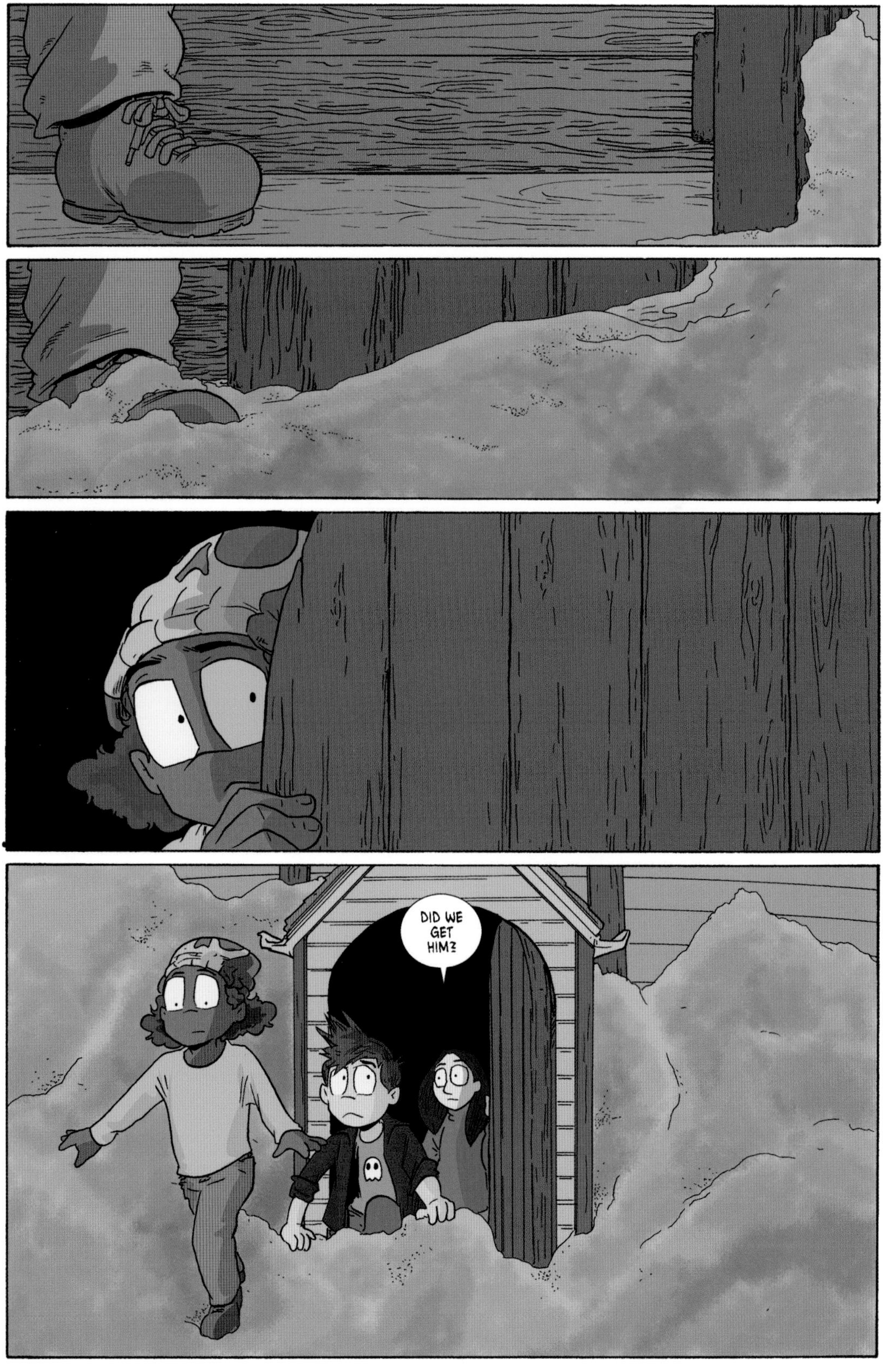
DID WE GET HIM?

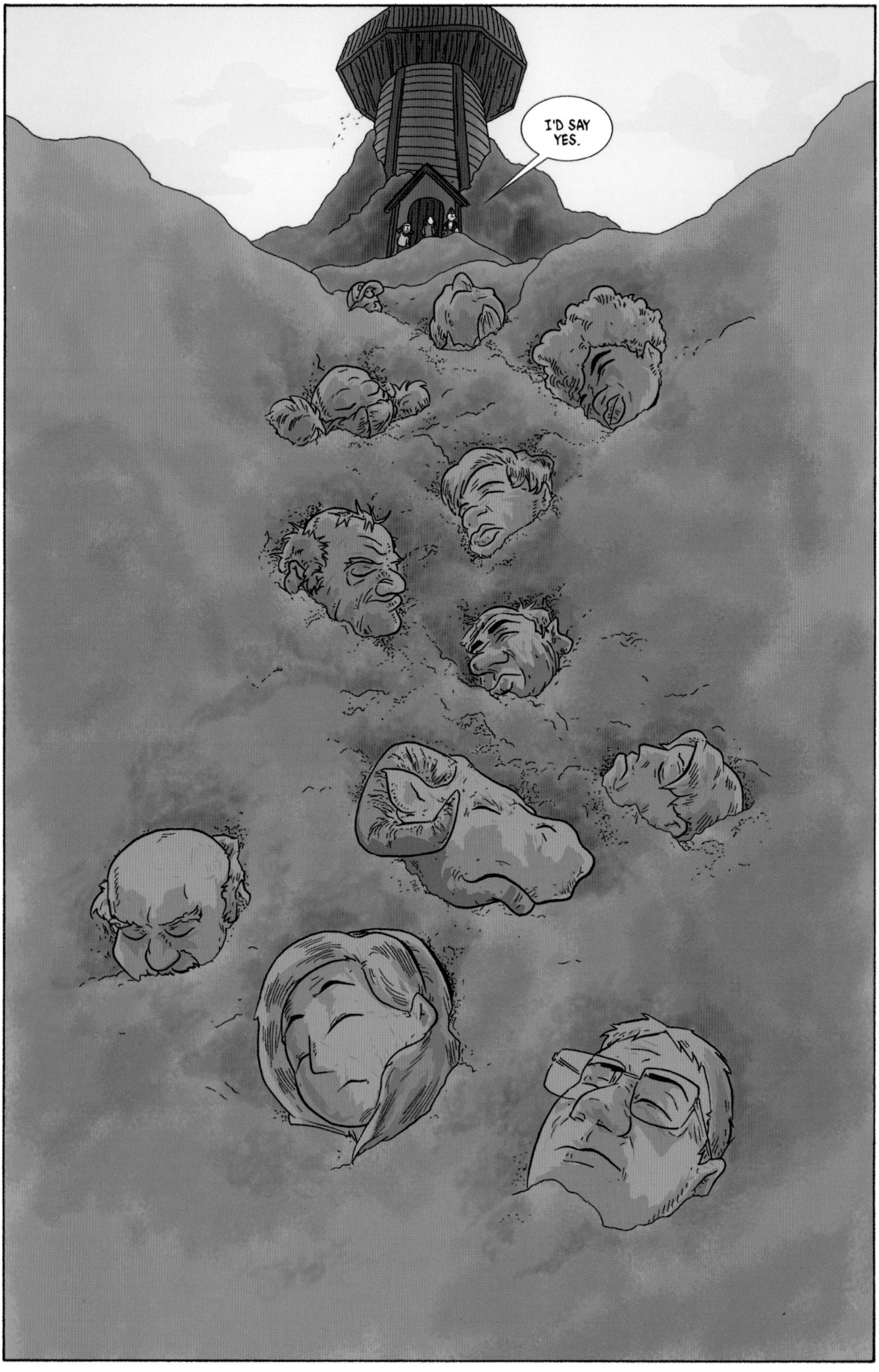
I'D SAY YES.

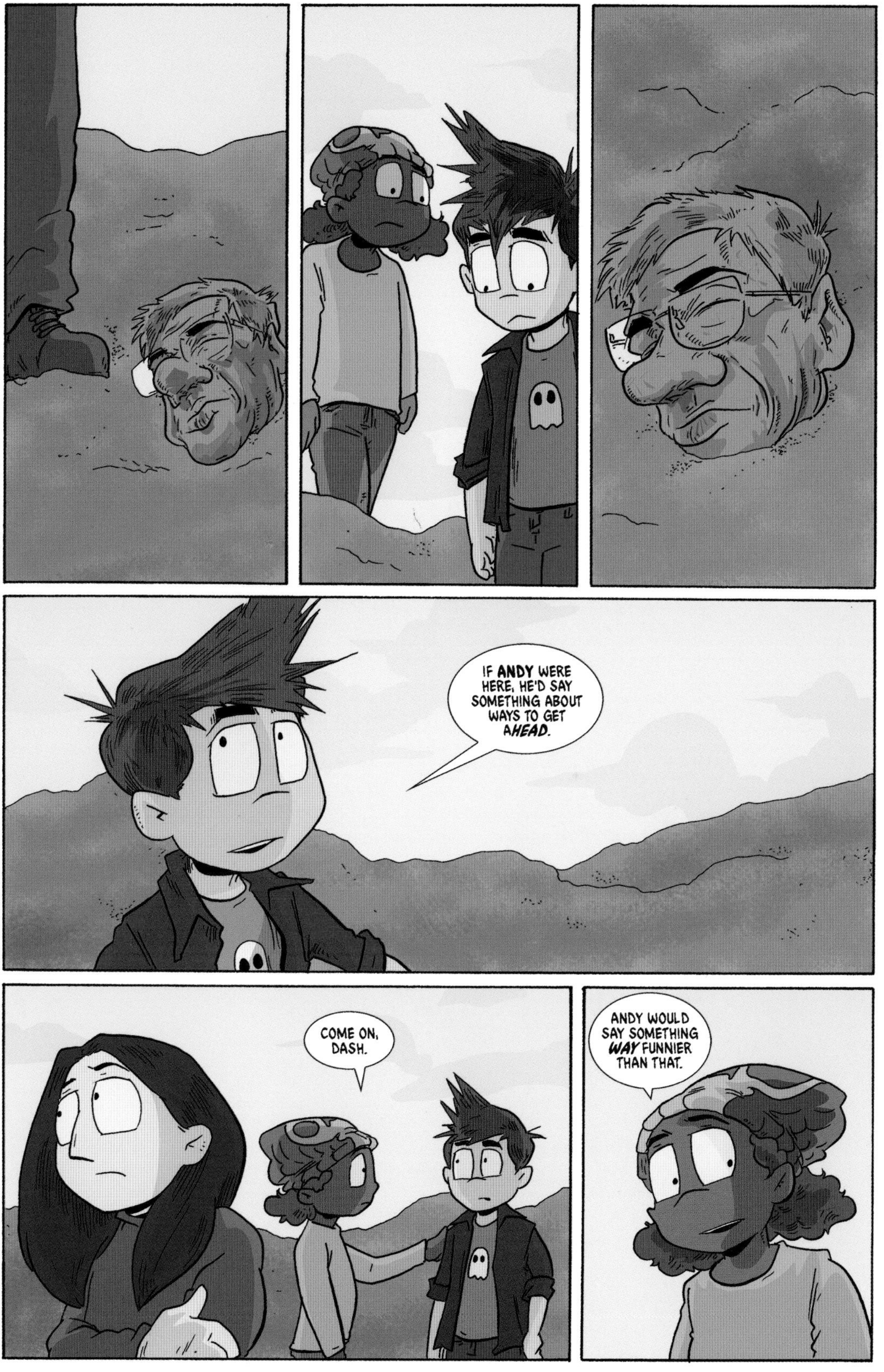
IF ANDY WERE HERE, HE'D SAY SOMETHING ABOUT WAYS TO GET AHEAD.
COME ON, DASH.
ANDY WOULD SAY SOMETHING WAY FUNNIER THAN THAT.

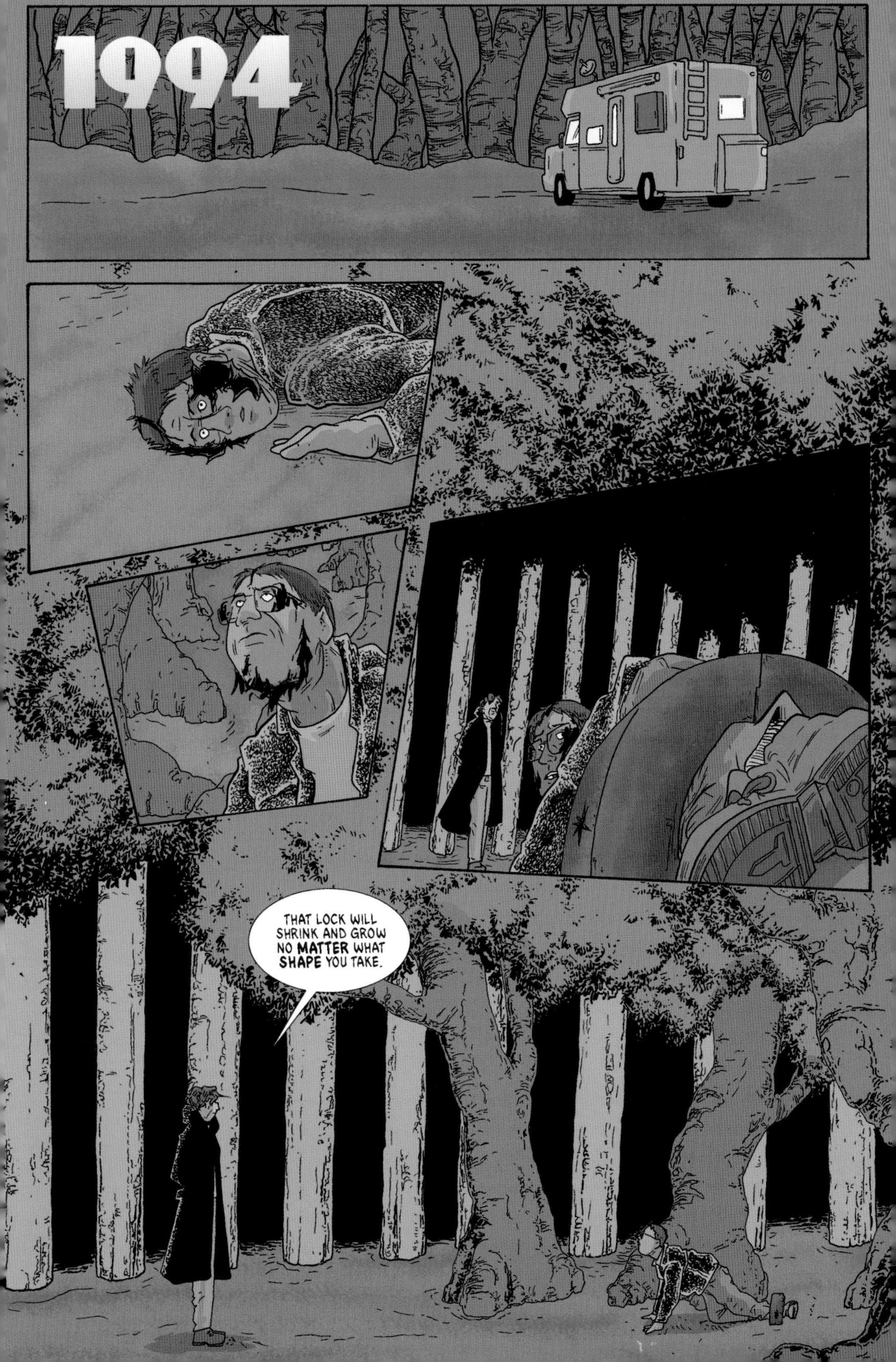
1994
THAT LOCK WILL SHRINK AND GROW NO **MATTER** WHAT **SHAPE** YOU TAKE.

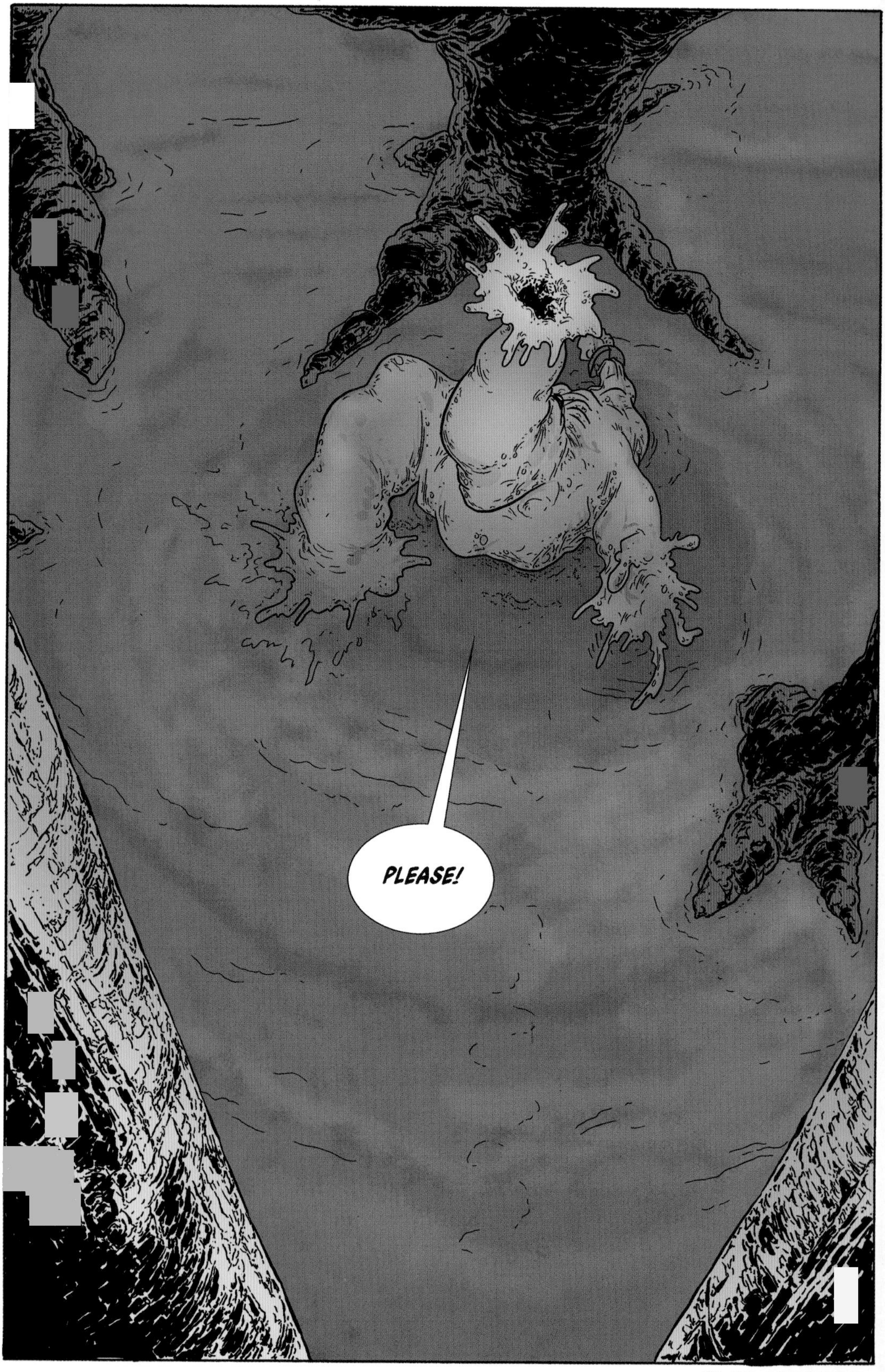
PLEASE!

TO BE CONTINUED.

NOT ALONE IN THE DARK

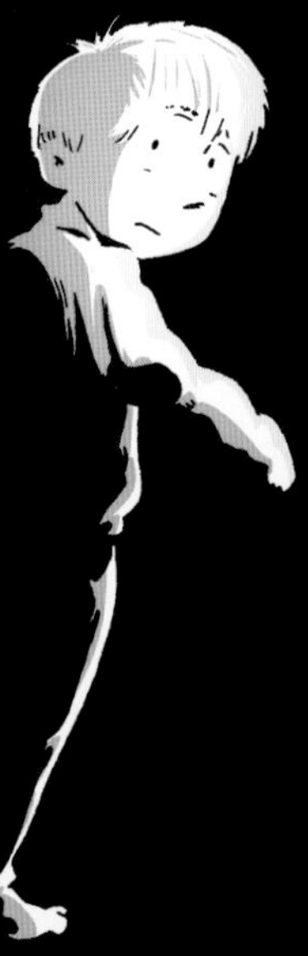

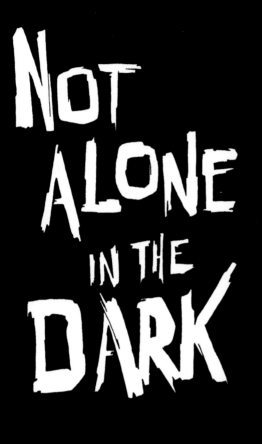

NOT ALONE IN THE DARK

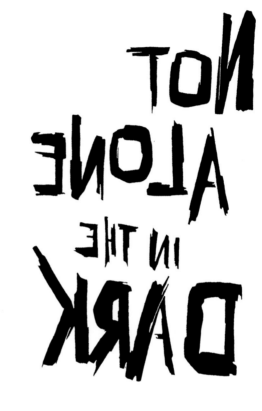

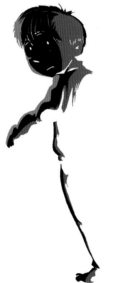

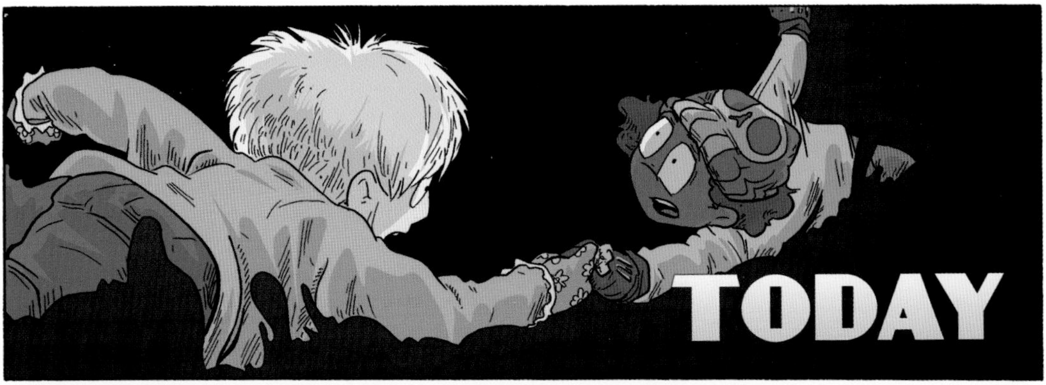
TODAY

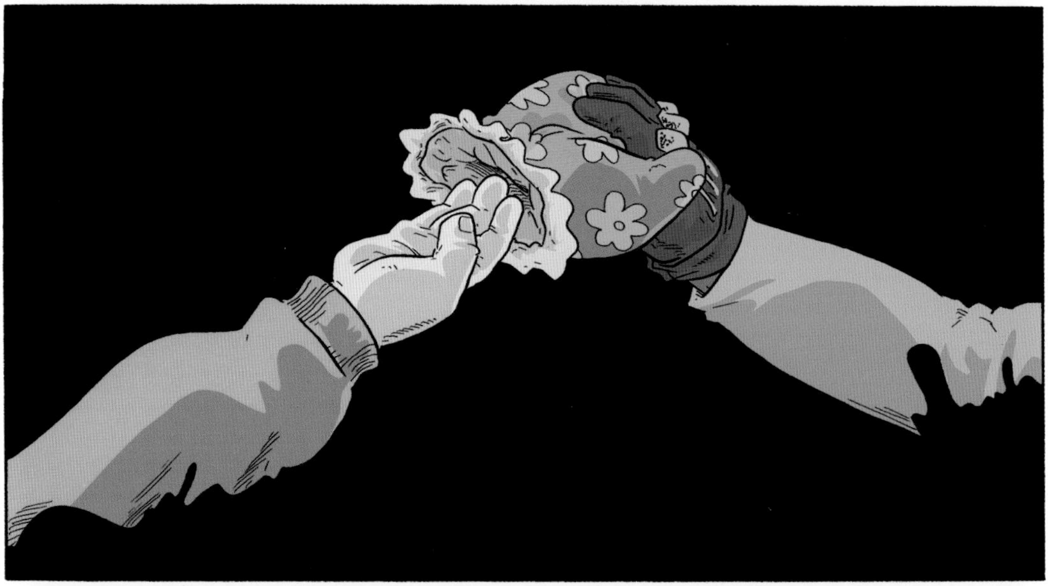

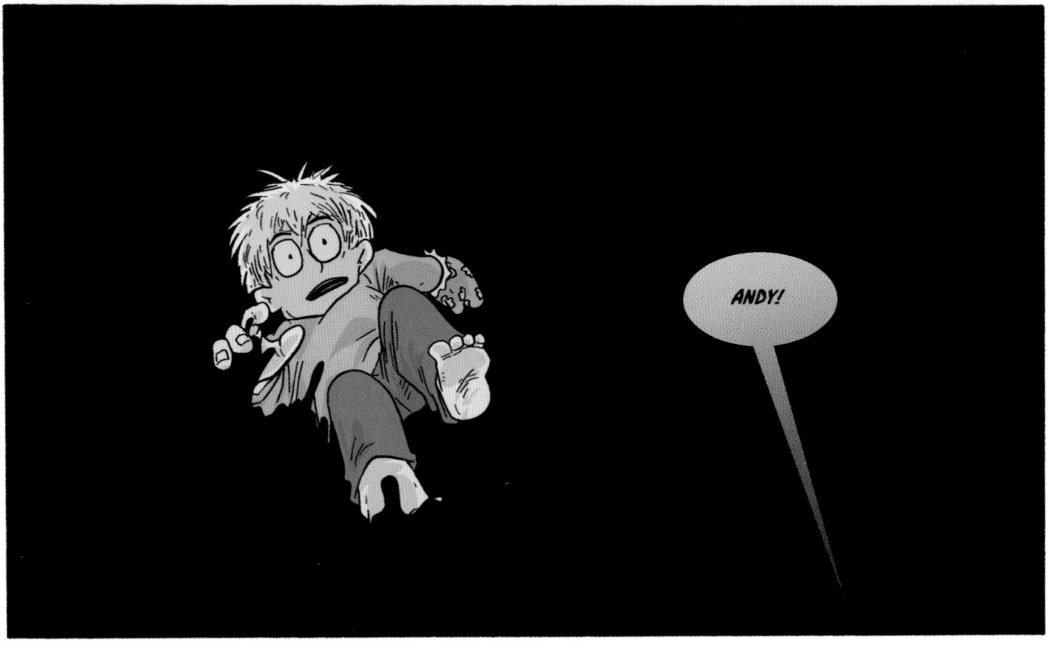
ANDY!

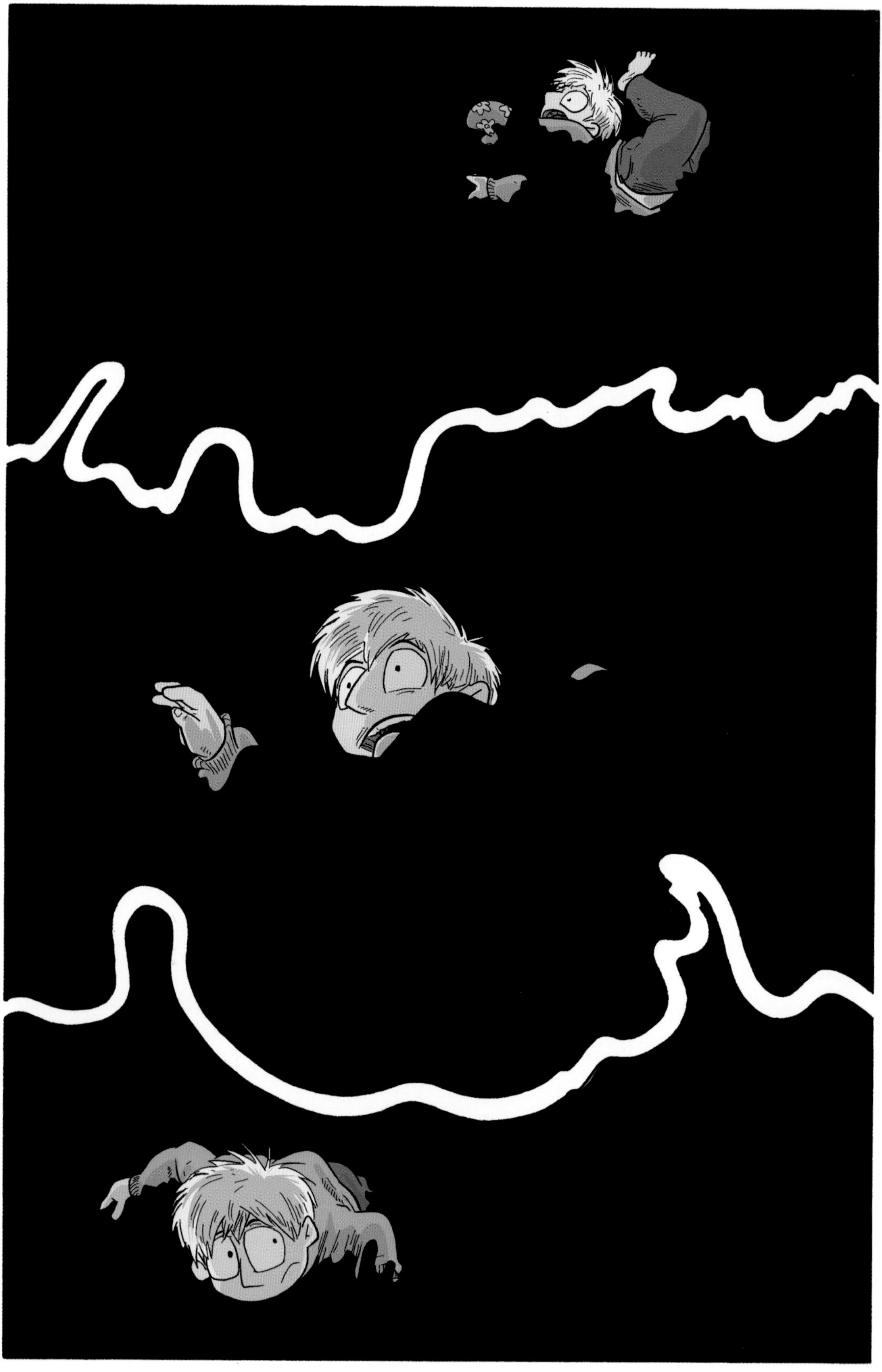

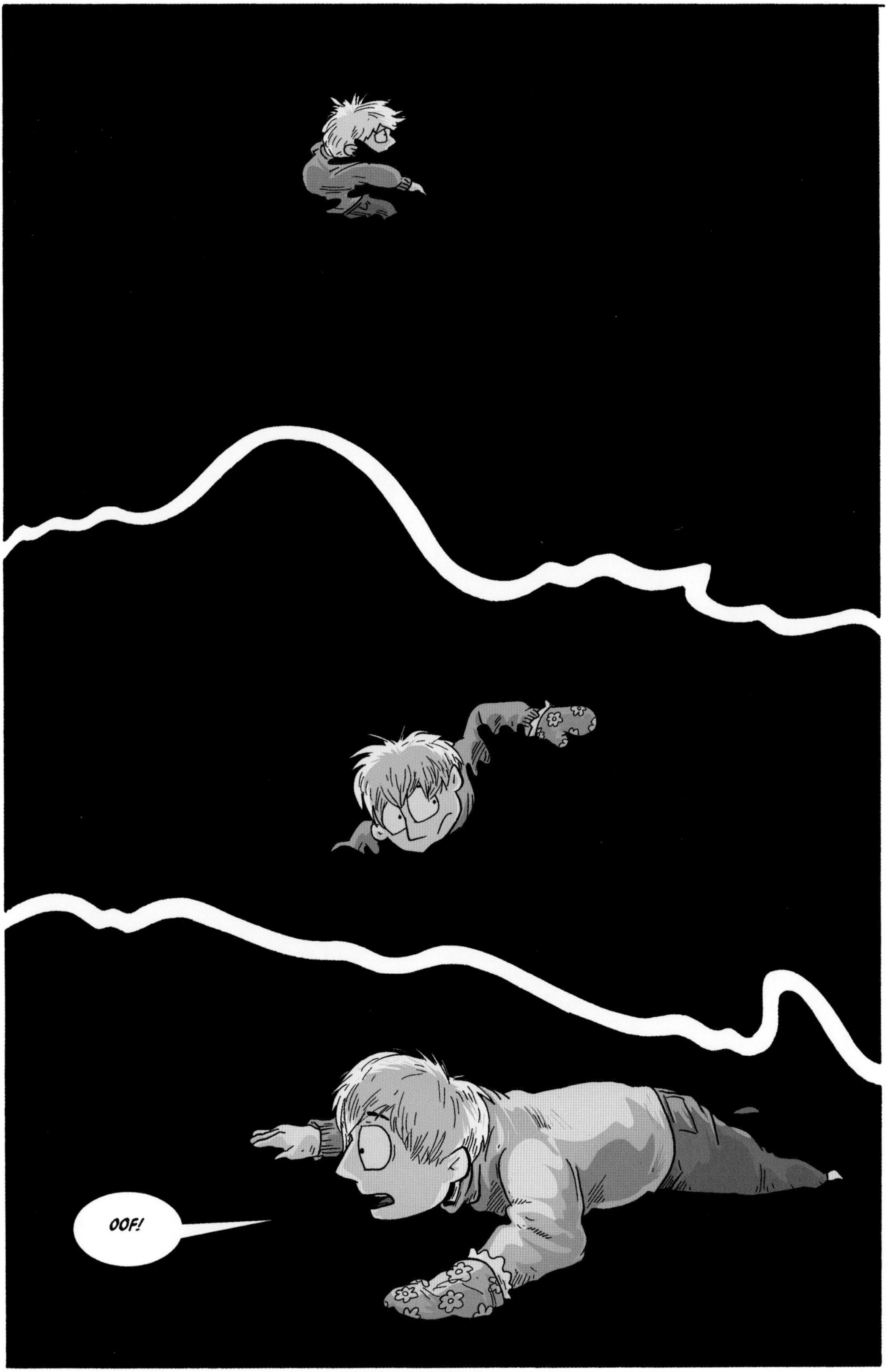
OOF!

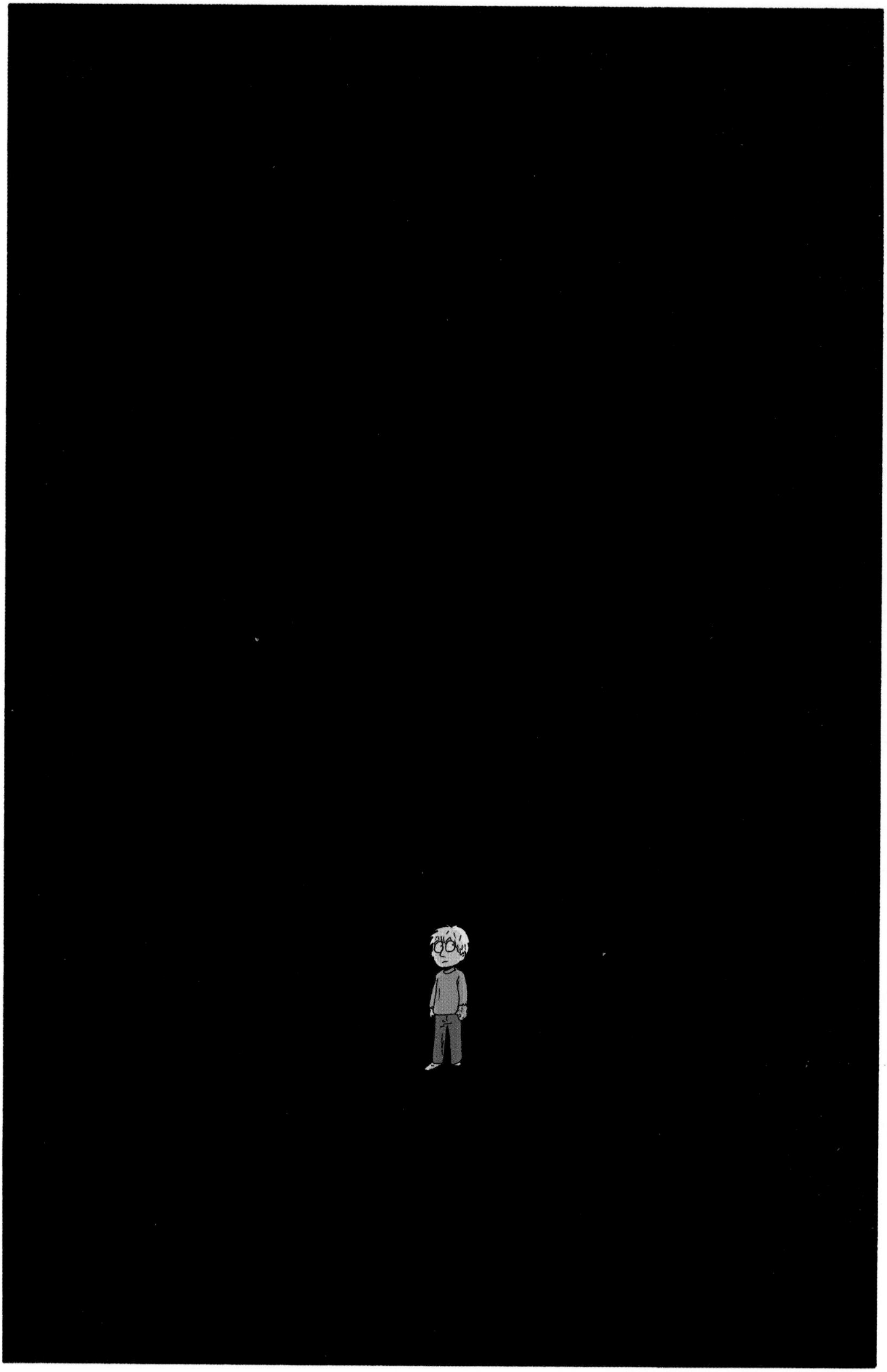

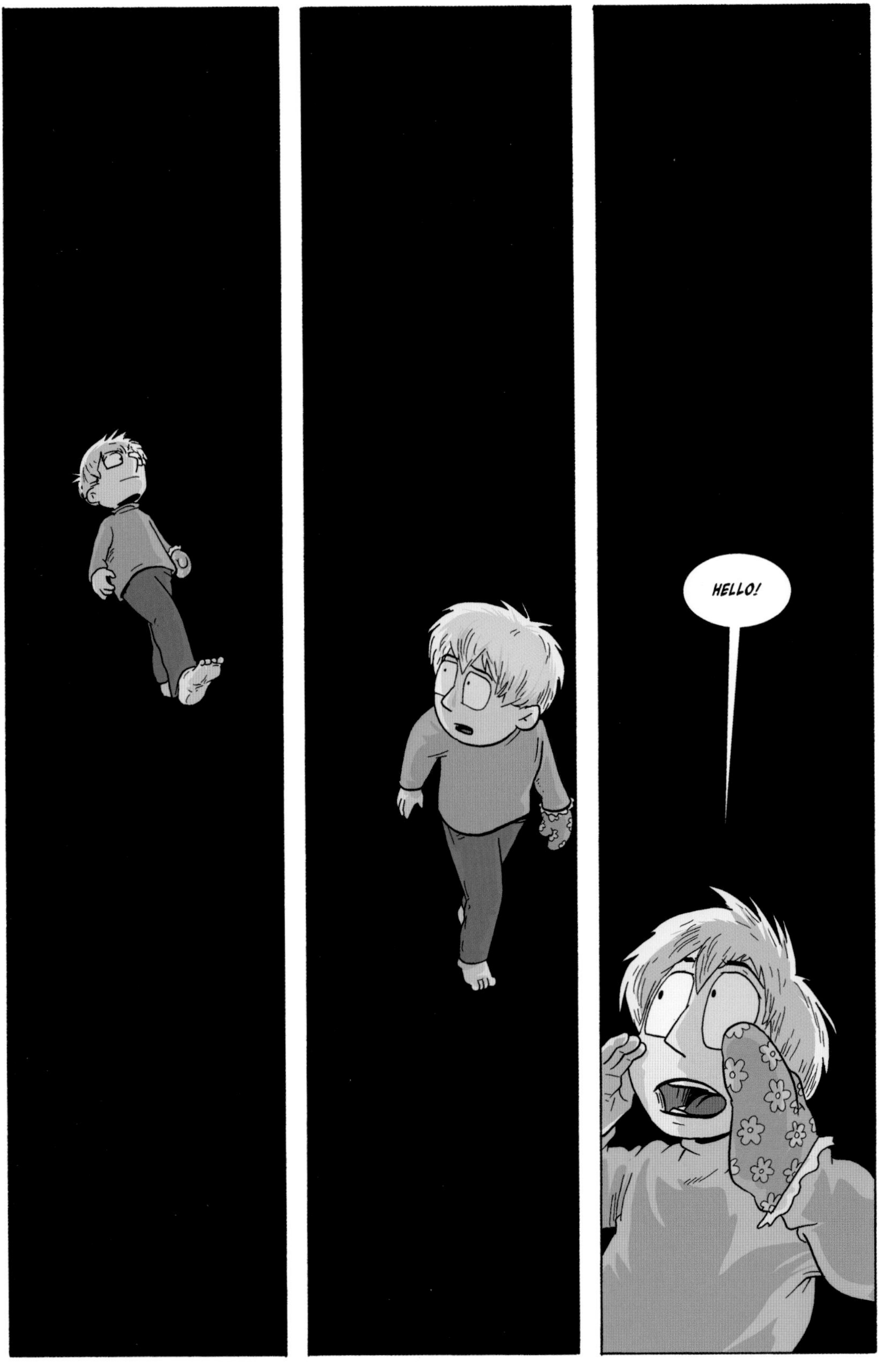
HELLO!

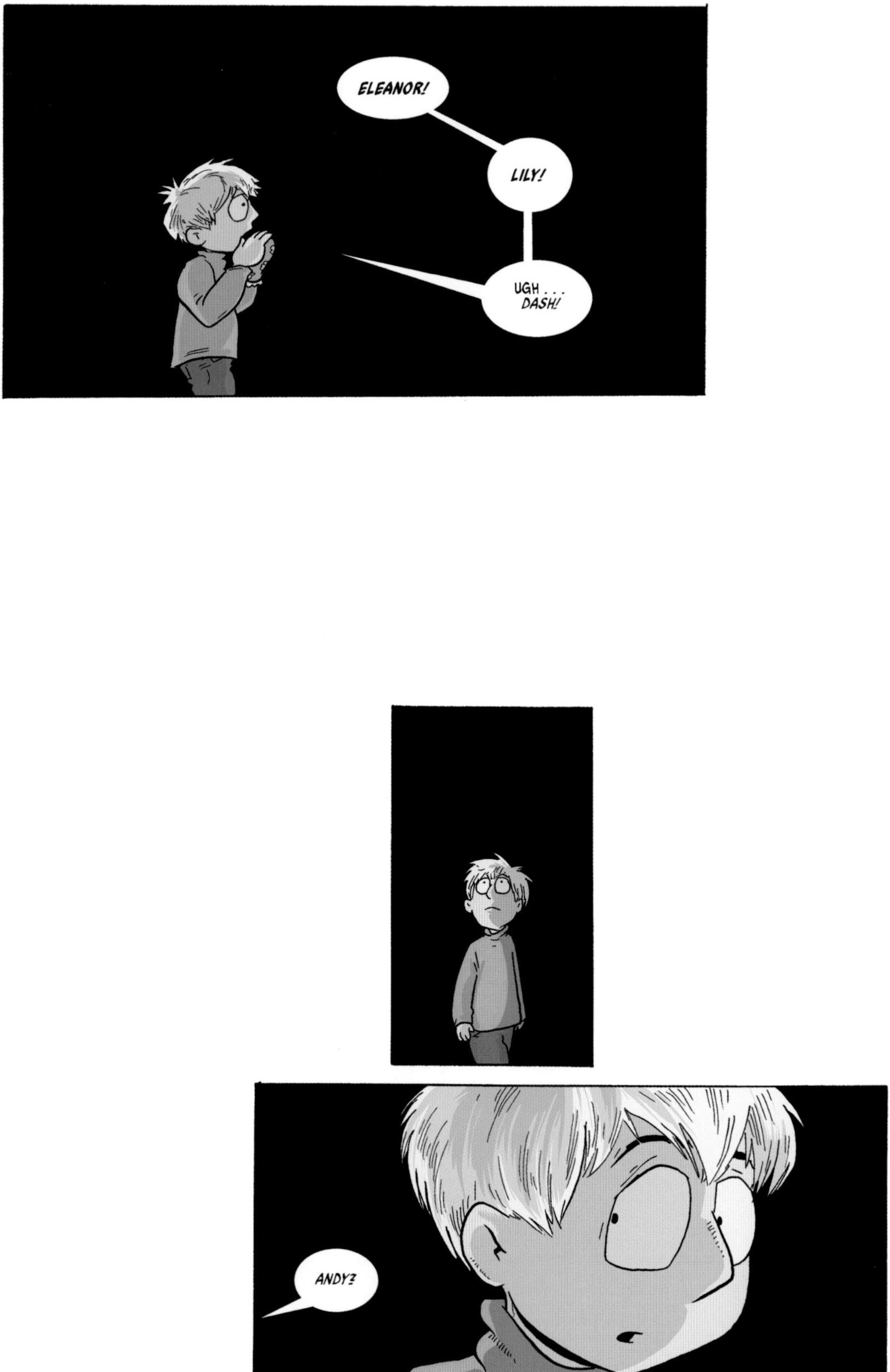
ELEANOR!
LILY!
UGH . . . DASH!
ANDY?

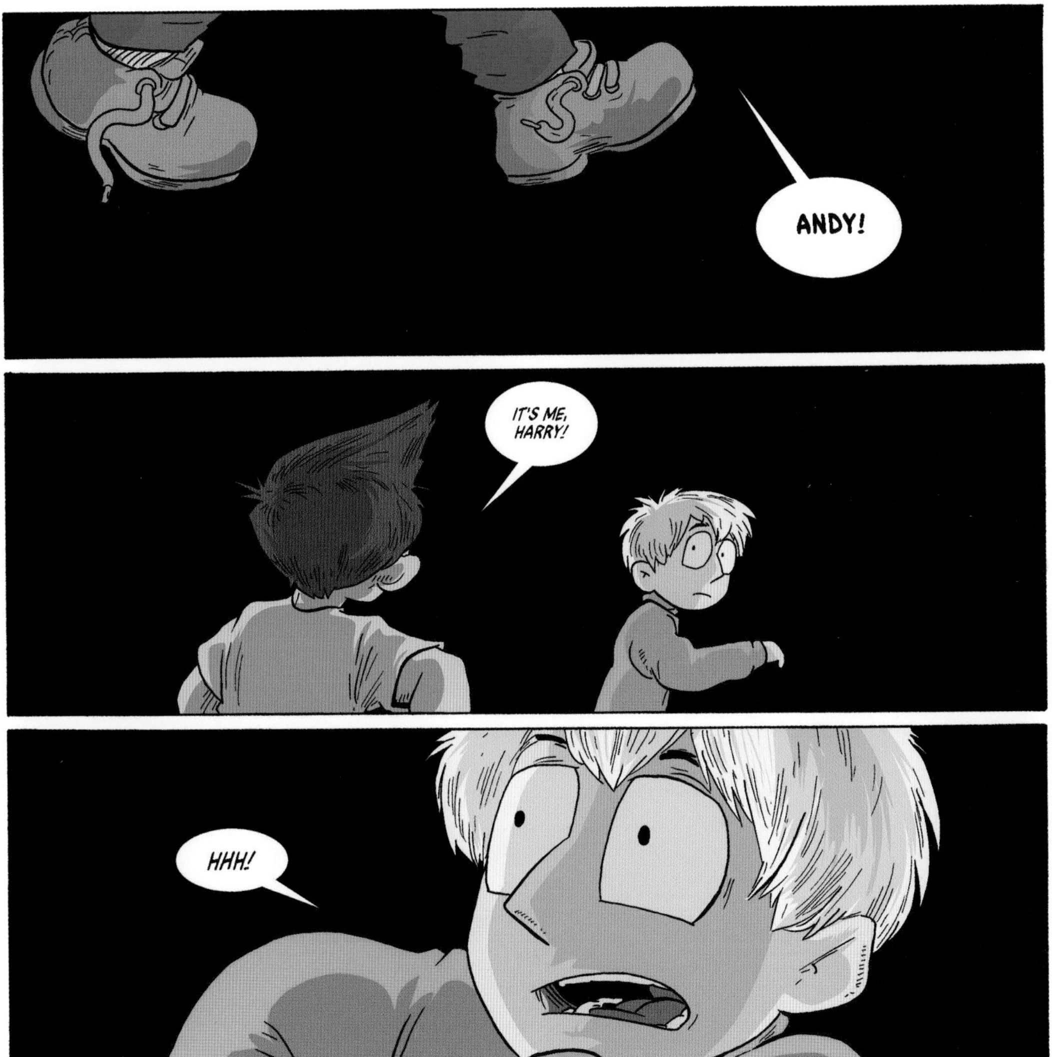
ANDY!
IT'S ME, HARRY!
HHH!

TO BE CONTINUED.

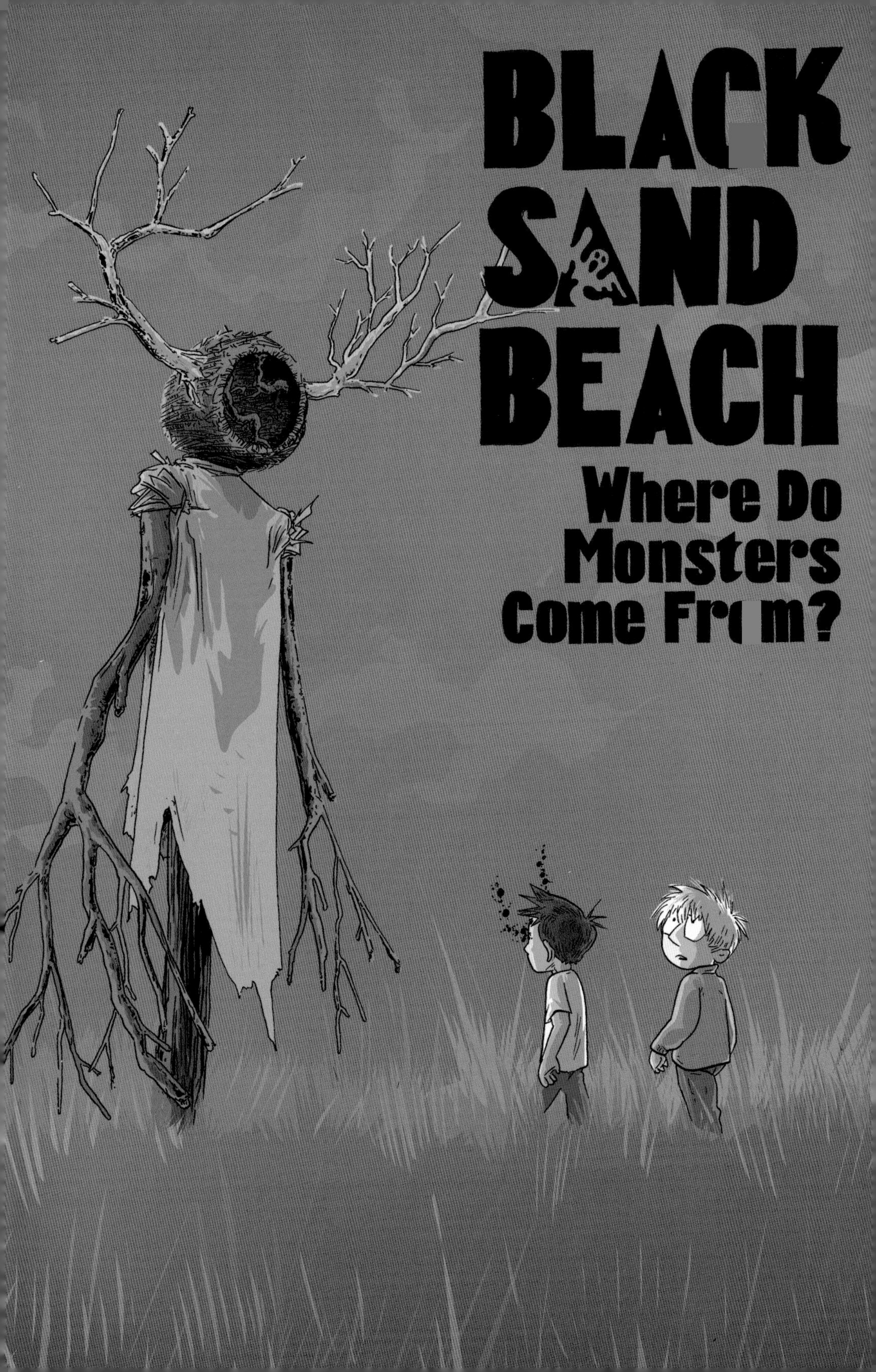
BLACK
SAND
BEACH
Where Do
Monsters
Come From?

RICHARD FAIRGRAY

Somewhere in the frozen depths of Canada sits Richard Fairgray. He hunches over his table scribbling trees and sand and monsters as his mind races to come up with new stories. Pink noise crackles through speakers on either side to drown out the world. His home is filled with skeletons and teeth and dogs of varying sizes.

Each night he stops for five hours to sleep and refuel. His dreams are filled with octopuses and ghosts and a low rumbling sound that he is sure is going to start telling him things any day.

His back hurts and his hand is cramping, but he has no choice but to get these stories onto paper.

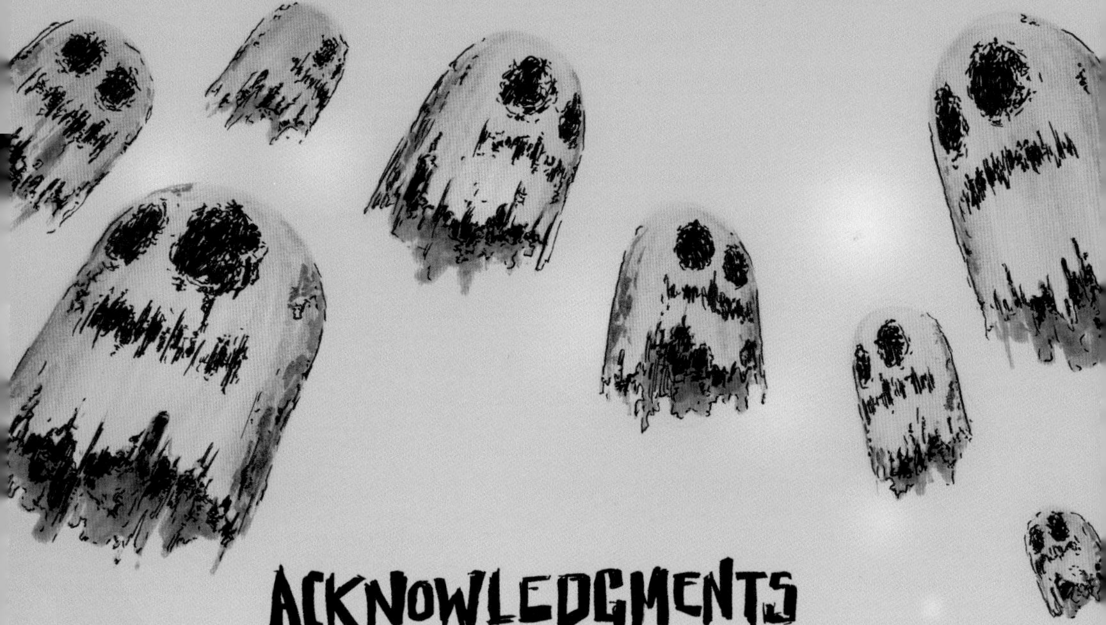

ACKNOWLEDGMENTS

This book was made during a very difficult year, not just for me, but for the whole world. Our ability to reach out to friends and family was tested and limited, and those of us who got through it relied on small handfuls of people.

Hierarchies of distance were wiped out and unexpected connections were made across continents. For me, those people were a lifeline.

This book also helped. This story kept me focused (obsessed, perhaps) and the world of Black Sand Beach became my refuge within my own house.

Tony, RE, Charlie, Lucy, Indira, Alex, Barbra, Bryant, Tilly, Susan, David, and the rest of the Saturday morning Zoom calls, and (of course) my husband, Raymond - this book could easily have been discarded with so many other things if it hadn't been for your presence in my life.

The support of Vicki and Bethany was as invaluable as ever.

The engineering genius of Paul Wolff cannot and will not be understated.

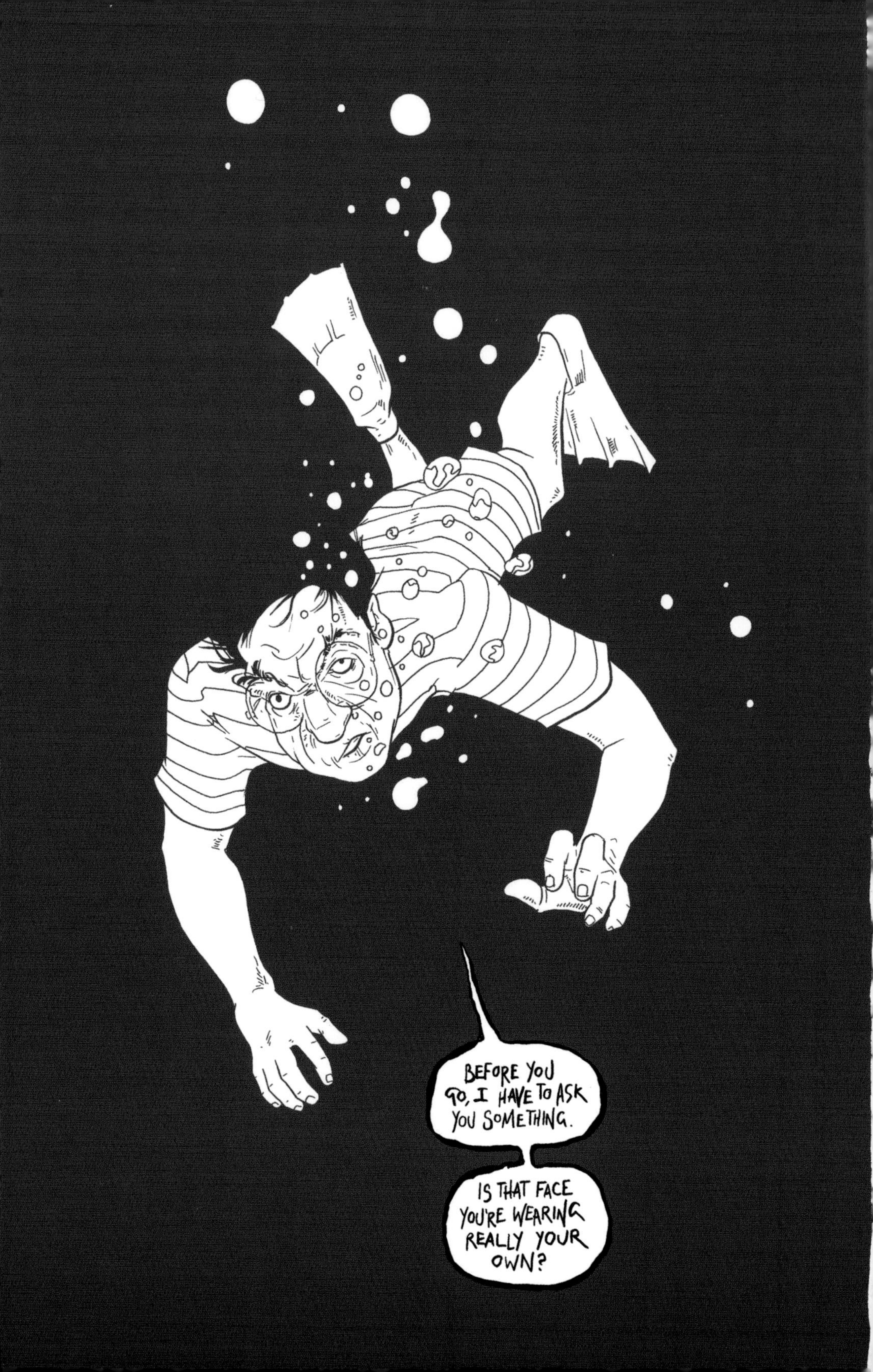
BEFORE YOU GO, I HAVE TO ASK YOU SOMETHING.
IS THAT FACE YOU'RE WEARING REALLY YOUR OWN?